SCHOOL STORIES

SCHOOL STORIES

Edited by
Janet Sacks

Illustrated by
Hilda Offen

Contents

First published 1980 by
Octopus Books Limited
59 Grosvenor Street
London W1

Reprinted 1983, 1985

ISBN 0 7064 1172 2

This arrangement © 1980 Octopus Books Limited

Printed in Czechoslovakia

50396/3

VILLAGE SCHOOL
Laurie Lee

The village to which our family had come was a scattering of some twenty to thirty houses down the south-east slope of a valley. The valley was narrow, steep, and almost entirely cut off; it was also a funnel for winds, a channel for the floods and a jungly, bird-crammed, insect-hopping sun-trap whenever there happened to be any sun. It was not high and open like the Windrush country, but had secret origins, having been gouged from the Escarpment by the melting ice-caps some time before we got there. The old flood-terraces still showed on the slopes, along which the cows walked sideways. Like an island, it was possessed of curious survivals – rare orchids and Roman snails; and there were chemical qualities in the limestone-springs which gave the women pre-Raphaelite goitres. The sides of the valley were rich in pasture and the crests heavily covered in beechwoods.

Water was the most active thing in the valley, arriving in the long rains from Wales. It would drip all day from clouds and trees, from roofs and eaves and noses. It broke open roads, carved its way through gardens, and filled the ditches with sucking noises. Men and horses walked about in wet sacking, birds shook rainbows from sodden branches, and streams ran from holes, and back into holes, like noisy underground trains.

I remember, too, the light on the slopes, long shadows in tufts and hollows, with cattle, brilliant as painted china, treading their echoing shapes. Bees blew like cake-crumbs through the golden air, white butterflies like sugared wafers, and when it wasn't raining a diamond dust took over which veiled and yet magnified all things.

Most of the cottages were built of Cotswold stone and were roofed by split-stone tiles. The tiles grew a kind of golden moss which sparkled like crystallized honey. Behind the cottages were long steep gardens full of cabbages, fruit-bushes, roses, rabbit-hutches, earth-closets, bicycles, and pigeon-lofts. In the very sump of the valley wallowed the Squire's Big House – once a fine, though modest sixteenth-century manor, to which a Georgian façade had been added.

The villagers themselves had three ways of living: working for the Squire, or on the farms, or down in the clothmills at Stroud. Apart from the Manor, and the ample cottage gardens – which were an insurance against hard times – all other needs were supplied by a church, a chapel, a vicarage, a wooden hut, a pub – and the village school.

The village school at that time provided all the instruction we were likely to ask for. It was a small stone barn divided by a wooden partition into two rooms – The Infants and The Big Ones. There was one dame teacher, and perhaps a young girl assistant. Every child in the valley crowding there, remained till he was fourteen years old, then was presented to the working field or factory with nothing in his head more burdensome than a few mnemonics, a jumbled list of wars, and a dreamy image of the world's geography. It seemed enough to get by with, in any case; and was one up on our poor old grandparents.

This school, when I came to it, was at its peak. Universal education and unusual fertility had packed it to the walls with pupils. Wild boys and girls from miles around – from the outlying farms and half-hidden hovels way up at the ends of the valley – swept down each day to add to our numbers, bringing with them strange oaths and odours, quaint garments and curious pies. They were my first amazed vision of any world outside the womanly warmth of my family; I didn't expect to survive it for long, and I was confronted with it at the age of four.

The morning came, without any warning, when my sisters surrounded me, wrapped me in scarves, tied up my bootlaces, thrust a cap on my head, and stuffed a baked potato in my pocket.

'What's this?' I said.

'You're starting school today.'

'I ain't. I'm stopping 'ome.'

'Now, come on, Loll. You're a big boy now.'

'I ain't.'

'You are.'

'Boo-hoo.'

They picked me up bodily, kicking and bawling, and carried me up to the road.

'Boys who don't go to school get put into boxes, and turn into rabbits, and get chopped up Sundays.'

I felt this was overdoing it rather, but I said no more after that. I arrived at the school just three feet tall and fatly wrapped in my scarves. The playground roared like a rodeo, and the potato burned through my thigh. Old boots, ragged stockings, torn trousers and skirts, went skating and skidding around me. The rabble closed in; I was encircled; grit flew in my face like shrapnel. Tall girls with fizzled hair, and huge boys with sharp elbows, began to prod me with hideous interest. They plucked at my scarves, spun me round like a top, screwed my nose, and stole my potato.

I was rescued at last by a gracious lady – the sixteen-year-old junior-teacher – who boxed a few ears and dried my face and led me off to The Infants. I spent that first day picking holes in paper, then went home in a smouldering temper.

'What's the matter, Loll? Didn't he like it at school, then?'

'They never gave me the present!'

'Present? What present?'

'They said they'd give me a present.'

'Well, now, I'm sure they didn't.'

'They did! They said: "You're Laurie Lee, ain't you? Well, just you sit there for the present." I sat there all day but I never got it. I ain't going back there again!'

But after a week I felt like a veteran and grew as ruthless as anyone else. Somebody had stolen my baked potato, so I swiped somebody else's apple. The Infant Room was packed with toys such as I'd never seen before – coloured shapes and rolls of clay, stuffed birds and men to paint. Also a frame of counting beads which our young teacher played like a harp, leaning her bosom against our faces and guiding our wandering fingers. . . .

The beautiful assistant left us at last, and was replaced by an opulent widow. She was tall, and smelt like a cart-load of lavender; and wore a hair net, which I thought was a wig. I remember going close up and having a good look – it was clearly too square to be hair.

'What are you staring at?' the widow inquired.

I was much too soft-hearted to answer.

'Go on. Do tell. You needn't be shy.'

'You're wearing a wig,' I said.

'I can assure you I'm not!' She went very red.

'You are. I seen it,' I said.

The new teacher grew flustered and curiously cross. She took me upon her knee.

'Now look very close. Is that really a wig?'

I looked hard, saw the net, and said, 'Yes.'

'Well, really!' she said, while the Infants gaped. 'I can assure you it's *not* a wig! And if you only could watch me getting dressed in the morning you'd know it wasn't one either.'

She shook me from her knee like a sodden cat, but she'd stirred my imagination. To suggest I might watch her getting dressed in the morning seemed to me both outrageous and wonderful.

★   ★   ★   ★

This tiny, white-washed Infants' room was a brief but cosy anarchy. In that short time allowed us we played and wept, broke things, fell asleep, cheeked the teacher, discovered the things we could do to each other, and exhaled our last guiltless days.

My desk companions were those two blonde girls, already puppyishly pretty, whose names and bodies were to distract and haunt me for the next fifteen years of my life. Poppy and Jo were limpet chums; they sat holding hands all day; and there was a female self-possession about their pink sticky faces that made me shout angrily at them.

Vera was another I studied and liked; she was lonely, fuzzy, and short. I felt a curious compassion for stumpy Vera; and it was through her, and no beauty, that I got into trouble and received the first public shock of my life. How it happened was simple, and I was innocent, so it seemed. She came up to me in the playground one morning and held her face close to mine. I had a stick in my hand, so I hit her on the head with it. Her hair was springy, so I hit her again and watched her mouth open up with a yell.

To my surprise a commotion broke out around me, cries of scandal from the older girls, exclamations of horror and heavy censure mixed with Vera's sobbing wails. I was intrigued, not alarmed, that by wielding a beech stick I was able to cause such a stir. So I hit her again, without spite or passion, then walked off to try something else.

The experiment might have ended there, and having ended would have been forgotten. But no; angry faces surrounded me, very red, all spitting and scolding.

'Horrid boy! Poor Vera! Little monster! Urgh! We're going to tell teacher about you!'

Something was wrong, the world seemed upset, I began to feel vaguely uneasy. I had only hit Vera on her wiry black hair, and now everybody was shouting at me. I ran and hid, feeling sure it would pass, but they hunted me down in the end. Two big righteous girls hauled me out by the ears.

'You're wanted in the Big Room, for 'itting Vera. You're 'alf going to cop it!' they said.

So I was dragged to that Room, where I'd never been before, and under the savage eyes of the elder children teacher gave me a scalding lecture. I was confused by now and shaking with guilt. At last I smirked and ran out of the room. I had learnt my first lesson, that I could not hit Vera, no matter how fuzzy her hair. And something else too; that the summons to the Big Room, the policeman's hand on the shoulder, comes almost always as a complete surprise, and for the crime that one has forgotten.

★   ★   ★   ★

My brother Jack, who was with me in the Infants, was too clever to stay there long. Indeed he was so bright he made us uncomfortable, and we were all of us glad to get rid of him. Sitting pale in his pinafore, gravely studying, commanding the teacher to bring him fresh books, or to sharpen his pencils, or to make less noise, he was an Infant Freak from the start. So he was promoted to the Big Room with unprece- dented promptness, given a desk and a dozen atlases to sit on, from which he continued to bully the teachers in that cold clear voice of his.

But I, myself, was a natural Infant, content to serve out my time, to slop around and whine and idle: and no one suggested I shouldn't. So I remained long after bright Jack had moved on, the fat lord of my nursery life, skilled at cutting out men from paper, chalking suns on the walls, making snakes from clay, idling voluptuously through the milky days with a new young teacher to feed on. But my time was slowly running out; my Big Room bumps were growing. Suddenly, almost to my dismay, I found that I could count up to a hundred, could write my name in both large and small letters, and subtract certain numbers from each other. I had even just succeeded in subtracting Poppy from Jo, when the call came down from on high. Infant no longer, I was being moved up – the Big Room was ready for me.

I found there a world both adult and tough, with long desks and inkwells, strange maps on the walls, huge boys, heavy boots, scratching pens, groans of labour, and sharp and sudden persecutions. Gone for ever were the infant excuses, the sanctuary of lisping charms. Now I was alone and unprotected, faced by a struggle which required new techniques, where one made pacts and split them, made friends and betrayed them, and fought for one's place near the stove.

The stove was a symbol of caste among us, the tub of warmth to which we cleaved during the long seven months of winter. It was made of cast-iron and had a noisy mouth which rattled coke and breathed out fumes. It was decorated by a tortoise labelled 'Slow But Sure', and in winter it turned red hot. If you pressed a pencil against it, the wood burst into flames; and if you spat on the top, the spit hopped and gam- bolled like tiny ping-pong balls.

My first days in the Big Room were spent in regret for the young teacher I'd left in the Infants, for her braided breasts and unbuttoning hands and her voice of sleepy love. Quite clearly the Big Room boasted no such comforts; Miss B, the Head Teacher, to whom I was now delivered, being about as physically soothing as a rake.

She was a bunched and punitive little body and the school had christened her Crabby; she had a sour yellow look, lank hair coiled in earphones, and the skin and voice of a turkey. We were all afraid of the gobbling Miss B; she spied, she pried, she crouched, she crept, she pounced – she was a terror.

Each morning was war without declaration; no one knew who would catch it next. We stood to attention, half-crippled in our desks, till Miss B walked in, whacked the walls with a ruler, and fixed us with her squinting eye. 'Good a-morning, children!' 'Good morning, Teacher!' The greeting was like a rattling of swords. Then she would scowl at the floor and begin to growl 'Ar Farther . . .'; at which we said the Lord's Prayer, praised all good things, and thanked God for the health of our King. But scarcely had we bellowed the last Amen than Crabby coiled, uncoiled, and sprang, and knocked some poor boy sideways.

One seldom knew why; one was always off guard, for the punishment preceded the charge. The charge, however, followed hard upon it, to a light shower of angry spitting.

'Shuffling your feet! Playing with the desk! A-smirking at that miserable Betty! I will not have it. I repeat – I will not have it!'

Many a punch-drunk boy in a playground battle, outnumbered and beaten to his knees, would be heard to cry: 'I will not have it! I'll not, I say! I repeats I will not have it!' It was an appeal to the code of our common suffering, and called for immediate mercy.

So we did not much approve of Crabby – though she was responsible for our excellent reflexes. Apart from this, her teaching was not memorable. She appears in my recollection as merely a militant figure, a hunched-up little creature all spring-coils and slaps – not a monster by any means, but a natural manifestation of what we expected of school.

For school in my day, that day, Crabby's day, seemed to be designed simply to keep us out of the air and from following the normal pursuits of the fields. Crabby's science of dates and sums and writing seemed a typical invention of her own, a sour form of fiddling or prison-labour like picking oakum or sewing sacks.

So while the bright times passed, we sat locked in our stocks, our bent backs turned on the valley. The June air infected us with primitive hungers, grass-seed and thistle-down idled through the windows, we smelt the fields and were tormented by cuckoos, while every out-of-door sound that came drifting in was a sharp nudge in the solar plexus.

13

The creaking of wagons going past the school, harness-jingle, and the cries of the carters, the calling of cows from the 17-Acre, Fletcher's chattering mower, gunshot from the warrens – all tugged and pulled at our active wishes till we could have done Miss B a murder.

And indeed there came the inevitable day when rebellion raised its standard, when the tension was broken and a hero emerged whom we would willingly have named streets after. At least, from that day his name was honoured, though we gave him little support at the time. . . .

Spadge Hopkins it was, and I must say we were surprised. He was one of those heavy, full-grown boys, thick-legged, red-fisted, bursting with flesh, designed for the great outdoors. He was nearly fourteen by then, and physically out of scale – at least so far as our school was concerned. The sight of him squeezed into his tiny desk was worse than a bullock in ballet-shoes. He wasn't much of a scholar; he groaned as he worked, or hacked at his desk with a jack-knife. Miss B took her pleasure in goading him, in forcing him to read out loud; or asking him sudden unintelligible questions which made him flush and stumble.

The great day came; a day of shimmering summer, with the valley outside in a state of leafy levitation. Crabby B was at her sourest, and Spadge Hopkins had had enough. He began to writhe in his desk, and roll his eyes, and kick with his boots, and mutter; 'She'd better look out. 'Er, – Crabby B. She'd better, that's all. I can tell you. . . .'

We didn't quite know what the matter was, in spite of his meaning looks. Then he threw down his pen, said; 'Sod it all,' got up, and walked to the door.

'And where are you going, young man, may I ask?' said Crabby.

Spadge paused and looked her straight in the eye.

'If it's any business of yourn.'

We shivered with pleasure at this defiance, Spadge leisurely made for the door.

'Sit down this instant!' Crabby suddenly screamed. 'I won't have it!'

'Ta-ta,' said Spadge.

Then Crabby sprang like a yellow cat, spitting and clawing with rage. She caught Spadge in the doorway and fell upon him. There was a shameful moment of heavy breathing and scuffling, while the teacher tore at his clothes. Spadge caught her hands in his great red fists and held her at arm's length, struggling.

Crabby stayed where she was, on top of the cupboard.

'Come and help me, someone!' wailed Crabby, demented. But nobody moved; we just watched. We saw Spadge lift her up and place her on the top of the cupboard, then walk out of the door and away. There was a moment of silence, then we all laid down our pens and began to stamp on the floor in unison. Crabby stayed where she was, on top of the cupboard, drumming her heels and weeping.

We expected some terrible retribution to follow, but nothing happened at all. Not even the trouble-spark, Spadge, was called to account – he was simply left alone. From that day Crabby never spoke to him, or crossed his path, or denied him anything at all. He perched idly in his desk, his knees up to his chin, whistling in a world of his own. Sometimes Miss B would consider him narrowly and if he caught her glance he just winked. Otherwise he was free to come and go, and to take time off as he pleased.

But we never rebelled again; things changed. Crabby B was replaced by a new Head Teacher – a certain Miss Wardley from Birmingham. This lady was something quite new in our lives. She wore sharp glass jewellery which winked as she walked, and she sounded her 'gees' like gongs. But she was fond of singing and she was fond of birds, and she encouraged us in the study of both. She was more sober than Crabby, her reins looser but stronger; and after the first hilarity of her arrival and strangeness, we accepted her proper authority.

Not that she approved very much of me. 'Fat-and-Lazy' was the name she called me. After my midday dinner of baked cabbage and bread I would often nod off in my desk. 'Wake up!' she would cry, cracking my head with a ruler, 'you and your little red eyes!' She also took exception to my steady sniff, which to me came as natural as breathing. 'Go out into the road and have a good blow, and don't come back till you're clear.' But I wouldn't blow, not for anyone on earth, especially if ordered to do so: so I'd sit out on the wall, indignant and thunderous, and sniff away louder than ever. I wouldn't budge either, or come back in, till a boy was sent to fetch me. Miss Wardley would greet me with freezing brightness. 'A little less beastly now? How about bringing a hanky tomorrow? I'm sure we'd all be grateful.' I'd sit and scowl, then forget to scowl, and would soon be asleep again. . . .

My brothers, by this time, were all with me at school. Jack, already the accepted genius, was long past our scope or help. It was agreed that his brains were of such distinction that they absolved him from mortal contacts. So he was left in a corner where his flashes of brilliance kept him twinkling away like a pin-table. Young Tony came last, but he again was different, being impervious either to learning or authority, importing moreover a kind of outrageous cheekiness so inspired that it remained unanswerable. He would sit all day picking holes in blotting paper, his large eyes deep and knowing, his quick tongue scandalous, his wit defiant, his will set against all instruction. There was nothing anyone could do about him, except to yelp at the things he said.

I alone, the drowsy middleman of these two, found it hard to win Miss Wardley's approval. I achieved this in the end by writing long faked essays on the lives and habits of otters. I'd never seen an otter, or even gone to look for one, but the essays took her in. They were read out aloud, and even earned me medals, but that's nothing to boast about.

Our village school was poor and crowded, but in the end I relished it. It had a lively reek of steaming life: boys' boots, girls' hair, stoves and sweat, blue ink, white chalk, and shavings. We learnt nothing abstract or tenuous there – just simple patterns of facts and letters, portable tricks of calculation, no more than was needed to measure a shed, write out a bill, read a swine-disease warning. Through the dead hours of the morning, through the long afternoons, we chanted away at our tables. Passers-by could hear our rising voices in our bottled-up room on the bank; 'Twelve-inches-one-foot. Three-feet-make-a-yard. Fourteen-pounds-make-a-stone. Eight-stone-a-hundred-weight.' We absorbed these figures as primal truths declared by some ultimate power. Un-hearing, unquestioning, we rocked to our chanting, hammering the gold nails home. 'Twice-two-are-four. One-God-is-Love. One-Lord-is-King. One-King-is-George. One-George-is-Fifth. . . .' So it was always; had been, would be for ever; we asked no questions; we didn't hear what we said; yet neither did we ever forget it.

So do I now, through the reiterations of those days, recall that schoolroom which I scarcely noticed – Miss Wardley in glory on her high desk throne, her long throat tinkling with glass. The bubbling stove with its chink of red fire; the old world map as dark as tea; dead field-flowers in jars on the windowsills; the cupboard yawning with dog-eared books. Then the boys and the girls, the dwarfs and the cripples; the slow fat ones and the quick bony ones; giants and louts,

17

angels and squinters – Walt Kerry, Bill Timbrell, Spadge Hopkins, Clergy Green, the Ballingers and Browns, Betty Gleed, Clarry Hogg, Sam and Sixpence, Poppy and Jo – we were ugly and beautiful, scrofulous, warted, ring-wormed, and scabbed at the knees, we were noisy, crude, intolerant, cruel, stupid, and superstitious. But we moved together out of the clutch of the Fates, inhabitors of a world without doom; with a scratching, licking and chewing of pens, a whisper and passing of jokes, a titter of tickling, a grumble of labour, a vague stare at the wall in a dream. . . .

'Oh, miss, please miss, can I go round the back?'

An unwilling nod permits me. I stamp out noisily into a swoop of fresh air and a musical surge of birds. All around me now is the free green world, with Mrs Birt hanging out her washing. I take stock of myself for a moment, alone. I hear the schoolroom's beehive hum. Of course I don't really belong to that lot at all; I know I'm something special, a young king perhaps placed secretly here in order to mix with the commoners. There is clearly a mystery about my birth, I feel so unique and majestic. One day, I know, the secret will be told. A coach with footmen will appear suddenly at our cottage, and Mother (my mother?) will weep. The family will stand very solemn and respectful, and I shall drive off to take up my throne. I'll be generous, of course, not proud at all; for my brothers there shall be no dungeons. Rather will I feed them on cakes and jellies, and I'll provide all my sisters with princes. Sovereign mercy shall be their portion, little though they deserve it. . . .

I return to the schoolroom and Miss Wardley scowls (she shall curtsy when I am king). But all this is forgotten when Walt Kerry leans over and demands the results of my sums. 'Yes, Walt. Of course, Walt. Here, copy them out. They ain't hard – I done 'em all.' He takes them, the bully, as his tributary right, and I'm proud enough to give them. The little Jim Fern, sitting beside me, looks up from his ruined pages. 'Ain't you a good scholar! You and your Jack. I wish I was a good scholar like thee.' He gives me a sad, adoring look, and I begin to feel much better.

Playtime comes and we charge outdoors, releasing our steamed-up cries. Somebody punches a head. Somebody bloodies their knees. Boys cluster together like bees. 'Let's go round the back then, shall us, eh?'

To the dark narrow alley, rich with our mysteries, we make our clattering way. Over the wall is the girl's own place, quite close, and we shout
them greetings.

'I 'eard you, Bill Timbrell! I 'eard what you said! You be careful,
I'll tell our teacher!'

Flushed and refreshed, we stream back to our playground, whistling,
indivisibly male.

'D'you 'ear what I said then? Did you then, eh? I told 'em! They 'alf
didn't squeal!'

We all double up; we can't speak for laughing, we can't laugh without hitting each other.

Miss Wardley was patient, but we weren't very bright. Our books
showed a squalor of blots and scratches as though monkeys were being
taught to write. We sang in sweet choirs, and drew like cavemen, but
most other faculties escaped us. Apart from poetry, of course, which
gave no trouble at all. I can remember Miss Wardley, with her squeak-
ing chalk, scrawling the blackboard like a shopping list:

'Write a poem – which must scan – on one or more of the following;
A Kitten. Fairies. My Holidays. An Old Tinker. Charity. Sea Wrack . . .'
('What's that, miss?')

But it was easy in those days, one wrote a dozen an hour, one simply
didn't hesitate, just began at the beginning and worked steadily through
the subjects, ticking them off with indefatigable rhymes.

Sometimes there was a beating, which nobody minded – except an
occasional red-faced mother. Sometimes a man came and took out our
teeth. ('My mum says you ain't to take out any double-'uns. . . .'
'. . . Fourteen, fifteen, sixteen, seventeen. . . .' 'Is they all double-'uns?'
'Shut up, you little horror.') Sometimes the Squire would pay us a
visit, hand out prizes, and make a misty-eyed speech. Sometimes an
Inspector arrived on a bicycle and counted our heads and departed.
Meanwhile Miss Wardley moved jingling amongst us, instructing,
appealing, despairing:

'You're a grub, Walter Kerry. You have the wits of a hen. You're a
great hulking lout of an oaf. You can just stay behind and do it over
again. You can all stay behind, the lot of you.'

When lessons grew too tiresome, or too insoluble, we had our
traditional ways of avoiding them.

'Please, miss, I got to stay 'ome tomorrow, to 'elp with the washing – the pigs – me dad's sick.'

'I dunno, miss; you never learned us that.'

'I 'ad me book stole, miss. Carry Burdock pinched it.'

'Please, miss, I got a gurt 'eadache.'

Sometimes these worked, sometimes they didn't. But once, when some tests hung over our heads, a group of us boys evaded them entirely by stinging our hands with horseflies. The task took all day, but the results were spectacular – our hands swelled like elephants' trunks. ''Twas a swarm, please, miss. They set on us. We run, but they stung us awful.' I remember how we groaned, and that we couldn't hold our pens, but I don't remember the pain.

At other times, of course, we forged notes from our mothers, or made ourselves sick with berries, or claimed to be relations of the corpse at funerals (the churchyard lay only next door). It was easy to start wailing when the hearse passed by, 'It's my auntie, miss – it's my cousin Wilf – can I go miss, please miss, can I?' Many a lone coffin was followed to its grave by a straggle of long-faced children, pinched, solemn, raggedly dressed, all strangers to the astonished bereaved.

So our school work was done – or where would we be today? We would be as we are; watching a loom or driving a tractor, and counting in images of fives and tens. This was as much as we seemed to need, and Miss Wardley did not add to the burden. What we learned in her care were the less formal truths – the names of flowers, the habits of birds, the intimacy of objects in being set to draw them, the treacherous innocence of boys, the sly charm of girls, the idiot's soaring fancies, and the tongue-tied dunce's informed authority when it came to talking about stoats. We were as merciless and cruel as most primitives are. But we learnt at that school the private nature of cruelty; and our inborn hatred for freaks and outcasts was tempered by meeting them daily.

There was Nick and Edna from up near the Cross, the children of that brother and sister – the boy was strong and the girl was beautiful, and it was not at school that we learned to condemn them. And there was the gipsy boy Rosso, who lived up the quarry where his tribe had encamped for the summer. He had a chocolate-smooth face and crisp black curls, and at first we cold-shouldered him. He was a real outsider (they ate snails, it was said) and his slant Indian eyes repelled us. Then one day, out of hunger, he stole some sandwiches and was given the cane by Miss Wardley. Whatever the rights and wrongs of the case, that made him one of us.

We saw him run out of school, grizzling from the beating, and kneel down to tie up his boots. The shopkeeper's wife, passing by at that moment, stopped to preach him a little sermon. 'You didn't have to steal, even if you was that hungry. Why didn't you come to me?' The boy gave her a look, picked himself up, and ran off without a word. He knew, as we did, the answer to that one: we set our dogs on the gipsies here. As we walked back home to our cabbage dinners we were all of us filled with compassion. We pictured poor Rosso climbing back to his quarry, hungry to his miserable tents, with nothing but mud and puddles to sit in and the sour banks to scavenge for food. Gipsies no longer seemed either sinister or strange. No wonder they eat snails, we thought.

★   ★   ★   ★

The narrow school was just a conveyor belt along which the short years drew us. We entered the door marked 'Infants', moved gradually to the other, and were then handed back to the world. Lucky, lucky point of time; our eyes were on it always. Meanwhile we had moved to grander desks, saw our juniors multiplying in number, Miss Wardley suddenly began to ask our advice and to spoil us as though we were dying. There was no more to be done, no more to be learned. We began to look round the schoolroom with nostalgia and impatience. During playtime in the road we walked about gravely, patronizing the younger creatures. No longer the trembling, white-faced battles, the flights, the buttering-up of bullies; just a punch here and there to show our authority, then a sober stroll with our peers.

At last Miss Wardley was wringing our hands, tender and deferential. 'Good-bye, old chaps, and jolly good luck! Don't forget to come back and see me.' She gave each one of us a coy sad glance. She knew that we never would.

ROSES AND THORNS
Susan Coolidge

'Oh! what is it? What has happened?' cried Clover, starting up in bed, the next morning, as a clanging sound roused her suddenly from sleep. It was only the rising-bell, ringing at the end of Quaker Row.

Katy held her watch up to the dim light. She could just see the hands. Yes, they pointed to six. It was actually morning! She and Clover jumped up, and began to dress as fast as possible.

'We've only got half an hour,' said Clover, unhooking the rules, and carrying them to the window – 'half an hour; and this says we must turn the mattress, smooth the under-sheet over the bolster, and spend five minutes in silent devotion. We'll have to be quick to do all that, besides dressing ourselves!'

It is never easy to be quick, when one is in a hurry. Everything sets itself against you. Fingers turn into thumbs; dresses won't button, nor pins keep their place. With all their haste, Katy and Clover were barely ready when the second bell sounded. As they hastened downstairs, Katy fastening her breast-pin, and Clover her cuffs, they met other girls, some looking half asleep, others half dressed; all yawning, rubbing their eyes, and complaining of the early hour.

'Isn't it horrid?' said Lilly Page, hurrying by with no collar on, and her hair hastily tucked into a net. 'I never get up till nine o'clock when

I'm at home. Ma saves my breakfast for me. She says I shall have my sleep out while I have the chance.'

'You don't look quite awake now,' remarked Clover.

'No, because I haven't washed my face. Half the time I don't before breakfast. There's that old mattress has to be turned; and when I sleep too long, I just do that first, and then scramble my clothes on the best way I can. Anything not to be marked!'

After prayers and breakfast were done, the girls had half an hour for putting their bedrooms to rights, during which interval it is to be hoped that Lilly found time to wash her face. After that, lessons began, and lasted till one o'clock. Dinner followed, with an hour's 'recreation'; then the bell rang for 'silent study-hour', when the girls sat with their books in their bedrooms, but were not allowed to speak to each other. Next came a walk.

'Who are you going to walk with?' asked Rose Red, meeting Clover in Quaker Row.

'I don't know. Katy, I guess.'

'Are you, really? You and she like each other, don't you? Do you know, you're the first sisters I ever knew at school who did! Generally, they quarrel awfully. The Stearns girls, who were here last term, scarcely spoke to each other. They didn't even sleep together; and Sarah Stearns was always telling tales against Sue, and Sue against Sarah.'

'How disgusting! I never heard of anything so mean,' cried Clover, indignantly. 'Why I wouldn't tell tales about Katy if we quarrelled ever so much. We never do, though – Katy is so sweet.'

'I suppose she is,' said Rose, rather doubtfully; 'but, do you know, I'm half afraid of her. It's because she's so tall. Tall people always scare me. And then she looks so grave and grown up! Don't tell her I said so though; for I want her to like me.'

'Oh, she isn't a bit grave or grown up. She's the funniest girl in the world. Wait till you know her,' replied loyal Clover.

'I'd give anything if I could walk with you part of this term,' went on Rose, putting her arm round Clover's waist. 'But you see, unluckily, I'm engaged straight through. All of us old girls are. I walk with May Mather this week and next; then Esther Dearborn for a month; then Lilly Page for two weeks; and all the rest of the time with Mary. I can't think why I promised Lilly. I'm sure I don't want to go with her. I'd ask Mary to let me off, only I'm afraid she would not like it. I say, suppose we engage now to walk with each other for the first half of next term.'

'Why, that's not till October!' said Clover.

'I know it; but it's nice to be beforehand. Will you?'

'Of course I will – provided that Katy has somebody pleasant to go with,' replied Clover, immensely flattered at being asked by the popular Rose. Then they ran downstairs, and took their places in the long procession of girls, who were ranged two and two, ready to start. Miss Jane walked at the head; and Miss Marsh, another teacher, brought up the rear. Rose Red whispered that it was like a funeral and a caravan mixed – 'as cheerful as hearses at both ends, and wild beasts in the middle.'

The walk was along a wooded road – a mile out and a mile back. The procession was not permitted to stop, or straggle, or take any of the liberties which make walking pleasant. Still, Katy and Clover enjoyed it. There was a spring smell in the air, and the woods were beginning to be pretty. They even found a little trailing arbutus blossoming in a sunny hollow. Lilly was just in front of them, and amused them with histories of different girls whom she pointed out in the long line. That was Esther Dearborn – Rose Red's friend. Handsome, wasn't she? but terribly sarcastic. The two next were Amy Alsop and Ellen Gray. They always walked together, because they were so intimate. Yes; they were nice enough, only so distressingly good. Amy did not get one single mark last term! That child with pig-tails was Bella Arkwright. Why on earth did Katy want to know about her? She was a nasty little thing.

'She's just about Elsie's height,' replied Katy. 'Who's that pretty girl with pink velvet on her hat?'

'Dear me! Do you think she's pretty? I don't. Her name is Louisa Agnew. She lives at Ashburn – quite near us; but we don't know them. Her family are not at all in good society.'

'What a pity! She looks so sweet and ladylike.'

Lilly tossed her head. 'They're quite common people,' she said. 'They live in a little mite of a house, and her father paints portraits.'

'But I thould think that would be nice. Doesn't she ever take you to see his pictures?'

'Take me!' cried Lilly, indignantly. 'I should think not, I tell you we

don't visit. I just speak when we're here, but I never see her when I'm
at home.'

'Move on, young ladies. What are you stopping for?' cried Miss
Jane.

'Yes; move on,' muttered Rose Red, from behind. 'Don't you hear
Policeman X?'

From walking-hour till tea-time was 'recreation' again. Lilly improved this opportunity to call at No. 6. She had waited to see how the
girls were likely to take in the school before committing herself to
intimacy; but, now that Rose Red had declared in their favour, she
was ready to begin to be friendly.

'How lovely!' she said, looking about. 'You got the end room, after
all, didn't you? What splendid times you'll have! Oh, how plainly you
can see Berry Searles's window! Has he spoken to you yet?'

'Spoken to us? Of course not! Why should he?' replied Katy. 'He
doesn't know us, and we don't know him.'

'That's nothing. Half the girls in the school bow, and speak, and
carry on with young men they don't know. You won't have a bit of
fun if you're so particular.'

'I don't want that kind of fun,' replied Katy, with energy in her voice;
'neither does Clover. And I can't imagine how the girls can behave so.
It isn't lady-like at all.'

Katy was very fond of this word, 'lady-like'. She always laid great
stress upon it. It seemed in some way to be connected with Cousin
Helen, and to mean everything that was good, and graceful, and sweet.

'Dear me! I'd no idea you were so dreadfully proper,' said Lilly,
pouting. 'Mother said you were as prim and precise as your grandmother; but I didn't suppose—'

'How unkind!' broke in Clover, taking fire, as usual, at any affront
to Katy. 'Katy prim and precise! She isn't a bit! She's twice as much
fun as the rest of you girls; but it's nice fun – not this horrid stuff about
students. I wish your mother wouldn't say such things.'

'I didn't – she didn't – I don't mean exactly that,' stammered Lilly,
frightened by Clover's indignant eyes. 'All I meant was, that Katy is
dreadfully dignified for her age, and we bad girls will have to look out.
You needn't be so mad, Clover; I'm sure it's very nice to be proper and
good, and set an example.'

'I don't want to preach to anybody,' said Katy, colouring, 'and I wasn't thinking about examples. But really and truly, Lilly, wouldn't your mother, and all the girls' mothers, be shocked if they knew about these performances here?'

'Gracious! I should think so; ma would kill me. I wouldn't have her know of my goings on for all the world.'

Just then Rose pulled out a drawer, and called through to ask if Clover would please come in and help her a minute. Lilly took advantage of her absence to say –

'I came on purpose to ask you to walk with me for four weeks. Will you?'

'Thank you; but I'm engaged to Clover.'

'To Clover! But she's your sister; you can get off.'

'I don't want to get off. Clover and I like dearly to go together.'

Lilly stared. 'Well, I never heard of such a thing,' she said; 'you're really romantic. The girls will call you "The Inseparables".'

'I wouldn't mind being inseparable from Clover,' said Katy, laughing.

Next day was Saturday. It was nominally a holiday; but so many tasks were set for it, that it hardly seemed like one. The girls had to practise in the gymnasium, to do their mending, and have all their drawers in apple-pie order, before afternoon, when Miss Jane went through the rooms on a tour of inspection. Saturday, also, was the day for writing home letters; so, altogether, it was the busiest of the week.

Early in the morning Miss Jane appeared in Quaker Row with some slips of paper in her hand, one of which she left at each door. They told the hours at which the girls were to go to the bath-house.

'You will carry each a bath towel, a sponge, and soap,' she announced to Katy, 'and will be in the entry, at the foot of the stairs, at twenty-five minutes after nine precisely. Failures in punctuality will be punished by a mark.' Miss Jane always delivered her words like a machine, and closed her mouth with a snap at the end of the sentence.

'Horrid thing! Don't I wish her missionary would come and carry her off. Not that I blame him for staying away,' remarked Rose Red, from her door; making a face at Miss Jane as she walked down the entry.

'I don't understand about the bath-house,' said Katy. 'Does it belong to us? And where is it?'

'No, it doesn't belong to us. It belongs to Mr Perrit, and anybody can use it; only on Saturday it is reserved for us nuns. Haven't you ever noticed it when we have been out walking? It's in that street by the bakery, which we pass to take the Lebanon Road. We go across the green, and down by Professor Seccomb's, and we are in plain sight from the college all the way; and, of course, those abominable boys sit there with spy-glasses, and stare as hard as ever they can. It's perfectly horrid. 'A bath towel, a sponge, and soap,' indeed! I wish I could make Miss Jane eat the pieces of soap which she has forced me to carry across this village.'

'Oh, Rose!' remonstrated Mary Silver.

'Well, I do. And the bath towels afterwards, by way of a dessert,' replied the incorrigible Rose. 'Never mind! Just wait! A bright idea strikes me.'

'Oh! what?' cried the other three; but Rose only pursed up her mouth, arched her eyebrows, and vanished into her own room, locking the door behind her. Mary Silver, finding herself shut out, sat down meekly in the hall till such time as it should please Rose to open the door. This was not till the bath hour. As Katy and Clover went by, Rose put her head out, and called that she would be down in a minute.

The bathing party consisted of eight girls, with Miss Jane for escort. They were half way across the common before Miss Jane noticed that everybody was shaking with stifled laughter, except Rose, who walked along demurely, apparently unconscious that there was anything to laugh at. Miss Jane looked sharply from one to another for a moment, then stopped short. 'Rosamund Redding! how dare you?'

'What is it, ma'am?' asked Rose, with the face of a lamb.

'Your bath towel! your sponge!' gasped Miss Jane.

'Yes, ma'am, I have them all,' replied the audacious Rose, putting her hand to her hat. There, to be sure, was the long towel, hanging down behind like a veil, while the sponge was fastened on one side like a great cockade; and in front appeared a cake of pink soap, neatly pinned into the middle of a black velvet bow.

Miss Jane seized Rose and removed these ornaments in a twinkling. 'We shall see what Mrs Florence thinks of this conduct,' she grimly remarked. Then, dropping the soap and sponge in her own pocket, she made Rose walk beside her, as if she were a criminal in custody.

'*Your bath towel! your sponge!*' *gasped Miss Jane.*

The bath-house was a neat place, with eight small rooms, well supplied with hot and cold water. Katy would have found her bath very nice, had it not been for the thought of the walk home. They must look so absurd, she reflected, with their sponges and damp towels.

Miss Jane was as good as her word. After dinner, Rose was sent for by Mrs Florence, and had an interview of two hours with her; she came out with red eyes, and shut herself into her room with a disconsolate bang. Before long, however, she revived sufficiently to tap on the drawers and push through a note with the following words:

'My heart is broken!

'R. R.'

Clover hastened in to comfort her. Rose was sitting on the floor, with a very clean pocket-handkerchief in her hand. She wept, and put her head against Clover's knee.

'I suppose I'm the nastiest girl in the world,' she said. 'Mrs Florence thinks so. She said I was an evil influence in the school. Wasn't that unkind?' with a little sob.

'I meant to be so good this term,' she went on; 'but what's the use? A codfish might as well try to play the piano! It was always so, even when I was a baby. Sylvia says I have got a little fiend inside of me. Do you believe I have? Is it that makes me so horrid?'

Clover purred over her. She could not bear to have Rose feel unhappy. 'Wasn't Miss Jane funny?' went on Rose, with a sudden twinkle; 'and did you see Berry, and Alfred Seccomb?'

'No; where were they?'

'Close to us, standing by the fence. All the time Miss Jane was unpinning the towel, they were splitting their sides, and Berry made such a face at me that I nearly laughed out. That boy has a perfect genius for faces. He used to frighten Sylvia and me into fits, when we were little tots, up here on visits.'

'Then you knew him before you came to school?'

'Oh dear, yes! I know all the Hillsover boys. We used to make mud pies together. They're grown up now, most of them, and in college; and when we meet we're very dignified, and say, "Miss Redding", and "Mr Seccomb", and "Mr Searles", but we're just as good friends as ever. When I go to take tea with Mrs Seccomb, Alfred always invites

Berry to drop in, and we have the greatest fun. Mrs Florence won't let me go this term, though, I guess, she's so mad about the towel.'

Katy was quite relieved when Clover reported this conversation. Rose, for all her wickedness, seemed to be a little lady. Katy did not like to class her among the girls who flirted with students whom they did not know.

It was wonderful how soon they all settled down, and became accustomed to their new life. Before six weeks were over, Katy and Clover felt as if they had lived at Hillsover for years. This was partly because there was so much to do. Nothing makes time fly like having every moment filled, and every hour set apart for a distinct employment.

They made several friends, chief among whom were Ellen Gray and Louisa Agnew; this last intimacy Lilly resented highly, and seemed to consider as an affront to herself. With no one, however, was Katy so intimate as Clover was with Rose Red. This cost Katy some jealous pangs at first. She was so used to considering Clover her own exclusive property that it was not easy to share her with another; and she had occasional fits of feeling resentful, and injured, and left out. These were but momentary, however. Katy was too good of heart to let unkind feelings grow, and by and by she grew fond of Rose and Rose of her, so that in the end the sisters shared their friend as they did other nice things, and neither of them was jealous of the other.

But, charming as she was, a certain price had to be paid for the pleasure of intimacy with Rose. Her overflowing spirits, and 'the little fiend inside her', were always provoking scrapes in which her friends were apt to be more or less involved. She was very penitent and afflicted after these scrapes, but it didn't make a bit of difference; the next time she was just as naughty as ever.

'What are you doing?' said Katy one day, meeting her in the hall with a heap of black shawls and aprons on her arm.

'Hush!' whispered Rose, mysteriously; 'don't say a word. Senator Brown is dead – our senator, you know. I'm going to put my window into mourning for him, that's all. It's a proper token of respect.'

Two hours later, Mrs Nipson, walking sedately across the common, noticed quite a group of students in the President's side yard, looking up at the Nunnery. She drew nearer. They were admiring Rose's window, hung with black, and decorated with a photograph of the deceased senator, suspended in the middle of a wreath of weeping-willow. Of course she hurried upstairs, and tore down the shawls and aprons; and, equally of course, Rose had a lecture and a mark. But, dear me! what good did it do? The next day but one, as Katy and Clover sat together in silent-study hour, their lower drawer was pushed open very noiselessly and gently, till it came out entirely, and lay on the floor, and in the aperture thus formed appeared Rose's saucy face, flushed with mischief. She was crawling through from her own room.

'Such fun!' she whispered; 'I never thought of this before! We can have parties in study hours, and all sorts of things.'

'Oh, go back, Rosy!' whispered Clover, in agonized entreaty, though laughing all the time.

'Go back? Not at all! I'm coming in,' answered Rose, pulling herself through a little farther. But at that moment the door opened; there stood Miss Jane! She had caught the buzz of voices as she passed in the hall, and had entered to see what was going on.

Rose, dreadfully frightened, made a rapid movement to withdraw. But the space was narrow, and she had wedged herself, and could move neither backward nor forward. She had to submit to being helped through by Miss Jane, in a series of pulls, while Katy and Clover sat by, not daring to laugh or offer assistance. When Rose was on her feet, Miss Jane released her with a final shake, which she seemed unable to refrain from giving.

'Go to your room,' she said. 'I shall report all of you young ladies for this flagrant act of disobedience.'

Rose went, and in two minutes the drawer, which Miss Jane had replaced, opened again, and there was this note:

'If I am never heard of more, give my love to my family, and mention how I died. I forgive my enemies, and leave Clover my band bracelet.

'My blessings on you both.
'With the deepest regard,
Your afflicted friend,
'R. R.'

Mrs Florence was very angry on this occasion, and would listen to no explanations, but gave Katy and Clover a 'disobedience mark' also.

31

This was very unfair, and Rose felt dreadfully about it. She begged and entreated, but Mrs Florence only replied, 'There is blame on both sides, I have no doubt.'

'She's entirely changed from what she used to be,' declared Rose. 'I don't know what's the matter; I don't like her half so much as I did.'

The truth was, that Mrs Florence had secretly determined to give up her connection with the school at Midsummer; and, regarding it now rather as Mrs Nipson's school than her own, she took no pains to study character or mete out justice carefully among scholars with whom she was not likely to have much to do.

SCHOOL
Flora Thompson

School began at nine o'clock, but the hamlet children set out on their mile-and-a-half walk there as soon as possible after their seven o'clock breakfast, partly because they liked plenty of time to play on the road and partly because their mothers wanted them out of the way before house-cleaning began.

Up the long, straight road they straggled, in twos and threes and in gangs, their flat, rush dinner-baskets over their shoulders and their shabby little coats on their arms against rain. In cold weather some of them carried two hot potatoes which had been in the oven, or in the ashes, all night, to warm their hands on the way and to serve as a light lunch on arrival.

They were strong, lusty children, let loose from control, and there was plenty of shouting, quarrelling, and often fighting among them. In more peaceful moments they would squat in the dust of the road and play marbles, or sit on a stone heap and play dibs with pebbles, or climb into the hedges after birds' nests or blackberries, or to pull long trails of bryony to wreathe round their hats. In winter they would slide on the ice on the puddles, or make snowballs – soft ones for their friends, and hard ones with a stone inside for their enemies.

After the first mile or so the dinner-baskets would be raided; or they would creep through the bars of the padlocked field gates for turnips to pare with the teeth and munch, or for handfuls of green pea shucks, or ears of wheat, to rub out the sweet, milky grain between the hands and devour. In spring they ate the young green from the hawthorn hedges, which they called 'bread and cheese', and sorrel leaves from the way-side, which they called 'sour grass', and in autumn there was an abundance of haws and blackberries and sloes and crab-apples for them to feast upon. There was always something to eat, and they ate, not so much because they were hungry as from habit and relish of the wild food.

At that early hour there was little traffic upon the road. Sometimes, in winter, the children would hear the pounding of galloping hoofs and a string of hunters, blanketed up to the ears and ridden and led by grooms, would loom up out of the mist and thunder past on the grass verges. At other times the steady tramp and jingle of the teams going afield would approach, and, as they passed, fathers would pretend to flick their offspring with whips, saying, 'There! that's for that time you deserved it an' didn't get it'; while elder brothers, themselves at school only a few months before, would look patronizingly down from the horses' backs and call: 'Get out o' th' way, you kids!'

Going home in the afternoon there was more to be seen. A farmer's gig, on the way home from market, would stir up the dust; or the miller's van or the brewer's dray, drawn by four immense, hairy-legged, satin-backed carthorses. More exciting was the rare sight of Squire Harrison's four-in-hand, with ladies in bright, summer dresses, like a garden of flowers, on the top of the coach, and Squire himself, pink-cheeked and white-hatted, handling the four greys.

When the four-in-hand passed, the children drew back and saluted, the Squire would gravely touch the brim of his hat with his whip, and the ladies would lean from their high seats to smile on the curtsying children.

A more familiar sight was the lady on a white horse who rode slowly on the same grass verge in the same direction every Monday and Thursday. It was whispered among the children that she was engaged to a farmer living at a distance, and that they met half-way between their two homes. If so, it must have been a long engagement, for she rode past at exactly the same hour twice a week throughout Laura's school-days, her face getting whiter and her figure getting fuller and her old white horse also putting on weight.

It has been said that every child is born a little savage and has to be civilized. The process of civilization had not gone very far with some of the hamlet children; although one civilization had them in hand at home and another at school, they were able to throw off both on the road between the two places and revert to a state of Nature. A favourite amusement with these was to fall in a body upon some unoffending companion, usually a small girl in a clean frock, and to 'run her', as they called it. This meant chasing her until they caught her, then dragging her down and sitting upon her, tearing her clothes, smudging her face, and tousling her hair in the process. She might scream and cry and say she would 'tell on' them; they took no notice until, tiring of the sport, they would run whooping off, leaving her sobbing and exhausted.

The persecuted one never 'told on' them, even when reproved by the schoolmistress for her dishevelled condition, for she knew that, if she had, there would have been a worse 'running' to endure on the way home, and one that went to the tune of:

> Tell-tale tit!
> Cut her tongue a-slit,
> And every little puppy-dog shall have a little bit!

It was no good telling the mothers either, for it was the rule of the hamlet never to interfere in the children's quarrels. 'Let 'em fight it out among theirselves,' the women would say; and if a child complained the only response would be: 'You must've been doin' summat to them. If you'd've left them alone, they'd've left you alone; so don't come bringing your tales home to me!' It was harsh schooling; but the majority seemed to thrive upon it, and the few quieter and more sensitive children soon learned either to start early and get to school first, or to linger behind, dipping under bushes and lurking inside field gates until the main body had passed.

When Edmund was about to start school, Laura was afraid for him. He was such a quiet, gentle little boy, inclined to sit gazing into space, thinking his own thoughts and dreaming his own dreams. What would he do among the rough, noisy crowd? In imagination she saw him

35

A favourite amusement was to fall upon some unoffending companion.

struggling in the dust with the runners sitting on his small, slender body, while she stood by, powerless to help.

At first she took him to school by a field path, a mile or more round; but bad weather and growing crops soon put an end to that and the day came when they had to take the road with the other children. But, beyond snatching his cap and flinging it into the hedge as they passed, the bigger boys paid no attention to him, while the younger ones were definitely friendly, especially when he invited them to have a blow each on the whistle which hung on a white cord from the neck of his sailor suit. They accepted him, in fact, as one of themselves, allowing him to join in their games and saluting him with a grunted 'Hello, Ted,' when they passed.

When the clash came at last and a quarrel arose, and Laura, looking back, saw Edmund in the thick of a struggling group and heard his voice shouting loudly and rudely, not gentle at all, 'I shan't! I won't! Stop it, I tell you!' and rushed back, if not to rescue, to be near him, she found Edmund, her gentle little Edmund, with face as red as a turkey-cock, hitting out with clenched fists at such a rate that some of the bigger boys, standing near, started applauding.

So Edmund was not a coward, like she was! Edmund could fight! Though where and how he had learned to do so was a mystery. Perhaps, being a boy, it came to him naturally. At any rate, fight he did, so often and so well that soon no one near his own age risked offending him. His elders gave him an occasional cuff, just to keep him in his place; but in scuffles with others they took his part, perhaps because they knew he was likely to win. So all was well with Edmund. He was accepted inside the circle, and the only drawback, from Laura's point of view, was that she was still outside.

Although they started school so early, the hamlet children took so much time on the way that the last quarter of a mile was always a race, and they would rush, panting and dishevelled, into school just as the bell stopped, and the other children, spick and span, fresh from their mothers' hands, would eye them sourly. 'That gipsy lot from Lark Rise!' they would murmur.

Fordlow National School was a small grey one-storied building, standing at the cross-roads at the entrance to the village. The one large classroom which served all purposes was well lighted with several windows, including the large one which filled the end of the building which faced the road. Beside, and joined on to the school, was a tiny two-roomed cottage for the schoolmistress, and beyond that a playground with birch trees and turf, bald in places, the whole being enclosed within pointed, white-painted palings.

The only other building in sight was a row of model cottages occupied by the shepherd, the blacksmith, and other superior farmworkers. The school had probably been built at the same time as the houses and by the same model landlord; for, though it would seem a hovel compared to a modern council school, it must at that time have been fairly up-to-date. It had a lobby with pegs for clothes, boys' and girls' earth-closets, and a backyard with fixed wash-basins, although there was no water laid on. The water supply was contained in a small bucket, filled every morning by the old woman who cleaned the schoolroom, and every morning she grumbled because the children had been so extravagant that she had to 'fill 'un again'.

The average attendance was about forty-five. Ten or twelve of the children lived near the school, a few others came from cottages in the fields, and the rest were the Lark Rise children. Even then, to an outsider, it would have appeared a quaint, old-fashioned little gathering; the girls in their ankle-length frocks and long, straight pinafores, with their hair strained back from their brows and secured on their crowns by a ribbon or black tape or a bootlace; the bigger boys in corduroys and hobnailed boots, and the smaller ones in homemade sailor suits or, until they were six or seven, in petticoats.

Baptismal names were such as the children's parents and grandparents had borne. The fashion in Christian names was changing; babies were being christened Mabel and Gladys and Doreen and Percy and Stanley; but the change was too recent to have affected the names of the older children. Mary Ann, Sarah Ann, Eliza, Martha, Annie, Jane, Amy, and Rose were favourite girls' names. There was a Mary Ann in almost every family, and Eliza was nearly as popular. But none of them were called by their proper names. Mary Ann and Sarah Ann were contracted to Mar'ann and Sar-ann. Mary, apart from Ann, had, by stages, descended through Molly and Polly to Poll. Eliza had become Liza, then Tiza, then Tize; Martha was Mat or Pat; Jane was Jin; and every Amy had at least one 'Aim' in life, of which she had constant reminder. The few more uncommon names were also distorted. Two sisters named at the font Beatrice and Agnes, went through life as Beat and Agg, Laura was Lor, or Low, and Edmund was Ned or Ted.

Laura's mother disliked this cheapening of names and named her third child May, thinking it would not lend itself to a diminutive. However, while still in her cradle, the child became Mayie among the neighbours.

There was no Victoria in the school, nor was there a Miss Victoria or a Lady Victoria in any of the farm-houses, rectories, or mansions in the district, nor did Laura ever meet a Victoria in later life. That great name was sacred to the Queen and was not copied by her subjects to the extent imagined by period novelists of today.

The schoolmistress in charge of the Fordlow school at the beginning of the 'eighties had held that position for fifteen years and seemed to her pupils as much a fixture as the school building; but for most of that time she had been engaged to the squire's head gardener and her long reign was drawing to a close.

She was, at that time, about forty, and was a small, neat little body with a pale, slightly pock-marked face, snaky black curls hanging down to her shoulders, and eyebrows arched into a perpetual inquiry. She wore in school stiffly starched, holland aprons with bibs, one embroidered with red one week, and one with blue the next, and was seldom seen without a posy of flowers pinned on her breast and another tucked into her hair.

Every morning, when school had assembled, and Governess, with her starched apron and bobbing curls appeared in the doorway, there was a great rustling and scraping of curtsying and pulling of forelocks. 'Good morning, children,' 'Good morning, ma'am,' were the formal, old-fashioned greetings. Then, under her determined fingers the harmonium wheezed out 'Once in Royal', or 'We are but little children weak', prayers followed, and the day's work began.

Reading, writing, and arithmetic were the principal subjects, with a Scripture lesson every morning, and needle work every afternoon for the girls. There was no assistant mistress; Governess taught all the classes simultaneously, assisted only by two monitors – ex-scholars, aged about twelve, who were paid a shilling a week each for their services.

Every morning at ten o'clock the Rector arrived to take the older children for Scripture. He was a parson of the old school; a commanding figure, tall and stout, with white hair, ruddy cheeks and an aristocratically beaked nose, and he was as far as possible removed by birth, education, and worldly circumstances from the lambs of his flock. He spoke to them from a great height, physical, mental, and spiritual. 'To order myself lowly and reverently before my betters' was the clause he underlined in the Church Catechism, for had he not been divinely appointed pastor and master to those little rustics and was it not one of his chief duties to teach them to realize this? As a man, he was kindly disposed – a giver of blankets and coals at Christmas, and of soup and milk puddings to the sick.

His lessons consisted of Bible reading, turn and turn about round the class, of reciting from memory the names of the kings of Israel and repeating the Church Catechism. After that, he would deliver a little lecture on morals and behaviour. The children must not lie or steal or be discontented or envious. God had placed them just where they were in the social order and given them their own especial work to do; to envy others or to try to change their own lot in life was a sin of which he hoped they would never be guilty. From his lips the children heard nothing of that God who is Truth and Beauty and Love; but they learned for him and repeated to him long passages from the Authorized Version, thus laying up treasure for themselves.

Scripture over and the Rector bowed and curtsied out of the door, ordinary lessons began. Arithmetic was considered the most important of the subjects taught, and those who were good at figures ranked high in their classes. It was very simple arithmetic, extending only to the first four rules, with the money sums, known as 'bills of parcels', for the most advanced pupils.

The writing lesson consisted of the copying of copper-plate maxims: 'A fool and his money are soon parted'; 'Waste not, want not'; 'Count ten before you speak', and so on. Once a week composition would be set, usually in the form of writing a letter describing some recent event. This was regarded chiefly as a spelling test.

History was not taught formally; but history readers were in use containing such picturesque stories as those of King Alfred and the cakes, King Canute commanding the waves, the loss of the White Ship, and Raleigh spreading his cloak for Queen Elizabeth.

There were no geography readers, and, excepting what could be gleaned from the descriptions of different parts of the world in the ordinary readers, no geography was taught. But, for some reason or other, on the walls of the schoolroom were hung splendid maps: The World, Europe, North America, South America, England, Ireland, and Scotland. During long waits in class for her turn to read, or to have her copy or sewing examined, Laura would gaze on these maps until the shapes of the countries with their islands and inlets became photographed on her brain. Baffin Bay and the land around the poles were especially fascinating to her.

Once a day, at whatever hour the poor, overworked mistress could find time, a class would be called out to toe the chalked semicircle on the floor for a reading lesson. This lesson, which should have been pleasant, for the reading matter was good, was tedious in the extreme. Many of the children read so slowly and haltingly that Laura, who was impatient by nature, longed to take hold of their words and drag them out of their mouths, and it often seemed to her that her own turn to read would never come. As often as she could do so without being detected, she would turn over and peep between the pages of her own *Royal Reader*, and, studiously holding the book to her nose, pretend to be following the lesson while she was pages ahead.

There was plenty there to enthral any child: 'The Skater Chased by Wolves'; 'The Siege of Torquilstone', from *Ivanhoe*; Fenimore Cooper's *Prairie on Fire*; and Washington Irving's *Capture of Wild Horses*.

Then there were fascinating descriptions of such far-apart places as Greenland and the Amazon; of the Pacific Ocean with its fairy islands and coral reefs; the snows of Hudson Bay Territory and the sterile heights of the Andes. Best of all she loved the description of the Himalayas, which began: 'Northward of the great plain of India, and along its whole extent, towers the sublime mountain region of the Himalayas, ascending gradually until it terminates in a long range of summits wrapped in perpetual snow.'

Interspersed between the prose readings were poems: 'The Slave's Dream'; 'Young Lochinvar'; 'The Parting of Douglas and Marmion'; Tennyson's 'Brook' and 'Ring out, Wild Bells'; Byron's 'Shipwreck'; Hogg's 'Skylark', and many more. 'Lochiel's Warning' was a favourite

with Edmund, who often, in bed at night, might be heard declaiming:
'Lochiel! Lochiel! beware of the day!' while Laura, at any time, with
or without encouragement, was ready to 'look back into other years'
with Henry Glassford Bell, and recite his scenes from the life of Mary
Queen of Scots, reserving her most impressive tone for the concluding
couplet:

Lapped by a dog. Go think of it in silence and alone,
Then weigh against a grain of sand the glories of a throne.

But long before their schooldays were over they knew every piece in
the books by heart and it was one of their greatest pleasures in life to
recite them to each other. By that time Edmund had appropriated Scott
and could repeat hundreds of lines, always showing a preference for
scenes of single combat between warrior chiefs. The selection in the
Royal Readers, then, was an education in itself for those who took to
it kindly; but the majority of the children would have none of it; saying
that the prose was 'dry old stuff' and that they hated 'poetry'.

Those children who read fluently, and there were several of them in
every class, read in a monotonous sing-song, without expression, and
apparently without interest. Yet there were very few really stupid
children in the school, as is proved by the success of many of them in
after life, and though few were interested in their lessons, they nearly
all showed an intelligent interest in other things – the boys in field work
and crops and cattle and agricultural machinery; the girls in dress, other
people's love affairs and domestic details.

It is easy to imagine the education authorities of that day, when
drawing up the scheme for that simple but sound education, saying,
'Once teach them to read and they will hold the key to all knowledge.'
But the scheme did not work out. If the children, by the time they left
school, could read well enough to read the newspaper and perhaps an
occasional book for amusement, and write well enough to write their
own letters, they had no wish to go farther. Their interest was not in
books, but in life, and especially the life that lay immediately about
them. At school they worked unwillingly, upon compulsion, and the
life of the schoolmistress was a hard one.

As Miss Holmes went from class to class, she carried the cane and
laid it upon the desk before her; not necessarily for use, but as a reminder,

for some of the bigger boys were very unruly. She punished by a smart stroke on each hand. 'Put out your hand,' she would say, and some boys would openly spit on each hand before proffering it. Others murmured and muttered before and after a caning and threatened to 'tell me feyther'; but she remained calm and cool, and after the punishment had been inflicted there was marked improvement – for a time.

It must be remembered that in those days a boy of eleven was nearing the end of his school life. Soon he would be at work; already he felt himself nearly a man and too old for petticoat government. Moreover, those were country boys, wild and rough, and many of them as tall as she was. Those who had failed to pass Standard IV and so could not leave school until they were eleven, looked upon that last year as a punishment inflicted upon them by the school authorities and behaved accordingly. In this they were encouraged by their parents, for a certain section of these resented their boys being kept at school when they might be earning. 'What do our young Alf want wi' a lot o' book-larnin'?' they would say. 'He can read and write and add up as much money as he's ever likely to get. What more do he want?' Then a neighbour of more advanced views would tell them: 'A good educa-tion's everything in these days. You can't get on in the world if you ain't had one,' for they read their newspapers and new ideas were per-colating, though slowly. It was only the second generation to be forcibly fed with the fruit of the tree of knowledge: what wonder if it did not always agree with it.

Meanwhile, Miss Holmes carried her cane about with her. A poor method of enforcing discipline, according to modern education ideas; but it served. It may be that she and her like all over the country at that time were breaking up the ground that other, later comers to the field, with a knowledge of child psychology and with tradition and experi-ment behind them, might sow the good seed.

She seldom used the cane on the girls and still more seldom on the infants. Standing in a corner with their hands on their heads was their punishment. She gave little treats and encouragements, too, and, al-though the children called her 'Susie' behind her back, they really liked and respected her. Many times there came a knock at the door and a smartly dressed girl on holidays, or a tall young soldier on leave, in his scarlet tunic and pill-box cap, looked in to see Governess'.

43

That Laura could already read when she went to school was never discovered. 'Do you know your A B C?' the mistress asked her on the first morning. 'Come, let me hear you say it: A–B–C—'

'A–B–C—' Laura began; but when she got to F she stumbled, for she had never memorized the letters in order. So she was placed in the class known as 'the babies' and joined in chanting the alphabet from A to Z. Alternately they recited it backward, and Laura soon had that version by heart, for it rhymed:

> Z–Y–X and W–V
> U–T–S and R–Q–P
> O–N–M and L–K–J
> I–H–G and F–E–D
> And C—B—A!

Once started, they were like a watch wound up, and went on alone for hours. The mistress, with all the other classes on her hands, had no time to teach the babies, although she always had a smile for them when she passed and any disturbance or cessation of the chanting would bring her down to them at once. Even the monitors were usually engaged in giving out dictation to the older children, or in hearing tables or spelling repeated; but, in the afternoon, one of the bigger girls, usually the one who was the poorest needlewoman (it was always Laura in later years) would come down from her own form to point to and name each letter on a wall-sheet, the little ones repeating them after her. Then she would teach them to form pot-hooks and hangers, and, afterwards, letters, on their slates, and this went on for years, as it seemed to Laura, but perhaps it was only one year.

At the end of that time the class was examined and those who knew and could form their letters were moved up into the official 'Infants'. Laura, who by this time was reading *Old St Paul's* at home, simply romped through this Little-Go; but without credit, for it was said she 'gabbled' her letters, and her writing was certainly poor.

It was not until she reached Standard I that her troubles really began. Arithmetic was the subject by which the pupils were placed, and as Laura could not grasp the simplest rule with such small help as the mistress had time to give, she did not even know how to begin working out the sums and was permanently at the bottom of the class. At needlework in the afternoon she was no better. The girls around her in class were making pinafores for themselves, putting in tiny stitches and biting off their cotton like grown women, while she was still struggling with her first hemming strip. And a dingy, crumped strip it was before she had done with it, punctuated throughout its length with blood spots where she had pricked her fingers.

'Oh, Laura! What a dunce you are!' Miss Holmes used to say every time she examined it, and Laura really was the dunce of the school in those two subjects. However, as time went on, she improved a little, and managed to pass her standard every year with moderate success until she came to Standard V and could go no farther, for that was the highest in the school. By that time the other children she had worked with had left, excepting one girl named Emily Rose, who was an only child and lived in a lonely cottage far out in the fields. For two years Standard V consisted of Laura and Emily Rose. They did few lessons and those few mostly those they could learn from books by themselves, and much of their time was spent in teaching the babies and assisting the schoolmistress generally.

That mistress was not Miss Holmes. She had married her head gardener while Laura was still in the Infants and gone to live in a pretty old cottage which she had renamed 'Malvern Villa'. Immediately after her had come a young teacher, fresh from her training college, with all the latest educational ideas. She was a bright, breezy girl, keen on reform, and anxious to be a friend as well as a teacher to her charges.

She came too early. The human material she had to work on was not ready for such methods. On the first morning she began a little speech, meaning to take the children into her confidence:

'Good morning, children. My name is Matilda Annie Higgs, and I want us all to be friends—' A giggling murmur ran round the school. 'Matilda Annie! Matilda Annie! Did she say Higgs or pigs?' The name made direct appeal to their crude sense of humour, and, as to the offer of friendship, they scented weakness in that, coming from one whose office it was to rule. Thenceforth, Miss Higgs might drive her pigs in the rhyme they shouted in her hearing; but she could neither drive nor lead her pupils. They hid her cane, filled her inkpot with water, put young frogs in her desk, and asked her silly, unnecessary questions

45

about their work. When she answered them, they all coughed in chorus.

The girls were as bad as the boys. Twenty times in one afternoon a hand would shoot upward and it would be: 'Please miss, can I have this or that from the needlework box?' and poor Miss Higgs, trying to teach a class at the other end of the room, would come and unlock and search the box for something they had already and had hidden.

Several times she appealed to them to show more consideration. Once she burst into tears before the whole school. She told the woman who cleaned that she had never dreamed there were such children anywhere. They were little savages.

One afternoon, when a pitched battle was raging among the big boys in class and the mistress was calling imploringly for order, the Rector appeared in the doorway.

'Silence!' he roared.

The silence was immediate and profound, for they knew he was not one to be trifled with. Like Gulliver among the Lilliputians, he strode into the midst of them, his face flushed with anger, his eyes flashing blue fire. 'Now, what is the meaning of this disgraceful uproar?

Some of the younger children began to cry; but one look in their direction froze them into silence and they sat, wide-eyed and horrified, while he had the whole class out and caned each boy soundly, including those who had taken no part in the fray. Then, after a heated discourse in which he reminded the children of their lowly position in life and the twin duties of gratitude to and respect towards their superiors, school was dismissed. Trembling hands seized coats and dinner-baskets and frightened little figures made a dash for the gate. But the big boys who had caused the trouble showed a different spirit. 'Who cares for him?' they muttered, 'Who cares? Who cares? He's only an old parson!' Then, when safely out of the playground, one voice shouted:

> Old Charley-wag! Old Charley-wag!
> Ate the pudden and gnawed the bag!

The other children expected the heavens to fall; for Mr Ellison's Christian name was Charles. The shout was meant for him and was one of defiance. He did not recognize it as such. There were several Charleses in the school, and it must have been unconceivable to him that his own Christian name should be intended. Nothing happened, and, after a few moments of tense silence, the rebels trooped off to get their own account of the affair in first at home.

After that, it was not long before the station fly stood at the school gate and Miss Higgs's trunk and bundles and easy-chair were hauled on top. Back came the married Miss Holmes, now Mrs Tenby. Girls curtsied again and boys pulled their forelocks. It was 'Yes, ma'am', and 'No, ma'am', and 'What did you please to say, ma'am?' once more. But either she did not wish to teach again permanently or the education authorities already had a rule against employing married-women teachers, for she only remained a few weeks until a new mistress was engaged.

This turned out to be a sweet, frail-looking, grey-haired, elderly lady named Miss Shepherd, and a gentle shepherd she proved to her flock. Unfortunately, she was but a poor disciplinarian, and the struggle to maintain some degree of order wore her almost to shreds. Again there was always a buzz of whispering in class; stupid and unnecessary questions were asked, and too long intervals elapsed between the word of command and the response. But, unlike Miss Higgs, she did not give up. Perhaps she could not afford to do so at her age and with an invalid sister living with and dependent upon her. She ruled, if she can be said to have ruled at all, by love and patience and ready forgiveness. In time, even the blackest of her sheep realized this and kept within certain limits; just sufficient order was maintained to avoid scandal, and the school settled down under her mild rule for five or six years.

Perhaps these upheavals were a necessary part of the transition which was going on. Under Miss Holmes, the children had been weaned from the old free life; they had become accustomed to regular attendance, to sitting at a desk and concentrating, however imperfectly. Although they had not learned much, they had been learning to learn. But Miss Holmes's ideas belonged to an age that was rapidly passing. She believed in the established order of society, with clear divisions, and had done her best to train the children to accept their lowly lot with gratitude to and humility before their betters. She belonged to the past; the children's lives lay in the future, and they needed a guide with at least some inkling of the changing spirit of the times. The new mistresses, who came from the outside world, brought something of this spirit with them.

Miss Shepherd taught the children that it was not what a man or woman had, but what they were which mattered. That poor people's souls are as valuable and that their hearts may be as good and their minds as capable of cultivation as those of the rich. She even hinted that on the material plane people need not necessarily remain always upon one level. Some boys, born of poor parents, had struck out for themselves and become great men, and everybody had respected them for rising upon their own merits. She would read them the lives of some of these so-called self-made men (there were no women, Laura noticed!) and though their circumstances were too far removed from those of her hearers for them to inspire the ambition she hoped to awaken, they must have done something to widen their outlook on life.

Meanwhile the ordinary lessons went on. Reading, writing, arithmetic, all a little less rather than more well taught and mastered than formerly. In needlework there was a definite falling off. Miss Shepherd was not a great needle-woman herself and was inclined to cut down the sewing time to make way for other work. Infinitesimal stitches no longer provoked delighted exclamations, but more often a 'Child! You will ruin your eyes!' As the bigger girls left who in their time had won county prizes, the standard of the output declined, until, from being known as one of the first needlework schools in the district, Fordlow became one of the last.

I MITE HAV KNOWN
Geoffrey Willans

Well i mite hav expected it. The game's up. They got me just when i thort i was safe. So here i am back at SKOOL agane for a joly term chiz chiz chiz.

St custard's, i regret to report, hav not changed in my absence, though perhaps it may hav got worse. It is just the same as any other first day since i started my akademic hem-hem career there some few semesters ago. (It seme as if it were yesterday, my dere). Same cobwebs, same smell of wet flannel, soap, carbolik ect poo gosh: inside the skool piano there is now a nest of mice, 1 cig. card, 3 katerpillers and pikture of marylyn monro pinched no doubt from the master's comon room.

As for my merry felow students, they are still here worse luck. Just look at them – grabber who arrive in a swank-pot rolls, peason my frend who hav a face like a squashed tomato, gillibrand, molesworth 2 my bro. And who is this who skip weedily up to me, eh? 'Hullo clouds, hullo sky,' he sa. 'Hullo birds, hullo poetry books, hullo skool sossages, hullo molesworth 1.' You hav guessed it is basil fotherington-tomas.

Wot brethless adventures lie before these stout little chaps? (And none stouter than fatpot peason.) Wot wizard japes and priceless pranks will they get up to? Before them lie the bright future of a new term – will they accept the chalenge?

49

(*Now read on.*)

On arrival all boys stand about with hands in pokets looking utterly fed up and dejected. Finally someone speke.

'Did you hav a good hols, molesworth?'

'Not bad.'

(*Silence.*)

'Did you have a good hols peason?'

'Not bad.'

The dialogue is positively scintilating, my dere. Surely they canot kepe it up? There is no chance of that for the wit of these skolars is interupted by a dread sound e.g.

CLANG-PIP. CLANG-PIP. CLANG-PIP.

It is the skool bell which sumon us to asemble in big skool into which enter anon GRIMES, the headmaster surounded by a posse of thugs and strong-arm men in black gowns. The beaks, of course, alias 'my devoted staff'. You can imagine it a few minits before.

Scene: GRIMES study. A candle is burning in a bottle. A bottle of GIN stand on the table. A beak is fixing an iron spike on a kane, another is fixing a knuckle-duster, a third practise with a broken botle.

GRIMES: Are they all in, Slugsy?

G. A. POSTLETHWAITE m.a. (leeds): Yep, they're all in, boss.

GRIMES: o.k. then we're ready to pull the job. You kno the plan. Slugsy, you cover me from the door. Lefty, cover my right flank. Butch, on the other side. Killer, bring up the rear, If there's any trouble, let them hav it. That clear Butch?

P. ST. J. NETLETON, b.a. (exeter): Wot about our cut? You still owe us for last terms jobs.

GRIMES: How can you be so sordid?

ect, ect. ect.

Now GRIMES stand on the platform, smiling horribly at the pitiable colection of oiks, snekes, cads, oafs and dirty roters below.

'Welcome back,' he snarl, 'Welcom back to st. custards for a new term. I hope you had a good hols? i did myself – spane, the s. of france, then on for a couple of weeks to the italian riviera. This term, of course, the fees will be higher to meet the mounting costs.'

But this evidence of good humour is short-lived. Without warning, he bare his fangs.

'Now listen, scum,' he yell, 'The last mum hav departed in tears. You are in my clutches agane and there is no escape. And its going to be this way this term. More work, increased production, trades unions supresed and the first boy i hear who sa poo gosh at a skool sossage will get 6. And strikes won't help you. If you go out the shop stewards will be flogged.'

'Remember this,' he leer, 'You never had it so good.'

Well, this is just wot we expect. We hav it every term and our tiny harts sink to our boots. It will be nothing but *lat. fr. arith. geom. algy. geog.* ect. and with the winter coming on it would be warmer in siberia in a salt mine. Oh well – we wait for wot we kno full well will come next.

'And wot,' sa GRIMES, 'have we all been reading in the hols?'

Tremble tremble moan drone, i hav read nothing but red the redskin and Guide to the Pools. i hav also sat with my mouth open looking at lassie, wonder horse ect on t.v. How to escape? But i hav alreddy made a plan.

'fotherington-tomas,' sa GRIMES, 'wot hav you read?'

'Ivanhothevicarofwakefieldwutheringheightstreasureislandvanity fairwestwardhothewaterbabies and—'

'That is enuff. Good boy. And molesworth?'

He grin horibly.

'What hav you read, molesworth?'

gulp gulp a rat in a trap.

'Proust, sir.'

'Come gane?'

'Prous, sir. A grate fr. writer. The book in question, sir, was swan's way.'

'Gorblimey. Wot did you think of it, eh?'

'The style was exquisite, sir, and the characterization superb. The long evocative passages—'

'SILENCE!' thunder GRIMES. 'There is no such book, impertinent boy. I shall hav to teach you culture the hard way. Report for the kane after prayers.'

Chiz chiz to think i hav learned all that by hart. It's not fair they get you every way. And so our first day end when we join together singing our own skool song.

> *St custard's is brave*
> SWISH
> *St. custard's is fair.*
> BIFF BANG WALOP.
> *Hurrah hurrah for st custard's.*
> SWISH SWISH SWISH

As lashed by the beaks we join our boyish trebles in this fine old song we feel positively inspired i do not think. We are in for the joliest term on record. In fakt, i am back in the jug agane.

TELEVISION

Out of 62 pupils at st. custard's, $61\frac{1}{2}$ stay up late at nite gawping at the t.v. To do this they employ unbelievable cuning saing mum, can we? ect. o please, mum, just till 7.30 when that grate dog who rescue people and bark like mad will be finished. $61\frac{1}{2}$ mums out of 62 fall for this becos it means a little quiet in the house (xcept for the grate dog barking, this, however, appere preferable to our boyish cries.) Wot hapen next? The grate dog is folowed by an even grater fool i.e. plunket of the yard. This is a program highly suitable for small boys as there is murder and various other CRIMES in it. The grate thing is to manage to sit gawping until the new program begin: then, when yore mum come in and sa britely 'Time for bed, chaps' ect, she will get wrapped up in the brutal crime which go on. This takes $61\frac{1}{2}$ boys out of 62 until 8 p.m. when there is a quiz chiz. Pater storm in and sa 'aren't these boys in bed yet?' He then kno the answer to the first q. *i.e.* wot is the capital of england? This set him going since he wish to give a demonstration of his prowess.

'Any fule would kno that,' he sa.

$61\frac{1}{2}$ boys out of 62 restrane any comment on this, knoing they will get sent to bed. Pater go on saing weedy things *i.e.* china, of corse, edison, e.a.poe also that he ought to go in for it he would win a lot of money. mum do not restrane coment on the last point and by the time the argument is over we can have a little peace v.ith the play. This is about LUV and of no interest but it do kepe you on the job until 10. The $61\frac{1}{2}$ boys then get into there pajamas and come back to sa good nite. They stretch forward for loving embrace when suddenly they are turned into pilar of salt, *e.g.* lot's wife becos a HORSE is in terrible trubble on the screen with a ruough master. 11 p.m. bed and swete dreams.

SMOKING

Enuff said. Just count the cig ends behind the skool potting shed. It look as if the skool gardner must smoke 500 a day.

CONVERSATION IN DORMS

The news is grave. 62 boys out of 62 indulge in this forbiden practise after lights out. Moreover the conversation is not on a high level *i.e.* you hav a face like a squished tomato same to you with no returns ass silly ass i said it first yes i did no i didn't. This frequently end up in BLOWS with ye olde concrete pilows. From 1 boy alone do we get GOOD CONVERSATION i think you kno to whom i refer. Oui! c'est basil fotherington- (hullo clouds, hullo sky) tomas who bore us to slepe with proust and t.s.eliot.

RUSHING DOWN THE PASSAGE

There is something about the sight of a passage which raise the worst in a boy. No sooner than he see the end of it than he wish to sa charge ta-ran-ta-rah and do so, sliding the soles off his house shoes. ½ a boy, however, do walk slowly and with corekt deportment, one hand on hip, until overtaken and troden on by the mob. And good ridance.

MOB VIOLENCE

We must do something about this: we canot hav it, you kno. In future there must be no more scrums in the gim. The honor of the skool is at stake. And the answer is easy. Organize some morris dancing and all will be well. Or not.

And wot is GRIMES conklusion, eh? Modern youth is on the way down. But he was a boy once (i suppose). Can it get any lower?

MUSIC THE FOOD OF LUV

Sooner or later yore parents decide that they ought to give you a chance to hav a bash at the piano. So wot happen, eh? They go up to GRIMES, headmaster, who is dealing in his inimitable way, my dere, with a number of problems from other parents *e.g.* fotherington-tomas's vests, peason's cough drops, grabber's gold pen and pore, pore mrs gillibrand thinks that ian (who is so sensitive) is the tiniest bit unhappy about the condukt of sigismund the mad maths master. (Who wouldn't be? He is utterly bats and more crooked than the angle A.) Finally come the turn o those super, smashing and cultured family hem-hem the molesworths. Mum step forward britely:

Oh, mr GRIMES, she sa, we think it would be so nice for nigel and his wee bro, molesworth 2, to learn the piano this term.

(GRIMES thinks: Another mug. One born every minit.)

GRIMES: Yes, yes, mrs molesworth, i think we could manage to squeeze them in. Judging from their drawings both yore sons hav strong artistik tendencies. i see them in their later years drawing solace from bach and beethoven ect in some cloistered drawing room. It'll cost you ten nicker and not a penny less.

PATER: (*feebly*) I sa—

GRIMES: Look at the wear and tear on the piano – it's a bektenstein, you kno. Then there's the metronome – had to have new sparking plugs last hols and the time is coming when we've got to hav a new pianoforte tutor.

Pater and Mater weakly agree and the old GRIMES cash register ring merily out again. It is in this way that that grate genius of the keyboard, molesworth 2, learned to pla that grate piece fairy bells chiz chiz chiz.

The first thing when you learn to pla the piano is to stare out of the window for 20 minits with yore mouth open. Then scratch yore head and carve yore name, adding it to the illustrious list already inscribed on the top of the piano. Should, however, GRIMES or any of the other beaks becom aware that there is no sound of mery musick, the pupil should pretend to be studdying the KEYBOARD in his instruktion book.

This is meant to teach the eager pupil the names of the notes ect. The skool piano may hav looked like that once, but toda it is very different. Before getting on to rimski-korsakov it is as well you kno wot you are up aganst. Here is the guide –

C – this one go plunk.

D – the top hav come off the note and you strike melody from something like a cheese finger.

E – sticks down when you hit it. Bring yore screwdriver to lever it up.

F – have never been the same since molesworth 2 put his chewing gum under it.

G – nothing hapen when you hit this note at all.

★   ★   ★   ★

'Wot is yore opinion of colin wilson, the new philosopher?' sa fother-ington-tomas, hanging by his weedy heels from the cross bar.

'Advanced, forthright, significant,' i repli, kicking off the mud from my footer boots.

'He takes, i think, the place of t.s.eliot in speaking for the younger genneration. Habe you any idea of the score?

'Not a clue.'

'Those rufians hav interrupted us 6 times. So one must assume half a dozen goles. If only our defence was more lively, quicker on the takle! Now as i was saying about colin wilson—'

Yes, clots, weeds, and fellow sufferers, it means the good old footer season is with us and jack the shepherd is a good deal warmer when he blows his nail than we are. Birds are frozen: little children sink with a vast buble in the mud and are not heard of agane: sigismund the mad maths master don his long white woollen hem-hems. Yes, this is the time when we are driven out with whip and lash upon ye old soccer field.

Mind you, there are some who think soccer is super. These are the ones who charge, biff, tackle and slam the leather first-time into the net ect. They hav badges and hav a horible foto taken at the end of term with their arms folded and the year chalked upon the pill. This foto cost there parents 7/6 on the skool bill and i hope they think it is worth it. i would not care for grabber's face on my walls, that's all.

Of corse i'm no good . . . no, i mean it . . . i simply am no good . . . no, please, grabber, my body-swerve . . . well, it go in the wrong direktion . . . o, i sa, no . . . wot a nice thing to hear about myself . . . if

Mind you, there are some who think soccer is super.

i try hard i'll be in *the seconds!* And then how much further on would i be in the career of life, eh?

I speke for millions when i sa i *AM NO GOOD AT SOCCER.* You can, of corse, watch it from the touchline in that case. Very diffrent.

'Pass . . . get it out to the wing . . . move in to the centre . . . wot are you plaing about at? . . . Get rid of it.'

I need hardly tell you the esential thing about a football *i.e.* nobody need tell *me* to get rid of it. i do not want it in the first place. Wot is the use of having a soaking wet piece of leather pushed at you? Give me a hadock every time, at least you can eat it.

However, where would headmaster GRIMES be without the good old game? No longer would he be able to look up from those delicious crumpets, which he eat before a roring fire and observe: 'The third game ort to be finished in about 20 minits. Cold out there. About 50 below zero. Damn it, forgot to stoke the baths! o well, a spot of cold water did nobody any harm, eh?'

However, there is no doubt about it the honour of the old skool depend a grate deal on whether you can score more than wot i may litely call 'the opposition'. Scoring more than the 'oposition' is practically imposible, but it sometimes hapen. Beware when it do becos you hav to bang yore spoon on the table, just when you want to help yourself to the jam, and yell RA, RA, RA! Well done SKOOL SKOOL, SKOOL!

And who is it who have achieved this sukcess? None other than the games master, who hav given his life, his time, his bootlaces and his premium bonds into making the 1st XI into a well-oiled footballing machine. There are lots of different kinds of games masters, but there are usually 2 types who are able to be distinguished by us weeds on the touchline *e.g.*

Type One: He do not sa anything: he puts his hands in his mack and watch. After about 17 minits of the first half he is heard to sa 'O, potts-rogers'. He knock out his pipe at half-time when the team are sucking lemons and whisper: 'good show, get on with it.' Then he relapse into silence and, about 2 minits from time, sa 'o god'.

The other type of games master is exactly the oposite. Remembering his own football prime (one day we must go into the rekords of games masters, must we not?) he think he can score a gole with his own voice. Some of them can: or ort to be able to.

'COME ON, ST CUSTARD'S . . . GET INTO HIM . . . PASS! . . . MARK YORE MAN! . . . BLOW YORE NOSE . . . INTO THE CENTRE . . . NO, THE CENTRE NOT THE ARTERIAL ROAD . . . GET IT IN! . . . COME ON NOW! SHOOT! . . .'

This is the last desparing cry. Lots of games masters have been carted awa murmuring faintly 'Shoot!' In 999 cases if they were aiming at gole someone missed: but ocasionaly the shot hit the mark. And it was an elfin-ray pistol with atommic atachment that do the damage.

*　　*　　*　　*

'The New Year stretches before us, molesworth,' sa fotherington-tomas, skipping weedily.

'Wot of it?' i sa 'Wot of it, o weedy wet? It will be the same as any other, all geom.fr. geog ect and weedy walks on sunda.'

'It was just – well, have you ever thort of becoming a skoolmaster when you grow up?'

Curses! Curses! That i should live to see the day when these things were spoken!

'Sa that agane,' i grit, 'and i will conk you on the head and/or thoroughly bash you up.'

'Do not,' he sa, 'get into a bate. i was only trying to help. A skool-master is better than a fashion designer. Besides, you hav all the qualifications.'

'Hav i?' i sa, in spite of myself. 'How super, fotherington-tomas. Tell me about them, go on o you mite.'

'You are qualified,' sa fotherington-tomas, 'becos you can frankly never pass an exam and have o branes. Obviously you will be a skool-master – there is no other choice.'

As it hapen this witty conversation take place during the 2nd XI footer match v porridge court. There comes a warning shout from the spektators. fotherington-tomas skip back weedily into gole and i remane where i am, a bleeding hart on the left wing.

All the same the conversation have me worried and affekt my game. (See report)

'*For the rest of the match molesworth 1 was not in the smashing form which have earned him the soobriquet of the "Dribbling Wizard".* *He was not fastening on to his passes.*' (m. thinks: you mean when someone hack a huge muddy ball in my direction? Wot a pass.) '*The opposition had him at sea.*' (m. thinks: it's amateurs still at prep skool, isn't it? Or are porridge court buying players?) '*Where was that body swerve? That familiar jink?* (m. thinks: Gone my dear. Absolument disparu like mother's mink.)

And so it is the old story. The better team won, ha-ha. And so it go on at football matches. But, as that nite i lie awake on my downy couch hem-hem in the PINK DORM the conversation came back to me as it was a nightmare. Me a Skoolmaster! Me a BEAK! Me an Usher! Wot an idea – and yet look around you. There are so many of them that it is obviously a fate which is difficult to avoid.

My head nods the tired brane drowses. i slip i slide (poetry THE BROOK) into merciful oblivion. Soon the dorm resound with a steady note plaster falls off the ceiling, the paint blisters pop. My snores join the others but there is no rest i am shaken by a terrible NIGHT-MARE.

i am sitting at the master's desk looking with horror at a see of faces, fat ones, thin ones, contorted, spotty, green, and black ones, there is no doubt of whose they are – it is 3B.

And who is that horrid creature dodging behind gillibrand and trying to conceal the fact that he is chewing buble gum? It is me, molesworth 1 chiz chiz chiz. *i am teaching myself!*

'Boy!' i rasp, in a voice i can scarcely recognize it is hoarse and thick with pasion. 'Boy, stand up. Wot is yore name?'

'molesworth 1, sir.'

'That is very interesting, molesworth very interesting indeed. Can it be, however, that you are having some difikulty in enunciating? i thort there was some slight suspicion of er congestion in the mouth? Some er impediment of the speech?'

'No – no, sir. Nnnnnnn – no, sir.'

'BOY HOW DARE YOU?'

My face is red as a tomato i shake with rage my eyes are those of a MANIAK. Like any other master i hav forgotten that i was ever a boy i have forgoten brave noble fearless youth cheers cheers. My hand go

59

back like a flash and i buzz the red chalk striking the victim on the nose. The rest of the klass titter they are sicophants and toadies i diskard them.

'If there is another sound i shall keep the whole klass in. Molesworth, go outside and remove that disgusting objekt.'

It is too horible. i struggle to awake but the nightmare continue.

It is still the same lesson and i am the master. Everything is normal i am feeling a trifle lazy and set the boys some geom propositions to get on with. Before me is a pile of uncorekted exercise books i pop outside for a quick cig and return to study a book on grips and tortures for boys. i am immersed in this when i hear a sound.

'Sir,'

(A spasm of anoyance run through my frame. i pretend not to hear.)

'Sir, sir, sir please sir.'

CURSES! Is the child not to be put off? am i never to be rid of his importunity? Wearily i raise my bespectakled face and gaze at him over a mountane of exercise books and bottles of red ink.

'Well, wot is it molesworth?'

'Wot is the verb–noun infinitiv, sir?'

'Eh?'

'The verb–noun infinitiv, sir. It sa in the Shorter Latin Primer ...'

'All right all right. i heard you the fust time' (thinks: verb–noun infinitiv? i dunno. search me.)

Open lat. grammer under cover of books. shufle shufle. Sweat pour from my brows i must play for time. i cover my action with stinging words.

'So molesworth you do not kno the verb–noun infinitiv? Wot crassness, wot ignorance ect ...'

Masters ushally keep their cribs and answer books in the dark depths of their desks and wot a collection there is in there – kanes, beetles, chalk, thumbscrews, old tin soldiers which hav been confiskated, fotos of gurls, bat oil, fleas and cobwebs.

in here i find the lat. grammer. i prop it against a tin of pineaple chunks and find the answer. My blak beak's heart is filled with relief. Also i thirst for revenge. i switch to geom and make the chalk squeak with the compass on the blackboard until all howl it is worse than molesworth 2's space ship.

SCREE SCREE SCREE SCREE delicious torture! i draw a

collossal Angle A and make it equal to Angle B. Gloat Gloat. Wot does it matter if it is half the size? pythagoras could make an elephant equal to a flea . . .

Restlessly i toss from side to side in my bed. Can it be that i have eaten too much skool cheese? Why can i not awake? The nightmare continue . . .

am i popular? Do the boys like me? O grief. perhaps they do not. i will do anything. tomorow i will read to them. i will give them the water babies that always sla them. it sla me too. Poor tom. And yet . . . are they making enuff progress? perhaps it should be the confidential clerk by t.s. eliot. But will that make me popular hem-hem?

THE BELL! The BELL!

I am telling a story about how i won the war. WEEE PING EEEAUOOWOO. Men, there is a nest of pea shooters under the map of that world i want you to silence them. CHARGE TA-RAN-TA-RA. BANG BONK BISH. Who zoom past then? it is molesworth 2 beating us up in his superjet speed hawk ur ur ur ur. Take cover, Sigismund, these boys are fiercer than the mau-mau and many look like them. This is rebelion and the boys mean business. Give me my kane i will die like a man.

THE BELL.

Why have not mrs grabber given me the ushual 50 cigs for an xmas box? Where are my yelow socks and pink tie? i am alone the skool is empty. Where are the boys? Gone. it is the old story, caruthers, too many masters chasing too few boys. To many . . .

THE BELL.

And this time it is the skool bell bidding me rise and face the chalenge of the new year hem-hem, Sun shine, birds sing, skool sossages frazzle in the kitchen – hurrah hurrah i am not a master after all. I stride forth with new knoledge *e.g.* even masters hav their problems. i will remember that in future.

MOLESWORTH WOT ARE YOU DOING WITH YORE HAIR UNBRUSHED YORE SHOES UNLACED AND WEARING ONE FOOTER SOCK ECT? 1000000000000 LINES.

So you see. There you are. There's nothing you can do about them.

THE SPORTS
Evelyn Waugh

Happily enough, it did not rain next day, and after morning school everybody dressed up to the nines. Dr Fagan appeared in a pale grey morning coat and sponge-bag trousers, looking more than ever *jeune premier*; there was a spring in his step and a pronounced sprightliness of bearing that Paul had not observed before. Flossie wore a violet frock of knitted wool made for her during the preceding autumn by her sister. It was the colour of indelible ink on blotting paper, and was ornamented at the waist with flowers of emerald green and pink. Her hat, also home-made, was the outcome of many winter evenings of ungrudged labour. All the trimmings of all her previous hats had gone to its adornment. Dingy wore a little steel brooch made in the shape of a bull-dog. Grimes wore a stiff evening collar made of celluloid.

'Had to do something to celebrate the occasion,' he said, 'so I put on a "choker". Phew, though, it's tight. Have you seen my fiancée's latest creation? Ascot ain't in it. Let's get down to Mrs Roberts for a quick one before the happy throng rolls up.'

'I wish I could, but I've got to go round the ground with the Doctor.'

'Righto, old boy! See you later. Here comes Prendy in his coat of many colours.'

Mr Prendergast wore a blazer of faded stripes, which smelt strongly of camphor.

'I think Dr Fagan encourages a certain amount of display on these occasions,' he said. 'I used to keep wicket for my college, you know, but I was too short-sighted to be much good. Still, I am entitled to the blazer,' he said with a note of defiance in his voice, 'and it is more appropriate to a sporting occasion than a stiff collar.'

'Good old Prendy!' said Grimes. 'Nothing like a change of clothes to bring out latent pep. I felt like that my first week in khaki. Well, so long. Me for Mrs Roberts. Why don't you come too, Prendy?'

'D'you know,' said Mr Prendergast, 'I think I will.'

Paul watched them disappear down the drive in amazement. Then he went off to find the Doctor.

'Frankly,' said the Doctor, 'I am at a loss to understand my own emotions. I can think of no entertainment that fills me with greater detestation than a display of competitive athletics, none – except possibly folk-dancing. If there are two women in the world whose company I abominate – and there are very many more than two – they are Mrs Beste-Chetwynde and Lady Circumference. I have, moreover, had an extremely difficult encounter with my butler, who – will you believe it? – waited at luncheon in a mustard-coloured suit of plus-fours and a diamond tie-pin, and when I reprimanded him, attempted to tell me some ridiculous story about his being the proprietor of a circus or swimming-bath or some such concern. And yet,' said the Doctor, 'I am filled with a wholly delightful exhilaration. I can't understand it. It is not as though this was the first occasion of the kind. During the fourteen years that I have been at Llanabba there have been six sports days and two concerts, all of them, in one way or another, utterly disastrous. Once Lady Bunyon was taken ill; another time it was the matter of the press photographers and the obstacle race; another time some quite unimportant parents brought a dog with them which bit two of the boys very severely and one of the masters, who swore terribly in front of everyone. I could hardly blame him, but of course he had to go. Then there was the concert when the boys refused to sing "God Save the King" because of the pudding they had had for luncheon. One way and another, I have been consistently unfortunate in my efforts at festivity. And yet I look forward to each new fiasco with the

63

utmost relish. Perhaps, Pennyfeather, you will bring luck to Llanabba; in fact, I feel confident you have already done so. Look at the sun!'

Picking their way carefully among the dry patches in the water-logged drive, they reached the playing-fields. Here the haphazard organization of the last twenty-four hours seemed to have been fairly successful. A large marquee was already in position, and Philbrick – still in plus-fours – and three gardeners were at work putting up a smaller tent.

'That's for the Llanabba Silver Band,' said the Doctor. 'Philbrick, I required you to take off those loathsome garments.'

'They were new when I bought them,' said Philbrick, 'and they cost eight pounds fifteen. Anyhow, I can't do two things at once, can I? If I go back to change, who's going to manage all this, I'd like to know?'

'All right! Finish what you are doing first. Let us just review the arrangements. The marquee is for the visitors' tea. That is Diana's province. I expect we shall find her at work.'

Sure enough, there was Dingy helping two servants to arrange plates of highly-coloured cakes down a trestle table. Two other servants in the background were cutting sandwiches. Dingy, too, was obviously enjoying herself.

'Jane, Emily, remember that that butter has to do for three loaves. Spread it thoroughly, but don't waste it, and cut the crusts as thin as possible. Father, will you see to it that the boys who come in with their parents come in *alone?* You remember last time how Briggs brought in four boys with him, and they ate all the jam sandwiches before Colonel Loder had had any. Mr Pennyfeather, the champagne-cup is *not* for the masters. In fact, I expect you will find yourselves too much occupied helping the visitors to have any tea until they have left the tent. You had better tell Captain Grimes that, too. I am sure Mr Prendergast would not think of pushing himself forward.'

Outside the marquee were assembled several seats and tubs of palms and flowering shrubs. 'All this must be set in order,' said the Doctor; 'our guests may arrive in less than an hour.' He passed on. 'The cars shall turn aside from the drive here and come right into the ground. It will give a pleasant background to the photographs, and, Pennyfeather, if you would with tact direct the photographer so that more promi-nence was given to Mrs Beste-Chetwynde's Hispano Suiza than to

Lady Circumference's little motor car, I think it would be all to the good. All these things count, you know.'

'Nothing seems to have been done about marking out the ground,' said Paul.

'No,' said the Doctor, turning his attention to the field for the first time, 'nothing. Well, you must do the best you can. They can't do everything.'

'I wonder if any hurdles have come?'

'They were ordered,' said the Doctor. 'I am certain of it. Philbrick, have any hurdles come?'

'Yes,' said Philbrick with a low chuckle.

'Why, pray, do you laugh at the mention of hurdles?'

'Just you look at them!' said Philbrick. 'They're behind the tea-house there.'

Paul and the Doctor went to look and found a pile of spiked iron railings in sections heaped up at the back of the marquee. They were each about five feet high and were painted green with gilt spikes.

'It seems to me that they have sent the wrong sort,' said the Doctor. 'Yes.'

'Well, we must do the best we can. What other things ought there to be?'

'Weight, hammer, javelin, long-jump pit, high-jump posts, low hurdles, eggs, spoons, and greasy pole,' said Philbrick.

'Previously competed for,' said the Doctor imperturbably. 'What else?'

'Somewhere to run,' suggested Paul.

'Why, God bless my soul, they've got the whole park! How did you manage yesterday for the heats?'

'We judged the distance by eye.'

'Then that is what we shall have to do today. Really, my dear Pennyfeather, it is quite unlike you to fabricate difficulties in this way. I am afraid you are getting unnerved. Let them go on racing until it is time for tea; and remember,' he added sagely, 'the longer the race the more time it takes. I leave the details to you. I am concerned with *style*. I wish, for instance, we had a starting pistol.'

'Would this be any use?' said Philbrick, producing an enormous service revolver. 'Only take care; it's loaded.'

65

'The very thing,' said the Doctor. 'Only fire into the ground, mind. We must do everything we can to avoid an accident. Do you always carry that about with you?'

'Only when I'm wearing my diamonds,' said Philbrick.

'Well, I hope that is not often. Good gracious! Who are these extraordinary-looking people?'

Ten men of revolting appearance were approaching from the drive. They were low of brow, crafty of eye, and crooked of limb. They advanced huddled together with the loping tread of wolves, peering about them furtively as they came, as though in constant terror of ambush; they slavered at their mouths, which hung loosely over their receding chins, while each clutched under his ape-like arm a burden of curious and unaccountable shape. On seeing the Doctor they halted and edged back, those behind squinting and moulting over their companions' shoulders.

'Crikey!' said Philbrick. 'Loonies! This is where I shoot.'

'I refuse to believe the evidence of my eyes,' said the Doctor. 'These creatures simply do not exist.'

After brief preliminary shuffling and nudging, an elderly man emerged from the back of the group. He had a rough black beard and wore on his uneven shoulders a druidical wreath of brass mistletoe.

'Why, it's my friend the stationmaster!' said Philbrick.

'We are the silver band the Lord bless and keep you,' said the stationmaster in one breath, 'the band that no one could beat whatever but two indeed in the Eisteddfod that for all North Wales was look you.'

'I see,' said the Doctor; 'I see. That's splendid. Well, will you please go into your tent, the little tent over there.'

'To march about you would not like us?' suggested the stationmaster; 'we have a fine yellow flag look you that embroidered for us was in silks.'

'No, no. Into the tent!'

The stationmaster went back to consult with his fellow-musicians. There was a baying and growling and yapping as of the jungle at moonrise, and presently he came forward again with an obsequious, sidelong shuffle.

'Three pounds you pay us would you said indeed to at the sports play.'

'Yes, yes, that's right, three pounds. Into the tent!'

'Nothing whatever we can play without the money first.'

'How would it be,' said Philbrick, 'if I gave him a clout on the ear?'

'No, no, I beg you to do nothing of the kind. You have not lived in Wales as long as I have.' He took a note-case from his pocket, the sight of which seemed to galvanize the musicians into life; they crowded round, twitching and chattering. The Doctor took out three pound notes and gave them to the stationmaster. 'There you are, Davies!' he said. 'Now take your men into the tent. They are on no account to emerge until after tea; do you understand?'

The band slunk away, and Paul and the Doctor turned back towards the Castle.

'The Welsh character is an interesting study,' said Dr Fagan. 'I have often considered writing a little monograph on the subject, but I was afraid it might make me unpopular in the village. The ignorant speak of them as Celts, which is of course wholly erroneous. They are of pure Iberian stock – the aboriginal inhabitants of Europe who survive only in Portugal and the Basque district. Celts readily intermarry with their neighbours and absorb them. From the earliest times the Welsh have been looked upon as an unclean people. It is thus that they have preserved their racial integrity. Their sons and daughters rarely mate with human-kind except their own blood relations. In Wales there was no need for legislation to prevent the conquering people intermarrying with the conquered. In Ireland that was necessary, for there inter-marriage was a political matter. In Wales it was moral. I hope, by the way, you have no Welsh blood?'

'None whatever,' said Paul.

'I was sure you had not, but one cannot be too careful. I once spoke of this subject to the sixth form and learned later that one of them had a Welsh grandmother. I am afraid it hurt his feelings terribly, poor little chap. She came from Pembrokeshire, too, which is of course quite a different matter. I often think,' he continued, 'that we can trace almost all the disasters of English history to the influence of Wales. Think of Edward of Caernarvon, the first Prince of Wales, a perverse life, Penny-feather, and an unseemly death, then the Tudors and the dissolution of the Church, then Lloyd George, the temperance movement, Non-conformity, and lust stalking hand in hand through the country, wasting and ravaging. But perhaps you think I exaggerate? I have a certain rhetorical tendency, I admit.'

'No, no,' said Paul.

'The Welsh,' said the Doctor, 'are the only nation in the world that has produced no graphic or plastic art, no architecture, no drama. They just sing,' he said with disgust, 'sing and blow down wind instruments of plated silver. They are deceitful because they cannot discern truth from falsehood, depraved because they cannot discern the consequences of their indulgence. Let us consider,' he continued, 'the etymological derivations of the Welsh language. . . .'

But here he was interrupted by a breathless little boy who panted down the drive to meet them. 'Please, sir, Lord and Lady Circumference have arrived sir. They're in the library with Miss Florence. She asked me to tell you.'

'The sports will start in ten minutes,' said the Doctor. 'Run and tell the other boys to change and go at once to the playing-fields. I will talk to you about the Welsh again. It is a matter to which I have given some thought, and I can see that you are sincerely interested. Come in with me and see the Circumferences.'

Flossie was talking to them in the library.

'Yes, isn't it a sweet colour?' she was saying. 'I do like something bright myself. Diana made it for me; she does knit a treat, does Diana, but of course I chose the colour, you know, because, you see, Diana's taste is all for wishy-washy greys and browns. Mournful, you know. Well, here's the dad. Lady Circumference was just saying how much she likes my frock what you said was vulgar, so there!'

A stout elderly woman dressed in a tweed coat and skirt and jaunty Tyrolean hat advanced to the Doctor. 'Hullo!' she said in a deep bass voice, 'how are you? Sorry if we're late. Circumference ran over a fool of a boy. I've just been chaffing your daughter here about her frock. Wish I was young enough to wear that kind of thing. Older I get the more I like colour. We're both pretty long in the tooth, eh?' She gave Dr Fagan a hearty shake of the hand, that obviously caused him acute pain. Then she turned to Paul.

'So you're the Doctor's hired assassin, eh? Well, I hope you keep a firm hand on my toad of a son. How's he doin'?'

'Quite well,' said Paul.

'Nonsense!' said Lady Circumference. 'The boy's a dunderhead. If he wasn't he wouldn't be here. He wants beatin' and hittin' and knockin' about generally, and then he'll be no good. That grass is shockin' bad on the terrace, Doctor; you ought to sand it down and re-sow it, but you'll have to take that cedar down if you ever want it to grow properly at the side. I hate cuttin' down a tree – like losin' a tooth – but you have to choose, tree or grass; you can't keep 'em both.'

As she was talking Lord Circumference emerged from the shadows and shook Paul's hand. He had a long fair moustache and large watery eyes which reminded Paul a little of Mr Prendergast.

'How do you do?' he said.

'How do you do?' said Paul.

'Fond of sport, eh?' he said. 'I mean these sort of sports?'

'Oh, yes,' said Paul. 'I think they're so good for the boys.'

'Do you? Do you think that,' said Lord Circumference very earnestly: 'you think they're good for the boys?'

'Yes,' said Paul; 'don't you?'

'Me? Yes, oh yes. I think so, too. Very good for the boys.'

'So useful in the case of a war or anything,' said Paul.

'Do you think so? D'you really and truly think so? That there's going to be another war, I mean?'

'Yes, I'm sure of it; aren't you?'

'Yes, of course. I'm sure of it too. And that awful bread, and people coming onto one's own land and telling one what one's to do with one's own butter and milk, and commandeering one's horses! Oh, yes all over again! My wife shot her hunters rather than let them go to the army. And girls in breeches on all the farms! All over again! Who do you think it will be this time?'

'The Americans,' said Paul stoutly.

'No, indeed, I hope not. We had German prisoners on two of the farms. That wasn't so bad, but if they start putting Americans on my land, I'll just refuse to stand it. My daughter brought an American down to luncheon the other day, and, do you know . . . ?'

'Dig it and dung it,' said Lady Circumference. 'Only it's got to be dug deep, mind. Now how did your calceolarias do last year?'

'I really have no idea,' said the Doctor. 'Flossie, how did our calceolarias do?'

'Lovely,' said Flossie.

'I don't believe a word of it,' said Lady Circumference. 'Nobody's calceolarias did well last year.'

'Shall we adjourn to the playing-fields?' said the Doctor. 'I expect they are all waiting for us.'

Talking cheerfully, the party crossed the hall and went down the steps.

'Your drive's awful wet,' said Lady Circumference. 'I expect there's a blocked pipe somewhere. Sure it ain't sewage?'

'I was never any use at short distances,' Lord Circumference was saying. 'I was always a slow starter, but I was once eighteenth in the Crick at Rugby. We didn't take sports so seriously at the 'Varsity when I was up: everybody rode. What college were you at?'

'Scone.'

'Scone, were you? Ever come across a young nephew of my wife's called Alastair Digby-Vane-Trumpington?'

'I just met him,' said Paul.

'That's very interesting, Greta. Mr Pennyfoot knows Alastair.'

'Does he? Well, that boy's doing no good for himself. Got fined twenty pounds the other day, his mother told me. Seemed proud of it. If my brother had been alive he'd have licked all that out of the young cub. It takes a man to bring up a man.'

'Yes,' said Lord Circumference meekly.

'Who else do you know at Oxford? Do you know Freddy French-Wise?'

'No.'

'Or Tom Obblethwaite or that youngest Castleton boy?'

'No, I'm afraid not. I had a great friend called Potts.'

'*Potts!*' said Lady Circumference, and left it at that.

All the school and several local visitors were assembled in the field. Grimes stood by himself, looking depressed. Mr Prendergast, flushed and unusually vivacious, was talking to the Vicar. As the headmaster's party came into sight the Llanabba Silver Band struck up *Men of Harlech*.

'Shockin' noise,' commented Lady Circumference graciously.

The head prefect came forward and presented her with a programme, be-ribboned and embossed in gold. Another prefect set a chair for her.

Clearly Tangent was not going to win.

She sat down with the Doctor next to her and Lord Circumference on the other side of him.

'Pennyfeather,' cried the Doctor above the band, 'start them racing.'

Philbrick gave Paul a megaphone. 'I found this in the pavilion,' he said. 'I thought it might be useful.'

'Who's that extraordinary man?' asked Lady Circumference.

'He is the boxing coach and swimming professional,' said the Doctor. 'A finely developed figure, don't you think?'

'First race,' said Paul through the megaphone, 'under sixteen. Quarter-mile!' He read out Grimes's list of starters.

'What's Tangent doin' in this race?' said Lady Circumference. 'The boy can't run an inch.'

The silver band stopped playing.

'The course,' said Paul, 'starts from the pavilion, goes round that clump of elms . . .'

'Beeches,' corrected Lady Circumference loudly.

'. . . and ends in front of the bandstand. Starter, Mr Prendergast; timekeeper, Captain Grimes.'

'I shall say, "Are you ready? one, two, three!" and then fire,' said Mr Prendergast. 'Are you ready? One' – there was a terrific report. 'Oh dear! I'm sorry' – but the race had begun. Clearly Tangent was not going to win; he was sitting on the grass crying because he had been wounded in the foot by Mr Prendergast's bullet. Philbrick carried him, wailing dismally, into the refreshment tent, where Dingy helped him off with his shoe. His heel was slightly grazed. Dingy gave him a large slice of cake, and he hobbled out surrounded by a sympathetic crowd.

'That won't hurt him,' said Lady Circumference, 'but I think someone ought to remove the pistol from that old man before he does anything serious.'

'I knew that was going to happen,' said Lord Circumference.

'A most unfortunate beginning,' said the Doctor.

'Am I going to die?' said Tangent, his mouth full of cake.

'For God's sake, look after Prendy,' said Grimes in Paul's ear. 'The man's as tight as a lord, and on one whisky, too.'

'First blood to me!' said Mr Prendergast gleefully.

'The last race will be run again,' said Paul down the megaphone. 'Starter, Mr Philbrick; timekeeper, Mr Prendergast.'

'On your marks! Get set.' Bang went the pistol, this time without disaster. The six little boys scampered off through the mud, disappeared behind the beeches and returned rather more slowly. Captain Grimes and Mr Prendergast held up a piece of tape.

'Well run, sir!' shouted Colonel Sidebotham. 'Jolly good race.'

'Capital,' said Mr Prendergast, and dropping his end of the tape, he sauntered over to the Colonel. 'I can see you are a fine judge of a race, sir. So was I once. So's Grimes. A capital fellow, Grimes; a bounder, you know, but a capital fellow. Bounders can be capital fellows; don't you agree, Colonel Sidebotham? In fact, I'd go further and say that capital fellows *are* bounders. What d'you say to that? I wish you'd stop pulling at my arm, Pennyfeather. Colonel Sidebotham and I are just having a most interesting conversation about bounders.'

The silver band struck up again, and Mr Prendergast began a little jig, saying: 'Capital fellow!' and snapping his fingers. Paul led him to the refreshment tent.

'Dingy wants you to help her in there,' he said firmly, 'and, for God's sake, don't come out until you feel better.'

'I never felt better in my life,' said Mr Prendergast indignantly. 'Capital fellow! capital fellow!'

'It is not my affair, of course,' said Colonel Sidebotham, 'but if you ask me I should say that man had been drinking.'

'He was talking very excitedly to me,' said the Vicar, 'about some apparatus for warming a church in Worthing and about the Apostolic Claims of the Church of Abyssinia. I confess I could not follow him clearly. He seems deeply interested in Church matters. Are you quite sure he is right in the head? I have noticed again and again since I have been in the Church that lay interest in ecclesiastical matters is often a prelude to insanity.'

'Drink, pure and simple,' said the Colonel. 'I wonder where he got it? I could do with a spot of whisky.'

'Quarter-mile open!' said Paul through his megaphone.

Presently the Clutterbucks arrived. Both the parents were stout. They brought with them two small children, a governess, and an elder son. They debouched from the car one by one, stretching their limbs in evident relief.

'This is Sam,' said Mr Clutterbuck, 'just down from Cambridge.

He's joined me in the business, and we've brought his nippers along for a treat. Don't mind, do you, Doc? And last, but not least, my wife.'

Dr Fagan greeted them with genial condescension and found them seats.

'I am afraid you have missed all the jumping events,' he said. 'But I have a list of the results here. You will see that Percy has done extremely well.'

'Didn't know the little beggar had it in him. See that, Martha? Percy's won the high-jump and the long-jump and the hurdles. How's your young hopeful been doing, Lady Circumference?'

'My boy has been injured in the foot,' said Lady Circumference coldly.

'Dear me! Not badly, I hope? Did he twist his ankle in the jumping?'

'No,' said Lady Circumference, 'he was shot at by one of the assistant masters. But it is kind of you to inquire.'

'Three Miles Open!' announced Paul. 'The course of six laps will be run as before.'

'On your marks! Get set.' Bang went Philbrick's revolver. Off trotted the boys on another race.

'Father,' said Flossie, 'don't you think it's time for the tea interval?'

'Nothing can be done before Mrs Beste-Chetwynde arrives,' said the Doctor.

Round and round the muddy track trotted the athletes while the silver band played sacred music unceasingly.

'Last lap!' announced Paul.

The school and the visitors crowded about the tape to cheer the winner. Amid loud applause Clutterbuck breasted the tape well ahead of the others.

'Well run! Oh, good, jolly good, sir!' cried Colonel Sidebotham.

'Good old Percy! That's the stuff,' said Mr Clutterbuck.

'Well run, Percy!' chorused the two little Clutterbucks, prompted by their governess.

'That boy cheated,' said Lady Circumference. 'He only went round five times. I counted.'

'I think unpleasantness so mars the afternoon,' said the Vicar.

'How dare you suggest such a thing?' asked Mrs Clutterbuck. 'I appeal to the referee. Percy ran the full course, didn't he?'

'Clutterbuck wins,' said Captain Grimes.

'Fiddlesticks!' said Lady Circumference. 'He deliberately lagged behind and joined the others as they went behind the beeches. The little toad!'

'Really, Greta,' said Lord Circumference, 'I think we ought to abide by the referee's decision.'

'Well, they can't expect me to give away the prizes, then. Nothing would induce me to give that boy a prize.'

'Do you understand, madam, that you are bringing a serious accusation against my son's honour?'

'Serious accusation fiddlesticks! What he wants is a jolly good hidin'.'

'No doubt you judge other people's sons by your own. Let me tell you, Lady Circumference . . .'

'Don't attempt to browbeat me, sir. I know a cheat when I see one.'

At this stage of the discussion the Doctor left Mrs Hope-Brown's side, where he had been remarking upon her son's progress in geometry, and joined the group round the winning-post.

'If there is a disputed decision,' he said genially, 'they shall race again.'

'Percy has won already,' said Mr Clutterbuck. 'He has been adjudged the winner.'

'Splendid! splendid! A promising little athlete. I congratulate you, Clutterbuck.'

'But he only ran five laps,' said Lady Circumference.

'Then clearly he has won the five furlongs race, a very exacting length.'

'But the other boys,' said Lady Circumference, almost beside herself with rage, 'have run six lengths.'

'Then they,' said the Doctor imperturbably, 'are first, second, third, fourth, and fifth respectively in the Three Miles. Clearly there has been some confusion. Diana, I think we might now serve tea.'

Things were not easy, but there was fortunately a distraction, for as he spoke an enormous limousine of dove-grey and silver stole soundlessly onto the field.

'But what could be more opportune? Here is Mrs Beste-Chetwynde.'

Three light skips brought him to the side of the car, but the footman was there before him. The door opened, and from the cushions within emerged a tall young man in a clinging dove-grey overcoat. After him, like the first breath of spring in the Champs-Élysées, came Mrs Beste-Chetwynde – two lizard-skin feet, silk legs, chinchilla body, a tight little black hat, pinned with platinum and diamonds, and the high invariable voice that may be heard in any Ritz Hotel from New York to Budapest.

'I hope you don't mind my bringing Chokey, Dr Fagan?' she said. 'He's just crazy about sport.'

'I sure am that,' said Chokey.

'Dear Mrs Beste-Chetwynde!' said Dr Fagan; 'dear, dear, Mrs Beste-Chetwynde!' He pressed her glove, and for the moment was at a loss for words of welcome, for 'Chokey', though graceful of bearing and irreproachably dressed, was a Negro.

THE CRYSTAL GAZERS
Angela Brazil

It was about this time that a wave of the occult passed over the school. It begun with Daphne Johnson, who happened to read a magazine article on 'The Borderland of the Spirit World', and it spread like an epidemic of influenza. The supernatural was the topic of the hour. Ghost stories were at a premium, and any girl who could relate some creepy spiritual experience, which had happened to the second cousin of a friend of hers, was sure of a thrilled audience. This taste for the psychic was particularly strong among the girls of the Sixth Form, who leaned towards its intellectual and scientific aspects. They despised vulgar apparitions, but discussed such abstruse problems as phantasms of the living, thought transference, will power, hypnotism, and clairvoyance. Meta Wright dabbled a little in palmistry, and examined the hands of her schoolmates, prophesying startling events in their future careers. Lois Barlow sent half-a-crown to a ladies' newspaper to have her horoscope cast, and was terribly dejected at the gloomy prospects offered her by the planets, till she fortunately discovered that she had put the date of her birth wrong by three hours, which would, of course, completely alter the aspect of the heavenly bodies, and cause the best of astrologers to err. Veronica Terry talked darkly of experiences in the psychic world, of astral bodies, etheric doubles, elemental entities, and nature spirits. She went to sleep at night with her thumbs and big toes crossed, in the hope of bringing back the adventures of her dreams into her waking consciousness. She was a little hazy on the subject, but yearned for further instruction.

'It's called "Yoga",' she confided to her particular chum, Barbara Rowlands. 'You concentrate your mind before you go to sleep, and then you're able to function in the astral body. My cousin Winnie told me of a girl at College who did it, and she was seen standing in the room of a friend at the other side of the hostel, while all the time she was asleep in bed.'

'I hope you won't do that!' shuddered Barbara nervously. 'It would give me a fit if I woke up and found you staring at me.'

'It may be rather difficult to regulate one's movements, once one is out of the body,' returned Veronica guardedly.

Barbara did not crave for spiritual excursions, and secretly preferred the old days, when her chum talked tennis instead of psychology; but the occult was paramount, and she was obliged to follow the fashion. The atmosphere of the Grange was certainly conducive to superstition. The dim passages and panelled walls looked haunted. Every accessory of the old mansion seemed a suitable background for a ghost. The juniors were frankly frightened. They did not dare go upstairs alone. They imagined skeleton fingers clutching their legs through the banisters, or bodiless heads rolling like billiard balls along the landings. Having listened, awestruck, to Veronica's accounts of a séance, they were apprehensive lest the tables should turn sportive and caper about the rooms rapping out spirit messages, or boisterous elementals should bump the beds up and down and fling the china about.

'That only happens if there's a powerful medium in the house,' Veronica had assured them, and the girls devoutly hoped that none of their number possessed the required mystic properties.

'Look here,' said Raymonde one day to Ardiune, 'I'm getting rather fed up with this spook business.'

'So'm I,' agreed Ardiune. 'I thought it was fun at first, but it's got beyond the limit now. The sillies can talk of nothing else. I'm sick of sitting on Veronica's bed and hearing about mediums and messages. I'd like a potato race for a change. I vote we get up some progressive games.'

78

'It would be more jinky! I fancy a good many are tired of ghosts, only they don't like to say so. Ardiune! I've got an idea! While the school's still mad on these things, why shouldn't we have some fun out of it? Play a rag on them, you know.'

'Dress up in a sheet and rub wet matches on one's hands?' suggested Ardiune.

'No, no! Nothing so stale as that! Why, it would hardly take in the juniors for more than a minute. I'm angling for bigger fish. I want to hook the Sixth!'

'H'm! Not so easy, my good girl!'

'It needs a craft, of course, and one must have a suitable bait. The common or garden ghost trick would be useless. I want something subtle. If I could have developed mediumistic powers, now, and gone into a trance!'

'Couldn't you?' queried Ardiune eagerly.

Raymonde shook a regretful head.

'Veronica knows too much about séances. She says the great test of the trance is to stick pins into the medium. If she doesn't utter a groan, then her conscious entity is suspended, and a spirit is about to materialize. I couldn't stand being a living pin-cushion. I know I'd squeal.'

'But we might pad you with cushions. Séances are always held in the dark, so they wouldn't find out.'

'Trust Veronica to find my vulnerable spot! She detests me, and she'd just enjoy prodding me up with pins. No, we must have something less painful than that, please.'

'Table-turning might be possible?'

'The Sixth did it, and the table was beginning to go round quite nicely when they discovered that Linda was pushing the leg. I think pretty nearly everything occult has been tried here lately, except just one. We've not had any crystal gazing.'

'How d'you do that?'

'Don't you remember that chapter in *Zilla, the Sahara Queen*? How she goes to the Coptic magician, and he pours some ink into a little boy's hand, and sees all her future in it?'

'Ink would stain horribly,' commented Ardiune.

'Yes, I don't mean to use ink. What I want is a crystal. There's something on Gibbie's chimney-piece that would do jolly well. I believe

I'll borrow it! I know just how to manage, because Mabel and Sylvia went to consult a psychist in Bond Street, and they told me about it, and everything she said and did. As a matter of fact she described Mabel's fiancé quite wrong, and pretended she saw him sitting in a dug-out, while all the time he was on a battleship; but they thought it great fun, because they hadn't really intended to believe her.'

'Would the girls believe you?'

'Certainly not as Raymonde Armitage. I don't mean them to know me. We're going to disguise ourselves, so that our very mothers wouldn't own us.'

'Whew!'

Ardiune looked decidedly sceptical.

'Wait till I've done telling you before you pull faces, you old blue-bottle! Can't you trust me by now to get up a decent rag? Yes, I'm offended! All right, I'll accept apologies. Now if you're really listening, I'll explain. You know the gipsies are camping down by the river. Everybody in the school has noticed their caravans, and realizes they're there. Now what's more natural than for a couple of these gipsies to stroll round by the barn some evening during recreation time, and offer to predict the future? Katherine and Ave could be in the secret, have their fortunes told first, and then bring others. We'd install ourselves in the old cow-house; it's so dark, no one would see us very plainly.'

'Ray, you've enough imagination for a novelist!' murmured Ardiune admiringly.

Having settled their plan of campaign, the next step was to carry out details. The question of costume loomed largest.

'We must look real gipsies, not stage ones,' decreed Raymonde. 'The thing's got to be done properly, if it's done at all.'

They ransacked the property box used for school theatricals, and having selected some likely garments, set to work on an ideal of realism. Two skirts were carefully torn on nails, artistically stained with rust and mud, and rubbed on the barn floor to give them an extra tone. Some cotton bodices were similarly treated. Shoes were a knotty problem, for gipsies do not generally affect trim footwear, yet nobody at the Grange possessed worn-out or dilapidated boots. In the end Raymonde carefully unpicked the stitches in her oldest pairs to give them the requisite burst appearance, and with the aid of a file rubbed the respectability from them. A dip in the mud of the moat completed the transformation. Some cheap beads and coloured handkerchiefs, and a faint wash of vandyke brown over face and hands, gave the finishing touches.

In the interval between preparation and supper, when several members of the Sixth Form were pursuing carpentry and other industrial occupations in the barn, Aveline Kerby entered to borrow a screwdriver. She conversed casually on the topics of wood-carving, photography, pressed flowers, and kindred hobbies; then, just as she was leaving, turned back and remarked, apparently as an afterthought:

'Oh, by the by, do you know there are two gipsies in the cowhouse? They're from the caravan by the river. They came in through the back gate, begging, and Morvyth happened to meet them. They offered to tell her fortune, so she took them into the cow-house, so that Gibbie shouldn't see them. She says they're marvellous. They described her mother exactly, and her brother at the front. Isn't it wonderful how they can do it?'

'Are they there still?' asked Veronica, swallowing the bait.

'I believe so. At least they were, five minutes ago. Elsie Moseley and Cynthia Greene had gone to see them. I'd go myself, but I've spent all my allowance, and of course one has to cross their palms with the orthodox piece of silver, I suppose. It's hard luck to be stony-broke. Ta-ta! Thanks for the screw-driver!'

Aveline beat a judicious retreat, and left her words to work. As she had expected, the news of the arrival of the occultists was received with interest.

'It's an extraordinary thing that gipsies are so often gifted with psychic powers,' commented Meta.

'They're children of nature,' returned Veronica. 'I suppose our ultra-civilization blunts our astral perceptions. One finds marvellous things among the hill tribes in India – things that can't be explained by any known rules of science.'

'I suppose these ancient races have inherited secrets that we can't grasp?'

'Yes, they follow forgotten laws of nature. Some day, no doubt, science will rediscover them.'

Veronica spoke seriously. During the holidays she had studied the subject by the aid of books borrowed from the Free Library.

'I should like just to go and have a look at these gipsies,' she added. 'Will you come with me?'

She voiced the feelings of the others. They rose with one accord, and went in the direction of the cow-shed. They met Cynthia Greene, and Elsie Moseley coming out, half-awed, half-giggling. At the sight of monitresses they dived round the corner of the building, and escaped into the orchard.

'It's certainly our duty to investigate,' propounded Meta.

It is pleasant when duty and inclination coincide. The girls walked forward briskly. The interior of the cow-house was dark as an Eastern temple. The gipsies had established themselves in the dimmest corner, and were squatting on bundles of straw under a manger. Obviously they were extremely dirty and dilapidated. Their hands and faces appeared to be unacquainted with soap and water, their clothes were tattered, their shoes seemingly in the last stage of decrepitude.

'Tell your fortunes, my pretty ladies?' pattered one of the Romanys. Her voice was hoarse but conciliatory. Possibly she had a cold – tents are notoriously draughty sleeping-places.

'We don't care about vulgar fortunes, we are really interested,' commenced Veronica. 'What we'd like to know is how you get your powers. Where does your knowledge of the future come from? I've always wanted to ask this.'

The gipsy woman shook her head pityingly.

'Ah, lady! We don't know ourselves! It comes to us suddenly. Like a flash of light we see your future – then it fades. It's sixth sense that's given to the poor gipsies. They're born with it, and they can't explain it any more than you can explain the breath of your body.'

'I've often heard of this sixth sense,' whispered Daphne to Lois.

'Sometimes we feel what's going to be, and sometimes we see it,' continued the gipsy, fumbling with something in her lap. 'We can't tell beforehand which way the knowledge will come.'

'What's that you've got there?' asked Veronica sharply. 'Is it a crystal?'

'You're right, lady. It is a crystal, and a wonderful one too. My grandmother got it from – but no! I'd best not be telling that. I wouldn't

The gipsies had established themselves in the dimmest corner.

part with it, lady, if the Queen offered me her crown in exchange. Take it in your hand! Look how it sparkles! It doesn't often shine like that – only when someone with the sixth sense holds it.'

'I've sometimes suspected that I possess psychic powers!' murmured Veronica complacently.

'Would you like to learn the future lady?' queried the gipsy. 'Then hold it so, in your hands, for a minute. Now it has felt you and known you, and it will tell – oh yes! it will tell!'

She took the crystal again, and turned to the companion who squatted beside her on the floor.

'Zara! Look what is coming to the lady,' she commanded softly.

Zara, who had apparently been in a deep reverie, roused herself with a start, placed the crystal in her lap with the first finger and thumb of each hand lightly touching it, and stared fixedly into the magic glass. For a moment or two the future seemed obscured, then evidently it cleared. She began to speak in a deep, monotonous voice, as if talking in her sleep.

'I see the sea – waves – waves – everywhere. There is a ship – oh! it has changed. I see sand, and a white house, and palm trees. A soldier in khaki is coming out of the house. He stops to speak to a servant – a black man in a turban – he is angry – he frowns – he goes again into the white house. Oh, it is fading – it is gone!'

'My brother Leslie's in Egypt!' gasped Veronica, much impressed.

She would have requested a continuance of the vision, but at that moment the dressing-bell clanged loudly. It was plainly time to go and tidy up for supper.

'If you could come again tomorrow about five,' she suggested, pressing a coin into the gipsy's ready hand.

'Yes, lady, if we're still in the neighbourhood. We never know when we'll be moving on, you see. But we'll try to oblige you if we can.'

Raymonde's and Ardiune's toilets that evening would have done credit to quick-change variety artistes. With clean faces and hands, and their dresses at least half fastened, they slipped into their places at the supper-table just in time; a little flurried, perhaps, but preserving an outward calm. So far their scheme had succeeded admirably. The Sixth appeared to have no suspicions.

They repeated their performance on the following day, installing themselves in the cow-house, and receiving relays of enquirers who came to consult them as to their future. Knowing somewhat of the private history of each member of the school, they got on excellently, and their reputation spread till more than half the girls had paid surreptitious visits to their retreat. All might have gone well, and their secret might have remained undiscovered, had it not been for Veronica's friendship with Mademoiselle. Veronica was so impressed with the value of the crystal's information that she could not help confiding the news, and bringing the impressionable Belgian to consult the seer for herself.

Ardiune's vision of smoking ruins and rescued refugees left Mademoiselle almost speechless. She in her turn felt impelled to seek a confidante, and imparted the wonderful revelations to Miss Gibbs.

That worthy lady immediately set off for the cow-house. As she entered there was a scuttling of juniors, who sought safety behind the partition. Raymonde started for a moment aghast, then whispered to Ardiune: 'Bluff it out!'

Miss Gibbs proceeded in an absolutely business-like manner. She requested a consultation, and listened while the gipsy, decidedly nervous, gave a rambling description of a dark gentleman and an Indian temple.

'Thank you,' she said at last. 'I think it only fair to warn you that you can be prosecuted and fined twenty-five pounds for telling fortunes. I should like to know where you got that crystal! It's remarkably like the ball of glass that was broken off my Venetian vase. I missed it yesterday from my mantelpiece. By the by' – stooping down suddenly, and pulling aside the handkerchief from Zara's swarthy neck – 'you are wearing a locket and chain that I know to be the property of one of my pupils. It is my duty immediately to put you in the hands of the police.'

The game was up! The disconcerted gipsies rose from their alcove, and came back from the psychic to the material world. It was a hard, exacting, unsympathetic world as mirrored in Miss Gibbs's keen grey eyes. She told them briefly to go and wash their faces and change their attire, then to report themselves in the class-room, where she would be at work correcting exercises.

'You can bring with you the money that you have collected over this business,' she added.

Half an hour later, two clean, tidy, but dejected pupils entered the class-room, and placed the sum of thirteen and ninepence upon her desk. Miss Gibbs counted it over scrupulously.

'Any girls who were foolish enough to give you this, deserve to lose it,' she remarked, 'and I shall send it as a contribution to the Red Cross Fund. You will each learn two pages of Curtis's *Historical Notes* by heart, and repeat them to me tomorrow after morning school. I may mention that I consider it a great liberty for any girl to enter my bed-room and remove ornaments from my mantelpiece.'

That evening, after preparation and supper, the entire school, instead of being allowed to pursue fancy work, was summoned to the lecture hall, and harangued by Miss Beasley upon the follies and dangers of superstition. She touched upon ancient beliefs in witchcraft, and modern credulity in clairvoyance and spiritualism, and placed an equal ban upon both.

'In these enlightened times, with all the advantages of education to dispel ignorance,' she concluded, 'it is incredible to me that anybody can still be found ready to believe in such nonsense. I beg you all, and especially those elder girls who should be leaders of the rest, to turn your thoughts and conversation to some healthier topic, and to let these morbid fancies sink into the obscurity they deserve.'

'It was a nasty hit for the monitresses!' whispered Ardiune to Raymonde afterwards. 'Did you see Veronica turning as red as beet-root? We'll have to wake early tomorrow morning, and swat at those wretched dates. It was grizzly bad luck Gibbie found us out!'

'But on the whole the game was worth the candle!' proclaimed Raymonde unrepentantly.

THE IDEALIST
Frank O'Connor

I don't know how it is about education, but it never seemed to do anything for me but get me into trouble.

Adventure stories weren't so bad, but as a kid I was very serious and preferred realism to romance. School stories were what I liked best, and, judged by our standards, these were romantic enough for anyone. The schools were English, so I suppose you couldn't expect anything else. They were always called 'the venerable pile', and there was usually a ghost in them; they were built in a square that was called 'the quad', and, according to the pictures, they were all clock-towers, spires, and pinnacles, like the lunatic asylum with us. The fellows in the stories were all good climbers, and got in and out of school at night on ropes made of knotted sheets. They dressed queerly; they wore long trousers, short, black jackets, and top hats. Whenever they did anything wrong they were given 'lines' in Latin. When it was a bad case, they were flogged and never showed any sign of pain; only the bad fellows, and they always said: 'Ow! Ow!'

Most of them were grand chaps who always stuck together and were great at football and cricket. They never told lies and wouldn't talk to anyone who did. If they were caught out and asked a point-blank question, they always told the truth, unless someone else was with them, and then even if they were to be expelled for it they wouldn't give his name, even if he was a thief, which, as a matter of fact, he frequently was. It was surprising in such good schools, with fathers who never gave less than five quid, the number of thieves there were. The fellows in our school hardly ever stole, though they only got a penny a week, and sometimes not even that, as when their fathers were on the booze and their mothers had to go to the pawn.

I worked hard at football and cricket, though of course we never had a proper football and the cricket we played was with a hurley stick against a wicket chalked on some wall. The officers in the barrack played proper cricket, and on summer evenings I used to go and watch them, like one of the souls in Purgatory watching the joys of Paradise.

Even so, I couldn't help being disgusted at the bad way things were run in our school. Our 'venerable pile' was a red-brick building without tower or pinnacle a fellow could climb, and no ghost at all: we had no team, so a fellow, no matter how hard he worked, could never play for the school, and, instead of giving you 'lines', Latin or any other sort, Murderer Moloney either lifted you by the ears or bashed you with a cane. When he got tired of bashing you on the hands he bashed you on the legs.

But these were superficial things. What was really wrong was ourselves. The fellows sucked up to the masters and told them all that went on. If they were caught out in anything they tried to put the blame on someone else, even if it meant telling lies. When they were caned they snivelled and said it wasn't fair; drew back their hands as if they were terrified, so that the cane caught only the tips of their fingers, and then screamed and stood on one leg, shaking out their fingers in the hope of getting it counted as one. Finally they roared that their wrist was broken and crawled back to their desks with their hands squeezed under their armpits, howling. I mean you couldn't help feeling ashamed, imagining what chaps from a decent school would think if they saw it.

My own way to school led me past the barrack gate. In those peaceful days sentries never minded you going past the guardroom to have a look at the chaps drilling in the barrack square; if you came at dinner-time they even called you in and gave you plumduff and tea. Naturally, with such temptations I was often late. The only excuse, short of a letter from your mother, was to say you were at early Mass. The

Murderer would never know whether you were or not, and if he did anything to you you could easily get him into trouble with the parish priest. Even as kids we knew who the real boss of the school was.

But after I started reading those confounded school stories I was never happy about saying I had been to Mass. It was a lie, and I knew that the chaps in the stories would have died sooner than tell it. They were all round me like invisible presences, and I hated to do anything which I felt they might disapprove of.

One morning I came in very late and rather frightened.

'What kept you till this hour, Delaney?' Murderer Moloney asked, looking at the clock.

I wanted to say I had been at Mass, but I couldn't. The invisible presences were all about me.

'I was delayed at the barrack, sir,' I replied in panic.

There was a faint titter from the class, and Moloney raised his brows in mild surprise. He was a big powerful man with fair hair and blue eyes and a manner that at times was deceptively mild.

'Oh, indeed,' he said, politely enough. 'And what delayed you?'

'I was watching the soldiers drilling, sir,' I said.

The class tittered again. This was a new line entirely for them.

'Oh,' Moloney said casually, 'I never knew you were such a military man. Hold out your hand!'

Compared with the laughter the slaps were nothing, and besides, I had the example of the invisible presences to sustain me. I did not flinch. I returned to my desk slowly and quietly without snivelling or squeezing my hands, and the Murderer looked after me, raising his brows again as though to indicate that this was a new line for him, too. But the others gaped and whispered as I were some strange animal. At playtime they gathered about me, full of curiosity and excitement.

'Delaney, why did you say that about the barrack?'

'Because 'twas true,' I replied firmly. 'I wasn't going to tell him a lie.'

'What lie?'

'That I was at Mass.'

'Then couldn't you say you had to go on a message?'

'That would be a lie too.'

'Cripes, Delaney,' they said, 'you'd better mind yourself. The Murderer is in an awful wax. He'll massacre you.'

I knew that. I knew only too well that the Murderer's professional pride had been deeply wounded, and for the rest of the day I was on my best behaviour. But my best wasn't enough, for I underrated the Murderer's guile. Though he pretended to be reading, he was watching me the whole time.

'Delaney,' he said at last without raising his head from the book, 'was that you talking?'

''Twas, sir,' I replied in consternation.

The whole class laughed. They couldn't believe but that I was deliberately trailing my coat, and, of course, the laugh must have convinced him that I was. I suppose if people do tell you lies all day and every day, it soon becomes a sort of perquisite which you resent being deprived of.

'Oh,' he said, throwing down his book, 'we'll soon stop that.'

This time it was a tougher job, because he was really on his mettle. But so was I. I knew this was the testing-point for me, and if only I could keep my head I should provide a model for the whole class. When I had got through the ordeal without moving a muscle, and returned to my desk with my hands by my sides, the invisible presences gave me a great clap. But the visible ones were nearly as annoyed as the Murderer himself. After school half a dozen of them followed me down the school yard.

'Go on!' they shouted truculently. 'Shaping as usual!'

'I was not shaping.'

'You were shaping. You're always showing off. Trying to pretend he didn't hurt you – a blooming crybaby like you!'

'I wasn't trying to pretend,' I shouted, even then resisting the temptation to nurse my bruised hands. 'Only decent fellows don't cry over every little pain like kids.'

'Go on!' they bawled after me. 'You ould idiot!' And, as I went down the school lane, still trying to keep what the stories called 'a stiff upper lip', and consoling myself with the thought that my torment was over until next morning, I heard their mocking voices after me.

'Loony Larry! Yah, Loony Larry!'

I realized that if I was to keep on terms with the invisible presences I should have to watch my step at school.

So I did, all through that year. But one day an awful thing happened.

I saw a fellow called Gorman taking something from a coat on the rack.

I was coming in from the yard, and in the porch outside our school-room I saw a fellow called Gorman taking something from a coat on the rack. I always described Gorman to myself as 'the black sheep of the school'. He was a fellow I disliked and feared; a handsome, sulky, spoiled, and sneering lout. I paid no attention to him because I had escaped for a few moments into my dream-world in which fathers never gave less than fivers and the honour of the school was always saved by some quiet, unassuming fellow like myself – 'a dark horse', as the stories called him.

'Who are you looking at?' Gorman asked threateningly.

'I wasn't looking at anyone,' I replied with an indignant start.

'I was only getting a pencil out of my coat,' he added, clenching his fists.

'Nobody said you weren't,' I replied, thinking that this was a very queer subject to start a row about.

'You'd better not, either,' he snarled. 'You can mind your own business.'

'You mind yours!' I retorted, purely for the purpose of saving face. 'I never spoke to you at all.'

And that, so far as I was concerned, was the end of it.

But after playtime the Murderer, looking exceptionally serious, stood before the class, balancing a pencil in both hands.

'Everyone who left the classroom this morning, stand out!' he called. Then he lowered his head and looked at us from under his brows. 'Mind now, I said everyone!'

I stood out with the others, including Gorman. We were all very puzzled.

'Did you take anything from a coat on the rack this morning?' the Murderer asked, laying a heavy, hairy paw on Gorman's shoulder and staring menacingly into his eyes.

'Me, sir?' Gorman exclaimed innocently. 'No, sir.'

'Did you see anyone else doing it?'

'No, sir.'

'You?' he asked another lad, but even before he reached me at all I realized why Gorman had told the lie and wondered frantically what I should do.

'You?' he asked me, and his big red face was close to mine, his blue eyes were only a few inches away, and the smell of his toilet soap was in my nostrils. My panic made me say the wrong thing as though I had planned it.

'I didn't take anything, sir,' I said in a low voice.

'Did you see someone else do it?' he asked, raising his brows and showing quite plainly that he had noticed my evasion. 'Have you a tongue in your head?' he shouted suddenly, and the whole class, electrified, stared at me. 'You?' he added curtly to the next boy as though he had lost interest in me.

'No, sir.'

'Back to your desks, the rest of you!' he ordered. 'Delaney, you stay here.'

He waited till everyone was seated again before going on.

'Turn out your pockets.'

I did, and a half-stifled giggle rose, which the Murderer quelled with a thunderous glance. Even for a small boy I had pockets that were museums in themselves: the purpose of half the things I brought to light I couldn't have explained myself. They were antiques, prehistoric and unlabelled. Among them was a school story borrowed the previous evening from a queer fellow who chewed paper as if it were gum. The Murderer reached out for it, and holding it at arm's length, shook it out with an expression of deepening disgust as he noticed the nibbled corners and margins.

'Oh,' he said disdainfully, 'so this is how you waste your time! What do you do with this rubbish – eat it?'

''Tisn't mine, sir,' I said against the laugh that sprang up. 'I borrowed it.'

'Is that what you did with the money?' he asked quickly, his fat head on one side.

'Money?' I repeated in confusion. 'What money?'

'The shilling that was stolen from Flanagan's overcoat this morning.'

(Flanagan was a little hunchback whose people coddled him; no one else in the school would have possessed that much money.)

'I never took Flanagan's shilling,' I said, beginning to cry, 'and you have no right to say I did.'

'I have the right to say you're the most impudent and defiant puppy in the school,' he replied, his voice hoarse with rage, 'and I wouldn't put it past you. What else can anyone expect and you reading this dirty, rotten, filthy rubbish?' And he tore my school story in halves and flung them to the furthest corner of the classroom. 'Dirty, filthy, English rubbish! Now, hold out your hand.'

This time the invisible presences deserted me. Hearing themselves described in these contemptuous terms, they fled. The Murderer went mad in the way people do whenever they're up against something they don't understand. Even the other fellows were shocked, and, heaven knows, they had little sympathy with me.

'You should put the police on him,' they advised me later in the playground. 'He lifted the cane over his shoulder. He could get the gaol for that.'

'But why didn't you say you didn't see anyone?' asked the eldest, a fellow called Spillane.

'Because I did,' I said, beginning to sob all over again at the memory of my wrongs. 'I saw Gorman.'

'Gorman?' Spillane echoed incredulously. 'Was it Gorman took Flanagan's money? And why didn't you say so?'

'Because it wouldn't be right,' I sobbed.

'Why wouldn't it be right?'

'Because Gorman should have told the truth himself,' I said. 'And if this was a proper school he'd be sent to Coventry.'

'He'd be sent where?'

'Coventry. No one would ever speak to him again.'

'But why would Gorman tell the truth if he took the money?' Spillane asked as you'd speak to a baby. 'Jay, Delaney,' he added pityingly, 'you're getting madder and madder. Now, look at what you're after bringing on yourself!'

Suddenly Gorman came lumbering up, red and angry.

'Delaney,' he shouted threateningly, 'did you say I took Flanagan's money?'

Gorman, though I of course didn't realize it, was as much at sea as Moloney and the rest. Seeing me take all that punishment rather than give him away, he concluded that I must be more afraid of him than of Moloney, and that the proper thing to do was to make me more so. He couldn't have come at a time when I cared less for him. I didn't even bother to reply but lashed out with all my strength at his brutal face.

This was the last thing he expected. He screamed, and his hand came away from his face, all blood. Then he threw off his satchel and came at me, but at the same moment a door opened behind us and a lame teacher called Murphy emerged. We all ran like mad and the fight was forgotten.

It didn't remain forgotten, though. Next morning after prayers the Murderer scowled at me.

'Delaney, were you fighting in the yard after school yesterday?'

For a second or two I didn't reply. I couldn't help feeling that it wasn't worth it. But before the invisible presences fled forever, I made another effort.

'I was, sir,' I said, and this time there wasn't even a titter. I was out of my mind. The whole class knew it and was awestricken.

'Who were you fighting?'

'I'd sooner not say, sir.' I replied, hysteria beginning to well up in me. It was all very well for the invisible presences, but they hadn't to deal with the Murderer.

'Who was he fighting with?' he asked lightly, resting his hands on the desk and studying the ceiling.

'Gorman, sir,' replied three or four voices – as easy as that!

'Did Gorman hit him first?'

'No, sir. He hit Gorman first.'

'Stand out,' he said, taking up the cane. 'Now,' he added, going up to Gorman, 'you take this and hit him. And make sure you hit him hard,' he went on, giving Gorman's arm an encouraging squeeze. 'He thinks he's a great fellow. You show him now what we think of him.'

Gorman came towards me with a broad grin. He thought it a great joke. The class thought it a great joke. They began to roar with laughter. Even the Murderer permitted himself a modest grin at his own cleverness.

'Hold out your hand,' he said to me.

I didn't. I began to feel trapped and a little crazy.

'Hold out your hand, I say,' he shouted, beginning to lose his temper.

'I will not,' I shouted back, losing all control of myself.

'You what?' he cried incredulously, dashing at me round the classroom with his hand raised as though to strike me. 'What's that you said, you dirty little thief?'

'I'm not a thief, I'm not a thief,' I screamed. 'And if he comes near me I'll kick the shins off him. You have no right to give him that cane, and you have no right to call me a thief either. If you do it again, I'll go down to the police and then we'll see who the thief is.'

'You refused to answer my questions,' he roared, and if I had been in my right mind I should have known he had suddenly taken fright; probably the word 'police' had frightened him.

'No,' I said through my sobs, 'and I won't answer them now either. I'm not a spy.'

'Oh,' he retorted with a sarcastic sniff, 'so that's what you call a spy, Mr Delaney?'

'Yes, and that's what they all are, all the fellows here – dirty spies! – but I'm not going to be a spy for you. You can do your own spying.'

'That's enough now, that's enough!' he said, raising his fat hand almost beseechingly. 'There's no need to lose control of yourself, my dear young fellow, and there's no need whatever to screech like that. 'Tis most unmanly. Go back to your seat now and I'll talk to you another time.'

I obeyed, but I did no work. No one else did much either. The hysteria had spread to the class. I alternated between fits of exultation at my own successful defiance of the Murderer, and panic at the prospect of his revenge; and at each change of mood I put my face in my hands and sobbed again. The Murderer didn't even order me to stop. He didn't so much as look at me.

After that I was the hero of the school for the whole afternoon. Gorman tried to resume the fight, but Spillane ordered him away contemptuously – a fellow who had taken the master's cane to another had no status. But that wasn't the sort of hero I wanted to be. I preferred something less sensational.

Next morning I was in such a state of panic that I didn't know how I should face the school at all. I dawdled, between two minds as to whether or not I should mitch. The silence of the school lane and yard awed me. I had made myself late as well.

'What kept you, Delaney?' the Murderer asked quietly.

I knew it was no good.

'I was at Mass, sir.'

'All right. Take your seat.'

He seemed a bit surprised. What I had not realized was the incidental advantage of our system over the English one. By this time half a dozen of his pets had brought the Murderer the true story of Flanagan's shilling, and if he didn't feel a monster he probably felt a fool.

But by that time I didn't care. In my school sack I had another story. Not a school story this time, though. School stories were a washout. 'Bang! Bang!' – that was the only way to deal with men like the Murderer. 'The only good teacher is a dead teacher.'

THE MUSEUM OUTING
E. Braithwaite

After lunch the class received the news of the trip to the Victoria and Albert Museum with delight. I told them it was planned for the following Thursday, and that Miss Blanchard would be coming along to help keep order. At this there was some good-natured twittering, and Pamela Dare asked:

'Does she have to come, Sir?'

'Oh yes, Miss Dare. The Council wouldn't allow forty-odd children to go on an expedition in the care of only one teacher.'

'I like Miss Blanchard, she's smashing.' Tich Jackson's puckish face creased in a smile of delight.

'Oh, shut up Tich, who asked you?' Tich looked at Pamela Dare in surprise; her tone was unnecessarily hostile.

'Jackson,' he said softly, 'the name's Jackson.'

The girl made a face at him and tossed her red hair defiantly.

On Thursday morning when I arrived I went to the Headmaster's office to collect the travel voucher for our trip and reached my classroom some time after they were all seated and waiting. I was quite unprepared for what I saw – the children were scrubbed, combed and brushed and shining. The girls were beautifully turned out and there was more than a suggestion of lipstick in evidence; the boys were smartly dressed, and everyone was beaming happily at my delighted surprise.

One seat was empty. Tich Jackson's. I called the register merely as a formality, for by now I could quickly spot an absence, so much a part of me had the class become.

I collected their dinner money and was waiting for Miss Blanchard when there was a slight commotion outside the door: I went across and pulled it open. On the threshold was a huge laundry bundle; and from somewhere underneath it a voice was crying:

'It's me, Sir, Jackson. Gotta take the bagwash for me Mum. Don't go without me, Sir, I'll be back in a jiff.' Without pausing for any reply the bundle was withdrawn and disappeared down the passage to a chorus of laughter from the class in which I joined helplessly.

Gillian soon arrived and we divided the class into two groups for easier control; and when Jackson returned we set off for the Underground Station.

At Whitechapel we changed to a District Line for South Kensington. At that time of morning there were not many seats available, and the children were strung out among two carriages in groups of three or four. I was sandwiched near a door with Moira Joseph, Barbara Pegg and Pamela Dare, who were chattering excitedly to me about the things we were likely to see. They were especially anxious to look at some very fine complicated hand-stitching about which Gillian had told them, and it pleased me to be so closely identified with their lively enthusiasm. At Cannon Street two elderly, well-dressed women joined the train, and stood in the crowd close to us. The stare of disapproval they cast in our direction was made very obvious; and soon they were muttering darkly something about 'shameless young girls and these black men'.

I felt annoyed and embarrassed, and hoped the girls were too absorbed in discussion to notice the remarks, which were meant to be overheard.

Barbara Pegg who was closer to them than the others, was the first to hear them. She bent forward and whispered to Pamela, who moved around until she had changed places with Barbara and was next to the women. Suddenly she turned to face them, her eyes blazing with anger.

'He is our teacher. Do you mind?'

She had intended her voice to carry, and it did. The women looked away, shocked and utterly discomfited, as other people on the train turned to stare at the defiantly regal girl and the blushing busybodies who probably wished that they could sink through the floor.

At the museum the children were collected together for a final briefing. Equipped with paper and pencils they would work in groups of six or seven, each group concerning itself with some particular aspect of Mid-Victorian dress – design, material, stitchcraft, accessories, hair culture, wigs, etc. We would all meet in the Museum canteen at eleven o'clock for a cup of tea, and again at twelve preparatory to returning to school. They were reminded to be very quiet and to refrain from touching any of the exhibits.

Gillian and I moved about among the little groups, giving advice and assistance. She was graceful and charming and made quite a hit with the boys who vied with each other for her attention.

It was for me a pleasant and revealing experience; I had not supposed that the children would have shown so much interest in historical events. Weston had even hinted that their enthusiasm for this outing was just one more excuse to get away from anything concerned with education; yet here they were, keenly interested, asking the sort of questions which clearly showed that they had done some preparatory work. They took the whole thing quite seriously, sketching, making notes, discussing it in undertones.

Later, I sat down to a cup of tea with Gillian, Patrick Fernman, Pamela and Barbara. It would have been difficult for a stranger to have guessed which of the three girls was the teacher, for Gillian was much smaller than the other two, who also looked more grown up than usual with the extra touch of red on their lips. Pamela especially was very striking, in a pleated red skirt set off by high-heeled red shoes and a saucy red ribbon worn high on her auburn hair. Looking at her I could see that in a few years she would really blossom out into something rather splendid.

'. . . it must have been very uncomfortable.'

I only caught the tail-end of Gillian's remark and looked at her guiltily.

'All the same, they must have looked smashing. Think of all that material for only one dress!' Barbara's large face was alive with enthusiasm.

The conversation centred around the exhibits they had seen; it was

We moved about the little groups, giving advice and assistance.

all very much outside their previous experience and interest, yet their comments were surprisingly shrewd. Fernman, whose parents worked in the clothing industry, showed an unexpected knowledge of the art of the Flemish weavers, and told us that his grandmother still wove in silk on her own hand loom.

I was thoroughly pleased with the conduct of my class; they would have been a credit to the best of schools. Denham and Potter had apparently elected themselves lieutenants, and just before twelve o'clock I could see them going from group to group marshalling the class together, and at a sign from me they led off through the subway towards the station.

Once on the train and released at last from the unusual strain of more than two hours of quiet, they were themselves again, joking and chattering about the things they had seen like a band of cheerful monkeys. Every now and then I could overhear the now familiar 'Sir said . . .' expressed with positive finality, a constant reminder of the great responsibility I had undertaken. They now accepted the things I said completely, unquestioningly, because they had accepted me, and no one seemed disposed to query the authenticity of anything which bore the seal 'Sir said'.

Back at school the children scattered towards the dining hall or home and Gillian and I went off to the staffroom. I had seen very little of her on the way back, and now as we settled down to our sandwiches she told me how much she had enjoyed the visit.

'It was so much nicer than I expected, Rick, I mean being with them off the school premises.'

'I know what you mean. They're really nice people, as Mrs Drew says.'

'It's more than that. On the way back I was talking with Moira Joseph and Effie Crook; they spoke to me as equals, and I had the odd feeling that they knew more about life than I did.'

'That's not surprising. Moira's mother has been in a convalescent home for nine weeks, tuberculosis I think, and Moira has to mother the family. Two younger ones are at a Junior School near by; she's allowed to leave school early each afternoon to collect them.'

'God, how dreadful!'

'I don't think she minds in the least; rather enjoys it, I suppose. She told me about the way her father praises her cooking. I do think we often make the mistake of lumping them all together as "kids".'

'Oh, I wouldn't call them that, not all of them anyway. The Dare girl has quite a crush on you, I've noticed.'

I sat looking at her, completely lost for words; women say the damnedest things.

'Well, you have noticed it, haven't you?' The smile did not detract from the serious note in her voice.

'No, I haven't. I treat her no differently from any of the others.'

'Now don't be silly, Rick. I'm sure you don't, but that would make no difference. It's quite the usual thing, you know; I'm sure some of the small boys in my class are dying for love of me.' Her silvery laughter rang through the room; and I found it impossible to be annoyed with her.

'I hear you had a spot of bother on the train this morning.'

'Oh, nothing serious.' I described the incident and the way in which Pamela had effectively put the busybodies to rout. She gave me a long searching look.

'Rick, I think you're the one who's treating them like kids. But don't make that mistake with the Dare girl; she's a woman in every sense of the word.'

'Now, wait a moment, Gillian; there's nothing significant in Pamela's action in the train, at least, not to me.'

'Have it your own way. Not that I really blame the girl a bit – you are rather overpowering, you know.'

The following morning I was a bit late for school. Those damned trains were becoming more and more unpredictable; they always managed to get held up just outside a station, so that there was no alternative to waiting. The children were all in their places when I arrived, and as I stepped into the room they greeted me as with one voice:

'Good morning, Sir.'

I was so surprised I must have gaped at them for a moment before returning their greeting. This had never happened before. Usually I greeted them first just before registration and would receive a reply from those who felt like it. This was overwhelmingly different.

I recovered myself and walked towards my table, and there it was.

In the centre of my table was a large vase in which was neatly arranged a bunch of flowers. Some were slightly bedraggled; all had evidently been collected from the tiny backyards and window boxes of their homes. For me this was the most wonderful bouquet in the world; it was an accolade bestowed collectively by them on me. I turned to look at their pleased, smiling faces and said, with a full heart:

'Thank you, all of you.'

THE MAN'S WORLD
D.H. Lawrence

Ursula Brangwen had started her first job – teaching at St Philip's School. But her methods were not those of the harsh domineering headmaster, Mr Harby, and her class was becoming more and more unruly. One evening after school, stones were thrown at her by some schoolboys. Ursula realized that if she was to continue at the school, she would have to assert her authority to show she was in control.

It seemed she scarcely saw her class the next day. She could only feel her will, and what she would have of this class which she must grasp into subjection. It was no good, any more, to appeal, to play upon the better feelings of the class. Her swift-working soul realized this.

She, as teacher, must bring them all as scholars, into subjection. And this she was going to do. All else she would forsake. She had become hard and impersonal, almost avengeful on herself as well as on them, since the stone throwing. She did not want to be a person, to be herself any more, after such humiliation.

From now on she would assert herself for mastery, be only teacher. She was set now. She was going to fight and subdue.

She knew by now her enemies in the class. The one she hated most was Williams. He was a sort of defective, not bad enough to be so classed. He could read with fluency, and had plenty of cunning intelligence. But he could not keep still. And he had a kind of sickness very repulsive to a sensitive girl, something cunning and etiolated and degenerate. Once he had thrown an ink-well at her, in one of his mad little rages. Twice he had run home out of class. He was a well-known character.

And he grinned up his sleeve at this girl-teacher, sometimes hanging round her to fawn on her. But this made her dislike him more. He had a kind of leech-like power.

From one of the children she took a supple cane, and this she determined to use when real occasion came. One morning, at composition, she said to the boy Williams:

'Why have you made this blot?'

'Please, miss, it fell off my pen,' he whined out, in the mocking voice that he was so clever in using. The boys near snorted with laughter. For Williams was an actor, he could tickle the feelings of his hearers subtly. Particularly he could tickle the children with him into ridiculing his teacher, or indeed, any authority of which he was not afraid. He had that peculiar gaol instinct.

'Then you must stay in and finish another page of composition,' said the teacher.

This was against her usual sense of justice, and the boy resented it derisively. At twelve o'clock she caught him slinking out.

'Williams, sit down,' she said.

And there she sat, and there he sat, alone, opposite to her, on the back desk, looking up at her with his furtive eyes every minute.

'Please, miss, I've got to go an errand,' he called out insolently.

'Bring me your book,' said Ursula.

The boy came out, flapping his book along the desks. He had not written a line.

'Go back and do the writing you have to do,' said Ursula. And she sat at her desk, trying to correct books. She was trembling and upset. And for an hour the miserable boy writhed and grinned in his seat. At the end of that time he had done five lines.

'As it is so late now,' said Ursula, 'you will finish the rest this evening.'

The boy kicked his way insolently down the passage.

The afternoon came again. Williams was there, glancing at her, and her heart beat thick, for she knew it was a fight between them. She watched him.

During the geography lesson, as she was pointing to the map with her cane, the boy continually ducked his whitish head under the desk, and attracted the attention of other boys.

'Williams,' she said, gathering her courage, for it was critical now to speak to him, 'what are you doing?'

He lifted his face, the sore-rimmed eyes half smiling. There was something intrinsically indecent about him. Ursula shrank away.

'Nothing,' he replied, feeling a triumph.

'What are you doing?' she repeated, her heart-beat suffocating her.

'Nothing,' replied the boy, insolently, aggrieved, comic.

'If I speak to you again, you must go down to Mr Harby,' she said.

But this boy was a match even for Mr Harby. He was so persistent, so cringing, and flexible, he howled so when he was hurt, that the master hated more the teacher who sent him than he hated the boy himself. For of the boy he was sick of the sight. Which Williams knew. He grinned visibly.

Ursula turned to the map again, to go on with the geography lesson. But there was a little ferment in the class. Williams's spirit infected them all. She heard a scuffle, and then she trembled inwardly. If they all turned on her this time, she was beaten.

'Please, miss—' called a voice in distress.

She turned round. One of the boys she liked was ruefully holding out a torn celluloid collar. She heard the complaint, feeling futile.

'Go in front, Wright,' she said.

She was trembling in every fibre. A big, sullen boy, not bad but very difficult, slouched out to the front. She went on with the lesson, aware that Williams was making faces at Wright, and that Wright was grinning behind her. She was afraid. She turned to the map again. And she was afraid.

'Please, miss, Williams—' came a sharp cry, and a boy on the back row was standing up, with drawn, pained brows, half a mocking grin on his pain, half real resentment against Williams – 'Please, miss, he's nipped me,' – and he rubbed his leg ruefully.

'Come in front, Williams,' she said.

The rat-like boy sat with his pale smile and did not move.

'Come in front,' she repeated, definite now.

'I shan't,' he cried, snarling, rat-like, grinning. Something went click in Ursula's soul. Her face and eyes set, she went through the class straight. The boy cowered before her glowering, fixed eyes. But she advanced on him, seized him by the arm, and dragged him from his seat. He clung to the form. It was the battle between him and her. Her instinct had suddenly become calm and quick. She jerked him from his

With one hand she held him, and now and then the cane came down on him.

grip, and dragged him, struggling and kicking, to the front. He kicked her several times, and clung to the forms as he passed, but she went on. The class was on its feet in excitement. She saw it, and made no move.

She knew if she let go the boy he would dash to the door. Already he had run home once out of her class. So she snatched her cane from the desk, and brought it down on him. He was writhing and kicking. She saw his face beneath her, white, with eyes like the eyes of a fish, stony, yet full of hate and horrible fear. And she loathed him, the hideous writhing thing that was nearly too much for her. In horror lest he should overcome her, and yet at the heart quite calm, she brought down the cane again and again, whilst he struggled making inarticulate noises, and lunging vicious kicks at her. With one hand she managed to hold him, and now and then the cane came down on him. He writhed, like a mad thing. But the pain of the strokes cut through his writhing, vicious, coward's courage, bit deeper, till at last, with a long whimper that became a yell, he went limp. She let him go, and he rushed at her, his teeth and eyes glinting. There was a second of agonized terror in her heart: he was a beast thing. Then she caught him, and the cane came down on him. A few times, madly, in a frenzy, he lunged and writhed, to kick her. But again the cane broke him, he sank with a howling yell on the floor, and like a beaten beast lay there yelling.

Mr Harby had rushed up towards the end of this performance.

'What's the matter?' he roared.

Ursula felt as if something were going to break in her.

'I've thrashed him,' she said, her breast heaving, forcing out the words on the last breath. The headmaster stood choked with rage, helpless. She looked at the writhing, howling figure on the floor.

'Get up, she said. The thing writhed away from her. She took a step forward. She had realized the presence of the headmaster for one second, and then she was oblivious of it again.

'Get up,' she said. And with a little dart the boy was on his feet. His yelling dropped to a mad blubber. He had been in a frenzy.

'Go and stand by the radiator,' she said.

As if mechanically, blubbering, he went.

The headmaster stood robbed of movement or speech. His face was yellow, his hands twitched convulsively. But Ursula stood stiff not far from him. Nothing could touch her now: she was beyond Mr Harby.

The headmaster muttered something, turned, and went down the room, whence, from the far end, he was heard roaring in a mad rage at his own class.

The boy blubbered wildly by the radiator. Ursula looked at the class. There were fifty pale, still faces watching her, a hundred round eyes fixed on her in an attentive, expressionless stare.

'Give our the history readers,' she said to the monitors.

There was dead silence. As she stood there, she could hear again the ticking of the clock, and the chock of piles of books taken out of the low cupboard. Then came the faint flap of books on the desks. The children passed in silence, their hands working in unison. They were no longer a pack, but each one separated into a silent, closed thing.

'Take page 125, and read that chapter,' said Ursula.

There was a click of many books opened. The children found the page, and bent their heads obediently to read. And they read, mechanically.

Ursula, who was trembling violently, went and sat in her high chair. The blubbering of the boy continued. The strident voice of Mr Brunt, the roar of Mr Harby, came muffled through the glass partition. And now and then a pair of eyes rose from the reading-book, rested on her a moment, watchful, as if calculating impersonally, then sank again.

She sat still without moving, her eyes watching the class, unseeing. She was quite still, and weak. She felt that she could not raise her hand from the desk. If she sat there for ever, she felt she could not move again, nor utter a command. It was a quarter-past four. She almost dreaded the closing of the school, when she would be alone.

The class began to recover its ease, the tension relaxed. Williams was still crying. Mr Brunt was giving orders for the closing of the lesson. Ursula got down.

'Take your place, Williams,' she said.

He dragged his feet across the room, wiping his face on his sleeve. As he sat down, he glanced at her furtively, his eyes still redder. Now he looked like some beaten rat.

At last the children were gone. Mr Harby trod by heavily, without looking her way, or speaking. Mr Brunt hesitated as she was locking her cupboard.

'If you settle Clarke and Letts in the same way, Miss Brangwen, you'll be all right,' he said, his blue eyes glancing down in a strange fellowship, his long nose pointing at her.

'Shall I?' she laughed nervously.

As she went along the street, clattering on the granite pavement, she was aware of boys dodging behind her. Something struck her hand that was carrying her bag, bruising her. As it rolled away she saw that it was a potato. Her hand was hurt, but she gave no sign. Soon she would take the tram.

She was afraid, and strange. It was to her quite strange and ugly, like some dream where she was degraded. She would have died rather than admit it to anybody. She could not look at her swollen hand. Something had broken in her; she had passed a crisis. Williams was beaten, but at a cost.

Feeling too much upset to go home, she rode a little farther into the town, and got down from the tram at a small tea-shop. There, in the dark little place behind the shop, she drank her tea and ate bread-and-butter. She did not taste anything. The taking of tea was just a mechanical action, to cover over her existence. There she sat in the dark, obscure little place, without knowing. Only unconsciously she nursed the back of her hand, which was bruised.

When finally she took her way home, it was sunset red across the west. She did not know why she was going home. There was nothing for her there. She had, true, only to pretend to be normal. There was nobody she could speak to, nowhere to go for escape. But she must keep on, under this red sunset, alone, knowing the horror in humanity, that would destroy her, and with which she was at war. Yet it had to be so.

In the morning again she must go to school. She got up and went without murmuring even to herself. She was in the hands of some bigger, stronger, coarser will.

School was fairly quiet. But she could feel the class watching her, ready to spring on her. Her instinct was aware of the class instinct to catch her if she were weak. But she kept cold and was guarded.

Williams was absent from school. In the middle of the morning there was a knock at the door: someone wanted the headmaster. Mr Harby went out, heavily, angrily, nervously. He was afraid of irate parents. After a moment in the passage, he came again into school.

'Sturgess,' he called to one of his larger boys. 'Stand in front of the class and write down the name of anyone who speaks. Will you come this way, Miss Brangwen.'

He seemed vindictively to seize upon her.

Ursula followed him, and found in the lobby a thin woman with a whitish skin, not ill-dressed in a grey costume and a purple hat.

'I called about Vernon,' said the woman, speaking in a refined accent. There was about the woman altogether an appearance of refinement and of cleanliness, curiously contradicted by her half beggar's deportment, and a sense of her being unpleasant to touch, like something going bad inside. She was neither a lady nor an ordinary working man's wife, but a creature separate from society. By her dress she was not poor.

Ursula knew at once that she was Williams's mother, and that he was Vernon. She remembered that he was always clean, and well-dressed, in a sailor suit. And he had this same peculiar, half transparent unwholesomeness, rather like a corpse.

'I wasn't able to send him to school today,' continued the woman, with a false grace of manner. 'He came home last night so ill – he was violently sick – I thought I should have to send for the doctor. – You know he has a weak heart.'

The woman looked at Ursula with her pale, dead eyes.

'No,' replied the girl, 'I did not know.'

She stood still with repulsion and uncertainty. Mr Harby, large and male, with his overhanging moustache, stood by with a slight, ugly smile at the corner of his eyes. The woman went on insidiously, not quite human:

'Oh, yes, he has had heart disease ever since he was a child. That is why he isn't very regular at school. And it is very bad to beat him. He was awfully ill this morning – I shall call on the doctor as I go back.'

'Who is staying with him now, then?' put in the deep voice of the schoolmaster, cunningly.

'Oh, I left him with a woman who comes in to help me – and who understands him. But I shall call in the doctor on my way home.'

Ursula stood still. She felt vague threats in all this. But the woman was so utterly strange to her, that she did not understand.

'He told me he had been beaten,' continued the woman, 'and when

I undressed him to put him to bed, his body was covered with marks –
I could show them to any doctor.'

Mr Harby looked at Ursula to answer. She began to understand.
The woman was threatening to take out a charge of assault on her son
against her. Perhaps she wanted money.

'I caned him,' she said. 'He was so much trouble.'

'I'm sorry if he was troublesome,' said the woman, 'but he must have
been shamefully beaten. I could show the marks to any doctor. I'm sure
it isn't allowed, if it was known.'

'I caned him while he was kicking me,' said Ursula, getting angry
because she was half excusing herself, Mr Harby standing there with
the twinkle at the side of his eyes, enjoying the dilemma of the two
women.

'I'm sorry if he behaved badly,' said the woman. 'But I can't think he
deserved beating as he has been. I can't send him to school, and really
can't afford to pay the doctor. – Is it allowed for the teachers to beat the
children like that, Mr Harby?'

The headmaster refused to answer. Ursula loathed herself, and loathed
Mr Harby with his twinkling cunning and malice on the occasion. The
other miserable woman watched her chance.

'It is an expense to me, and I have a great struggle to keep my boy
decent.'

Ursula still would not answer. She looked out at the asphalt yard,
where a dirty rag of paper was blowing.

'And it isn't allowed to beat a child like that, I am sure, especially
when he is delicate.'

Ursula stared with a set face on the yard, as if she did not hear. She
loathed all this, and had ceased to feel or to exist.

'Though I know he is troublesome – but I think it was too much.
His body is covered with marks.'

Mr Harby stood sturdy and unmoved, waiting now to have done,
with the twinkling, tiny wrinkles of an ironical smile at the corners of
his eyes. He felt himself master of the situation.

'And he was violently sick. I couldn't possibly send him to school
today. He couldn't keep his head up.'

Yet she had no answer.

'You will understand why he is absent,' she said to Mr Harby.

'Oh, yes,' he said, rough and off-hand. Ursula detested him for his male triumph. And she loathed the woman. She loathed everything.

'You will try to have it remembered, sir, that he has a weak heart. He *is* so sick after these things.'

'Yes,' said the headmaster, 'I'll see about it.'

'I know he is troublesome,' the woman only addressed herself to the male now – 'but if you could have him punished without beating – he is really delicate.'

Ursula was beginning to feel upset. Harby stood in rather superb mastery, the woman cringing to him to tickle him as one tickles trout.

'I had come to explain why he was away this morning, sir. You will understand.'

She held out her hand. Harby took it and let it go, surprised and angry.

'Good morning,' she said, and she gave her gloved, seedy hand to Ursula. She was not ill-looking, and had a curious insinuating way, very distasteful yet effective.

'Good morning, Mr Harby, and thank you.'

The figure in the grey costume and the purple hat was going across the school yard with a curious lingering walk. Ursula felt a strange pity for her, and revulsion from her. She shuddered. She went into the school again.

The next morning Williams turned up, looking paler than ever, very neat and nicely dressed in his sailor blouse. He glanced at Ursula with a half-smile: cunning, subdued, ready to do as she told him. There was something about him that made her shiver. She loathed the idea of having laid hands on him. His elder brother was standing outside the gate at playtime, a youth of about fifteen, tall and thin and pale. He raised his hat, almost like a gentleman. But there was something subdued, insidious about him too.

'Who is it?' said Ursula.

'It's the big Williams,' said Violet Harby roughly. 'She was here yesterday, wasn't she?'

'Yes.'

'It's no good her coming – her character's not good enough for her to make any trouble.'

Ursula shrank from the brutality and the scandal. But it had some vague, horrid fascination. How sordid everything seemed! She felt sorry for the queer woman with the lingering walk, and those queer, insidious boys. The Williams in her class was wrong somewhere. How nasty it was altogether.

So the battle went on till her heart was sick. She had several more boys to subjugate before she could establish herself. And Mr Harby hated her almost as if she were a man. She knew now that nothing but a thrashing would settle some of the big louts who wanted to play cat and mouse with her. Mr Harby would not give them the thrashing if he could help it. For he hated the teacher, the stuck-up, insolent high-school miss with her independence.

'Now, Wright, what have you done this time?' he would say genially to the boy who was sent to him from Standard Five for punishment. And he left the lad standing, lounging, wasting his time.

So that Ursula would appeal no more to the headmaster, but, when she was driven wild, she seized her cane, and slashed the boy who was insolent to her, over head and ears and hands. And at length they were afraid of her, she had them in order.

But she had paid a great price out of her own soul, to do this. It seemed as if a great flame had gone through her and burnt her sensitive tissue. She who shrank from the thought of physical suffering in any form, had been forced to fight and beat with a cane and rouse all her instincts to hurt. And afterwards she had been forced to endure the sound of their blubbering and desolation, when she had broken them to order.

Oh, and sometimes she felt as if she would go mad. What did it matter, what did it matter if their books were dirty and they did not obey? She would rather, in reality, that they disobeyed the whole rules of the school, than that they should be beaten, broken, reduced to this crying, hopeless state. She would rather bear all their insults and insolences a thousand times than reduce herself and them to this. Bitterly she repented having got beside herself, and having tackled the boy she had beaten.

Yet it had to be so. She did not want to do it. Yet she had to. Oh, why, why had she leagued herself to this evil system where she must brutalize herself to live? Why had she become a school-teacher, why, why?

The children had forced her to the beatings. No, she did not pity them. She had come to them full of kindness and love, and they would have torn her to pieces. They chose Mr Harby. Well then, they must know her as well as Mr Harby, they must first be subjugate to her. For she was not going to be made nought, no, neither by them, nor by Mr Harby, nor by all the system around her. She was not going to be put down, prevented from standing free. It was not to be said of her, she could take her place and carry out her task. She would fight and hold her place in this state also, in the world of work and man's convention.

NO ANGELS
Francesca Enns

'We are losing Mitchell and we are getting two new children instead.'
'How is that?'
'Because Mary is leaving. Moving. We are going to have Coxen.'
'Coxen?' There was no great enthusiasm for Coxen.
'Coxen has to sit next to Halliday.'
'No, I am not going to have Coxen next to me.'
All of Halliday's pimples seemed to stand up like bristles.
'Look, Halliday, you are the biggest and strongest boy in class. That's why I want to sit Coxen next to you. He won't be able to bully you.'
Halliday was either flattered or saw sense in my suggestion. He made no further objections.
'Macnab is also joining our class.'
'Macnab!'
'Macnab is a thief.'
'You must not say such a thing.'
'But it is true.'
'Well, if you have any suspicions keep your eyes open. It is a pity we shall have to lock up everything. We never had any thieving.'
'What about Barry Lee?'
Yes, indeed. None of us will ever forget Barry Lee.

Barry Lee came at the beginning of the winter term. The Head had prepared me for the boy. 'Barry Lee is coming from a convalescent home. Before that he spent six months in hospital. Be very careful with him. He was at this school and was very naughty and disobedient. He gave a lot of trouble. There is no question of not punishing him, but don't forget he is a sick child. He was found unconscious in the street: beaten up, supposedly by some of our boys. It has never been proved. There was a story that he had interfered with the fourth-year boys' bicycles. In hospital they discovered a tuberculous lung which had to be removed. He also suffers from a heart condition. I tried to persuade his mother to send him to a school for delicate children. She does not want to. It is her only child. There is no shortage of money in the home. I know you will do your best.'

I assured the Head that I was against corporal punishment, theoretically I must confess.

The Head said that there was a place for corporal punishment in a school like this; not to be used indiscriminately of course.

'If you have any difficulties with Barry Lee send him to me.'

I was surprised when I saw the boy. He was so small and looked like a child of eight. His face was angelic if an angel could have a blotchy, unhealthy complexion. Saucer eyes fringed with lashes which were so long that they appeared artificial. How could anybody have harmed this sweet babe . . . a cockney version of Lord Fauntleroy?

Barry Lee was seated right in front of me. He could not be quiet, sit still or concentrate. He broke pencils, bent pen-nibs, spilled ink and continually interrupted all work. Only at Drama lesson did he behave perfectly normally.

His acting was superb.

Soon things became very difficult for me. I had made up my mind not to be provoked but Barry Lee's continuous clamour for attention grew worse. If I ignored him he started swearing in the most filthy manner.

I might have overlooked the swearing; after all for many children it was the language they heard at home, but swearing was forbidden in the school and had to be punished. Furthermore the girls and some of the boys considered swearing as something the teacher must not allow.

His face was angelic if an angel could have a blotchy, unhealthy complexion.

He was supposed to be kept in after school; I knew that if I gave him lines to write he would not do them so when he swore I sent him to the Senior Master. What he did to him I don't know, but the relief of having him out of the class was so great that I regretted it when he did not swear and I had no excuse to send him to the main building. Luckily he had to take some medicine after which he pretended he did not feel well. Very sympathetically I offered, on fine days, to let him sit in the yard. The whole class appreciated these respites from his irritating, restless presence.

One day he had to go to court for stealing a bicycle. Why he had done so no one knew because he had a perfectly good machine which he rode, against all regulations, in the yard, displaying a circus-like agility. With him it was not only a question of no hands, it was practically no feet either. Barry was put on probation and returned to school.

It happened that soon after this I had to stay at home for a few days with a severe cold. The day I returned to school I went very early and met one of the cleaners.

'Oh, Mrs Enns,' she said. 'You have no idea what a state your Art Room was in last Friday. There was ink and crayons all over the place. And a little boy was jumping about like a demon. Some others tried to clean up after him. They could not stop him.'

The first thing I noticed were the ink splashes over a large group picture on which the fourth-year boys had worked for months. This was the lowest stream of the fourth-year boys who had often exasperated me until I had the idea of this very large painting: The Greatest Show on Earth. I had promised them I would hang it up in the dining-room indicating clearly that it was their work.

After my first shock I realized that it could be painted over and no permanent damage had been done. On the other hand, most of the clay models were permanently ruined. They were kept in airtight tins and I had no doubt from the cleaner's description that it was Barry Lee who had filled them with ink.

The door to the store-room stood wide open. Obviously the teacher who had taken Art in my absence had forgotten to lock it. Twenty-four packets of new wax crayons had disappeared or more correctly the traces of broken crayons were scattered everywhere. Countless packets of powder paste had been emptied and formed a white heap on the floor. The bristles of paint-brushes had been cut off. Both sinks were blocked with small paint-brushes which jammed the pipes.

Barry Lee was not present. I found out who the boys were who had witnessed the orgy of destruction. I knew one of them was Sasso because the cleaner had recognized him (who did not know Sasso?) but she had assured me that he was one of the boys who had tried to restrain the little 'un, which I well believed because Sasso, except for his vile temper, which often made him utter abuse, was not destructive. Other boys assured me that they too had tried to prevent the damage but it turned out that they themselves had taken part in the orgy of flinging the crayons about and emptying the powder paste, and furthermore, that they had taken quite a lot of crayons and paste home.

My position was difficult. I did not want to 'tell' on the teacher who had left the store-room unlocked or on the other who had enabled these boys to be in the hut after school hours. On the other hand, the crayons and the powder paste had to be replaced. Most of the crayons, though broken, were found and the ones taken home brought back. Some of the emptied powder paste could be salvaged. I told the boys that I had not enough for my next lesson and that they had to buy me a packet.

One of the culprits was Halliday, the large pimply boy who was the football captain. I was very much surprised that he had been involved because he was turning into a quiet and, as I had thought, reliable person whom I had made librarian.

'I want the powder paste this afternoon.' (I told them the shop where they could get it.)

'How much?'

'I daresay it costs two bob.'

Halliday fished in his pockets and retrieved two shillings.

'How much have you got?' he asked the other boys.

They had none. I got the packet in time for the afternoon lesson, not realizing that Halliday, who had no school dinners but bought himself food in the pie-shop, had spent his dinner money to make good the damage. The other boys paid him their share back in pennies.

*   *   *   *

Halliday, Sasso and a boy called Platts were the three boys who had given so much trouble to their teacher in the first year that the Head had decided on a 'report book' for them.

A 'report book' was just an ordinary small exercise book in which each teacher recorded the behaviour of these boys. This was sent to the Head at the end of the week. When I took over the class in their second year I discontinued the 'report book'. Sasso and I had quite a lot of brushes. Sasso would easily burst into tears of rage and shout 'I hate you'. When I sent him out of the room he would slam the door and scream, 'I am not coming back', but he soon sobered down and his swarthy urchin-face would peep in and he would mildly ask, 'Can I come back and work?' Halliday had the habit of calling me 'cheeky woman' but I understood that he did not realize he was being rude. He had the reputation of being very aggressive and in one of his compositions he mentioned it:

In the first school I went to I was kicked out because I used to hit all of the little boys so they would not keep me any longer. . . .

I did not find him aggressive, perhaps because he had turned into a very tall boy who commanded respect.

The incident with the crayons which he had taken home was amazing because from one of his compositions I had thought him on the side of the law:

Plans for the Future

When I leave school I would like to be a printer and in my spare time I would like to play football. I think I have the ability to be a printer and a footballer. I have an uncle in the printing trade and he will get me in and my dad's friend runs a little football team on Sunday mornings.

My Mum and Dad would like me to be a Bobby but I do not. My other uncle is a Bobby. I fort I go in for the best.

Halliday sustained a lot of injuries playing football. Nothing would stop him practising though one day he was obviously in great pain. Another boy told me: 'Halliday said he would play football if he had a tin leg.'

Later on when I gave the class the subject 'The Turning Point' for composition, he wrote:

A couple of years ago there was a footballer called Joe Briggs, who played football for Oldham Town and England. As he was driving home after playing for England at Wembley (they had beaten Scotland 3–0) and he had scored all three goals he was very happy for it was his fiftyth cap. As he was approaching London a big lorrie came out of a side turning and hit his car and Joe was badly hurt, and he had to have his leg taken off, and that was the end of his football career, and the man who was driving the lorrie was an Oldham supporter and that year they were seeking promotion to the first division and if anyone could help them it would be Joe Briggs but now he had only one leg.

Oldham gave him a job in the club as assistant manager after he had his artifisal leg and liked it very much and he bought another centre-forward for the Club and they got into the first division and that new player took Joe's place in the England team after their first season in the first division they found that they had won the Championship. And the new centre forward had scored 61 goals that season and 20 the season before. After another two years they had won the F.A. cup twice and the manager retired so they made Joe manager of the club and he did a very good job of it.

Halliday's writing leaned very much back to the left. He was the only child in the class who wrote in this way. He was a nuisance in Poetry lesson as he would giggle and make faces and could never be persuaded to read aloud. His silly behaviour made me believe that he did not like poetry. However, when I gave the children a test in which they had to write down some poetry they had learned by heart, it appeared that it was Halliday who knew the most. He also disliked Art and I allowed him to read during this period. He never volunteered for Drama and refused to make a speech. It was unfortunate as the P.T. Master had decided that he did not assert himself enough and he made another boy, who was in D class, captain. This boy could hardly read or write and all attempts to make him work had failed. Yet this sullen, morose boy possessed amazing qualities.

One day I had the boys in his class for Art. They came into the hut shouting and pushing and I sent them out again and told them they would not have a lesson until they walked in properly. The boys thought that was great fun and jeered and cheered outside. I let them go on for a minute. Suddenly the noise stopped. In came the new football captain.

'They are all right, now,' he said. 'I have lined them up.' Indeed the boys of Class 2D stood like guardsmen according to their size in perfect line. 'Walk in quietly,' he commanded. They did. The lesson began. The boy himself, as usual, refused to work. 'Can I just sit and have a kip?' he asked. After the help he had given me I could not easily refuse.

Halliday could keep order during a football practice but he would not have dreamed of taking action in a case like that. I believe he did not want to become a policeman because he was really shy.

The third boy who had had a report book, Platts, was not involved in the incident with the crayons. He had never been typed as aggressive: he was a boy who was inclined to pranks and practical jokes; he concentrated badly and chattered all the time. Unlike Halliday he was an extrovert, always clamouring that his stories should be read to the class and eager to make a speech or play-act. In an essay he wrote:

Plans for the Future

I would like to be an artist because I like painting and drawing. I think I have the ability but I do not think I have the opportunity because I cannot go to an Art school.

My mother would encourage me but my father would not because he wants me to be a printer. So I will probably be a printer because my father wants me to and I will most probably like it.

It will be possible because I know a friend in the trade his name is John Turner.

I think I have the ability because I am a good speller and a fairly good reader.

Through Platts, who was a great tell-tale and gossip, I learned the names of the boys who had helped Barry Lee in damaging the hut. I then told the Head that some of my boys had been involved in Barry Lee's destructive pranks and as he was a bad influence my hut was not the best place for him. I could not lock everything up. Added to this the boy was not up to standard in work as he was quite incapable of concentrating. I felt there was something to be said in favour of the other boys since they had all confessed and partly made good the damage.

The Head agreed that it would be better to keep the boy in the main building. The E class was in the hands of a young, enthusiastic teacher who wanted to specialize in backward children. The D class, to which Barry should have gone, had no regular teacher at that moment. One could not expect an untrained graduate from the London School of Economics or a Law student, who were filling in the gap, to deal with such a case.

When Barry heard of his transfer to the E class he refused to go there and walked out of school. The next morning he was seen playing football before school; when the whistle sounded for lining up he had disappeared.

The school attendance officer had a word with his mother and Barry turned up for his lessons. The young teacher said he had behaved very well the first day.

Next morning the Housecraft Mistress found that somebody had broken into her department. Flour, margarine, sugar and salt had been flung about. Nothing was taken and no great damage was done. Barry Lee had boasted of the exploit.

When interviewed by the Head, Barry admitted the deed. The Head at that time was a substitute – our regular one was ill.

'Why did you do this dreadful thing?' he had asked the boy.

'And you know what he told me?' The 'supply' Head had come to my hut and had started telling me the story with an apologizing smile. ' "I did it," the boy said, "because I want to go back to Mrs Enns." I know it is bad news for you.'

I picked up one of the brushes which had been scalped by Barry Lee. 'This brush cost one-and-six. I simply cannot prevent the boy from doing damage to school property and other children's work.'

'He won't stay long. I told him the slightest misdemeanour and out he goes. Back to 2E for good.'

Not only I but the whole form was depressed. Yet the first day back Barry behaved like a perfectly normal child. He worked, he did not speak out of turn. The next day he exploded. He had lost his pencil and asked me for another. Quietly I reminded him that I had given him a new one only yesterday. The boy grew excited and started shouting that it was not his fault he could not find his pencil, somebody 'thieved' it. I felt the undercurrent of annoyance of the class. To avoid a scene

I said I would lend him one and handed him a small pencil which I had in my pocket. The fact that this was a small and old pencil enraged the child. He started swearing and Barry Lee's swearing is unprintable.

'He is swearing!' the class said, with some relief.

'Now he's had it.' The children knew of Barry's promise to be good.

Barry threw his books down, picked up his satchel and, banging the door, walked out.

I asked the Head to make Barry's transfer permanent. Barry appeared at school for registration but was found to disappear between lessons. So the young teacher appointed a bodyguard for him: a boy who was extremely tall for his age and had quite uncommonly long arms. This was a very backward boy indeed who could read no better than a child of five. He took his job very seriously and stuck to Barry in an octopus-like fashion, even following and keeping him under observation in the lavatory (though he did not prevent him from smoking there, as I heard). Barry was rather flattered. It also pleased him to become top of the class.

I still had him for Art where he always treated me as his dearest friend. I kept a watchful eye. He did not cause any more malicious damage.

DON'T KNOCK THE CORNERS OFF
Caroline Glyn

The Monday after that was the day of the eleven-plus for Class One. Sir wandered around before it started, looking almost ill with anxiety. In prayers the headmaster had told us to be very quiet all day, very quiet indeed. Miss Lovely made Valerie spend the morning writing out 'Silence Please during the Examination' on all the spare blackboards in the school, in italic. The rest of us had to prop them up in conspicuous places all over the school. We crashed round with them, shouting and fooling. Poor Sir came out and yelled at us in a whisper, but nobody except me took any notice of him.

The rest of the school, too, took care to be even noisier than usual, and the boys spent half playtime on the landing outside the room where the exam was going on, smashing milk bottles. Sir came out in a fury and caned half of them on the spot, which gave them a good excuse to howl the place down.

I was just setting out to go home at lunchtime when I remembered that I was to eat at school in future. I joined on to the end of a queue of Class Fourers who looked as if they might be going to have some lunch. I was feeling as lost and helpless as I had on my first day. We trailed down to the basement.

'Look at 'er – she's got lost!' shouted a voice, with a scream of laughter. I recognized it with a start. It was the leader of Pooh-Pooh-Pants. I turned and bolted back up the stairs. I didn't care if I didn't have any lunch, I wasn't hungry anyway, but I was not going to eat with those little harpies of Class Fourers.

I arrived at the top of the stairs again and cannoned into Tatley.

'Where on earth are you going?' she said loudly.

'I'm having school dinner today,' I said, trying to look superior, as she did.

'Well, whatever were you doing there?' she said in a voice that echoed all over the school and made everyone look at me. 'You ought to be at the end of the line, over there. Go on, silly.' She gave me a push that almost knocked me downstairs again.

We went into a room that I never knew existed. I had begun to think I had got the school straight, but I couldn't find a place for this anywhere. There were lots of oilcloth-topped tables and low chairs from the kindergarten. A strange woman in a white dressing-gown was arranging us at the tables. She stood me at a table beside Skinner. There were more women dressed like her dishing up brown stuff from a great cauldron through a hatchway. Some villainous-looking boys I didn't know came and stood next to Skinner, shepherded by the woman. The din was quite incredible. We were all screaming at the top of our voices. I found myself shouting too, for no reason. At the end of the room stood Miss Lovely on a wooden platform. She was shouting as well, quite inaudibly. The cooks were fussing round like nannies. They stood a boy I recognized from Class One beside me on the other side, and then Felicity Dearchild, and then O'Brien. They were all yelling hard. I looked at them in apprehension, and wished I were on the table with all the Valeries and Sandras.

Suddenly Miss Lovely rang a bell. Screaming more loudly than ever, everyone ran across the room and stood against the wall opposite the hatch. I followed, and was almost squashed to a pulp between Dearchild and one of the ruffianly looking boys. They had all got plates from somewhere. I looked wildly round. All I could see was a pile of broken vegetable dishes beside one of the hatches. When my part of the queue arrived there I snatched a bit of one and held that through the hatch. The cook didn't notice. She put a bit of pastry on it that might or might not have meat underneath, and then to my horror half emptied a bottle of ketchup over it. I grabbed it away. The ketchup ran off the broken edge of the dish all over my dress. I went back to my place next to Skinner hating Daddy for making me have school lunches, and thinking what I would say to him at home.

Miss Lovely blew a whistle. That seemed to be the signal for us to scream a shade less loudly. At least, by looking very hard at her mouth I could make out what she was saying.

'Benedictus benedicat per Jesum Christum dominum nostrum,' said Miss Lovely very slowly, 'Amen.'

I looked at my plate. The pastry had disappeared, and there was only a bit of meat and some unattractive gristle. As I looked Dearchild leant across, yelling, speared the meat with her fork and put it on her own plate. I looked at my plate disbelievingly. One of the boys flicked a large lump of fat across the table onto it. I sat down on the tiny chair, thinking it was as well that I wasn't hungry. My head came just above the table. O'Brien and Skinner, who I had always thought were no bigger than me, didn't seem to have any trouble.

'Whee! Smash!' shouted one of the boys, rushing his mug of water across the table and spilling it into my ketchup. 'Watch out! It's the Ferrari 216. Whoo!'

I said to the boy from Class One next to me,

'I suppose you've just been taking your eleven-plus. What did you think of it?'

He punched me in the face.

Miss Lovely rang a bell. All the children in the room jumped onto their chairs and put their hands on their heads.

'Now, silence, please!' she said. She checked us on the lunch register. 'All right, get on.'

We all screamed, and got down again. Instead of sitting down and finishing, however, we took our plates and rushed to queue at the hatches. I followed. We queued for ages. By the time they reached the hatch the others had finished and were served out some more, but I had had no intention of eating their leftovers that they had dumped on my plate, and was sent back in disgrace.

'Go on! You haven't finished. You can't have anything more till you do,' said the cook. I went back to my place and waited till the rest of my table had eaten their second and third helpings. It took a long time because they kept taking things off each others' plates and fighting and playing cars with the water mugs. Twice more Miss Lovely rang a bell for silence, and we all jumped onto our chairs and put our hands on our heads. At last they finished, and the cook came to clear away the plates. Inside the hatches I could see piles of some steaming pudding which the cooks were dousing with treacle. It really didn't look too bad. I began to feel almost hungry.

'Just look at that! You haven't eaten a mouthful,' said the cook, poking at my cold gristle. 'Now you're just going to sit there till you finish it, if it takes all night.' She stood beside me and made me do it while the rest ate the pudding.

I tried, unsuccessfully, to be sick down her.

*   *   *   *

In the afternoon, Miss Lovely made us strip to our vest and knickers and go outside in the back playground to play relay races. We stood in lines shuddering with cold and cheering feebly, while a few of us ran around with rounders pins. It was January 23rd, I remembered, and might be going to snow tonight.

'Oh, come on, Buddersmud! Oh, you, get a move on,' someone was shouting. 'Quick, run!'

I ran, but had not got a notion what to do and got lost and had to round the course twice. Everybody shrieked at me.

'Oh, Buddersmud, you great idiot, now we're miles behind.'

I said I was sorry, and shivered, and missed my second turn. Everyone booed me and despised me. I concentrated very hard and remembered the course and came in on time on my third turn. Unfortunately, Miss Lovely had changed the race while I wasn't looking, and although I was most conscientious about running round the chair and changing over rounders I still had to go round again and lost my team the second race too. It really did begin to snow after a while, but Miss Lovely said it wouldn't hurt us and made us play ball games instead of going in. We stayed out the whole afternoon.

'In future we will have outdoor P.E. twice a week,' said Miss Lovely afterwards, 'and I'm not having anyone crying off. Is that understood?

Not even those of us whose parents seem to think we're too soft to go out,' she said, looking hard at me. 'Do you all a world of good.'

'It's absolutely lunatic! Lunatic!' said Mummy in a frenzy afterwards. 'She might have given you pneumonia. It's enough to kill the lot of you. Better take your temperature at once.'

I put the thermometer in my mouth, and said, 'We're going to do it twice a week.'

'It's wicked! I won't have it,' said Mummy. 'I don't think the thermometer would taste very nice crunched up, Antonia, I shouldn't try it. Now do you hear, you're not to do it. You are not to go out without a coat and that's that. Ninety-five! Oh, it's a shame! Out in the snow with nothing on and a temperature of ninety-five! Next time just say 'Mummy says I'm to do games with my clothes on,' and if she bullies you again she ought to be sacked.'

'I thought your parents would say something of the sort,' said Miss Lovely glaring at me. 'Have you got a medical certificate? Of course not. Right, out you come, then.'

I wondered whether to warn her that she was now going to be sacked, but thought on the whole better not.

'Last night my temperature was only ninety-five and Mummy said I wasn't to go out without my coat,' I said bravely.

She stared at me until I was practically not there any more, and then said. 'Very well. Today I'll let it go. You can bring me a medical certificate tomorrow, and now instead of P.E. you can start on this.' She rummaged in her drawer and brought out a big card covered with italic writing. 'I was going to make you do it while the others did arithmetic anyway, as you're so bad at italic. Copy this out neatly until you know it.'

I ventured to say, 'Please, I haven't got a pen.'

She flared up at me. 'No, you never have anything, do you, you lazy, careless child! Well, here's one, but it's the last you'll ever have off me, mind. Now go and get on and stop making a nuisance of yourself.'

I went and sat down and looked miserably at the card she had given me. I had only written out about half of it when she came back with the others from P.E. It was all spotted and smudged with tears. She said it was a horrible mess and made me start again.

I spent the whole day slaving over that italic, while the others wrote compositions and did arithmetic. Tatley's composition was read aloud and given a star. That nearly set me crying again, because I knew I could have written an even better composition and perhaps got two stars.

At the end of the day Miss Lovely looked at my italic and said it was shocking.

'You ought to be ashamed of yourself. I think you'll have to work on it again tomorrow,' she said, and tore it up.

'Mummy, if I have to spend another minute writing out italic I shall run away from school,' I said.

'It's so pointless. You say you didn't do any lessons all day, just spent the time learning to write?' said Mummy. 'Why, you could write perfectly when you were five. Well, of all the stupid women your Miss Lovely must be the worst. Look, give me a bit of paper. I'll write to the headmaster about it now and he'll get it tomorrow and see you do some proper lessons. Really, what does that woman think I sent you to school for?'

Miss Lovely didn't make me write out that card again next day after all. Instead she said.

'Now, I've noticed that all your handwritings are perfectly disgusting, and so now you are all to write italic for all your work, and it will gradually replace your ordinary writing for good, I hope.'

I decided that the headmaster couldn't have spoken to her yet.

She set us a composition to write. It was on 'The Happiest Day of My Life.' I had dozens of wonderful ideas and couldn't wait to begin.

'Now, don't forget. Your best italic,' she said.

My dozens of ideas went down like a punctured balloon. I knew very well that I would hardly get half a line down in italic. I had cherished hopes of making up for yesterday with a brilliant essay that would beat Tatley's. I felt rebellious. Which mattered more, what I wrote or how I wrote?

'Hurry up,' said Miss Lovely.

All right, I will, I thought, and wrote my brilliant composition in a sort of ungainly print that hardly even pretended to be italic. Valerie Barker next to me was writing perfect italic without a single mistake. She had written, 'The hapest day of my life was my cosan Gorgy came too stay.' Nothing more. Hurrah! I thought. My turn for the star.

After lunch, Miss Lovely said.

'I've marked your compositions. Most of you did very well. I don't know what happened to yours, Rutherford, it was appalling. Barker got a star for hers. Give them out, please, Johnson.'

I stared at her, dumbfounded.

'However, I've been having a talk with the headmaster, and he says that after all he would rather that you didn't write italic all the time just yet.' She was looking very hard at me as she spoke, just like the eyes in my poem. She really is hypnotizing me with hate, I thought, mentally congratulating Mummy.

★   ★   ★   ★

'Valentine's Day,' said Mummy on the doorstep, 'I expect there'll be some high jinks at school.'

'Oh, I wonder,' I said doubtfully. 'Still, you can't tell.'

'Just supposing a boy sent you a valentine!'

'More likely a black eye,' I said. 'School's not a place for romance. I'm so sorry, Mummy.' She looked quite crestfallen.

Just as I had expected, nobody even knew that it was Valentine's Day. 'And Leap Year too,' I said to Valerie Barker. 'That's when the girls do the proposing, isn't it? You ought to propose to someone.'

'Ooh, I know who,' she said, and put her arms round my neck. 'I'll marry you.'

'Oh,' I said, wriggling uncomfortably and wishing I'd never brought the subject up.

At the end of the afternoon I went into the cloakroom to get my raincoat. I heard a great trampling of feet behind me. Usually I waited for my raincoat until the boys had gone.

'Look out – here comes the rush hour,' I tried to say to someone, but before I had finished speaking I was swallowed up in a wave of stamping boys. I lost my balance and fell over, and tried to wriggle away. Skinner, charging through, gave me such a kick in the face that I was knocked backwards again, feeling dizzy, under the boys' feet. I tried to clutch at the coat hook for support.

The boys rushed out again, treading on me as they went. I really did feel a bit peculiar from the kick Skinner had given me. My head was

The boys rushed out again, treading on me as they went.

buzzing, my face was stinging. I felt sick and giddy, and I could hardly see. I sat down on the floor again.

'Oh, hullo, Antonia,' said Valerie Smith falling over me. 'What are you doing down there? Are you all right?'

'Yes, I'm all right, thank you,' I said, getting up. 'A boy kicked me in the face. No matter. It's not as if it were the first time. See you to-morrow!'

I aimed at the door, and lurched out, very cross with myself for forgetting to wait until the boys had gone before getting my coat, and even more cross because I felt so ill over nothing at all. At the end of the street a group of strange boys came past, staring at me.

'One – lovely – black eye!' sang one of them. They all laughed. Quite batty, I thought. Then it occurred to me that perhaps they were referring to me.

'What, back already?' called Mummy from the kitchen as I came in. 'We're just finishing lunch. Well, how did you get on? Get any valentines? Come on down and talk to us.'

I didn't think I could face the stairs just yet. I called down,

'Everything happened just as I said. No valentines, but I got a whacking great black eye. I'll come down in a minute.'

'What's that? A black eye?' cried Mummy, and came running up. 'Wow! So you have! Eeh, you poor child, the things they do to you at this awful school!'

'A black eye? Someone's given our Totty a black eye?' said Daddy, coming up. 'A knockout!'

Wrestling was one of Daddy's hobbies. He watched it avidly every Saturday on television, and sometimes threatened to try out some of the holds on me.

'Yes. A knockout decided the winner,' I said weakly. 'It happened just now.'

'It's too awful to think of. Come and lie down on the sofa. What brute did it?' said Mummy, tucking me down.

'Oh, I only got Skinner's foot in my face. It's my own fault for being where his foot wanted to go. Anyway, it's always happening. I'm getting quite used to the taste of boys' boots,' I said.

'I don't see that that's any consolation at all,' said Mummy. 'Do you feel all right? No, you don't look it, either. By the way, I wrote to Dr

Harvey for your medical certificate. He said that after all your flu, he would willingly send one. Your poor eye does look awful.'

'Why not complain about it to the headmaster?' suggested Daddy.

'Oh, not again!' I said, involuntarily.

'Good idea. I don't believe he has any idea what goes on behind his back. Skinner, you say it was? I'll ring him up now.'

When she came back she said,

'The headmaster was horrified and promised to "put the fear of God into him," so I hope he'll be more careful in future.'

'Will the headmaster cane him?' I asked anxiously.

'I sincerely hope so. Yes, sure to,' she answered.

'Oh,' I said miserably. 'Oh, I wish you hadn't!'

'You wish we hadn't? Why I hope it'll teach him to leave you alone in future,' Mummy said.

'But he didn't kick me on purpose. Now he really will want to get at me,' I said, thinking of that dark place under the fire-escape in the playground where the boys dragged the girls and made them scream.

The medical certificate that Mummy had written for arrived the next morning. It said that on no account was I to go outside without warm clothes and a coat. I showed it triumphantly to Miss Lovely. She looked at it as if it were a rattlesnake and opened and shut her mouth without saying anything.

Finally she managed to say, 'Very well. I suppose this doctor knows what he's doing, although I'm sure it wouldn't hurt you to get a little air to your body. You may do P.E. fully dressed.' She said it as if she were granting a great honour. 'Though mind you I asked for it several days ago.' She looked in disgust at my black eye. 'You face is a disgrace. I suppose you've been fighting,' she snorted, and stalked out of the room to go to prayers.

After prayers she told Skinner that the headmaster would like to see him. I felt a pang of remorse. The poor boy got into trouble often enough without my interfering. It wasn't as if he'd deliberately set on me. He came back presently looking none the worse for wear, but that didn't mean anything. I dreaded playtime.

When it came I crept downstairs behind the others, and peeped round the door into the playground. I couldn't see him, and stepped outside. Skinner was standing behind the door, and I found myself facing him.

I prepared to fight for my life. He grinned at me, and stepped back to let me pass. As I went by I looked at him anxiously. He just grinned again. I ran to the lavatories, not knowing what to think; I wondered whether anything the headmaster could say would stop him bashing me up if he wanted to.

After play, as I was going upstairs, he put out his foot just in front of me in one of the dark corners. I fell over it, and tumbled down two flights of stone stairs, and was only saved by Tatley, standing duty as stair monitor from going further. I decided not to say anything at home. After all, it might have been an accident.

★   ★   ★   ★

On the door of the classroom there hung a great chart with everyone's points marked on it. I used to get quite a lot when Sir took our class, but now that we had Miss Lovely, I noticed sadly, I hadn't had a single one all term.

'Good gracious!' I said to Valerie Barker standing beside me, 'look at all the marks Roberts has got! Six! Now how on earth did Roberts get six points! You see, he got nothing but minuses last term.'

Didn't you know?' said Valerie, looking at me in surprise. 'Miss Lovely's just made him House captain for Green and he gets all the points for sport. Anyway, he's one of her favourites.'

'Funny, I wouldn't have thought he was at all the type to make a good House captain,' I said, putting things mildly.

'Perhaps that's why Green came bottom last week,' giggled Valerie.

While the others were still changing after P.E. Miss Lovely and Roberts came up together. I was there already, not having to change.

'Now, don't you think it's fun, being in a responsible position? Don't you get a wonderful feeling when you think that other people are relying on you?' she was saying.

'No, I don't,' said Roberts, scowling.

'Oh, really now, Derek, try not to look at things like that. Of course, when one is put in authority life isn't so comfortable for oneself afterwards. But I'm sure you'll find that the pleasure of being able to make other people comfortable quite makes up for that. Now, your team isn't getting on very well at the moment, but you'll soon settle down and then if you really work hard it might come top at the end of term. Yes, it really might, if you work hard, as I'm sure you will. And wouldn't that be a lovely surprise for your form master to come back to? To see that you've improved so much that you can help your House to be top? Now then, you try really hard, and let everyone see how good you can be,' said Miss Lovely, talking very gently and putting on an encouraging smile.

Roberts snarled in her face. She smiled more sweetly than ever. Roberts looked as if he would like to be sick down her. I found myself sympathizing with him.

'Now, Derek. I should very much like you to bring my tea to me in playtime, instead of Linda, in future,' she said.

'Oh, blast you, you old bag,' growled Roberts into his shirt. Everyone else suddenly finished changing and charged into the room, interrupting Miss Lovely before she could look shocked.

Miss Lovely broke the news to Tatley that she had been deprived of her special privilege of bringing her form teacher's tea. Tatley had a wonderful time being offended, and then saying in a hurt way that of course it was perfectly all right, although she didn't really see why Roberts. . . . But Miss Lovely wouldn't give in, and Tatley just had to go and sit down in a sulk.

Roberts didn't take Miss Lovely's tea up at playtime the next day. I had had a suspicion he wouldn't, and wondered whether I would have either. She had a little talk with him afterwards. I couldn't help admiring her patience and determination, or was it bone-headedness? Roberts played the fool with such energy throughout the next lesson that we didn't get any work done at all. Miss Lovely didn't say anything to him, and blamed everything on me instead, because I had leant across to ask Valerie the page.

'If you won't sit still and work, Rutherford, there are plenty of people who have to go to less good schools who would be only too glad to take your place at this one!' she roared. I shut my eyes and held on to my chair while the blast of words went over me.

Sandra King, at the front of the class, suddenly screamed and tucked her feet up under her chair. All the other girls did the same, giggling and squealing. The boys kept their feet resolutely on the floor, watching the girls in amusement.

'Now what's the matter?' snapped Miss Lovely.

'There's a spider, Miss Lovely,' squeaked Sandra Pope.

'A spider? What a lot of fuss for nothing!' said Miss Lovely, moving nervously across to the other side of the class-room.

'You scared of spiders then, Miss Lovely?' called Mason.

'Of course not. Don't be rude,' said Miss Lovely, coming back again.

The girls in front began to scream extra loudly, and the spider ran past them to the front of the room, almost to Miss Lovely's feet. It certainly was the biggest, blackest spider I had ever seen, even bigger than the ones that came out of the walls in our country cottage. Miss Lovely squeaked and retreated again. The spider ran on a bit further, as if it were chasing her. She marched all the way over to the door, pretending to be looking for the board rubber, and the spider followed. The whole class began to giggle. I felt really sorry for her.

Roberts got up with a matchbox, caught the spider and put it in the box. Miss Lovely shuddered all the way down when he picked it up in his hand.

'Oh, thank you, Derek,' gasped Miss Lovely. 'Now throw the nasty thing away, and let's have no more of this nonsense.'

Roberts didn't throw the spider away. He put it, in its box, in his pocket. He was as good as gold all the rest of the lesson, which made me suspicious anyway, and when next day he actually took up a cup of tea at playtime, I should have thought that even Miss Lovely might have guessed what was coming. She didn't however. As we all tore down the stairs to the playground, we heard a hysterical scream come from inside the staff room. Everyone stopped instantly, absolutely still, listening. I saw that the others all had an expression of great glee on their faces, and I suspected I had the same.

'Look, it's all right now, I've thrown it away. I'll get you some more tea,' said Sir's voice, sounding most embarrassed. Someone was gasping, almost sobbing. Sir came out, pink in the face.

'Go on. Get out,' he said, waving us downstairs. We had to go.

Later I noticed that Andrews was wearing the Green House captain badge instead of Roberts. The rumour went round that the headmaster had been caning someone in the lunch hour, and Roberts certainly looked peculiarly pink and snarled extra defiantly all the afternoon. Tatley took up Miss Lovely's tea next day.

A SCHOOL STORY
William Trevor

Every night after lights-out in the dormitory there was a ceremonial story-telling. One by one we contributed our pieces, holding the stage from the gloom for five or six minutes apiece. Many offerings were of a trite enough order: the Englishman, the Irishman and the Scotsman on a series of desert islands, and what the drunk said to the Pope. But often the stories were real: reminiscences from a short past, snippets of overheard conversation, descriptions of the naked female body in unguarded moments. Only Markham deliberately repeated himself, telling us again and again, and by unanimous demand, about the death of his mother. On a night when no one had much to say, Markham would invariably be called upon; and none of us ever expected to hear anything new. We were satisfied that it was so; because Markham told his story well and it was, to us, a fascinating one.

'It was like this, you see. One Sunday morning my father and I were walking up Tavistock Hill and I asked him to tell me about my mother. It was a good sunny morning in early May and my father looked up at the sky and started on about how beautiful she'd been. So then, when I could get a word in, I asked him about how she'd died and that. Well, he took an extra breath or two and said to prepare myself. I assured him I was well prepared, and then he told me about how they had been staying with these friends in Florence and how they had set out to the hills to do some shooting. They rode out in a great Italian shooting-brake and soon they were slaying the birds like nobody's business. But in the middle of everything there was this accident and my mother was lying in a pool of blood and all the Italians were throwing up their hands and saying "Blessed Mother of Jesus, what a terrible thing!" I said: "Did her gun go off by accident? Was she not carrying it correctly or what?" And my father said it wasn't like that at all, it was his gun that went off by accident and what a shocking thing it was to be the instrument of one's wife's slaughter. Well, sharp as a knife I could see the lie in his face and I said to myself: "Accident, forsooth! Murder more like." Or, anyway, words to that effect. You'll understand with a discovery like that fresh on the mind one is in an emotional tizzy and apt to forget the exact order of thinking. Why was I certain? I'll tell you, boys, why I was certain: because within a six-month the father had married the dead mother's sister. My stepmother to this day. And I'll tell you another thing: I have plans laid to wipe out those two with a couple of swoops of a butcher's knife. Am I not, when all's said and done, a veritable pocket Hamlet? And isn't it right that I should dream at night of the sharpening of the knife?'

Markham had a long, rather serious face; deeply set, very blue eyes; and smooth fair hair the colour of yellow terracotta. People liked him, but nobody knew him very well. His stories about his family and the threats they exposed were taken only half seriously; and when he talked in this way he seemed to be speaking outside his role. Markham was too quiet, too pleasant, too attractive to be mixed up in this way. There was something wrong, not so much with what he said – which we quite understood, whether we thought of it as fact or not – as with Markham's saying it. That at least is how it appears in retrospect, to me and to the others with whom I have since discussed it. Then, we scarcely analysed our feelings; after all, we were only fifteen at the time of the Markham affair.

'I've got some bread from Dining Hall,' Williams said. 'Let's toast it in the boiler-house.' He drew from beneath his jacket four rounds of hard-looking bread and a couple of pieces of straightened wire. His small red-rimmed eyes darted about my face as though seeking some minute, mislaid article. He held out a piece of wire and I took it from him, already recognizing its utter uselessness for the task in hand. One had to open the top of the boiler and toast from above, guiding the bread far into the bowels of the ironwork until it was poised nearly above the glowing coke. It was a business of expertise, and a single length of wire in place of an expanding toasting fork indicated rudimentary disaster.

It was mid-afternoon and, recovering from a cold, I was 'off games'. Williams, who suffered from asthma, was rarely seen on the games field. He disliked any form of physical exercise and he used his disability as an excuse to spend solitary afternoons hanging around the classrooms or enjoying a read and a smoke in the lavatories. He was despised for his laziness, his unprepossessing appearance, and his passion for deception. I said I would join him on his expedition to the boiler-house.

'I've snitched some jam,' he said, 'and a pat or two of butter.'

We walked in silence, Williams occasionally glancing over his shoulder in his customary furtive manner. In the boilerhouse he laid the bread on the seat of the boilerman's chair and extracted the jam and butter from the depths of his clothes. They were separately wrapped in two sheets of paper torn from an exercise book. The jam was raspberry and contact with the paper had caused the ruled lines to run. Fearing the effects of this, I said at once that as far as I was concerned the addition of butter was quite sufficient.

The toast was badly burnt and tasted of smoke. Williams ate his ravenously, wiping his fingers on his trouser pockets. I nibbled at mine and eventually threw it into the corner. At this Williams expostulated, picked up the discarded piece, wiped it and smeared on the remains of the jam. He made a crunching noise as he ate, and explained that his inordinate appetite was due to the presence of worms in his body.

There was a football on the steps outside and a moment later a figure appeared, sharply silhouetted in the doorway. We could not at first establish its identity, and Williams, speaking loudly, said to me: 'It has been well worth while. The knowledge we have gained of our school's heating system will stand us in good stead. It is well to put a use to one's time in this way.' The figure advanced, and Williams, seeing that it was not the headmaster, sniggered. 'It's only bloody Markham,' he said. 'I thought it was Bodger at least.'

'I have come to smoke,' Markham announced, offering us cigars.

A moment later a figure appeared, sharply silhouetted in the doorway.

'When I am fully grown and equipped for life,' Williams said, 'I intend to pursue a legal career. As well, I shall smoke only the most expensive cigars. One can well afford such a policy if one makes a success of the law.'

Markham and I, concerned with the lighting of our tobacco, heard this pronouncement in silence.

'It may be,' Williams went on, 'that I shall learn in time to roll the leaves together myself. The female thigh, I understand, is just the instrument for such a chore.'

'Williams will make an excellent lawyer,' Markham remarked.

'Certainly he will be splendid beneath his wig,' I said.

'And what,' Williams asked, 'do you intend to do with your years, Markham?'

'Oh, they are well numbered. I shall hang quite soon for the slaughter of my father.'

'Would you not wait a while that I might defend you?'

'It is not an action you could readily defend surely? I am guilty already. I would prefer not to die, but I would not wish to dissociate myself from my crime.'

Williams, puffing hard and with the cigar clamped in the centre of his teeth, said:

'Markham's a bloody madman, eh?'

'Damn it, isn't it correct that I should be hatching schemes of vengeance? Wasn't it my own mother? Would you do less, Mr Williams?'

'Ah Markham, I wouldn't go about with the noose around my neck before it was time for it. I'd hold my peace on that account.'

'Puny, Williams, puny.'

'But wise, none the less.' He kicked a piece of coke across the floor, following it with his glance. He said: 'Anyway, Markham will never do it. Markham is all talk.'

'This is a good cigar,' Markham said. 'May we enjoy many another.'

'Yes,' said Williams agreeably enough. 'A fine drag.'

We smoked in silence. Looking back on it, it seems certain that it all began that afternoon in the boiler-house. Had I not met Williams on the way to his toasting session, had Markham not later shared his cigars with us, how different the course of events might have been. My friendship with Markham might never have come about; Williams might never have been transformed from a cunning nonentity into a figure of mystery and power; and Markham, somehow, might have dodged the snare he had already set for himself.

★   ★   ★   ★

Becoming friends with Markham was an odd thing. Markham was so silent, so unforthcoming on any subject except the death of his mother. Yet he was sunny rather than sullen; thoughtful rather than brooding. We walked together on the hills behind the school, often without exchanging more than a dozen words. In spite of this our friendship grew. I discovered that Markham's father and stepmother were now in Kenya. Markham saw them only once a year, during the summer holidays; he spent Easter and Christmas with a grandmother on the south coast.

The other odd aspect of this new relationship between Markham and me was the attitude of Williams. He hung around us. Often, uninvited, he accompanied us on our walks. He took to sidling up to us and whispering: 'Markham will never do it. Markham's just a madman, eh?' Markham rarely replied. He stared at Williams with a puzzled expression and smiled.

When he came on walks with us Williams would ask Markham to tell us about the shooting accident in Florence, and this of course Markham never tired of doing. He didn't seem to resent Williams. I think he was more generous than the rest of us about people like Williams. Certainly he was more generous than I was. Frankly, Williams used to set my teeth on edge. I found him alone one day and asked him bluntly what he was up to. He sniffed at me and asked me what I meant.

'Why do you follow Markham and me around?' I said. 'Why don't you leave Markham alone?'

Williams laughed. 'Markham's an interesting bird.'

'What are you up to, Williams?'

But he wouldn't tell me. He said: 'I'm an unhealthy personage.' He laughed again and walked away.

This exchange had no effect on Williams. He still haunted our movements, chattering of his future in the legal world or retailing the fruits of an hour's eavesdropping. When we were alone together Markham no longer repeated his famous story or made any allusion to this particular aspect of life. I came to realize that although he truly hated his father it had become a joke with him to talk about it. I was the first close friend Markham had known, and he was quite unused to the communication that such a relationship involved. It was only very gradually that new topics of conversation developed between us.

But there was always Williams, devotedly determined, it seemed, to wrap Markham and his story closer and closer together. We formed, I suppose, an odd kind of triangle.

★   ★   ★   ★

At the beginning of the autumn term the headmaster, Bodger, addressed us at length about this and that, announcing the names of the new prefects and supplying us with fresh items of school routine. When he had finished this part of his peroration he paused for a suitable moment and then he said:

'There are times, boys, in the lives of us all when we must display the ultimate bravery. When we must face the slings and arrows with a fortitude we may perhaps have never had call to employ before. Such a fearful moment has come to one of our number. I would ask you to show him kindness and understanding. I would ask you this term to help him on his way; to make that way as easy as you may. For us it is a test as it is for him. A test of our humanity. A test of our Christian witness. It is with the greatest grief, boys, that I must report to you the sudden and violent death of Ian Markham's father and stepmother.'

★   ★   ★   ★

Markham had not yet returned. During the fortnight of his absence speculation and rumour ran high. Neither Bodger nor his henchmen seemed to know about the threats he had been wont to issue. Only we who were in their care questioned the accuracy of the facts as they had been presented to us: that a Mau Mau marauder armed with a heavy knife had run berserk through the Markham farm in Kenya. Was not the coincidence too great? Was it not more likely that Markham had finally implemented his words with action?

'Markham's a madman, eh?' Williams said to me.

When he did return, Markham was changed. He no longer smiled. Waiting expectantly in the dormitory for a new and gory story, his companions received only silence from Markham's bed. He spoke no more of his mother; and when anyone sympathized with him on his more recent loss he seemed not to know what was being spoken of. He faded into the background and became quite unremarkable. Pointedly rejecting my companionship, he ended our brief friendship. Instead, he and Williams became inseparable.

*   *   *   *

It was, I remember, a particularly beautiful autumn. Red, dead leaves gleamed all day in the soft sunlight. On warm afternoons I walked alone through the gorse-covered hills. I did not make friends easily; and I missed the company of Markham.

As the weeks passed it became clear the murder of Markham's parents by Mau Mau was now generally accepted. It might be thought that against a background of Markham's stories and avowed intentions a certain fear would have developed; an uneasiness about sharing one's daily existence with such a character. It was not so. Markham seemed almost dead himself; he was certainly not a figure to inspire terror. The more one noticed him the more unlikely it appeared that he could possibly have had any hand in the events in Kenya, although he had been in the house at the time and had himself escaped undamaged.

I thought that only I must have been aware of the ominous nature of Markham's association with Williams. Williams, I knew, was up to no good. He whispered constantly to Markham, grinning slyly, his small eyes drilling into Markham's face. I didn't like it and I didn't know what to do.

One afternoon I walked into the town with a boy called Block. We went to a café with the intention of passing an hour over tea and cakes and, if the coast seemed clear, a surreptitious smoke.

'This is an uncivilized place,' Block remarked as we sat down. 'I cannot imagine why we came here.'

'There is nowhere else.'

'It is at least too revolting for the Bodger or any of his band. Look, there's our dreaded Williams. With Markham.'

They were sitting at a table in an alcove. Williams, talking as usual, was fiddling with the spots on his face. As I watched him, he picked a brightly coloured cake from the plate between them. It looked an uninviting article, indeed scarcely edible. He nibbled at one corner and replaced it on the plate.

'Whatever does Markham see in him?' Block asked.

I shook my head. Block was a simple person, but when he next spoke he revealed a depth I had not before had evidence of. He cocked his head to one side and said: 'Williams hates Markham. You can see it easily enough. And I believe Markham's terrified of him. You used to know Markham rather well. D'you know why?'

Again I shook my head. But there was no doubt about it, Block was quite right.

The nub of the relationship was William's hatred. It was as though hatred of some kind was essential to Markham; as though, since he had no father to hate now, he was feeding on this unexplained hatred of himself. It all seemed a bit crazy, but I felt that something of the kind must be true.

'I feel I should do something about it all,' I said. 'Williams is a horribly untrustworthy fellow. God knows what his intentions are.'

Did Williams know something that we others were ignorant of? Something of the double death in Kenya?

'What can you do?' Block said, lighting the butt of a cigarette.

'I wonder if I should talk to Pinshow?'

Block laughed. Pinshow was a fat, middle-aged master who welcomed the personal problems of his pupils. He was also a bit of an intellectual. It was enough to tell Mr Pinshow that one had an ambition to become a writer or an actor to ensure endless mugs of black coffee in Mr Pinshow's room.

'I often wonder if we don't underestimate Pinshow,' I said. 'There's lots of goodwill in the man. And good ideas quite often originate in unexpected quarters. He just might be able to suggest something.'

'Perhaps. You know more about Markham than I do. I mean, you probably know more about what the matter is. He doesn't seem much good at anything any more, does he?'

I looked across the room at his sad, lost-looking face. 'No, I'm afraid he doesn't.'

Block suddenly began to laugh. 'Have you heard Butler's one about the sick budgerigar?'

I said I didn't think I had, and he leaned forward and told me. Listening to this obscene account of invalid bird-life, I made up my mind to see Pinshow as soon as possible.

★   ★   ★   ★

The evening light faded and Mr Pinshow continued to talk. I tried in the gloom to take some biscuits without his observing my action. He pushed the box closer to me, oblivious, or so I hoped, of my deceit. 'Out of the slimy mud of words,' said Mr Pinshow, 'out of the sleet and hail of verbal imprecision, come approximate thoughts and feelings, words that have taken the place of thoughts and feelings, and the beauty of incantation.' Mr Pinshow often said this. I think it may have been his favourite quotation. I drained my coffee mug, filling my mouth with bitter sediment as I did so.

I said: 'There is a land of the living and a land of the dead and the bridge is love.'

'Ah, Wilder.' Mr Pinshow drew a large coloured handkerchief from his trouser pocket and blew his nose.

'The only survival,' I added, 'the only meaning.'

Mr Pinshow replaced his handkerchief. He scratched a match along the side of its box and held the flame to his pipe. 'Love,' he said, puffing, 'or love? One sort or the other sort?'

'The other sort, sir?'

'You question such a division? Good. Good.'

I said: 'I wanted to speak to you, sir.'

'Quite right. Fire away, then.'

'In confidence, sir, I think Williams is a bad influence on Markham.'

'Ah.'

'I think Markham may be very upset about his parents' death, sir. Williams is the last person . . .'

'Come now, in what way a bad influence? Speak freely, my friend. We must straightway establish the facts of the case.'

I knew then that the whole thing was going to be useless. It had been a mistake to come to Pinshow. I could not reveal to him the evidence on which my fears were based. I said nothing, hoping he would not press me.

'I see,' he said.

'Perhaps I am making a mountain out of a molehill, sir.'

Mr Pinshow, however, did not think so at all. 'This is a serious business,' he said. 'Though it is unusual in these matters, I am glad you came to me.'

Clearly, I had given the man a completely false impression. I attempted to rectify this, but Mr Pinshow waved me to silence.

'Say no more, my friend. Leave the matter with me. You can rely on me to speak with discretion in the right directions.'

'Sir, I hope I have not misled you.'

'No, no, no.'

'It is not a *serious* thing, sir. It is just that Markham was once a friend of mine and I am sure that now he . . .'

Mr Pinshow held up his hand. He smiled. 'You are a good fellow. Do not despair. All will be well.'

God knows, I thought, what damage I have done.

★ ★ ★ ★

'Mind your own bloody business,' Williams muttered to me. 'Any more of this kind of stuff to Pinshow and I'll have you for slander. Don't you know that man's a menace?'

'Go to hell, Williams.' And Williams, seeming a fit candidate for such a destination, shuffled angrily away.

After that, I decided to forget about Markham and Williams. After all, it had nothing to do with me; and in any case I appeared to have no option. I settled down to concentrating a little harder on my work and then, when I really had forgotten all about this strange alliance, I was summoned from class one day by the headmaster.

He stood by the window of his study, a terrible, sickly figure of immense height. He remained with his back to me when I entered the room and spoke to me throughout the interview from this position. 'You will tell me what you know about Markham and the boy Williams,' he said. 'Do not lie, boy. I know a lie. I feel a lie on its utterance. Likewise, do not exaggerate. You will repeat to me simply and honestly all that is apposite. Unburden yourself, boy, that you may leave the room with your duty well done.'

I did not intend to lie. To conceal three-quarters of the story was not to lie. I said: 'The whole truth, sir, is that . . .' I paused not knowing how to go on. The headmaster said:

'Well, boy, let us have haste with the whole truth.'

'I can tell you nothing, sir.'

'Nothing?'

'Yes, sir. I know nothing of Markham and Williams.'

'They are boys in this school. You know that, I presume? You have associated with them. You have spoken to Mr Pinshow of these boys. If their relationship is an illicit one I wish to know it. You will achieve little by reticence.'

'There is nothing illicit, sir, in their friendship. I spoke to Mr Pinshow merely because I felt Williams to be the wrong sort of friend for Markham at this particular time.'

'That is a presumptuous decision for you to make, boy.'

'Yes, sir.'

'Why, then, did you so perversely make it?'

'I like Markham, sir.'

'Why, then, did you not see to it that his days were made easier by persuading him personally against an ill influence?'

'Markham no longer wished for my companionship, sir.'

'You had harmed him in some manner?'

'No, sir. At least not that I know of.'

'Yes or no, boy? Do not leave yourself a cowardly loophole.'

'No, sir. I had not harmed him.'

'Well then, why did he not wish to converse with you?'

'I'm afraid I don't know.'

'You do not know. It is unnecessary to be afraid as well.'

'Yes, sir.'

'You see, boy, that you have placed me in an intolerable position with your wild irresponsibilities? I am the fount of authority in this school. You have made me uneasy in my mind. You have forced me to pursue a course I see no good reason for pursuing. Yet because there may be one tittle of reality in your guarded suspicions I must act as I do not wish to act. Have you ever placed yourself in a headmaster's shoes?'

'No, sir.'

'No, sir. I had sensed as much. They are shoes that pinch, boy. It is well to remember that.'

'Yes, sir.'

'Walk forward to my desk, boy, and press the bell you see there. We will order this affair one way or the other.'

Markham and Williams were summoned. When they entered, the headmaster turned from the window and faced us. He said to them:

'Your friendship is in dispute. Your accuser stands beside you. Do not lie, boys. I know a lie. I can feel a lie on its utterance. Have you reason for shame?'

Williams, whose eyes were fastened on the legs of the headmaster's desk, shook his head. Markham replied that he had no cause to be ashamed.

'On what then is your relationship based? Have you like interests? Of what do you speak together?'

'Of many things, sir,' Williams said. 'Politics and affairs of state. Of our ambitions, sir. And our academic progress as the term passes.'

'We talk of one subject only, sir,' Markham said. 'The death of my father and stepmother.'

'Yet you, boy,' the headmaster said to Williams, 'would claim a wider conversational field. The air is blackened with the lie. Which boy are we to believe?'

'Markham is ill, sir. He is not at all himself. I give him what help I can. He does not recall the full extent of our conversation.'

'We speak of one subject,' Markham repeated.

'Why, boy, do you speak of this subject to the exclusion of all others?'

'Because I killed my father, sir. And my stepmother too.'

'Markham is ill, sir. He . . .'

'Leave the room, you boys. Markham, you shall remain.'

Neither Williams nor I spoke as we walked away from the head-master's door. Then, as our ways were about to divide, I said:

'You know he didn't. You know it is not true.'

Williams did not look at me. He said: 'That's right. Why didn't you tell Bodger that?'

'You've made him believe he did it, Williams.'

'Markham's all talk. Markham's a madman, eh?'

'You're an evil bastard, Williams.'

'That's right. I'm an unhealthy personage.'

He went on his way and I stood where he had left me, looking back at the closed door of the headmaster's study. The little red light which indicated that for no reason whatsoever should the headmaster be disturbed gleamed above it. Within, I guessed that the curtains were by now closely drawn, since to do so was the headmaster's practice on all grave occasions.

Suddenly I had the absurd notion of returning to this darkened room and demanding to be heard, since now I was free to speak. I felt for the moment that I could put his case more clearly, more satisfactorily than Markham himself. I felt that I knew everything: the horror of the thought that had leapt in Markham's mind when first his father told him of the accident in Florence; the game he had made of it, and the later fears that Williams had insidiously played upon. But as I paused in doubt I heard the urgent chiming of a bell, and, like the object of some remote control, I answered the familiar summons.

That same evening Markham was driven away. He was seen briefly in the headmaster's hall, standing about in his overcoat, seeming much as usual.

'They've sent him up to Derbyshire,' said Mr Pinshow when later I attempted to elicit information. 'Poor lad; so healthy in the body, too.' He would say no more, but I knew what he was thinking; and often since I have thought of Markham, still healthy in his body, growing up and getting older in the place they had found for him in Derbyshire. I have thought of Williams too, similarly growing older though in other circumstances, marrying perhaps and begetting children, and becoming in the end the man he had said he would one day be.

TREACLE TART
Robert Graves

The news travelled from group to group along the platform of Victoria Station, impressing our parents and kid-sisters almost as much as ourselves. A lord was coming to our prep school. A real lord. A new boy, only eight years old. Youngest son of the Duke of Downshire. A new boy, yet a lord. Lord Julius Bloodstock. Same name! Crikey!

Excitement strong enough to check the rebellious tears of home-lovers, and make our last good-byes all but casual. None of us having had any contact with the peerage, it was argued by some, as we settled in our reserved Pullman carriage, that on the analogy of policemen there couldn't be boy-lords. However, Mr Lees, the Latin Master (declined: *Lees, Lees, Lem, Lei, Lei, Lee*) confirmed the report. The lord was being driven to school that morning in the ducal Rolls-Royce. Crikey, again! *Cricko, Crickere, Crickey, Crictum!*

Should we be expected to call him 'your Grace', or 'Sire', or something? Would he keep a coronet in his tuck-box? Would the masters dare cane him if he broke school rules or didn't know his prep?

Billington Secundus told us that his father (the famous Q.C.) had called Thos a 'tuft-hunting toad-eater', as meaning that he was awfully proud of knowing important people, such as bishops and Q.C.s and lords. To this Mr Lees turned a deaf ear, though making ready to crack down on any further disrespectful remarks about the Rev. Thomas Pearce, our Headmaster. None came. Most of us were scared stiff of Thos; besides, everyone but Billington Secundus considered pride in knowing important people an innocent enough emotion.

Presently Mr Lees folded his newspaper and said: 'Bloodstock, as you will learn to call him, is a perfectly normal little chap, though he happens to have been born into the purple – if anyone present catches the allusion. Accord him neither kisses nor cuffs (*nec oscula, nec verbera*, both neuter) and all will be well. By the way, this is to be his first experience of school life. The Duke has hitherto kept him at the Castle under private tutors.'

At the Castle, under private tutors! Crickey! *Crickey, Crikius, Crikissime!*

We arrived at the Cedars just in time for school dinner. Thos, rather self-consciously, led a small, pale, fair-haired boy into the dining-hall, and showed him his seat at the end of the table among the other nine newcomers. 'This is Lord Julius Bloodstock, boys,' he boomed. 'You will just call him Bloodstock. No titles or other honorifics here.'

'Then I prefer to be called Julius.' His first memorable words.

'We happen to use only surnames at Brown Friars,' chuckled Thos; then he said Grace.

None of Julius's table-mates called him anything at all, to begin with, being either too miserable or too shy even to say 'Pass the salt, please.' But after the soup, and half-way through the shepherd's pie (for once not made of left-overs) Billington Tertius, to win a bet, leant boldly across the table and asked: 'Lord, why didn't you come by train, same as the rest of us?'

Julius did not answer at first, but when his neighbours nudged him, he said: 'The name is Julius, and my father was afraid of finding newspaper photographers on the platform. They can be such a nuisance. Two of them were waiting for us at the school gates, and my father sent the chauffeur to smash both their cameras.'

This information had hardly sunk in before the third course appeared: treacle tart. Today was Monday: onion soup, shepherd's pie and carrots, treacle tart. Always had been. Even when Mr Lees-Lees-Lem had been a boy here and won top scholarship to Winchester. 'Treacle. From the Greek *theriace*, though the Greeks did not, of course . . .' With this,

Mr Lees, who sat at the very end of the table, religiously eating treacle tart, looked up to see whether anyone were listening; and noticed that Julius had pushed away his plate, leaving the oblong of tough burned pastry untouched.

'Eat it, boy!' said Mr Lees. 'Not allowed to leave anything here for Mr Good Manners. School rule.'

'I never eat treacle tart,' explained Julius with a little sigh.

'You are expected to address me as "sir",' said Mr Lees.

Julius seemed surprised. 'I thought we didn't use titles here, or other honorifics,' he said, 'but only surnames?'

'Call me "sir",' insisted Mr Lees, not quite certain whether this were innocence or impertinence.

'Sir,' said Julius, shrugging faintly.

'Eat your tart,' snapped Mr Lees.

'But I never eat treacle tart – sir!'

'It's my duty to see that you do so, every Monday.'

Julius smiled. 'What a queer duty!' he said incredulously.

Titters, cranings of necks. Then Thos called jovially down the table: 'Well, Lees, what's the news from your end? Are the summer holidays reported to have been wearisomely long?'

'No, Headmaster. But I cannot persuade an impertinent boy to sample our traditional treacle tart.'

'Send him up here,' said Thos in his most portentous voice. 'Send him up here, plate and all! Oliver Twist asking for less, eh?'

When Thos recognized Julius, his face changed and he swallowed a couple of times, but having apparently lectured the staff on making not the least difference between duke's son and shopkeeper's son, he had to put his foot down. 'My dear boy,' he said, 'let me see you eat that excellent piece of food without further demur; and no nonsense.'

'I never eat treacle tart, Headmaster.'

Thos started as though he had been struck in the face. He said slowly: 'You mean perhaps: "I have lost my appetite, sir." Very well, but your appetite will return at supper time, you mark my words – and so will the treacle tart.'

The sycophantic laughter which greeted this prime Thossism surprised Julius but did not shake his poise. Walking to the buttery-table, he laid down the plate, turned on his heel, and walked calmly back to his seat.

Thos led a small, pale, fair-haired boy into the dining hall.

'Cocky ass, I'd like to punch his lordly head for him,' growled Billington Secundus later that afternoon.

'You'd have to punch mine first,' I said. 'He's a . . . the thing we did in Gray's *Elegy* – a village Hampden. Standing up to Lees and Thos in mute inglorious protest against that foul treacle tart.'

'You're a tuft-hunting toad-eater.'

'I may be. But I'd rather eat toads than Thos's treacle tart.'

A bell rang for supper, or high tea. The rule was that tuck-box cakes were put under Matron's charge and distributed among all fifty of us while they lasted. 'Democracy', Thos called it (I can't think why); and the Matron, to cheer up the always dismal first evening, had set the largest cake she could find on the table: Julius's. Straight from the ducal kitchens, plastered with crystallized fruit, sugar icing and marzipan, stuffed with raisins, cherries and nuts.

'You will get your slice, my dear, when you have eaten your treacle tart,' Matron gently reminded Julius. '*Noblesse oblige.*'

'I never eat treacle tart, Matron.'

It must have been hard for him to see his cake devoured by strangers before his eyes, but he made no protest; just sipped a little tea and went supperless to bed. In the dormitory he told a ghost story, which is still, I hear, current in the school after all these years: about a Mr Gracie (why 'Gracie'?) who heard hollow groans in the night, rose to investigate and was grasped from behind by an invisible hand. He found that his braces had caught on the door knob; and, after other harrowing adventures, traced the groans to the bathroom, where Mrs Gracie . . .

Lights out! Sleep. Bells for getting up; for prayers; for breakfast.

'I never eat treacle tart.' So Julius had no breakfast, but we pocketed slices of bread and potted meat (Tuesday) to slip him in the playground afterwards. The school porter intervened. His orders were to see that the young gentleman had no food given him.

Bell: Latin. Bell: Maths. Bell: long break. Bell: Scripture. Bell: wash hands for dinner.

'I never eat treacle tart,' said Julius, as a sort of response to Thos's Grace; and this time fainted.

Thos sent a long urgent telegram to the Duke, explaining his predicament: school rule, discipline, couldn't make exceptions, and so forth.

The Duke wired back non-committally: 'Quite so. Stop. The lad never eats treacle tart. Stop. Regards. Downshire.'

Matron took Julius to the sickroom, where he was allowed milk and soup, but no solid food unless he chose to call for treacle tart. He remained firm and polite until the end, which came two days later, after a further exchange of telegrams.

We were playing kick-about near the Masters' Wing, when the Rolls-Royce pulled up. Presently Julius, in overcoat and bowler hat, descended the front steps, followed by the school porter carrying his tuck-box, football boots and hand-bag. Billington Secundus, now converted to the popular view, led our three cheers, which Julius acknowledged with a gracious tilt of his bowler. The car purred off; and thereupon, in token of our admiration of Julius, we all swore to strike against treacle tart the very next Monday, and none of us eat a single morsel, even if we liked it, which some of us did!

When it came to the point, of course, the boys sitting close to Thos took fright and ratted, one after the other. Even Billington Secundus and I, not being peers' sons or even village Hampdens, regretfully conformed.

FROM MY SCHOOLDAYS
Herman Hesse

Twice during my years at school I had a teacher whom I could honour and love, in whom I could freely recognize the highest authority and who could direct me by a wink. The first was called Schmid, a teacher at the Calw Latin School, a man much disliked by all the other pupils as being severe and bitter, evil-tempered and terrifying. He became important to me because in his class (we students were twelve years old) instruction in Greek began. In this little half-rural Latin school we had grown accustomed to teachers whom we either feared and hated, avoided and deceived, or laughed at and despised. They possessed power, that was unalterably true, an overwhelming power completely undeserved, often frightfully and inhumanly exercised – it frequently happened in those days that the paddling of hands or the pinching of ears was carried to the point of drawing blood – but this pedagogic power was simply a hostile force, dreaded, hated. That a teacher might possess power because he stood high above us, because he represented intellect and humanity, because he instilled into us inklings of a higher world, this was something we had not yet experienced with any of our teachers in the lower classes of the Latin school. We had encountered a few good-natured teachers who lightened the boredom of school for themselves and for us by indifference and by gazing out the window or reading novels while we busily copied one another's written exercises. We had also encountered evil, dark, raging, maniacal teachers and had our hair pulled by them and been hit over the head (one of them, a particularly ruthless tyrant, used to accompany his lectures to bad students by rhythmically thumping them on the head with his heavy latchkey). That there might also be teachers whom a student would follow gladly and with enthusiasm, for whom he would exert himself and even overlook injustice and bad temper, to whom he would be grateful for the revelation of a higher world and eager to render thanks – this possibility had remained hitherto beyond our ken.

And now I came to Professor Schmid in the fourth form. Of the approximately twenty-five students in this form, five had decided upon humanistic studies and were called 'humanists' or 'Grecians', and while the rest of the class were engaged in profane subjects such as drawing, natural history, and the like, we five were initiated into Greek by Professor Schmid. The professor was by no means beloved; he was a sickly, pale, careworn, morose-looking man, smooth-shaven, dark-haired, usually solemn and severe in mood, and if on occasion he was witty it was in a sarcastic tone. What really won me over against the unanimous judgement of the class I do not know. Perhaps it was a response to his unhappiness. He was frail and looked as if he were suffering, had a delicate, sickly wife who was almost never visible, and he lived like all our teachers in shabby poverty. Some circumstance, very likely his wife's health, prevented him from increasing his small income as the other teachers did, by taking in boarders, and this fact gave him a certain air of distinction in contrast to our other teachers. To this was now added Greek. We five chosen ones always seemed to ourselves like an intellectual aristocracy in the midst of our fellow students. Our goal was the higher studies, while the others were destined to be hand workers or tradesmen – and now we began to learn this mysterious, ancient language, much older, more mysterious, and more distinguished than Latin, this language that one did not learn for the purpose of earning money or to be able to travel about in the world but simply to become acquainted with Socrates, Plato, and Homer. Certain features of that world were already known to me, for Greek scholarship had been familiar to my parents and grandparents, and in Schwab's *Myths of the Classical World* I had long since made the acquaintance of Odysseus and Polyphemus, of Phaëthon, Icarus, the Argonauts, and Tantalus. And in the reader which we had recently been using in school there was amid a crowd of most prosaic pieces, lonesome as a bird of paradise, a marvellous poem by Hölderlin which, to be sure, I only half understood, but which sounded infinitely sweet and seductive and whose secret connection with the world of Greece I dimly perceived.

This Herr Schmid did nothing to make our school year easy. Indeed, he made it extra hard, often unnecessarily hard. He demanded a great deal, at least from us 'humanists', and was not only severe but often harsh and frequently ill-tempered as well; he would have attacks of sudden anger and was then feared, with reason, by all of us, including me, very likely as the young fish fry in a weir fear the pursuing pike. Now I had become acquainted with this under other teachers. With Schmid I experienced something new. I experienced, besides fear, respect, I discovered that you can love and honour a man even when he happens to be your enemy. Sometimes in his dark hours, when his haggard face beneath the black hair looked so tragic, oppressed, and malicious, I was forced to think of King Saul in his periods of gloom. But then he would recover, his face would grow smooth, he would draw Greek letters on the blackboard and say things about Greek grammar and language that I felt were more than pedagogic rigmarole. I fell deeply in love with Greek, although I was terrified of the Greek class, and I would draw in my schoolbook certain Greek letters such as upsilon, psi, omega, quite entranced and obsessed, as though they were magic signs.

During this first year of the humanities, I suddenly fell ill. It was a sickness that so far as I know is unknown and unregarded today, but that the doctors at that time called 'growing pains'. I was given cod-liver oil and salicylic acid, and for a while my knees were massaged with ichthyol. I enjoyed my sickness thoroughly, for despite my humanistic idealism I was far too accustomed to hate and fear school not to regard a halfway bearable illness as a gift of grace and a release. For a long time I lay in bed, and since the wall beside my bed was of wood painted white I began to work on this convenient surface with water colours, and at the level of my head I painted a picture that was supposed to represent the Seven Swabians and was heartily laughed at by my brothers and sisters. But when the second and third weeks had gone by and I was still sick abed, some concern was felt lest, if this were to last much longer, I might be left too far behind in Greek. One of my classmates was summoned to keep me in touch with what went on in class, and then it became apparent that Herr Schmid with his humanists had by that time got through a formidable number of chapters in the Greek grammar. These I must now make up, and under the eyes of the Seven Swabians I struggled through many lonesome hours against my own indolence and the problems of Greek conjugation. At times my father helped me, but when I was well again and allowed to be up and around I was still very far behind, and some private lessons from Professor Schmid were thought necessary. He was willing to give them, and so for a short period I went every other day to his dim and cheerless apartment where Schmid's pale, taciturn wife was fighting a mortal illness. I seldom got to see her, she died shortly thereafter. The hours in this oppressive apartment were as though bewitched; the moment I crossed the threshold I stepped into a different, unreal, terrifying world; I found the honoured wise man, the feared tyrant whom I had known in school, strangely and uncannily changed. Intuitively I began to understand his tormented expression, I suffered for him, suffered under him, for his mood was usually very bad. But twice he took me out for walks, strolled about with me in the open air unburdened by grammar or Greek, and on these short walks he was gracious and friendly to me; without sarcasm, without attacks of temper, he asked about my hobbies and about my dreams for the future, and from then on I loved him, although, as soon as I was back in his classroom once more, he seemed to have forgotten the walks completely. After his wife was buried I remember that he made his characteristic gesture of pushing his long hair back from his forehead more often and more abruptly. As a teacher he was very difficult at that time, and I believe I was the only one of his pupils who loved him, despite his harshness and his unpredictability.

Not long after I finished Schmid's class I left my home town and its school for the first time. This happened for disciplinary reasons, for at that time I had become a very difficult and wayward son and my parents did not know what to do with me. In addition to that, however, I had to be as well prepared as possible for the 'district examination'. This

I waited, holding my mother's hand, outside the famous rector's study.

official examination, which was held every summer for the whole province of Württemberg, was very important, for whoever passed it was granted room and board in a theological 'seminary' and could study there on a scholarship. This course had been decided upon for me. Now there were certain schools in the district in which preparation for this examination was a speciality, and so to one of these schools I was sent. It was the Latin school in Göppingen, where for years the old rector, Bauer, had been cramming students for the provincial exam; he was famous for it in the whole district, and year after year a throng of ambitious students flocked around him, sent there from all parts of the province.

In earlier years Rector Bauer had had the reputation of being a harsh pedagogue, fond of caning; an older relation of mine who years before had been his pupil had been severely beaten by him. Now an old man, Bauer was regarded as a marvellous eccentric and also as a teacher who demanded a great deal from his students but could be nice to them. Nevertheless, it was with no little dread that I, after the first painful farewell to my family's house, waited, holding my mother's hand, outside the famous rector's study. I believe my mother was not at first enchanted by him as he came towards us and invited us into his den, a bent, aged man with tangled grey hair, somewhat protuberant eyes marked with red veins, dressed in an indescribably old-fashioned garment stained with greenish discolourations, wearing spectacles low on his nose and holding in his right hand a long pipe with a porcelain bowl reaching almost to the floor, from which he continuously blew mighty clouds of smoke into the already smoke-filled room. Even in class he would not be parted from his pipe. This strange old man with his bent, careless posture, his untidy old clothes, his sad, moody expression, his shapeless slippers, his long fuming pipe, seemed to me like an aged magician into whose custody I was now to be given. It would perhaps be terrifying with this dusty, grey, other-worldly ancient; also conceivably it could be pleasant and enchanting – in any case, it would be something strange, an adventure, an experience. I was ready and willing to meet him halfway.

But first I had to endure the moment at the station when my mother kissed me and gave me her blessing and got into the train and the train moved off, and for the first time I stood outside and alone in 'the world',

in which I must now find my way and defend myself – I have not yet
been able to do so even up to the present moment when my hair is
beginning to grow grey. Before the parting, my mother had prayed
with me, and although at that time my piety was no longer anything to
boast about, nevertheless during her prayer and her blessing I had
solemnly resolved in my heart to behave myself here, away from home,
and not to disgrace my mother. In the long run I did not succeed! My
later school years brought her and me severe storms, trials, and dis-
illusionments, much sorrow, many tears, much strife and misunder-
standing. But at that time in Göppingen I remained completely true to
my resolve and behaved well. This, to be sure, was not discernible to
the model students or, for that matter, to the house mother with whom
I and four other boys lived, and ate, and by whom we were cared for,
but whom I could not respect and obey in the manner she expected
from her charges. No, I never stood very high in her regard, and
although there were many days when I could turn charmer and divert
her to smiles and good will, she was a judge in whom I acknowledged
neither power nor importance, and when on a bitter day after some
small boyish misdeed she once summoned her big, powerfully muscled
brother to inflict corporal punishment on me, I rebelled most stubbornly and would sooner have thrown myself out the window or sunk
my teeth into the man's throat than allow myself to be punished by
someone who in my opinion did not have the right to do it. He did not
dare touch me and had to withdraw without accomplishing his purpose.

I did not like Göppingen. The 'world' into which I had been thrust
did not appeal to me, it was barren and bleak, coarse and impoverished.
At that time Göppingen had not yet become the manufacturing city it
is today, but there were already six or seven tall factory chimneys there,
and the little river, in comparison with the one at home, was a prolet-
arian, creeping shabbily between piles of rubbish, and the fact that the
outer surroundings of the city were very beautiful was hardly known to
us since we had only brief periods when we could be away, and I got
onto the Hohenstaufen only a single time. Oh no, this Göppingen
displeased me completely, this prosaic manufacturing city could not
really compare with my home town, and if I told my schoolmates, all
of whom like me were languishing in a strange land and in durance vile,
about Calw and the life there, then I laid the colours on thick and

created romances out of yearning and love of boasting for which no one could call me to account, since I was the only one from Calw in our school. Almost all sections of the province and all the provincial cities were represented in the school, barely six or seven in the class being from Göppingen, all others having come from afar to make use of the approved springboard for the provincial examination.

And the springboard continued to be effective with our class as it had been with so many others. At the end of our Göppingen stay an impressive number of students had passed the examination, and I was among them. Göppingen was not to blame if nothing good ever came of me.

Now, although the dull, industrial city, the imprisonment under the supervision of a strict house mother, and the whole exterior side of my life in Göppingen were highly unpleasant for me, this period (it was almost a year and a half) was nevertheless extraordinarily fruitful and important in my life. That relationship between teacher and pupil of which I had had an inkling in Calw with Professor Schmid, that infinitely rewarding and yet so subtle relationship between an intellectual leader and a gifted child, came to full bloom in the case of Rector Bauer and me. That strange, almost frightening-looking old man with his countless eccentricities and whimsies, who stared out, watchful and moody, from behind his small, greenish eyeglasses, who constantly filled the crowded schoolroom with smoke from his long pipe, became for a time in my eyes leader, exemplar, judge, demigod. We had two other teachers too, but as far as I was concerned, they did not exist; they receded like shadows behind the beloved, feared, honoured figure of the old man, as though they had one less dimension. And just so the unappealing life in Göppingen disappeared for me, and even my friendships with fellow students, they too dwindled to nothing beside this looming figure. At that time when my boyhood was in full flower and when even the first intimations and premonitions of sexual love began to stir, school, a generally so despised institution, was for more than a year the central point of my life around which everything else revolved, even my dreams, even my thoughts during vacation time. I, who had always been a sensitive and critical pupil used to defending myself tooth and nail against every form of dependence and subjugation, had been completely caught and enchanted by this mysterious old man, simply because he called upon my highest efforts and ideals, seemed not to see at all my immaturity, my awkwardness, my inferiority, assumed the best in me and regarded the highest accomplishment as natural. He did not need many words to express his praise. If he commented on a Latin or Greek exercise: 'You have done that quite nicely, Hesse', then for days I was happy and fired with enthusiasm. And if just in passing he happened to whisper without looking at me: 'I'm not entirely satisfied with you, you can do better', then I suffered and went to mad lengths to propitiate the demigod. He often talked to me in Latin, translating my name as Chattus.

Now there was no way for me to tell how far this experience of a completely special relationship was shared by my fellow students. Certain favoured ones, to be sure, my closest friends and rivals, were obviously, just like me, under the spell of the old catcher of souls and, just as I had been handed the boon of vocation, felt themselves initiates on the bottom step of the sanctuary. If I attempt to understand my youthful psyche, I find that the best and most productive part of it, despite many rebellions and many negations, was the ability to feel reverence, and that my soul prospered most and blossomed most beautifully when it could revere, adore, strive for that highest goal. This happiness, the beginnings of which my father had earlier recognized and cultivated in me, and which under a series of mediocre, lacklustre teachers had almost withered away, which had burgeoned a bit once more under the dyspeptic Professor Schmid, came into full flower, for the first and last time in my life, under Rector Bauer.

Had our rector been able to do nothing except cause some of his better students to fall in love with Latin and Greek and inspire in them a belief in an intellectual vocation and its responsibilities, even that would have been a great and praiseworthy accomplishment. However, the unique, the extraordinary thing about our teacher was his ability not only to nose out the more intelligent of his pupils and to supply their idealism with nourishment and support but to give proper due to the age of his pupils, to their boyishness and passion for play. For Bauer, an honoured Socrates, was also a clever, a highly original schoolmaster who again and again found ways to make school attractive to thirteen-year-old youngsters. This sage, able with such wit to teach us Latin syntax and the rules of Greek accent, had constant pedagogic inspirations too, and they delighted us boys. One must have some inkling of the severity, stiffness, and boredom of a Latin school at that time to be able to imagine how fresh, original, and inspired this man seemed in the midst of the usual crowd of dry bureaucrats. Even his exterior, the fantastic appearance which at first made you want to laugh, soon became the instrument of his authority and discipline. Out of his oddities and hobbies, which seemed by no means suited to support his authority, he made new aids for education. For example, his long pipe, which had so horrified my mother, in the shortest time was no longer for us pupils a laughable or annoying appanage but rather a kind of sceptre and symbol of might. Whoever was allowed to hold his pipe for a moment, whoever he entrusted with the office of knocking it out and keeping it in working order, he was the envied favourite. There were other honorary posts for which we pupils competed eagerly. There was the office of 'windbag', which for a time I proudly filled. The windbag had to dust off the teacher's desk every day and he had to do this with two rabbit's feet which lay on top of the desk. When this job was taken away from me one day and given to another student, I felt severely punished.

On a winter day, if we were sitting in the overheated, smoke-filled schoolroom and the sun was shining on the frost-covered windows, our rector might suddenly say: 'Boys, it stinks hideously in here and outside the sun is shining. Have a race around the house. And before you do, open up the windows!' Or, at those times when we candidates for the provincial examination were much overloaded with extra work, he would invite us unexpectedly to come up to his apartment, and there we would find in a strange room a huge table and on it a quantity of cardboard boxes filled with toy soldiers which we would then arrange in armies and battle array, and when the conflict was joined, the rector would solemnly puff clouds of smoke from his pipe between the battalions.

Beautiful things are transitory and fine times never last long. If I think of those Göppingen days, of the single short period in my school years when I was a good scholar, when I honoured and loved my teacher and was heart and soul absorbed in study, then I always have to think too of the summer vacation in the year 1890, which I spent at my parents' home in Calw. For that vacation we were not assigned any school work. However, Rector Bauer had called our attention to the

'rules of life' of Isocrates, which were included in our Greek chresto-
mathy, and he told us that formerly some of his best students had
learned these rules of life by heart. It was left to each one of us to take
this hint or not.

Of that summer vacation, a few walks with my father linger in my
memory. Sometimes we spent an afternoon in the woods above Calw;
under the old white pines there were barberries and raspberries
aplenty, and in the clearings loosestrife bloomed, and summer butterflies, the red admiral and the tortoiseshell, fluttered about. There was a
strong smell of pine resin and mushrooms, and occasionally we came
face to face with deer. My father and I would wander through the
forest or race here and there in the heather at the forest's edge. And once
in a while he would ask me how far I had got with Isocrates. For I sat
for a while every day with the book, memorizing those 'rules of life'.
And even today the first sentence of Isocrates is the single bit of Greek
prose I know by heart. That sentence from Isocrates and a few verses of
Homer are the sole remnant of my whole Greek education. Also, I
never attained a mastery of all the 'rules of life'. Several dozen sentences
which I did learn by heart, and for a time carried around with me and
could produce at will, have crumbled away and been lost in the course
of the years, like everything a man possesses and believes is really his
own.

Today I no longer know any Greek, and most of my Latin has long
since disappeared – I would have forgotten it completely were it not for
one of my Göppingen classmates who is still alive and still my friend.
From time to time he writes me a letter in Latin and when I read it,
working my way through the beautifully constructed classic sentences,
then there is a faint smell of the garden of my youth and the pipe smoke
of old Rector Bauer.

LAST YEAR AT SCHOOL
Simone de Beauvoir

I was working even harder than ever. The imminence of the examinations and the hope that I would soon be at the university spurred me on. It was a great year for me. My face got into better shape, and I was no longer incommoded by my growing body; my secrets did not weigh so heavily. My friendship with Zaza ceased to be the torment it had been. I had regained confidence in myself; and Zaza was changing too: I didn't wonder why, but, by a stroke of irony, she became all dreamy and romantic. She began to like Musset, Lacordaire, and Chopin. She still inveighed against the pharisaism of her surroundings, but no longer extended her criticisms to the whole of humanity. From now on she spared me her sarcasms.

There was a very select little group of us at the Cours Désir. The school only prepared for the Latin–modern languages examinations. Monsieur Mabille wanted his daughter to have a good grounding in science; I myself liked things I could get my teeth into, like mathematics. An extra teacher was appointed who taught algebra, trigonometry, and physics. Mademoiselle Chassin was young, lively, and very competent; she didn't need to waste time on moral exhortations: we did serious work. She was very fond of us. Whenever Zaza stayed up in the clouds too long, Mademoiselle would say sweetly: 'Where are you, Elizabeth?' Zaza would start and smile. We had for classmates twins who were always in mourning and almost never said a word. I was enchanted by the intimate atmosphere of our classes. In Latin we had been allowed to skip a year and go on to a higher grade; the struggle to keep up with the pupils in the top class kept me on my toes. When I found myself back with my normal classmates in the year when I was to take my school-leaving certificate there was no longer the spice of novelty and Abbé Trécourt's knowledge seemed a little thin; he frequently made mistakes in translation; but this big fellow with the blotchy complexion was more forthcoming and more jovial than our old school-marms and we had a genuine affection for him which he obviously reciprocated. Our parents thought it would be fun if we also offered Latin–modern languages in our examination, and in January we began to learn Italian; we were soon able to translate *Cuore* and *le mie prigioni*. Zaza took German; but as my English teacher showed herself to be well-disposed towards me I followed her lessons with pleasure. On the other hand, we had to put up with the patriotic tub-thumping of Mademoiselle Gontran, our history teacher; and Mademoiselle Lejeune exasperated us by the narrowness and pettiness of her literary tastes. In order to broaden our horizons we read a great deal and had long discussions among ourselves. Often we would stubbornly defend our points of view in class; I don't know if Mademoiselle Lejeune was perspicacious enough to see through me but she now seemed to distrust me far more than Zaza.

We struck up friendships; we would meet to play cards and chatter; in summer we would go on Saturdays to an open-air tennis court in the rue Boulard. None of our other friends meant much to Zaza or myself. If the truth were told, the older pupils at the Cours Désir were not attractive. When, after eleven years' hard work, I won a silver-gilt medal, my father agreed without much enthusiasm to attend the prize-giving; he complained afterwards that he had never seen such a collection of ugly girls. A few of my schoolmates had quite pleasant features; but when we made public appearances we were done up like dogs' dinners: the severe hair-styles and the violent or sickly-sweet colours of our satin or taffeta dresses drained all the life from our faces. The thing that must have struck my father most forcibly was the depressed, mournful look those adolescents had. I was so accustomed

He complained that he had never seen such a collection of ugly girls.

to it that when a new girl arrived one day and I saw her laughing – it was a real, hearty laugh – I opened my eyes wide in astonishment; she was an international golf champion and she had travelled widely; her bobbed hair, her well-cut jumper and box-pleated skirt, her sporty manner, and her uninhibited voice were obvious signs that she had not been brought up under the influence of Saint Thomas Aquinas; she spoke perfect English and knew enough Latin to be able to present the subject for her school-leaving certificate at the age of fifteen and a half; Corneille and Racine bored her to tears. 'Literature makes me sick,' she told me. 'Oh, don't say that!' I protested. 'Why not?' she retorted. 'It's the truth.' Her gay personality enlivened the funereal 'lecture-study room'. Some things she found tedious, but there were other things in her life which gave her pleasure, and one felt that she had a future ahead of her. The air of sadness that emanated from my other school-mates was due less to their appearance than to their hopeless resignation. Once they had passed their school-leaving certificate they would follow a few lecture-courses on history and literature, they would attend classes at the École du Louvre or the Red Cross where they would learn how to decorate china, make batik prints and fancy bindings, and occupy themselves with good works. From time to time they would be taken out to a performance of *Carmen* or for a walk round the tomb of Napoleon in order to make the acquaintance of some suitable young man; with a little luck, they would marry him. This was the elder Mabille girl's life; she did cooking and went to dances, acted as secretary to her father, and helped her sisters to make their clothes. Her mother dragged her from one meeting with a young man to another. Zaza told me that one of her aunts had a theory about 'the sacrament of love at first sight': at that very moment when the fiancés said 'yes' before the priest, they were filled with grace, and at once fell in love with one another. These tribal rites disgusted Zaza; she declared one day that she couldn't see any difference between a woman who married 'for convenience' and a prostitute; she had been taught that a Christian woman should respect her body: she would not be respecting it if she gave it to a man without love, for financial or family reasons. Her vehemence astounded me; it was as if she felt her own body was defiled by the ignominy of this bartering of human souls. The question did not arise for me. I would earn my own living, I would be free. But in Zaza's family you either had to get married or become a nun. 'Celibacy,' they used to repeat, 'is not a vocation.' She began to dread the future; was that the cause of her insomnia? She slept badly; often she would get up in the middle of the night and rub herself from top to toe, with eau de Cologne; in the morning, to get herself going, she would swallow quantities of black coffee and white wine. When she told me about these excesses, I realized that there were many things I did not know about her. But I encouraged her in her resistance to the family code and she was grateful to me for it: I was her only ally. We both agreed that many things were disgusting, and we both had a great longing for freedom and happiness.

Despite our differences, we often reacted to circumstances in the same manner. My father had received from his actor friend two free seats for a matinée at the Odéon; he made us a present of them; they were doing a play by Paul Fort, *Charles VI*. When I found myself alone with Zaza in a box, I was overjoyed. The three knocks sounded, the curtain rose, and we were watching a heavy melodrama; Charles went out of his mind; at the end of the first act, haggard-eyed, he was staggering round the stage in a long, incoherent monologue; I sank deeper and deeper into a gloomy despair that was as appallingly lonely as his own madness. I took a look at Zaza; she was white-faced. 'If it goes on like this let's leave,' I suggested. She agreed. When the curtain went up on the second act, Charles, in shirt-sleeves, was struggling to get out of the clutches of masked and hooded men. We left the box. The attendant stopped us: 'Why are you leaving?' 'It's too horrible,' I said. She burst out laughing. 'But it isn't *real*, my pets. It's just play-acting.' We knew that: all the same, we had seen something frightful.

My understanding with Zaza and her good opinion helped me to free myself from the grown-ups and to see myself with my own eyes. But one incident reminded me how much I still depended on their judgement. It exploded unexpectedly just as I was beginning to enjoy a care-free existence.

Just as I did every week, I made a careful word-for-word translation of my Latin text; I wrote it in a column opposite the original. Then I had to put it into 'good French'. As it happened, this particular piece of prose had been translated in my text book on Latin literature, and with an elegance which I felt could not be equalled: in comparison, all the expressions which came to my mind seemed to be painfully clumsy. I had not made any mistake in the meaning; I was certain to get a good mark, and I had no ulterior motives; but the requirements of the object, the phrase itself, had to be satisfied: each sentence had to be perfect. It was repugnant to me to substitute my heavy-handed inventions for the ideal model furnished by the text book. There and then I copied it straight out of the book.

We were never left alone with the Abbé Trécourt; one of our old school-marms would sit at a little table near the window and supervise us; before he handed us back our translations, she entered our marks in a register. On that day the task had fallen to Mademoiselle Dubois, the one with the degree, whose Latin classes I would have normally attended the year before had not Zaza and I turned our noses up at them in favour of the Abbé's: she did not like me. I could hear her making a fuss behind my back; she was whispering furious protests. In the end she drafted a note which she place on top of the pile of exercise books before giving them back to the Abbé. He wiped his eyeglasses, read the message, and smiled: 'Yes,' he said mildly, 'this passage from Cicero was already translated in your text books and many of you apparently noticed it. I have given the highest marks to those of you whose work showed the most originality.' Despite his indulgent tones, Mademoiselle Dubois' furious face, and the uneasy silence of my classmates filled me with terror. Whether through force of habit, absent-mindedness, or simple affection, the Abbé had given me the best mark. I had got 17. In any case, no one had got less than 12. Doubtless in order to justify his partiality he asked me to construe the text word by word: I kept my voice steady and did so without a mistake. He congratulated me and the tension eased a little. Mademoiselle Dubois didn't dare ask me to read out my final version; Zaza, sitting next to me, didn't so much as glance at it: she was scrupulously honest and I think refused to entertain any suspicions about me. But when the lesson was over certain of my other classmates started whispering together and Mademoiselle Dubois took me to one side: she felt she would have to inform Mademoiselle Lejeune of my perfidy. And so the thing I had often dreaded was finally going to happen: an action performed innocently and in secret would, by being brought to light, disgrace me. I still felt some respect for Mademoiselle Lejeune: the idea that she would despise me was torture. It was impossible to turn back the clock, to undo what I had done: I was marked for life! I had had a presentiment of danger: the truth can be unjust, unfair; all that evening and part of the night I tried to fight a way out of the trap into which I had so thoughtlessly fallen and which would not let me go. Usually I got round difficulties by running away from them, or keeping silent, or forgetting them; I rarely took any initiative; but this time I decided to fight it out. Lies would be needed to cover up the circumstances which conspired against me; so lie I must. I went to see Mademoiselle Lejeune in her study and I swore to her, with tears in my eyes, that I hadn't copied my Latin translation: only some involuntary recollections of the text book version had slipped into mine. Convinced that I had done nothing wrong, I defended myself with all the fervour of an injured innocent. But my tactics were absurd: I was guiltless, I should have taken my work with me as the chief evidence in me defence; but I merely gave my word. The principal did not believe me, told me so, and added impatiently that the subject was now closed. She did not tell me off, and she did not reproach me for what I had done: this indifference, and the crisp tone of her voice made me realize that she hadn't an ounce of affection for me. I had been afraid that my mistake would ruin the good opinion she had of me: but for a long time now I had had nothing more to lose. I recovered my equanimity. She had so categorically withheld her respect that I no longer wished for it.

During the weeks preceding the examination, my happiness was unalloyed. The weather was fine and my mother allowed me to go and study in the Luxembourg Gardens. I would sit in the 'English gardens', at the edge of a lawn, or near the Medici fountain. I was still wearing my hair down my back, caught together with a slide, but my cousin Annie, who often made me a present of her cast-off clothes, had given me that summer a white pleated skirt with a blue cretonne bodice; in my sailor-hat I fancied myself to be a real young lady. I was reading Faguet, Brunetière, and Jules Lemaître; I would sniff the fragrance of the lawns and feel I was as emancipated as the university students who strolled through the gardens. I would pass through the gates and go and rummage round the arcades of the Odéon; I felt the same thrill of delight there as I had felt at the age of ten in my mother's circulating library, the Bibliothèque Cardinale. Here there were displayed rows of leather-bound books, gilt-edged; their pages had been cut, and I would stand there reading for two or three hours without ever being asked to buy anything. I read Anatole France, the Goncourts, Colette, and whatever I could lay my hands on. I told myself that as long as there were books I could be sure of being happy.

I had also been given permission to sit up late: when Papa had left for the Café Versailles where he played bridge nearly every evening, and when Mama and my sister had gone to bed I would be left alone in the study. I would lean out of the window; the wind would bring me gusts of fragrance from the leafy trees; across the way, windows would be lighted. I would get Papa's opera glasses, take them out of their case and spy on the lives of strangers, just as I had used to do; I didn't care how trivial were the things I saw; I was – I still am – very conscious of the fascination of these little peep-shows, these lighted rooms hanging in the night. My gaze would wander from house to house, and I would tell myself, deeply affected by the balmy airs of the summer evening: 'Soon I'll be living my own life . . . *really* living.'

I enjoyed my examinations. In the amphitheatres of the Sorbonne I rubbed shoulders with boys and girls who had been educated in schools and colleges and *lycées* which I had never even heard of: I was struggling free from the Cours Désir and facing up to the realities of life. Having been assured by my teachers that I had done well in the written examination, I approached the oral with complete self-confidence and took a great fancy to myself in my unfashionably long dress of sky-blue voile. In front of those important gentlemen who had gathered on purpose to evaluate my merits, I regained the self-conceit of childhood. The examiner in literature particularly flattered me by talking in quite a conversational manner; he asked me if I were a relative of Roger de Beauvoir; I told him that it was only a pseudonym; he questioned me about Ronsard; as I sat there displaying my learning I was admiring all the time the fine, thoughtful head which he inclined in my direction: at last, I was face to face with one of those superior men whose approbation I so earnestly desired! But in the Latin–modern languages oral the examiner gave me an ironic greeting: 'Well, mademoiselle! Have you come to pick up a few more diplomas?' I was rather disconcerted, and I suddenly realized that my performances might have appeared somewhat comical; but I held my own. I was given a pass with 'distinction', and my old school-marms, delighted to have this success to their credit, made much of me. My parents were over the moon. Jacques, peremptory as ever, had declared: 'You must pass with distinction, or else not at all.' He gave me his warmest congratulations. Zaza passed also, but at that period I was too much occupied with myself to bother much about her.

My school life was coming to an end, and something else was going to begin: what would it be? In *Les Annales* I read a lecture which set me day-dreaming; a former student at the teachers' training college for women at Sèvres was recalling her experiences there: she described the gardens in which beautiful young women, athirst for knowledge, went walking by moonlight, the sound of their voices mingling with the murmur of fountains. But my mother didn't like the idea of the École Normale Supérieure at Sèvres. And when I came to think about it, I hardly wanted to shut myself up with a lot of women away from Paris. So what should I do? I dreaded the arbitrary side of any choice. My father, who at the age of fifty had the painful prospect of an uncertain future ahead of him, wanted me to have some sort of security above everything else; he thought I should go into the Civil Service, which would provide me with a fixed salary and a pension on retirement. Someone recommended the School of Palaeography and Librarianship – l'École des Chartes. I went with my mother to an interview with a lady behind the scenes at the Sorbonne. We went along seemingly endless corridors lined with books; here and there were doors leading to offices full of filing cabinets. As a child I had always dreamed of working in this dusty ante-room of learning, and today I felt as if I were penetrating into the Holy of Holies. The lady we went to see described to us the attractions and also the difficulties of librarianship; I was put off by the thought of having to learn Sanskrit; I wasn't interested in dry-as-dust erudition. What I should have liked was to continue my study of philosophy. I had read in an illustrated magazine an article about a woman philosopher who was called Mademoiselle Zanta: she had taken her doctorate; she had been photographed, in a grave and thoughtful posture, sitting at her desk; she lived with a young niece whom she had adopted: she had thus succeeded in reconciling her intellectual life with the demands of feminine sensibility. How I should love to have such flattering things written one day about *me*! In those days the women who had a degree or a doctorate in philosophy could be counted on the fingers of one hand: I wanted to be one of those pioneers. From a practical point of view, the only career that would be open to me if I had a degree in philosophy was teaching: I had nothing against that. My father did not object to this plan; but he wouldn't hear of my giving private tuition in pupils' homes: I would have to get a post in a *lycée*. Why not? This solution was very much to my taste, and also set his mind at rest. My mother went in fear and trembling to tell my teachers of my decision; their faces went rigid with disapproval. They had given their lives to combating secular institutions and to them a state school was nothing better than a licensed brothel. In addition, they told my mother that the study of philosophy mortally corrupts the soul: after one year at the Sorbonne, I would lose both my faith and my good character. Mama felt worried. As a degree in classics held out greater possibilities – or so my father thought – and as there was a possibility that Zaza might be allowed to follow a few of the courses, I agreed to sacrifice philosophy for literature. But I was still determined to teach in a *lycée*. How scandalous! Eleven years of sermons, careful grooming, and systematic indoctrination, and now I was biting the hand that had fed me! It was with complete unconcern that I read in my teachers' eyes their opinion of my ingratitude, my unworthiness, my treachery: I had fallen into the hands of Satan.

In July, I passed in elementary mathematics and philosophy. The Abbé's teaching had been so feeble that my dissertation, which he would have marked at 16, only scraped through with 11. I made up for this in my science papers. On the eve of the oral, my father took me to the Théâtre de Dix-Heures, where I saw Dorin, Colline, and Noël-Noël; I enjoyed myself immensely. How glad I was that I had finished with the Cours Désir! Yet a few days later, finding myself alone in the apartment, I was overcome by a strange uneasiness; I stood planted in the middle of the hall, feeling as utterly lost as if I had been transported to another planet! No family, no friends, no ties, no hope. My heart had died and the world was empty: could such an emptiness ever be filled? I was afraid. And then time started to flow again.

SNOWDROPS
Leslie Norris

Today Miss Webster was going to show them the snowdrops growing in the little three-cornered garden outside the school-keeper's house, where they weren't allowed to go. All through the winter, Miss Webster said, the snowdrops had been asleep under the ground, but now they were up, growing in the garden. He tried to think what they would look like, but all he could imagine was one flake of the falling snow, bitterly frail and white, and nothing like a flower.

It was a very cold morning. He leaned against the kitchen table, feeling the hard edge against his chest, eating his breakfast slowly. His brother, Geraint, who was only three, sat in an armchair close to the fire. He could see the shape of Geraint's head outlined against the flames and he saw with wonder that the fire had given to his brother's legs a glow of red only slightly less bright than the leaping flames. Geraint was eating a bowl of porridge, and what he did was this. He would make a crater in the porridge with his spoon, and then he'd watch the milk run in and fill the hole up. Then he would dip his spoon in the milk and drink it. The boy watched his brother.

'Hurry up,' said the boy's mother, 'or you'll never get to school on time!'

'Miss Webster is going to show us the snowdrops today,' he said.

'That's nice,' said his mother, looking out of the window at the grey morning. 'I wonder where your father is.'

His father came in and filled the room with bigness. He stood in front of the fire, because it was cold in the yard, and all the boy could see was a faint light each side of his father's wide body.

'It's a cold wind,' said his father. 'I can't remember a colder March.' The man turned around and faced them, smiling because he was much warmer and the cold March wind was safely locked outside.

'You're a big boy for six,' he said to the boy, 'and it's all because you eat your breakfast up.'

This was a joke his father always said, and the boy smiled, thinking all the time of the snowdrops. Would it be too cold to go and see them? Perhaps Miss Webster would take only the boys, he comforted himself, because they were stronger, and the girls could stay in school out of the cold.

'The Meredith boy is being buried this afternoon,' his father was saying to his mother. 'I'm sorry I shan't be able to go. I worked with his father for two and a half years, up at the rolling mill. A nice man, Charlie Meredith, very quiet. I hear he's very cut up, and his wife too. This was their only boy.'

'How old was he?' asked his mother.

'Twenty,' his father said. 'Twenty last January. Silly little fool. That bike was too powerful for him – well, to go at that speed on a wet, dark night. Over seventy, the police said, straight into the back of a stationary truck. A terrible mess.'

'He was a nice-looking boy, too,' said his mother.

'All the Merediths are,' said his father. 'This one was very friendly with the young teacher up at the school, Webber, is it? Something like that.'

But his mother coughed and looked sharply at the boy.

'Oh?' said his father. 'Of course. I should have remembered. Come on, son, or you'll be late.'

It seemed much warmer when he got to school and he took off his overcoat next to Edmund Jenkins. Edmund had a long blue scarf which his big sister had knitted for him. They each held an end of the scarf and raced up the corridor, seeing how many children they could catch, but Miss Lewis stopped them. Then Edmund told him a joke.

'What's the biggest rope in the world?' Edmund asked.

The boy didn't know.

'Europe,' said Edmund, and they both laughed.

They were still laughing as they went into the classroom, although Miss Webster wasn't there. After a time Miss Lewis came in and sent the children into other classrooms. Miss Lewis took the top class and she was very stern and strict. He and Edmund had to go to Miss Lewis's class.

'Europe,' said Edmund Jenkins to him, very quietly, as they went into the top class. Edmund was very brave.

It wasn't too bad in Miss Lewis's class, because they had some interesting books there and the arithmetic was not difficult. When you looked out of the window, too, you saw a different part of the playground. The boy could almost see a corner of the school-keeper's house, so he wasn't very far away from the snowdrops.

Just before playtime Miss Lewis told all the children from Miss Webster's class that they could go back to their own room after play. The boy grinned in delight. Everything would be all right, he told himself. After play they would surely go to see the flowers.

Out in the playground they all began to run about, except Gerald Davis, who seemed to fall over whatever he did. He was quite unable to make even the tiniest step without tumbling down, and his face was red from laughing and because he didn't know what was happening to him. Edmund Jenkins was standing close by and the boy could see that Edmund had been up to his tricks again.

'What's happening to Gerald?' he asked.

But Edmund only pointed to Gerald's boots, and then the boy saw that his laces had been tied together, the left boot to the right boot and the right boot to the left boot, so that Gerald was hobbled. Some boys were beginning to imitate Gerald, falling about although their boots weren't tied together. After a while he and Edmund untied the laces and Gerald went whooping up the gravel yard like a released pigeon.

He walked with Edmund towards the last corner of the playground, away from the wind, and they took their small packets of sandwiches from their pockets. Edmund had three sandwiches, with marmalade in them, and he had two sandwiches, but he didn't know what they were filled with. He bit one of them to find out.

The taste was incredibly new and marvellous, filling the whole of his mouth with delight and pleasure. He shook his head to show Edmund how wonderful the taste was, and then let Edmund have a bite.

'What's in it, Edmund?' he asked. 'What's in my sandwich?'

'Bacon,' said Edmund. 'It's only bacon.'

The boy was incredulous. He opened the second sandwich to inspect the filling. It didn't look like bacon.

'It can't be,' he said. 'I have bacon for my breakfast every morning. I had some *this* morning.'

'I know,' said Edmund, 'but it tastes different when it's cold.'

Together they walked as far as the shed in which the coal was stored. This was as far as they were allowed to go. Not very far away, but tantalizingly around the corner and down the little path that led to the garden, the snowdrops were growing.

'Do you wish,' said the boy, 'that Miss Webster will take us to see the flowers when play is over?'

'I don't care,' said Edmund, 'because I've seen some already, growing in my aunt's garden.'

The boy looked at his best friend, deciding carefully whether he would ask him to describe a snowdrop. But he would wait, he thought, to see them for himself, and then the bell was ringing to call them in.

The children cheered and clapped when they saw Miss Webster. She was dressed in a black frock, without any jewellery, but she smiled at them, holding her finger to her lips for them to be quiet. The bandage she had on one finger, where she had trapped it in the cupboard door and hadn't cried, looked very white and clean. She gave them some crayons and a big sheet of paper for each child and they could draw whatever they liked.

The boy drew a robin. He hadn't drawn a robin since Christmas, but just recently he had been watching one that came to his garden every day, and now he knew just how the bird's head fitted onto his round little body, and he had seen the way the legs, as thin as pieces of wire, splayed out underneath. Sometimes the robin looked like a hunchback, but he would draw this robin standing up bravely, throwing out his red chest before he sang. And the robin's song was odd. It wasn't very long, and it dropped and fell like threads of falling water. The boy closed his eyes a little while so that he could hear the robin, but he couldn't get

The children cheered and clapped when they saw Miss Webster.

it quite right. Soon he was engrossed in watching his robin grow on the paper. With infinite care he set its delicate feet on a brown twig, not just a flat stick as he had drawn at Christmas, but a real twig, with little knobs on it where the buds would be. At last it was finished and he leaned back in his chair, looking around as he did so. Nearly all the other children had completed their drawings some time before and they were reading their books. Miss Webster was sitting at her desk, her head in her hands. Everything was very still. The boy took out his book and began to read, but most of the time he looked at the robin he had drawn.

This is what he was doing when the bell ended morning school and they were dismissed for home. Miss Webster looked at his robin and she liked it. She took it from his desk and pinned it in a good place on the wall, where everybody could see it. The boy was pleased and surprised, because he had never before had a drawing pinned up in this way, although he knew he could draw at least as well as Edmund, who had a drawing selected nearly every week.

'Shall we be going to see the snowdrops this afternoon?' he asked Miss Webster before he went home.

'Yes,' she said, 'if Miss Lewis will allow us, we'll go to see them this afternoon.'

He ate his lunch quietly, thinking in his head of a story about a wizard who could change himself into anything at all. It was a good story, but something always seemed to happen before he got to the end of it. Sometimes he began it at night in bed, only to fall asleep long before the really exciting part. Now his mother was talking to him.

'Was Miss Webster in school this morning?' she asked.

His mother was knitting a pullover. The needles went over and under each other, with the same little slide and click, and a row of knitting grew magically behind them.

'Yes,' he said, 'but she came late. She didn't arrive until playtime.'

'Poor girl,' said his mother.

He thought about this for a long time.

'She's got a bad hand,' he said. 'She caught her finger in the cupboard door and her hand was bleeding. She's got a bandage on it today. She'll never be able to bend her finger again, that's what Edmund Jenkins said.'

'Oh, you and Edmund Jenkins,' said his mother.

He raced back to school, his boots ringing on the pavement as they always seemed to in cold weather. Every day he went a special way, over the river bridge, being very careful of the traffic, up Penry Street as far as the fruiterer's, then across the road by the fire station in case the doors were open; now he could balance along a low wall outside Jack Williams's garden, and at last he was in the small road where the school was. He never knew what would happen here, because he would meet many boys going to school and almost any adventure could happen. Once in this road Bernard Spencer had given him a glass marble, and once he and Edmund had found a silver medal which somebody had won for running. Edmund's father had taken it to the police, but they didn't have a reward.

But there was nobody about, except some girls skipping and giggling just inside the school yard, and he made his way inside the building. Everybody was sitting very quietly inside the classroom. They were allowed to go in early because it was very cold. Normally they would have stayed outside until Miss Lewis rang the bell, and some boys stayed outside however wet and cold it was, but today it seemed that they all wanted to sit quietly with Miss Webster, close to the cast-iron stove that had the figure of a tortoise on the top.

At two o'clock Miss Webster marked her register and then began to tell them a story. It was a good story, about a dragon who guarded a hoard of treasure in his den underground, where the snowdrops slept all through the winter. From time to time Miss Webster turned her head to look at the big clock in the hall. She could see it through the top half of the classroom door, which had four panes of glass in it. Her voice seemed to be hoarser than usual, which was fine when she read the dragon's bits, but not good for the knight nor the princess. She shut her book with a snap and stood up. She hadn't completed the story.

'Now we'll go to see the snowdrops,' she said. 'I want the girls to go quietly to the cloakroom and put on their coats. When they are ready, I'll come along with the boys. Everybody must wear a coat. If you have difficulty with buttons, please stand in front and I'll fasten them for you.'

He stood up with a sudden lightening of the heart. He had known all the time that Miss Webster would not forget, and at last she was taking him to see the miraculous flowers, pale and fragile as the falling snow. He looked at Miss Webster with gratitude. Her eyes were bright as frost, and she was making sure that the girls walked nicely through the door. Edmund Jenkins waved at him and that was funny, because Edmund had his black gloves on, with a hole in a place he could push his finger through. Edmund waved his finger like a fat white worm in the middle of his dark hand.

They all walked beautifully through the playground, in two rows holding hands, and he held Edmund's hand and they gave a little skip together every three steps. It didn't take long to get to the garden. The children bent down, four at a time, to look at the little clump of snowdrops and Miss Webster told them what to look at. He and Edmund would be the last to look. When they had finished, the other children went down to the garden gate which opened onto the road. It was a big gate with iron bars and your head could almost poke through. Somewhere a long way off the boy could hear men singing. They sang softly, mournfully, the words carried gently on the air over the school wall.

'It's a funeral,' said Edmund. 'My father's there and my Uncle Jim. It's a boy who was killed on a motor-bike.'

The boy nodded. Funerals often passed the school on their way to the cemetery at the top of the valley. All the men wore black suits and they walked slowly. Sometimes they sang.

He squatted down to look at the snowdrops. He felt a slow, sad disappointment. He looked around for Miss Webster to explain these simple flowers to him, but she had gone down to the gate and was staring through, looking up the road. Her back was as hard as a stone. He turned again to the snowdrops, concentrating, willing them to turn marvellous in front of his eyes. They hung down their four-petalled heads in front of him, the white tinged with minute green, the little green ball sturdily holding the petals, the greyish leaves standing up like miniature spears. The boy began to see their fragility. He saw them blow in a sudden gust of the cold March wind, shake, and straighten gallantly. He imagined them standing all night in the dark garden, holding bravely to their specks of whiteness. He put out a finger to touch the nearest flower, knowing now what snowdrops were. He lifted his face to tell Miss Webster, but she was standing right at the gate, holding the iron bars with her hands. Her shoulders were shaking.

Mor ddedwydd yw y rhai trwy ffydd
S'yn mynd o blith y byw . . .

sang the men as they filed solemnly past the school. The boy knew it was
Welsh because of his grandmother, and it was sad and beautiful.

After a while they couldn't hear the singing any more, but Miss
Webster continued to cry aloud in the midst of the frightened children.

FIRST DAY AT MILLINGTON
Jennifer Zabel

In the low golden sunshine of an early autumn morning, a bottle-green Rover, the dents in its bodywork dimmed by dust, slid cautiously through the open gates of Millington Comprehensive School.

Silence fell upon the occupants at the sight of the vast, alien stretches of pale concrete and gleaming glass. For the driver and passengers respectively, the busy corridors of Whitehall and the ivy-encrusted stone walls of boarding school seemed already to have faded into the family's folk memory.

It was an end and a beginning. Millington's new headmaster, Henry Diddlewick-Clack, and its two new pupils, Natasha and Simon Diddlewick-Clack, were on the threshold of a strange new world.

Natasha had known that everything was going to be all right from the moment she had read in the prospectus that the school uniform was cream and olive green. The colours would suit her long, copper-coloured hair beautifully. She shuddered, remembering the well-cut but dowdy brown tunics and brown check blouses of her old school. The girls went around looking as freckly and dull as the ducks on the school lake. Not that it mattered much, for Deepwood Academy was an all girls school.

The car passed a group of lanky sixth-form boys, carrying bulging

Natasha came out of a door in front of them.

briefcases and trendy sports bags. Natasha half-turned her head to look at them. The boys stared back, and interested smirks appeared on one or two of the faces.

Natasha felt a ripple of joy pass through her. What more could a sixteen-year-old girl want than to be as pretty as she was, with six O-levels behind her, maths, physics and chemistry over and done with forever, and a future bathed in the radiance of English literature before her?

She suddenly became aware of the fact that she was sitting bolt upright and clutching the strap of her satchel in excitement. She leaned back quickly, adopting her usual pose of sophisticated boredom. After all, she was even more of a somebody now, being the head-master's daughter.

The car drew up at the main door. Henry Diddlewick-Clack squeezed the contents of his rather tight, grey pin-striped suit from behind the wheel and stood up, coughing self-consciously as he looked around.

All this was far from being the comedown it had at first appeared to be. In fact, it was probably the greatest challenge of his life. Odd that it might never have presented itself had a series of family and financial disasters not shaken the pattern of his previous life out of all recognition.

It had all begun at the demise of his dreadful father Henry Diddlewick-Clack Senior. The provision of the mammoth marble tombstone which now dominated the country churchyard like a great inverted ice-cream cone proved to be the least expensive of his death duties. The Inland Revenue had soon made sure of that.

Worse was to come. He had invested a huge sum of money in a holiday camp that was being set up in a beautiful, seemingly stable Central African republic. There had promptly been an uprising. The holiday camp had been seized by rebel forces and was now being used as a guerrilla training base.

The last stage in the epic downfall of Henry Diddlewick-Clack came, oddly enough, when he uncovered a spy ring operating at the Foreign Office, where he worked. The catch was that his wife had turned out to be one of the ringleaders. This remote and beautiful creature was familiar to Natasha and Simon only as a pale, slant-eyed face peering over mysterious black fur to give instructions to a series of cheerful, round-faced governesses. She had managed to escape into exile and now sent the children furry boots once in a while, and 'Greetings from Moscow' postcards. As for Henry Diddlewick-Clack, he had been asked, very politely, to resign.

He now had no choice but to take his children out of their expensive boarding schools, put his elegant country house on the market, and scour the 'Situations Vacant' columns in the best Sunday newspapers.

'Er-hem!' he now declared from the bottom step of his new place of work. 'I think you two had better walk back and go in through the side door. Like the other pupils.' With the instinct of an old diplomat he felt that the wisest policy for the children of a new headmaster was to lie as low as possible for a while.

Simon shuffled untidily from the front seat of the Rover. He had hardly said a word to anyone all morning. When Natasha had asked him what he was sulking about as he slouched over his breakfast cereal he had told her to shut up, he was pondering his next move. This always meant his next move in a game of chess. He played himself a lot, and invariably won.

Natasha had shut up, disappearing into the bathroom to fiddle with her hair and leave him in peace. Not that Simon felt at all at peace. He was too busy turning over and over in his mind the idea of the new school, the new teachers, and, most of all, the new boys – the girls didn't count, of course. Would they decide to give him the cold shoulder because of the dreadful handicap of having the new headmaster for a father? And then, what about Dad? What if he made a mess of it? He'd made a mess of things before. It can't always have been just bad luck when things went terribly wrong. He couldn't understand how Dad had got the job in the first place. The other candidates must have been pretty hopeless. Or else there had been some old biddy on the education committee who had thought that Dad looked like her long-lost son or something.

Simon closed his eyes and mind against the possible agony of it all.

'Have a good day, Simon!' said his father, with deliberate briskness. 'I'll see you at 3.30, if not before.'

Natasha had already disappeared, swinging her new olive green skirt from side to side. She would be all right, thought Henry Diddlewick-Clack, sighing slightly. He sometimes thought she was a bit too much like her mother. A chameleon inside a hard, brightly enamelled shell, adapting easily to change but always presenting the same, self-assured, attractive exterior. When it came to new impressions it always seemed as if Natasha made them on others, rather than the other way round.

Not so old Simon. He was more like a defenceless sponge, visibly reacting against newness and change, but powerless to prevent himself becoming saturated with it all.

The father stood and watched until his son, small for his fourteen years, had been swallowed up by the swelling crowds of Millington pupils. Then the new headmaster turned and walked smartly up the steps towards his office.

As Simon was jostled through one of the side doors and found himself for the first time in the interior of Millington, the first thing that caught his eye and sent his already shaky courage plummeting, was the number on one of the wooden wall lockers that stretched down the corridor past an infinity of other swinging glass doors. It was nine hundred and sixty two. Nine hundred and sixty two. Fishworthy college for Boys, all four hundred and eleven of them, suddenly assumed a kind of family-like cosiness in Simon's mind.

The second thing that struck him, was that this school didn't smell of polish like Fishworthy. Particularly on the first day of a new term its dense, sweet, all-pervading smell of polish had hit you as you opened the doors: polish on the dark boards of the creaking wooden staircases, polish on the heavy oak desks in the library, polish on the brass door-knobs and the brass bowls of soft summer roses. The reek of polish had somehow managed to cut the school off from the outside, making it close, protective, rather like an animal's familiar lair.

Millington didn't only not smell of polish, it didn't smell of anything. It was too high, too light and airy, had too many doors and windows, too many open walks leading from one section of the school to the other, too many nameless faces to afford any protection against the great outside. The great outside was part of it, moving through it, undisturbed, like the wind.

On the wall above the lockers a large notice with a red arrow directed all the first-year pupils to the right. Presumably more information as to how to get to their destination would await them at the next parting of the ways. Pinned to an oak tree or drawn in the sand.

Simon watched as they obediently followed the arrow. They all looked much neater than the rest of the pupils, and their school uniforms still looked as if they didn't really belong to them. Simon glanced down at his own uniform. It must stand out a mile that he was new, too. He envied the first-years. At least they were all in it together.

A group of boys and girls who looked about his own age came through the door behind him. They were all eagerly laughing at something a tall blond boy was saying.

As Simon came up to them they fell silent and looked at him with a mocking curiosity that immediately excluded him from the group. Simon knew instantly, without being aware of it, that they had reacted to him in this way because the tall blond boy expected it of them.

'Excuse me,' began Simon, automatically addressing himself to their leader. 'I'm new here. I'm going into the third year. Could you tell me where I'll find my form room, please?'

'Form room? Form room?' declared the blond boy, throwing up his arms in feigned amazement. 'I don't know about that, but the third year TUTOR rooms are up there!' And he jerked his thumb in the direction of a flight of stairs.

'Nicholas!' murmured a plump little dark girl with thick black eyelashes and silver rings in her ears.

But it wasn't until Simon reached the bend in the stairs and saw the cluster of upturned, grinning faces, that he realized he'd been had. Angry and embarrassed he determined to avoid the confrontation that honour would demand if he turned back. So, feigning ignorance, he ran jauntily up the rest of the steps and began to peruse the noticeboard at the top, for all the world as if that had been his intention.

Sliding his eyes to the left he saw the chilly white rows of impossibly clean cookers that betokened the domestic science room. To the right a notice on the only other door on the landing read: 'Sixth Form Common Room. Keep Out. Trespassers enter at their peril.'

Peering round it Simon saw Natasha. It seemed odd, seeing someone so familiar in these alien surroundings. She was sitting on the edge of a formica-topped desk wearing a shy newcomer's smile but not looking in the least as if she felt like one. A group of sixth-formers, boys and girls, stood around her, chatting and laughing. As usual, Natasha was the centre of attention. She looked straight at Simon once, but by tacit consent they didn't acknowledge one another. At a time when each had its own battle to fight, the presence of a brother or sister in the same circumstances felt like an Achilles heel.

Wishing fervently that he could appear half as self-possessed as his sister, Simon went slowly back down the steps.

When he finally arrived at his tutor room, which was naturally in a completely different part of the school complex altogether, he was not at all surprised to find Nicholas and several other members of his pack already sitting there. Mr Greaves, the tutor, a preoccupied, bearded member of the Creative Studies faculty, introduced him with a vague wave of the hand as the son of the new headmaster. Nicholas greeted this information with a groan of mock despair, rolling his eyes heavenward and beating his hands on the desk top.

For over an hour Simon was bombarded with a stream of confusing information necessary for his survival. Then, being a new pupil, he was despatched to the photography room where he shuffled awkwardly along in a queue of first-years. Natasha floated out past him, escorted by a couple of sylph-like sixth-formers who had gone along to show her the way. Simon sniffed and thrust his hands deep into his pockets. They had probably jumped the queue, into the bargain.

On his way out of the photography room an electric bell sounded through the corridors. It was time for the morning break. Simon fought to buy a bar of chocolate and a plastic carton of orange at the school tuck shop, then perched on a low window sill in the third-year open area. All the chairs were already taken.

He watched as Nicholas, sitting in a bored-looking group some distance away, produced a travelling chess set from his battered briefcase and garbled out an open invitation to play through a mouthful of chocolate biscuit.

Unwittingly he had opened a door. Quickly Simon got his foot in.

'I'll play,' he said, walking over. The others moved over for him, alert now, and interested. Nicholas's face registered nothing, but he shrugged, moving forward to the edge of his chair to concentrate on the board.

Simon beat him. They were quite evenly matched as it happened, but that signified nothing in the circumstances. Simon had won.

'Good game!' he declared with deliberate enthusiasm, trying hard to conceal his jubilation. Nicholas was white-faced with humiliation. 'We could have another game at lunchtime if you like!'

Nicholas grabbed the game and stuffed it back into his briefcase, quite unable to cope with this mortifying loss of face.

'Lunchtime, lunchtime!' he mimicked. 'We call it dinner here, new boy!'

A member of staff walked up to them.

'Who left that wrapping paper on the floor?' she demanded, pointing to the silver foil from Nicholas's biscuit which was lying mid-way between his chair and Simon's.

'It's probably his, Miss Farraday!' grinned Nicholas gleefully, bubbling with a desire for revenge. 'He's a new boy and hasn't learnt the rules yet!'

Miss Farraday looked at Simon through cool, blue eyes.

'You must be Simon Diddlewick-Clack!' she said. 'Simon, anyone found leaving litter around or even walking past somebody else's litter' – here she turned and looked speculatively at Nicholas – 'will be given a detention. Is that clear?'

Simon nodded, choking back his anger.

'Now I'm taking you all for a double maths lesson in Room 25, I believe,' continued Miss Farraday. 'Off you go, all of you!'

In Room 25 the small dark girl with earrings deliberately plumped her satchel down on the table next to Simon's.

'You're very good at chess!' she declared, sitting down and resting her chin on her hand to look at him. 'I'm Susie, by the way, and this is Mike!' The boy called Mike grinned at Simon and said 'Hi!' He was a clever-looking boy with a cheerful, freckled face.

Simon beamed with pleasure, and felt the relief of being able to relax his face into a smile.

Two rows in front, Nicholas was nudged by one of his henchmen. He scowled sulkily over his shoulder. Susie made a face at him.

'You can come to dinner with Mike and me, if you like!' she declared airily, knowing that he would like, and that Nicholas would be furious.

Happily Simon nodded his thanks.

At twelve o'clock the first sitting spilled out of their classrooms and converged on the dining-hall to grab metal trays and shuffle past the steaming ladles of the white-overalled dinner ladies. Simon was overawed to find that here at Millington there was actually a choice of food on the menu. He sat with Mike and Susie at a table by the window. Over their plates of Spaghetti Bolognese – Susie had salad – and apple crumble – Susie had yoghurt – they talked football. An England versus West Germany football match was going to be televised live that evening. The boys wouldn't have missed it for the world. Neither would Susie. She was an ardent supporter of the local Millington team, and declared that she would knit Simon an appropriately striped scarf if he would promise to go to all their home matches. Simon promised that he would.

As the three of them wandered across the courtyard towards the science block, where they were due to spend their afternoon in the chemistry lab, Natasha came out of a door in front of them, walking quickly, her small, neat heels tapping purposefully across the concrete slabs and her hair gleaming and flying back in the wind.

'Hello, Simon!' she cried gaily as she passed by. Simon responded by swinging his heavy briefcase against her legs and giving a brotherly grunt. Vaguely he wondered what was the matter with her. He knew his sister well enough to know that the bright smile on her face was too bright, it had been put there deliberately.

The matter was quite simple. During dinner a group of boys had come up and invited Cheryl and Caroline to a disco. Neither of them could talk about anything else after that. In fact, they were still at it up there, mooning on about what they were going to wear. If none of the boys had been brave enough to invite her as well, the girls could at least have waited until she wasn't there to discuss all the boring details. They had been so nice to her all morning, too. Catty things. Never mind, a display of independence was what was called for here.

Which was why Natasha was now heading so determinedly towards the library. She would spend her free period studying there, alone. She marched over to the English section, and selected Wordsworth's Prelude, smiling disarmingly at the student English teacher who was searching in vain for one of the three copies the library was supposed to possess of *Lady Chatterley's Lover*.

Outside the chemistry lab everyone was waiting for Mr Randall to arrive. It was forbidden to enter any room in the science block before a member of staff was present.

A flustered little secretary in a pink jumper came hurrying anxiously along the corridor.

'Mr Randall has had a slight accident with his car,' she announced. 'The headmaster will be taking your class today. Please wait quietly until he arrives!'

There was a stir of anticipation. Simon went rigid with horror. For some reason he hadn't thought about his father all morning. He knew he had an honours degree in chemistry and had taught for a couple of years in a public school, but he hadn't realized that he might be called upon to teach here at Millington, too. He would make a real fool of himself in front of this hard-boiled lot. Just when things were getting better, too.

'Well, we all know who's going to be teacher's pet today, don't we?' came a jeering voice. It was Nicholas, slouched against a wall with his hands in his pockets. 'Have you seen this, what's his name – Fiddlewick-Slack – anyway? He goes marching around as if he owned the place! He could do with a new suit, too. A couple of sizes bigger, if you ask me!'

That was it. Simon didn't even give Nicholas time to stand up. He hit him, all over, thumping out the rage that had started on the bend of the stairs so long ago.

'And just what is going on here?' demanded a knife-edged voice.

The two boys fell apart, panting. Henry Diddlewick-Clack stared icily from one to the other. There was a breathless hush amongst the spectators.

'I have never seen such a disgusting display in all my life!' he continued, eyeing Nicholas's bleeding nose with distaste. 'Which one of you hooligans started this brawl?'

'I did, Sir!' muttered Simon, who had never called his father 'sir' before in his life.

'Why?' demanded the headmaster, curtly.

It was unthinkable to tell the truth. There was a split-second's silence.

'I didn't like his face, Sir!' said Simon.

Somebody snorted back a guffaw, and some of the girls began to giggle.

'Right then, Diddlewick-Clack!' said Diddlewick-Clack. 'It's a five hundred word essay for you tonight, entitled 'Crime and Punishment'.

To be on my desk tomorrow morning! I'll tell you all now that I don't believe in corporal punishment. Never have, not for any of my boys. But I warn you, don't try to convince me that I'm wrong. Now, you, get that nose seen to. Into the lab, everyone else, *in an orderly fashion!*'

In an awed silence, the children filed obediently between the benches. Simon caught the headmaster's eye, and for a fraction of a second father and son glanced at each other with a new kind of respect. Henry Diddlewick-Clack nodded almost imperceptibly, a glint of affectionate amusement in his eye.

'You won't be able to watch the football match now, will you?' whispered Mike, aghast. 'Not with that whopping essay to do!'

'I'll tape it for him!' hissed somebody else. 'My Dad's got a new tape recorder. Cheap. It fell off the back of a lorry!'

At three-thirty Simon was sitting in the car, brooding over his essay and the football match he wasn't going to see, when his father arrived.

'Feet off the dashboard, Simon!' said Henry Diddlewick-Clack briskly, as he started the engine to turn the car round.

'What have you got to look so pleased about?' said Simon grumpily, as Natasha ran up and bounced into the back seat. 'Got yourself a new boyfriend, by any chance?'

'What?' said Natasha, vaguely. 'Oh, don't be so silly, Simon. Daddy, we had English literature this afternoon and do you know which Shakespeare play we're doing for A-level? Oh, perhaps you do, I keep forgetting. Anyway, it's *King Lear*. We read the first act today – oh, and it's marvellous! And Mrs Burton – that's the English teacher, she's fantastic – wants us to describe and compare the characters of King Lear's three daughters. By Friday! Oh, hurry up, Dad! I'll have to start tonight, it'll take me *ages!*'

The bottle-green Rover slid confidently down the drive towards the open gates. It was part of the Millington scene now, for someone had scrawled a welcome in huge letters all over the dusty boot. It read 'This car is dirty. Get it washed.'

THE PATRON'S VISIT
Charlotte Brontë

My first quarter at Lowood seemed an age; and not the golden age either: it comprised an irksome struggle with difficulties in habituating myself to new rules and unwonted tasks. The fear of failure in these points harassed me worse than the physical hardships of my lot; though these were no trifles.

During January, February, and part of March, the deep snows, and, after their melting, the almost impassable roads, prevented our stirring beyond the garden walls, except to go to church; but within these limits we had to pass an hour every day in the open air. Our clothing was insufficient to protect us from the severe cold; we had no boots, the snow got into our shoes and melted there; our ungloved hands became numbed and covered with chilblains, as were our feet: I remember well the distracting irritation I endured from this cause every evening, when my feet inflamed; and the torture of thrusting the swelled, raw, and stiff toes into my shoes in the morning. Then the scanty supply of food was distressing: with the keen appetites of growing children, we had scarcely sufficient to keep alive a delicate invalid. From this deficiency of nourishment resulted an abuse, which pressed hardly on the younger pupils: whenever the famished great girls had an opportunity, they would coax or menace the little ones out of their portion. Many a time

I have shared between two claimants the precious morsel of brown bread distributed at teatime; and after relinquishing to a third, half the contents of my mug of coffee, I have swallowed the remainder with an accompaniment of secret tears, forced from me by the exigency of hunger.

Sundays were dreary days in that wintry season. We had to walk two miles to Brocklebridge Church, where our patron officiated. We set out cold, we arrived at church colder: during the morning service we became almost paralysed. It was too far to return to dinner, and an allowance of cold meat and bread, in the same penurious proportion observed in our ordinary meals, was served round between the services.

At the close of the afternoon service we returned by an exposed and hilly road, where the bitter winter wind, blowing over a range of snowy summits to the north, almost flayed the skin from our faces.

I can remember Miss Temple walking lightly and rapidly along our drooping line, her plaid cloak, which the frosty wind fluttered, gathered close about her, and encouraging us, by precept, and example, to keep up our spirits, and march forward, as she said, 'like stalwart soldiers.' The other teachers, poor things, were generally themselves too much dejected to attempt the task of cheering others.

How we longed for the light and heat of a blazing fire when we got back! But, to the little ones at least, this was denied: each hearth in the school-room was immediately surrounded by a double row of great girls, and behind them the younger children crouched in groups, wrapping their starved arms in their pinafores.

A little solace came at tea-time, in the shape of a double ration of bread – a whole, instead of a half, slice – with the delicious addition of a thin scrape of butter: it was the hebdomadal treat to which we all looked forward from Sabbath to Sabbath. I generally contrived to reserve a moiety of this bounteous repast for myself; but the remainder I was invariably obliged to part with.

The Sunday evening was spent in repeating, by heart, the Church Catechism, and the fifth, sixth, and seventh chapters of St Matthew; and in listening to a long sermon, read by Miss Miller, whose irrepressible yawns attested her weariness. A frequent interlude of these performances was the enactment of the part of Eutychus by some half dozen of little girls; who, overpowered with sleep, would fall down, if not out of the third loft, yet off the fourth form, and be taken up half dead. The remedy was, to thrust them forward into the centre of the school-room, and oblige them to stand there till the sermon was finished. Sometimes, their feet failed them, and they sank together in a heap; they were then propped up with the monitors' high stools.

I have not yet alluded to the visits of Mr Brocklehurst; and indeed that gentleman was from home during the greater part of the first month after my arrival; perhaps prolonging his stay with his friend the archdeacon: his absence was a relief to me. I need not say that I had my own reasons for dreading his coming: but come he did at last.

One afternoon (I had then been three weeks at Lowood), as I was sitting with a slate in my hand, puzzling over a sum in long division, my eyes, raised in abstraction to the window, caught sight of a figure just passing: I recognized almost instinctively that gaunt outline; and when, two minutes after, all the school, teachers included, rose *en masse*, it was not necessary for me to look up in order to ascertain whose entrance they thus greeted. A long stride measured the school-room, and presently beside Miss Temple, who herself had risen, stood the same black column which had frowned on me so ominously from the hearth-rug of Gateshead. I now glanced sideways at this piece of architecture. Yes, I was right: it was Mr. Brocklehurst, buttoned up in a surtout, and looking longer, narrower, and more rigid than ever.

I had my own reasons for being dismayed at this apparition: too well I remembered the perfidious hints given by Mrs Reed about my disposition, etc.; the promise pledged by Mr Brocklehurst to apprise Miss Temple and the teachers of my vicious nature. All along I had been dreading the fulfilment of this promise, – I had been looking out daily for the 'Coming Man', whose information respecting my past life and conversation was to brand me as a bad child for ever: now there he was. He stood at Miss Temple's side: he was speaking low in her ear: I did not doubt he was making disclosures of my villainy; and I watched her eye with painful anxiety, expecting every moment to see its dark orb turn on me a glance of repugnance and contempt. I listened too; and as I happened to be seated quite at the top of the room, I caught most of what he said: its import relieved me from immediate apprehension.

'I suppose, Miss Temple, the thread I bought at Lowton will do; it struck me that it would be just of the quality for the calico chemises, and I sorted the needles to match. You may tell Miss Smith that I forgot to make a memorandum of the darning needles, but she shall have some papers sent in next week; and she is not, on any account, to give out more than one at a time to each pupil: if they have more, they are apt to be careless and lose them. And, oh ma'am! I wish the woollen stockings were better looked to! – when I was here last, I went into the kitchen-garden and examined the clothes drying on the line; there was a quantity of black hose in a very bad state of repair: from the size of the holes in them I was sure they had not been well-mended from time to time.'

He paused.

'Your directions shall be attended to, sir,' said Miss Temple.

'And, ma'am,' he continued, 'the laundress tells me some of the girls have two clean tuckers in the week: it is too much; the rules limit them to one.'

'I think I can explain that circumstance, sir. Agnes and Catherine Johnstone were invited to take tea with some friends at Lowton last Thursday, and I gave them leave to put on clean tuckers for the occasion.'

Mr Brocklehurst nodded.

'Well, for once it may pass; but please not to let the circumstance occur too often. And there is another thing which surprised me: I find, in settling accounts with the house-keeper, that a lunch, consisting of bread and cheese, has twice been served out to the girls during the past fortnight. How is this? I look over the regulations, and I find no such meal as lunch mentioned. Who introduced this innovation? and by what authority?'

'I must be responsible for the circumstance, sir,' replied Miss Temple: 'the breakfast was so ill-prepared that the pupils could not possibly eat it; and I dared not allow them to remain fasting till dinner time.'

'Madam, allow me an instant. – You are aware that my plan in bringing up these girls is, not to accustom them to habits of luxury and indulgence, but to render them hardy, patient, self-denying. Should any little accidental disappointment of the appetite occur, such as the spoiling of a meal, the under or the over dressing of a dish, the incident ought not to be neutralized by replacing with something more delicate the comfort lost, thus pampering the body and obviating the aim of this institution; it ought to be improved to the spiritual edification of the pupils, by encouraging them to evince fortitude under the temporary privation. A brief address on those occasions would not be mistimed, wherein a judicious instructor would take the opportunity of referring to the sufferings of the primitive Christians; to the torments of martyrs; to the exhortations of our blessed Lord himself, calling upon His disciples to take up their cross and follow Him; to His warnings that man shall not live by bread alone, but by every word that proceedeth out of the mouth of God; to his divine consolations, "if ye suffer hunger or thirst for my sake, happy are ye." Oh, madam, when you put bread and cheese, instead of burnt porridge, into these children's mouths, you may indeed feed their vile bodies, but you little think how you starve their immortal souls!'

Mr Brocklehurst again paused – perhaps overcome by his feelings. Miss Temple had looked down when he first began to speak to her; but she now gazed straight before her, and her face, naturally pale as marble, appeared to be assuming also the coldness and fixity of that material; especially her mouth, closed as if it would have required a sculptor's chisel to open it, and her brow settled gradually into petrified severity.

Meantime, Mr Brocklehurst, standing on the hearth with his hands behind his back, majestically surveyed the whole school. Suddenly his eye gave a blink, as if it had met something that either dazzled or shocked its pupil: turning, he said in more rapid accents than he had hitherto used:

'Miss Temple, Miss Temple, what – *what* is that girl with curled hair? Red hair, ma'am, curled – curled all over?' And extending his cane he pointed to the awful object, his hand shaking as he did so.

'It is Julia Severn,' replied Miss Temple, very quietly.

'Julia Severn, ma'am! And why has she, or any other, curled hair? Why, in defiance of every precept and principle of this house, does she conform to the world so openly – here in an evangelical, charitable establishment – as to wear her hair one mass of curls?'

'Julia's hair curls naturally,' returned Miss Temple, still more quietly.

'Naturally! Yes, but we are not to conform to nature: I wish these girls to be the children of Grace: and why that abundance? I have again and again intimated that I desire the hair to be arranged closely, modestly, plainly. Miss Temple, that girl's hair must be cut off entirely;

I will send a barber tomorrow: and I see others who have far too much of the excrescence – that tall girl, tell her to turn round. Tell all the first form to rise up and direct their faces to the wall.'

Miss Temple passed her handkerchief over her lips, as if to smooth away the involuntary smile that curled them; she gave the order, however, and when the first class could take in what was required of them, they obeyed. Leaning a little back on my bench, I could see the looks and grimaces with which they commented on this manoeuvre: it was a pity Mr Brocklehurst could not see them too; he would perhaps have felt that, whatever he might do with the outside of the cup and platter, the inside was further beyond his interference than he imagined.

He scrutinized the reverse of these living medals some five minutes, then pronounced sentence. These words fell like the knell of doom:

'All those top-knots must be cut off.'

Miss Temple seemed to remonstrate.

'Madam,' he pursued, 'I have a Master to serve whose kingdom is not of this world: my mission is to mortify in these girls the lusts of the flesh; to teach them to clothe themselves with shame-facedness and sobriety, not with braided hair and costly apparel; each of the young persons before us has a string of hair twisted in plaits which vanity itself might have woven: these, I repeat, must be cut off; think of the time wasted, of——'

Mr Brocklehurst was here interrupted: three other visitors, ladies, now entered the room. They ought to have come a little sooner to have heard his lecture on dress, for they were splendidly attired in velvet, silk, and furs. The two younger of the trio (fine girls of sixteen and seventeen) had grey beaver hats, then in fashion, shaded with ostrich plumes, and from under the brim of this graceful head-dress fell a profusion of light tresses, elaborately curled; the elderly lady was enveloped in a costly velvet shawl, trimmed with ermine, and she wore a false front of French curls.

These ladies were deferentially received by Miss Temple, as Mrs and Misses Brocklehurst, and conducted to seats of honour at the top of the room. It seems they had come in the carriage with their reverend relative, and had been conducting a rummaging scrutiny of the rooms upstairs, while he transacted business with the housekeeper, questioned the laundress, and lectured the superintendent. They now proceeded to address divers remarks and reproofs to Miss Smith, who was charged with the care of the linen and the inspection of the dormitories: but I had no time to listen to what they said; other matters called off and enchained my attention.

Hitherto, while gathering up the discourse of Mrs Brocklehurst and Miss Temple, I had not, at the same time, neglected precautions to secure my personal safety; which I thought would be effected, if I could only elude observation. To this end, I had sat well back on the form, and while seeming to be busy with my sum, had held my slate in such a manner as to conceal my face: I might have escaped notice, had not my treacherous slate somehow happened to slip from my hand, and falling with an obtrusive crash, directly drawn every eye upon me; I knew it was all over now, and, as I stopped to pick up the two fragments of slate, I rallied my forces for the worst. It came.

'A careless girl!' said Mr Brocklehurst, and immediately after – 'It is the new pupil, I perceive.' And before I could draw breath, 'I must not forget I have a word to say respecting her.' Then aloud: how loud it seemed to me! 'Let the child who broke her slate, come forward!'

Of my own accord, I could not have stirred; I was paralysed: but the two great girls who sat on each side of me, set me on my legs and pushed me towards the dread judge, and then Miss Temple gently assisted me to his very feet, and I caught her whispered counsel, –

'Don't be afraid, Jane, I saw it was an accident; you shall not be punished.'

The kind whisper went to my heart like a dagger.

'Another minute, and she will despise me for a hypocrite,' thought I; and an impulse of fury against Reed, Brocklehurst, and Co. bounded in my pulses at the conviction. I was no Helen Burns.

'Fetch that stool,' said Mr Brocklehurst, pointing to a very high one from which a monitor had just risen: it was brought.

'Place the child upon it.'

And I was placed there, by whom I don't know: I was in no condition to note particulars; I was only aware that they had hoisted me up to the height of Mr Brocklehurst's nose, that he was within a yard of me, and that a spread of shot orange and purple silk pelisses, and a cloud of silvery plumage extended and waved below me.

Mr Brocklehurst hemmed.

They hoisted me up to the height of Mr Brocklehurst's nose.

'Ladies,' said he, turning to his family; 'Miss Temple, teachers, and children, you all see this girl?'

Of course they did; for I felt their eyes directed like burning glasses against my scorched skin.

'You see she is yet young; you observe she possesses the ordinary form of childhood; God has graciously given her the shape that He has given to all of us; no signal deformity points her out as a marked character. Who would think that the Evil One has already found a servant and agent in her? Yet such, I grieve to say, is the case.'

A pause – in which I began to steady the palsy of my nerves, and to feel that the Rubicon was passed; and that the trial, no longer to be shirked, must be firmly sustained.

'My dear children,' pursued the black marble clergyman, with pathos, 'this is a sad, a melancholy occasion; for it becomes my duty to warn you, that this girl, who might be one of God's own lambs, is a little castaway: not a member of the true flock, but evidently an interloper and an alien. You must be on your guard against her; you must shun her example: if necessary, avoid her company, exclude her from your sports, and shut her out from your converse. Teachers, you must watch her: keep your eyes on her movements, weigh well her words, scrutinize her actions, punish her body to save her soul: if, indeed, such salvation be possible, for (my tongue falters while I tell it) this girl, this child, the native of a Christian land, worse than many a little heathen who says its prayers to Brahma and kneels before Juggernaut – this girl is – a liar!'

Now came a pause of ten minutes; during which I, by this time in perfect possession of my wits, observed all the female Brocklehursts produce their pocket-handkerchiefs and apply them to the optics, while the elderly lady swayed herself to and fro, and the two younger ones whispered, 'How shocking!'

Mr Brocklehurst resumed.

'This I learnt from her benefactress; from the pious and charitable lady who adopted her in her orphan state, reared her as her own daughter, and whose kindness, whose generosity the unhappy girl repaid by an ingratitude so bad, so dreadful, that at last her excellent patroness was obliged to separate her from her own young ones, fearful lest her vicious example should contaminate their purity: she has sent her here to be healed, even as the Jews of old sent their diseased to the troubled pool of Bethesda; and, teachers, superintendent, I beg of you not to allow the waters to stagnate round her.'

With this sublime conclusion, Mr Brocklehurst adjusted the top button of his surtout, muttered something to his family, who rose, bowed to Miss Temple, and then all the great people sailed in state from the room. Turning at the door, my judge said:

'Let her stand half an hour longer on that stool, and let no one speak to her during the remainder of the day.'

There was I, then, mounted aloft: I, who had said I could not bear the shame of standing on my natural feet in the middle of the room, was now exposed to general view on a pedestal of infamy. What my sensations were, no language can describe; but just as they all arose, stifling my breath and constricting my throat, a girl came up and passed me: in passing, she lifted her eyes. What a strange light inspired them! What an extraordinary sensation that ray sent through me! How the new feeling bore me up! It was as if a martyr, a hero, had passed a slave or victim, and imparted strength in the transit. I mastered the rising hysteria, lifted up my head, and took a firm stand on the stool. Helen Burns asked some slight question about her work of Miss Smith, was chidden for the triviality of the inquiry, returned to her place, and smiled at me as she again went by. What a smile! I remember it now, and I know that it was the effluence of fine intellect, of true courage; it lit up her marked lineaments, her thin face, her sunken grey eye, like a reflection from the aspect of an angel. Yet at that moment Helen Burns wore on her arm 'the untidy badge'; scarcely an hour ago I had heard her condemned by Miss Scratcherd to a dinner of bread and water on the morrow, because she had blotted an exercise in copying it out. Such is the imperfect nature of man! such spots are there on the disc of the clearest planet; and eyes like Miss Scatcherd's can only see those minute defects, and are blind to the full brightness of the orb.

MR EVANS
Hayden McAllister

Philip Maddison and his cousin Stewart Johnson attended Sealyn School. Both boys were thirteen and shared the same desk in class, but whereas Philip was proficient only at English composition and Nature study, Stewart seemed to excel at most subjects.

According to Mr Tonks, their class teacher, the brown-haired Philip was a dreamer and didn't take his work seriously enough. Soon however, Mr Tonks's opinion would stand for nothing in the school for at the beginning of the autumn term a new teacher would be arriving to be Philip's class master. Rumour had it that the new teacher 'Mr Evans' was an ex-military man – but for the time being Philip wasn't too concerned with school, for it was still the summer break.

Both Philip and Stewart lived on the dockland housing estate and Philip's front door was less than three hundred yards from the North Sea. During the long summer evenings he would take his bicycle down to the beach and sometimes pedal, and sometimes walk along the shingle. He loved watching the fishing boats ploughing through the rough grey waters at full tide, followed by the hungry flocks of shrieking seagulls. On occasions when the tide was fully out he would kick his football along the sands.

To the east lay the dock area with two concrete piers stretching out like pincers. At the end of one pier was a lighthouse, while on the other stood a port beacon which acted as a warning light to guide vessels entering the docks at night. From his bedroom window Philip could see the beacon glowing like a red star above the North Sea.

Not far from the lighthouse was a barnacle-covered rock and seabirds, more especially cormorants and shags, often perched there after feeding with fish sticking out of their gullets. These tall black birds looked for all the world like passengers queuing for a bus.

At low tide Philip would walk out to this rock and climb up and stand at the 'Cormorants Bus Stop' and gazing out to sea he would watch the empty coal ships in the offshore waters till the tides changed. Then the boats would steam into Sealyn Docks to collect their cargoes of coal. Railway trucks brought the coal to the port side from the local pits and the dock was fitted with loading bays and mechanical coal chutes, enabling the coal to be poured directly into the holds of the coal ships.

Coal was big business in Sealyn and the town boasted three pits. One high on Sealyn Hill Road beyond the school and the other two near the coast road. The one called Sealyn Old Colliery had coal shafts probing out nearly two miles underneath the sea. Philip's father worked as a miner there and it was thought that Philip would one day take a job at the Old Colliery. But Philip's secret ambition was to become a professional footballer and when Sunderland Football Club played their home matches he travelled to the Roker Park ground with his father and cousin Stewart. Naturally he roared with delight when his team scored – but he also tried to learn as he watched, committing to memory some of the moves the more skilful players made.

But when Philip concentrated on playing his own game, all those skilful moves seemed to 'stick in his head', and when he was challenged for the ball, he found it very difficult to put his ideas and theories into practice. In fact the harder he tried, the harder it became. Often he would trip over the ball or lose possession in a tackle, and he knew he would have to improve a great deal before he was even considered for the school team.

Meanwhile he plodded on with his lessons, taking special interest in English composition and Nature study. But as for geometry and algebra – *they* made his head spin, and quite often when he was supposed to be doing his lessons he'd be day-dreaming about football – or thinking of the beach on a summer's day.

But the arrival of Mr Evans – his new class teacher – was to change all that.

★   ★   ★   ★

Sealyn School was situated halfway up Sealyn Hill Road, partially in the shadow of Hill Top Pit. On two sides of the school lay asphalt playgrounds, while at the rear of the building the playing fields stretched almost to the railway embankment.

Many years ago a pupil had been injured on the railway tracks and now a tall metal fence topped with coiled barbed-wire separated the sports field from the main Newcastle to Middlesborough railway line.

In Philip's class there were the usual mixture of pupils: Chambers the 'Swot' who spent all his spare time studying at home. This admirable sense of dedication did not give him pride of place at the head of the class however – that distinction went to Malcolm Keenan, the 'Prof', who casually designed micro-wave ovens and intergalactic transporters on the rear pages of his exercise books. What was even more astonishing was the fact that his inventions worked – in *theory* at least. There was a well-founded rumour that Keenan was a 'genius'; but Nature – as if to balance her gifts – had given him a trait of professorial absent-mindedness and a huge shock of carrot red hair – which he often 'forgot' to comb. Nevertheless the 'Prof' always had top marks in Maths, Science, Geography, History etc. . . .

Next on the list of school chums was Stewart Johnson – Philip's counsin. 'Stewie' was the sportsman of the class *and* the school. He was captain of the cricket and football teams and could give any boy ten yards start and beat him over half a mile. He was also a good scholar and generally finished in the top five. John Smith was the poet, and 'Smithers' often used his talent to make rhymes about his class mates and the most hated teachers.

The bully of the class was Bill Baxter. He was a big-boned lad with squinting eyes set in a face the colour of uncooked dough. He lived on fear – other people's fear. Most of his classmates hated him. Baxter reckoned that if he made enough noise and trouble, people would sit up and take notice of him. He was the type of boy who liked torturing weaklings and animals, not realizing that this was an outward sign of his own inner brutality. But for all that he also had a better side to his nature, if you dug deep enough to find it.

The first morning of the new term found Philip walking towards school alone. He'd called for cousin Stewart but Mrs Johnson told him that Stewart was in bed with tonsilitis.

On the way up Sealyn Hill Road, Philip began wondering how Sunderland Football Club were faring on their North American tour. For such a big nation Philip thought it odd that the Americans couldn't produce a decent soccer team. Still on the subject Philip made up his mind to be his level best to get into the school eleven and the thought of a football training session that morning sent his blood racing. To put in a good performance during the first sports' session would certainly heighten his chances of getting into the team.

Slowly he climbed the road leading to the school. Ahead lay the pit cages, and one of the huge slag-heaps where the pit authorities dumped slate and shale and other non-combustible materials. Directly to his right lay the Sealyn Sports' Centre.

Suddenly a stone skidded past his feet. He looked around. Along one side of the perimeter fence of the club ran a narrow alleyway. There he saw Bully Boy Baxter throwing stones at a tin can which lay on the ground. Philip was about to pass on when he heard a reedy squeak. There was something trapped inside the can!

Before he realized what he was doing, Philip had taken the few paces necessary to reach the can. As he bent to pick it up Bully Baxter yelled: 'Hands off. That's mine!' Philip hesitated, then the tiny squeal of terror came again.

In a flash Philip had prised off the lid with his pocket knife. Inside was a tiny field mouse shivering with fear. Philip laid down the can and the field mouse scuttled to freedom into the long grass at the side of the boundary fence. The next moment Philip felt a heavy blow on his forehead, then he was staring up at the menacing figure of Bully Baxter.

'Now I'll teach you to mess up my games!' sneered Baxter.

'Why don't you pick on someone your own size?' retorted Philip.

'That's what all white-livered cowards say.'

'Look,' said Philip, steadying himself on one knee. 'I don't mind you picking on me. I was talking about the mouse.'

'I don't like mice,' said Baxter. 'I don't like anything that creeps or crawls. . . .'

'You mean you don't like anything that reminds you of yourself,' provoked Philip.

At this the bigger boy kicked out towards the crouching figure of Philip, but Philip saw the blow coming and moved to one side, grabbing Baxter's foot and twisting it as he did so. The bully crashed onto the pavement with a curse.

Being of lighter build, Philip regained his feet first and sprinted up the alley with Baxter lumbering behind. The next second Philip collided with another figure at the alley entrance and almost stuck out a fist, thinking it to be one of Baxter's cronies. But he looked up into the eyes of a tall man with a military bearing who gazed at both boys in a detached manner. 'You boys seem to be in a great big hurry,' he said. 'Why are you so keen to get to school? Do you enjoy sitting in class-rooms on summer days?'

'No', blurted Philip. 'I was – I thought I would be late.' The stranger then looked at Baxter with an amused expression, but Baxter merely scowled.

'Well let me assure you boys that you have more than a quarter of an hour before school begins – which should give you ample time to walk the fifty yards necessary – or hop – or do whatever you like, so long as you get there in one piece and *don't harm anyone or anything* on the way.' This latter sentence seemed to be directed at Baxter, who stared morosely at his boots.

'Thank you sir,' said Philip, making to pass the stranger.

'Oh. Don't thank me boy,' said the man with a smile. 'My advice is free. But did you thank the sun for shining this morning?'

'The sun?' Philip laughed. 'No, I didn't sir.'

'Then why thank me for mere words and then not thank the sun for its life-giving light?' Disconcerted, Philip replied. 'Never thought about it sir.'

'Well *do* think about it boy. Why do we take life for granted, seeing one side and never the other. I call this "Evans' law of relativity" .'

215

'I've heard of Einstein's law . . .' began Baxter, 'but never Evans – '
Then he stopped. 'Evans!' he gasped. Mr Evans!?'

'Then you must be our new class master sir,' said Philip after an
awkward silence. The man nodded but said nothing. 'Oh, I'm Philip
Maddison, sir, and this is Bull – er Bill Baxter,' said Philip by way of
introduction.

'Pleased to meet you boys,' said Mr Evans. 'Now perhaps you'd like
to give me your thoughts on school life as we walk towards the
playground?'

★   ★   ★   ★

The first lesson on Nature study with their new class master started
abruptly.

' What can you tell me about bees?' asked Mr Evans.

'They fly, sir,' said Stewart. Someone snorted.

'They do indeed,' said Mr Evans, ignoring the suppressed laughter.
'What else?'

'They sting,' said Baxter.

'But only when severely provoked,' added Philip.

'They buzz', said the 'Prof' absent-mindedly. Everyone laughed. 'I
once designed an inter-galactic fuel transporter sir,' he continued,
'based on the aerodynamic flight potential of a bee outside the earth's
gravitational field.'

'Does it work?' asked Mr Evans.

'Don't know sir. Haven't had a chance to try it.'

'Let me tell you something about bees, Professor,' said Mr Evans.
'According to the earthly laws of aero-dynamics, bees should *not* be
able to fly.'

'You're joking, sir!' said Smithers.

'No. I'm quite serious, Smith. Bees – by flying – are actually defying
the laws of aero-dynamics. Furthermore, when a bee finds, let's say a
patch of clover, he can fly back to the hive and let his fellow bees know
exactly where that clover is. He can tell them what variety of clover it
is, how far the clover is and in what direction they'll find the plants in
relation to the sun.' Mr Evans looked up. 'What have you got to say
about that Baxter?'

'Don't like bees sir. They sting.'

'Do you like honey Baxter?'

'Yes, sir.'

'Bees make honey, Baxter. . . . Now what does honey remind you of boys?'

'Goodness, sir,' said Philip.

'Sunshine,' said Smithers.

'Energy,' said Prof.

'Now these creatures whom Baxter doesn't like – creatures which cannot fly according to textbooks on aero-dynamics – do an intricate dance in their hives and relay complicated information to other bees about food sources. This is just one insight into the miraculous world of Nature. And this is what I want you boys to understand, that the world isn't a dead billiard ball flying around a light bulb called the sun. It's a vast and sensitive organism linked to the solar system which is in turn linked to the heavens. . . . As one poet called Francis Thompson said: "Thou canst not stir a flower, without the troubling of a star." '

'Now on Friday morning I want to explore this subject further by taking half the class out on a Nature Trail. The other half can join Mr Billington's art class and their turn will come next Friday.

'Now, Keenan. Using your scientific mind, could you explain how trees get water up to their higher branches?'

'Capillary action, osmosis and atmospheric pressure, sir.'

'Explain capillary action, please.'

'Well' said the Prof. 'If you dip a long strip of blotting paper into a cup of water – the water will slowly rise up the blotting paper. This is capillary action.'

'Very good explanation Keenan. But according to science, capillary action, osmosis and atmospheric pressure can push the water in a tree up to the height of about 100 feet. Yet some trees – like the Australian Eucalyptus can grow to the height of 300 feet. How they manage to pump the water so high still remains a mystery.'

The Prof looked glum. Apparently science didn't have all the answers. . . .

★   ★   ★   ★

Philip turned up on Wednesday evening at Baydon Colliery School to watch the Sealyn School team play a practice match. Secretly he hoped that someone might drop out of the team at the last moment and that he'd be asked to play. No one did, and by half-time Baydon Colliery led 1–0. It was a goal brilliantly engineered by their outside right who ran fifty yards down the wing, jinking past two players before centring the ball. The centre-forward threw himself at the ball, and connected amidst a ruck of players. The ball ricocheted off his shin and grazed a post before it ended up in the back of the net.

Philip heard a voice say, 'Brave lad', and turning he saw Mr Evans dressed in an old tweed jacket and smoking a briar pipe.

'Hello, sir. I didn't know you liked football.'

'I love the game, Maddison,' replied the teacher, enthusiastically. 'It has all the elements of classical drama, skill, unpredictability – a villain – a hero, with occasional moves which have an almost poetical beauty.

'Of course, there's not always a story-book ending, for the script isn't written beforehand. In football, fate and the elements always take a hand.' Mr Evans looked at Philip. 'But why aren't you playing, Maddison? You're not injured, are you?'

Philip blushed. 'I've never been able to make the grade, sir. I guess I'm just not good enough.'

'Why not? Do you practise?'

'Yes, sir. But although I know how to play in theory – I can't do it when I'm playing for real.' Mr Evans looked thoughtful. 'Well – I can spare a couple of hours on Saturday morning. If your parents are agreeable, I'll meet you down on Sealyn Beach around ten o'clock. I believe the tide will be out. . . . And bring your football.'

'Gosh! Thanks sir!'

$$\star \qquad \star \qquad \star \qquad \star$$

Friday morning, the day of the proposed 'Nature Trail', dawned clear and Philip was happy to do as Mr Evans suggested. . . . He thanked the sun for shining, for if it had been raining, the expedition would certainly have been cancelled.

Nine pupils – one half of the class – Bully Baxter, Stewart, Smithers, Stevie, Prof, Lanky, the Swot, Tubby and Philip accompanied Mr

Evans out of the school gate. It was only when they got around the corner and out of sight of the school that he announced: 'I've hired a mini-bus to take us to the Baydon Black Beach gentlemen.'

'The Black Beach!' gasped Stewart. 'But that's out of bounds sir!'

'I've received permission from the National Coal Board to explore the beach, so let's get cracking. I presume you've all brought your sandwiches?'

The Black Beach lay seven miles up the coast from Sealyn Sands. And while the Sealyn sands were a bright surf-washed yellow, the Black Beach was a bizarre mixture of colours. For twenty years coal and shale dust had been poured into the sea and the level of the sands at Baydon had been slowly raised as waves spread the coal dust up to the edge of the limestone cliffs. As time passed, the colour of the beach had turned black. Soon the shore became shelved until gradually the waves began to fall well short of the cliffs. Now the sea had been forced back to a distance of nearly a mile from the cliff face. Marram grass had sprung up, followed by wild sea flowers; Common Tamarisk, Sea Campion, Bloody Cranesbill, Purple Thistle, Green Seablite and Golden Samphire. There were also great clumps of bleached driftwood strewn upon the vast beach, and due to chemical reaction, oxides caused red blushes to appear on the blackened sands, and these colours were in turn mingled with green and yellow sulphur marks.

Rare birds and butterflies, completely undisturbed, had found their way to the strange beach and made it their home. Because of the high cliffs, no one could descend and the one straggling footpath was barred by a fence warning off any would-be trespassers. It was an untouched wilderness, a paradise for wild life.

The first thing the boys did under Mr Evans's supervision was to build a small bonfire under the lee of the shelving beach. As the wind blew off the land, it was sheltered and with the sun shining clear in the late August sky the air was pleasantly warm. The fire was built to boil water so that the boys could have tea with their sandwiches. As the logs burned, Mr Evans pointed to the strange colours of the flames; red, green and yellow – due to the wood being impregnated with sea salt. He also remarked on 'lambent' flames. These flames played on the surface of the driftwood without burning the surface. This phenomenon was due to gases escaping from the driftwood and igniting.

Oddly striped 'digger wasps' were their first discovery once their Nature Trail began in earnest. These insects dug themselves small holes in the cleaner sand. Mr Evans explained briefly the difference between wasps and bees, then set the boys out on a 'discovery' ramble.

Amongst lumps of shale and shingle almost at the water's edge, Baxter found a white flower strangely fragile and incongruous against the black shore. He called out with a yell to Mr Evans who identified it as Sea Campion. Baxter wanted to take a section to grow at home, but Mr Evans pointed out that the sea and sand didn't inhabit Baxter's front garden and that the plant would die in such an alien environment.

Mr Evans told the boys about sea currents, about whales and porpoises and how gigantic marine forests had been found near Tierra del Guego with monster sea-weed growing nearly six hundred feet high.

Were these plants related to Baxter's flower, asked the Swot?

'Everything is linked in some way or another,' said Mr Evans. 'When a man looks through a telescope he sees a cluster of objects in space. When he peers through a microscope he sees a similar pattern as if to show that the same agency is at work. A sparrow, without being taught, recognizes a kestrel as an enemy. A swallow can find its way to South Africa. A pigeon is born with a star map in his head and homing instinct within its breast. Not in its tiny brain,' added Mr Evans – 'but in the pigeon *spirit*.'

'I don't understand when you say everything is linked,' said Philip, puzzled.

'Look,' said Mr Evans. 'We all need the sun – otherwise we couldn't survive. It's the same for plants and animals, they'd die too. And when we eat our food it's a kind of sacrament – so long as we eat the plant or vegetable in the right way. This is why people used to say Grace before meal times.

'An apple will thank you if you eat it in the right way. If you don't – you'll get bellyache. Right Baxter?'

'Dunno sir.'

'Try it Baxter. Have any of you heard of the experiments with plants. How even the scientists have proved that plants are sensitive and feel things?'

'Science is the greatest of all arts,' murmured Keenan dreamily.

'Mmm. I'm not sure about that,' said Mr Evans. 'Remember,

'I love the game, Maddison,' replied the teacher, enthusiastically.

Professor, that poets knew that plants were sensitive at least two thousand years before the scientists actually proved it by experiment.'

Keenan blinked. 'What instruments did they use sir?' he asked, face lined with suspicion.

'Intuition, Professor. And sensitivity. They found in a deeper part of themselves something which was linked to all things – showing that we are all interrelated. Have you ever spoken to a tree or smiled at the sun, Keenan?'

Keenan took off his spectacles and polished them gravely. 'You're surely not serious, sir?'

'Trees are the highest vegetables on the earth, Professor, the humans the highest animals – so why shouldn't they be friends? And as for the sun – which scientist discovered that?'

'It was already there, sir,' said the Prof.

'Exactly,' smiled Mr Evans. 'And can you tell me what has been discovered that wasn't *already* there?'

Deep thought lines bit into the Professor's brow. 'Theoretically – nothing, sir,' he answered at last. 'Because to be discovered – it already *had* to be there.'

'You're learning fast, Professor. Next question – what or who put all the things discovered and all the things *to be* discovered there?'

'I've yet to discover that, sir.'

'Drop me a line when you do,' said Mr Evans with a wry smile.

For the rest of the morning Mr Evans tried to let each boy express himself in his own way. Smithers wrote poetry about his experiences at the Black Beach. The Prof compiled a scientific thesis on the relationship between the environment and the multitude of plants and creatures growing and living at Baydon. The Swot made a list of plants, birds, weeds and butterflies, helped by Stewart who copied and sketched leaf formations, colourings and characteristics of plant and bird life.

Baxter climbed up to a high ledge with some crayons and a sketch pad and sketched the unusual scene which unfurled before him. Philip wrote an essay titled 'My day on Baydon Beach' and described his own feelings as a new world unfolded before his eyes.

'Can we do this more often sir?' asked Philip as they got ready to leave the beach at lunchtime. 'Of course,' said Mr Evans. 'We'll get out as much as possible and visit the Wild Fowl Trust, the parks, woods and other areas of the beach. But if you've enjoyed yourselves, why not take the initiative and form small groups – learning to look after yourselves – discovering for yourselves. Or if you wish to go alone, take your note-pad and sketch book and keep your eyes open. Be observant and you'll be amazed at what life has to tell you.

'Most people are so busy thinking about their own petty affairs that they never "see" the amazing world of Nature. So look out for every thing from the star constellations in the heavens to the daisies in the fields – and if you do it gently without trying to grab at the beauty of life – its spirit may bring you a gift much more precious than gold.'

★　　★　　★　　★

'Why is it that everything becomes so much more interesting when Mr Evans is around?' asked Philip's mother at Saturday morning breakfast.

Philip shrugged. 'Because he's different I suppose.'

'Different!?' His dad looked over the top of his newspaper. 'In what way?'

' 'Cos he seems to make ordinary things come alive,' said Philip. 'Take that water in your tea-cup. Where did it come from?'

'Out of the tank of course,' answered his father in astonishment. 'Where else?'

'But before that it was in the river or the sea, and before that maybe as a cloud passing over Russia. . . .'

Philip's dad looked at his tea with new found suspicion. 'Russian tea, you mean?!'

'I don't mean that, dad,' protested Philip. 'Everything is linked Mr Evans says. If it wasn't for the sun there'd be no tea, or people to drink it. No cows in the field to eat the grass and make the milk. No sugar cane and tea plants in foreign countries and ships that fetch them here. All that goes into making your cup of tea dad.'

'Knowing all that doesn't make it *taste* any different though,' said Philip's dad.

★　　★　　★　　★

When Philip arrived on the beach Mr Evans was already there, scouring the horizon with his binoculars. But as soon as Philip approached he laid them down.

'Good morning! Now – about this football, young Philip!'

'Good morning sir. Thank-you for coming.'

First Mr Evans helped Philip practise passing, trapping and heading the ball, then after half an hour he smiled. 'That's fine! Now you try and get past me with the ball at your feet and I'll tackle you. . . .'

Straight away Philip blundered, either pushing the ball too far forward or getting caught in possession. At the sixth attempt a frown of concentration puckered Philip's face – but as usual, the harder he tried, the worse he played.

Finally Mr Evans picked up the ball and beckoned Philip to him. 'Now when you see Pelé or Best playing soccer – what strikes you?'

'Their skill sir?'

'Apart from that?'

'Don't know sir.'

'How "natural" they appear? You see they are *relaxed*, almost casual, for their game is *instinctive*. Your game Philip is all in your head. You've got to trust your body and the *moment* of challenge to show you what to do.'

'How do you mean sir?'

'Well – you know the usual technique – how to pass, trap and head a ball. But when it comes to beating your man, you hesitate. So learn to trust yourself. Throw away all the clever ideas and take the situation as it comes.

'In a man to man situation you can take your eyes off the ball. Make a move one way. Tempt your man. Watch him. Once you've thrown him off balance use that moment to push the ball past him – and he's left tackling your shadow. Come on – try it!'

An hour passed – but Philip didn't improve at all and at the end of two hours he doubted his ability more than ever. At least now he knew that Mr Evans wasn't a miracle worker.

A cloud crossed the sun and at the same time a big black shadow passed over Philip's secret dream to become a professional footballer. Finally, Philip grew tired and dispirited, until Mr Evans suggested they call it a day.

As they reached the coast road Mr Evans spoke: 'I'm thinking of starting a school newspaper Philip. We can use some of the material we collected on the Baydon Beach expedition for a start, and there'll be room for various articles, quizzes, drawings puzzles and short stories. As there was so much promise in your essay on your day at the Black Beach – perhaps you'd like to do a football report on the next game played by the school team?'

'Football reporter . . . ?' said Philip, half to himself. The dream had escaped from the shadows, and this time it was more realistic. . . .

'It's nothing much, I know,' prompted Mr Evans, 'But it'll be a beginning.'

'Yes sir,' said Philip. 'I'd like to write about football matches very much!'

As Philip walked home to his dinner the sun came out and a brighter dream glowed in his heart.

AN ESCAPADE AT THE JOLLY HERRING
Frederic W. Farrar

> 'Tis one thing to be tempted, Escalus,
> Another thing to fall.
> *Measure for Measure, Act II, Scene I*

'The Anti-muffs request the honour of Eric Williams's company to a spread they are going to have tomorrow evening at half past four, in their smoking-room.'

A note to this effect was put into Eric's hand with much *empressement* by Wildney after prayers. He read it when he got into his study, and hardly knew whether to be pleased or disgusted at it.

He tossed it to Duncan, and said, 'What shall I do?'

Duncan turned up his nose, and chucked the note into the fire.

'I'd give them that answer, and no other.'

'Why?'

'Because, Eric,' said Duncan, with more seriousness than was usual with him, 'I can't help thinking things have gone too far lately.'

'How do you mean?'

'Well, I'm no saint myself, Heaven knows; but I do think that the fellows are worse now than I have ever known them – far worse. Your friend Brigson reigns supreme out of the studies; he has laid down a law that *no work* is to be done downstairs ever under any pretence, and it's only by getting into one of the studies that good little chaps like Wright can get on at all. Even in the classrooms there's so much row and confusion that the mere thought of work is ridiculous.'

'Well, there's no great harm in a little noise, if that's all.'

'But it isn't all. The talk of nearly the whole school is getting most blackguardly; shamelessly so. Only yesterday Wildney was chatting with Vernon up here (you were out, or Vernon would not have been here) while I was reading; they didn't seem to mind me, and I'm sure you'd have been vexed to the heart if you'd heard how they talked to each other. At last I couldn't stand it any longer, and bouncing up, I boxed both their ears smartly, and kicked them downstairs.'

As Eric said nothing, Duncan continued, 'And I wish it ended in talk, but—'

'But I believe you're turning Owenite. Why, bless me, we're only schoolboys; it'll be lots of time to turn saint some other day.'

Eric was talking at random, and in the spirit of opposition. 'You don't want to make the whole school such a muffish set as the Rosebuds, do you?'

There was something of assumed bravado in Eric's whole manner which jarred on Duncan exceedingly, 'Do as you like,' he said, curtly, and went into another study.

Immediately after came a rap at the door, and in walked Wildney, as he often did after the rest were gone to bed, merely slipping his trousers over his night-shirt, and running up to the studies.

'Well, you'll come to the Anti-muffs, won't you?' he said.

'To that pestilential place again? – not I.'

Wildney looked offended. 'Not after we've all asked you? The fellows won't half like your refusing.'

He had touched Eric's weak point.

'Do come,' he said, looking up in Eric's face.

'Confound it all,' answered Eric, hastily. 'Yes, I've no friends, I'll come, Charlie. Anything to please you, boy.'

'That's a brick. Then I shall cut down and tell the fellows. They'll be no end glad. No friends! what bosh! why, all the school like you.' And he scampered off, leaving Eric ill at ease.

Duncan didn't re-enter the study that evening.

The next day, about half-past four, Eric found himself on the way to Ellan. As he was starting, Ball caught him up and said –

'Are you going to the Anti-muffs?'

'Yes; why? are you going too?'

'Yes; do you mind our going together?'

'Not at all.'

In fact, Eric was very glad of someone – no matter who – to keep him in countenance, for he felt considerably more than half ashamed of himself.

They went to 'The Jolly Herring', as the pothouse was called, and passed through the dingy beery tap-room into the back parlour, to which Eric had already been introduced by Wildney. About a dozen boys were assembled, and there was a great clapping as the two new-comers entered. A long table was laid down the room, which was regularly spread for dinner.

'Now then, Billy; make haste with the goose,' called Brigson. 'I vote, boys, that Eric Williams takes the chair.'

'Hear! hear!' said half a dozen; and Eric, rather against his will, found himself ensconced at the end of the table, with Brigson and Ball on either hand. The villainous low-foreheaded man, whom they called Billy, soon brought in a tough goose at one end of the table, and some fowls at the other; and they fell to, doing ample justice to the δαίζ εἴση, while Billy waited on them. There was immense uproar during the dinner, everyone eating as fast, and talking as loud, as he could.

The birds soon vanished, and were succeeded by long roly-poly puddings, which the boys called Goliahs; and they, too, rapidly disappeared. Meanwhile beer was circling only too plentifully.

'Now for the dessert, Billy,' called several voices; and that worthy proceeded to put on the table some figs, cakes, oranges, and four black bottles of wine. There was a general grab for these dainties, and one boy shouted, 'I say. I've had no wine.'

'Well, it's all gone. We must get some brandy – it's cheaper,' said Brigson; and accordingly some brandy was brought in, which the boys diluted with hot water, and soon dispatched.

'Here! before you're all done swilling,' said Brigson, 'I've got a health: "Confound muffs and masters, and success to the antis".'

'And their chairman,' suggested Wildney.

'Confound muffs and masters, and success to the antis.'

'And their chairman, the best fellow in the school,' added Brigson.

The health was drunk with due clamour, and Eric (ridiculous and meaningless as he thought the toast) got up to thank them.

'I'm not going to spout,' he said; 'but boys must be boys, and there's no harm in a bit of fun. I for one have enjoyed it, and am much obliged to you for asking me; and now I call for a song.'

'Wildney! Wildney's song,' called several.

Wildney had a good voice, and struck up without the least bashfulness –

> 'Come, landlord, fill the flowing bowl
> Until it does run over!
> Come, landlord, fill,' etc.

'Now,' he said, 'join in the chorus!' The boys, all more or less excited, joined in heartily and uproariously—

> 'For to-night we'll merry merry be!
> For to-night we'll merry merry be!
> For to-night we'll merry merry be!
> To-morrow we'll be sober!'

While Wildney sang, Eric had time to think. As he glanced round the room at the flushed faces of the boys, some of whom he could not recognize in the dusky atmosphere, a qualm of disgust and shame passed over him. Several of them were smoking, and, with Ball and Brigson heading the line on each side of the table, he could not help observing what a bad set they looked. The remembrance of Russell came back to him. Oh, if Edwin could have known that he was in such company at such a place! And by the door stood Billy, watching them all like an evil spirit, with a leer of saturnine malice on his evil face.

But the bright little Wildney, unconscious of Eric's bitter thoughts, sang on with overflowing mirth. As Eric looked at him shining out like a sunbeam among the rest, he felt something like blood-guiltiness on his soul, when he felt that he was sanctioning the young boy's presence in that degraded assemblage.

Wildney meanwhile was just beginning the next verse, when he was interrupted by a general cry of 'cavé, cavé'. In an instant the room was in confusion; someone dashed the candles upon the floor, the table was overturned with a mighty crash, and plates, glasses, and bottles rushed onto the ground in shivers. Nearly everyone bolted for the door, which led through the passage into the street; and in their headlong flight and selfishness, they stumbled over each other, and prevented all egress, several being knocked down and bruised in the crush. Others made for the tap-room; but, as they opened the door leading into it, there stood Mr Ready and Mr Gordon! and as it was impossible to pass without being seen, they made no further attempt at escape. All this was the work of a minute. Entering the back parlour the two masters quickly took down the names of full half the boys who, in the suddenness of the surprise, had been unable to make their exit.

And Eric?

The instant that the candles were knocked over, he felt Wildney seize his hand, and whisper, 'This way; all serene'; following, he groped his way in the dark to the end of the room, where Wildney, shoving aside a green baize curtain, noiselessly opened a door, which at once led them into a little garden. There they both crouched down under a lilac tree beside the house, and listened intently.

There was no need for this precaution; their door remained unsuspected, and in five minutes the coast was clear. Creeping into the house again, they whistled, and Billy coming in, told them all was safe.

'Glad ye're not twigged, gen'lmen,' he said; 'but there'll be a pretty sight of damage for all this glass and plates.'

'Shut up with your glass and plates,' said Wildney. 'Here, Eric, we must cut for it again.'

It was the dusk of a winter evening when they got out from the close room into the open air, and they had to consider which way they would choose to avoid discovery. They happened to choose the wrong, but escaped by dint of hard running, and Wildney's old short cut. As they ran they passed several boys (who, having been caught, were walking home leisurely), and managed to get back undiscovered, when they both answered their names quite innocently at the roll-call, immediately after lock-up.

'What lucky dogs you are to get off,' said many boys to them.

'Yes; it's precious lucky for me,' said Wildney. 'If I'd been caught at this kind of thing a second time, I should have got something worse than a swishing.'

'Well, it's all through you I escaped,' said Eric, 'you knowing little scamp.'

'I'm glad of it, Eric,' said Wildney, in his fascinating way, 'since it was all through me you went. It's rather too hazardous though; we must manage better another time.'

During tea-time Eric was silent, as he felt pretty sure that none of the sixth form or other study-boys would particularly sympathize with his late associates. Since the previous evening he had been cool with Duncan, and the rest had long rather despised him as a boy who'd do anything to be popular; so he sat there silent, looking as disdainful as he could, and not touching the tea, for which he felt disinclined after the recent potations. But the contemptuous exterior hid a self-reproving heart, and he felt how far more noble Owen and Montagu were than he. Now gladly would he have changed places with them! how much he would have given to recover some of their forfeited esteem!

The master on duty was Mr Rose, and after tea he left the room for a few minutes while the tables were cleared for 'preparation', and the boys were getting out their books and exercises. All the study- and classroom boys were expected to go away during this interval; but Eric, not noticing Mr Rose's entrance, sat gossiping with Wildney about the dinner and its possible consequences to the school.

He was sitting on the desk carelessly, with one leg over the other, and bending down towards Wildney. He had just told him that he looked like a regular little sunbeam in the smoking-room of the Jolly Herring, and Wildney was pretending to be immensely offended by the simile.

'Hush! no more talking,' said Mr Rose, who did everything very gently and quietly. Eric heard him, but he was inclined to linger, and had always received such mild treatment from Mr Rose, that he didn't think he would take much notice of the delay. For the moment he did not, so Wildney began to chatter again.

'All study-boys to leave the room,' said Mr Rose.

Eric just glanced round and moved slightly; he might have gone away, but that he caught a satirical look in Wildney's eye, and besides wanted to show off a little indifference to his old master, with whom he had had no intercourse since their last-mentioned conversation.

'Williams, go away instantly; what do you mean by staying after I have dismissed you?' said Mr Rose sternly.

Everyone knew what a favourite Eric had once been, so this speech created a slight titter. The boy heard it just as he was going out of the room, and it annoyed him, and called to arms all his proud and dogged obstinacy. Pretending to have forgotten something, he walked conceitedly back to Wildney, and whispered to him, 'I shan't go if he chooses to speak like that.'

A red flush passed over Mr Rose's cheek; he took two strides to Eric, and laid the cane sharply once across his back.

Eric was not quite himself, or he would not have acted as he had done. His potations, though not deep, had, with the exciting events of the evening, made his head giddy, and the stroke of the cane, which he had not felt now for two years, roused him to madness. He bounded up, sprang towards Mr Rose, and almost before he knew what he was about, had wrenched the cane out of his hands, twisted it violently in the middle until it broke, and flung one of the pieces furiously into the fire.

For one instant, boy and master – Eric Williams and Mr Rose – stood facing each other amid breathless silence, the boy panting and passionate, with his brain swimming, and his heart on fire; the master pale, grieved, amazed beyond measure, but perfectly self-collected.

'After that exhibition,' said Mr Rose, with cold and quiet dignity, 'you had better leave the room.'

'Yes I had,' answered Eric bitterly; 'there's your cane.' And, flinging the other fragment at Mr Rose's head, he strode blindly out of the room, sweeping books from the table, and overturning several boys in his way. He then banged the door with all his force, and rushed up into his study.

Duncan was there, and remarking his wild look and demeanour, asked, after a moment's awkward silence, 'Is anything the matter, Williams?'

'Williams!' echoed Eric with a scornful laugh; 'yes, that's always the way with a fellow when he's in trouble. I always know what's coming when you begin to leave off calling me by my Christian name.'

'Very well, then,' said Duncan good-humouredly, 'what's the matter, Eric?'

'Matter?' answered Eric, pacing up and down the little room with an

233

angry to-and-fro like a caged wild beast, and kicking everything which came in his way; 'matter? hang you all, you are all turning against me, because you are a set of muffs, and—'

'Take care!' said Duncan; but suddenly he caught Eric's look, and stopped.

'—And I've been breaking Rose's cane over his head, because he had the impudence to touch me with it, and—'

'Eric, you're not yourself tonight,' said Duncan, interrupting, but speaking in the kindest tone; and taking Eric's hand, he looked him steadily in the face.

Their eyes met; the boy's false self once more slipped off. By a strong effort he repressed the rising passion which the fumes of drink had caused, and flinging himself on his chair, refused to speak again, or even to go downstairs when the prayer-bell rang

Seeing that in his present mood there was nothing to be done with him, Duncan, instead of returning to the study, went after prayers into Montagu's, and talked with him over the recent events, of which the boys' minds were all full.

But Eric sat lonely, sulky, and miserable, in his study, doing nothing, and when Montagu came in to visit him, felt inclined to resent his presence.

'So!' he said, looking up at the ceiling, 'another saint come to cast a stone at me! Well! I suppose I must be resigned,' he continued, dropping his cheek on his hand again; 'only don't let the sermon be long.'

But Montagu took no notice of his sardonic harshness, and seated himself by his side, though Eric pettishly pushed him away.

'Come, Eric,' said Montagu, taking the hand which was repelling him; 'I won't be repulsed in this way. Look at me. What? Won't you even look? Oh, Eric, one wouldn't have fancied this in past days, when we were so much together with one who is dead. It's a long time since we've even alluded to him, but *I* shall never forget those happy days.'

Eric heaved a deep sigh.

'I'm not come to reproach you. You don't give me a friend's right to reprove. But still, Eric, for your own sake, dear fellow, I can't help being sorry for all this. I did hope you'd have broken with Brigson after the thrashing I gave him for the foul way in which he treated me. I don't think you *can* know the mischief he is doing.'

The large tears began to soften the fire of Eric's eye. 'Ah!' he said, 'it's all of no use; you're all giving me the cold shoulder, and I'm going to the bad, that's the long and short of it.'

'Oh, Eric! for your own sake, for your parents' sake, for the school's sake, for all your real friends' sake, don't talk in that bitter, hopeless way. You are too noble a fellow to be made the tool or the patron of the boys who lead, while they seem to follow you. I *do* hope you'll join us even yet in resisting them.'

Eric had laid his head on the table, which shook with his emotion. 'I can't talk, Monty,' he said, in an altered tone; 'but leave me now; and if you like, we will have a walk tomorrow.'

'Most willingly, Eric.' And, again warmly pressing his hand, Montagu returned to his own study.

Soon after, there came a timid knock at Eric's door. He expected Wildney as usual; a little before, he had been looking out for him, and hoping he would come, but he didn't want to see him now, so he answered rather peevishly, 'Come in; but I don't want to be bothered tonight.'

Not Wildney, but Vernon appeared at the door. 'May I come in? not if it bothers you, Eric,' he said gently.

'Oh, Verny, I didn't know it was you; I thought it would be Wildney. You *never* come now.'

The little boy came in, and his pleading look seemed to say, 'Whose fault is that?'

'Come here, Verny'; and Eric drew him towards him, and put him on his knee, while the tears trembled large and luminous in the child's eyes.

It was the first time for many a long day that the brothers had been alone together, the first time for many a long day that any acts of kindness had passed between them. Both seemed to remember this, and, at the same time, to remember home, and their absent parents, and their mother's prayers, and all the quiet half-forgotten vista of innocent pleasures, and sacred relationships, and holy affections. And why did they see each other so little at school? Their consciences told them both, that either wished to conceal from the other his wickedness and forgetfulness of God.

They wept together; and once more, as they had not done since they were children, each brother put his arm round the other's neck. And remorseful Eric could not help being amazed how, in his cruel heartless selfishness, he had let that fair child go so far far astray; left him as a prey to such boys as were his companions in the lower school.

'Eric, did you know I was caught tonight at the dinner?'

'You!' said Eric, with a start and a deep blush. 'Good heavens! I didn't notice you, and should not have dreamt of coming, if I'd known you were there. Oh, Vernon, forgive me for setting you such a bad example.'

'Yes, I was there, and I was caught.'

'Poor boy! but never mind; there are such a lot that you can't get much done to you.'

'It isn't *that* I care for; I've been flogged before, you know. But – may I say something?'

'Yes, Vernon, anything you like.'

'Well, then – oh, Eric! I'm *so so* sorry that you did that to Mr Rose tonight. All the fellows are praising you up, of course; but I could have cried to see it, and I did. I wouldn't have minded if it had been anybody but Rose.'

'But why?'

'Because, Eric, he's been so good, so kind to both of us. You've often told me about him, you know, at Fairholm, and he's done such lots of kind things to me. And only tonight, when he heard I was caught, he sent for me to the library, and spoke so firmly, yet so gently, about the wickedness of going to such low places, and about so young a boy as I am learning to drink, and the ruin of it – and – and' – his voice was choked by sobs for a time – 'and then he knelt down and prayed for me, so as I have never heard anyone pray but mother; and do you know, Eric, it was strange, but I thought, I *did* hear our mother's voice praying for me too, while he prayed, and' – he tried in vain to go on; but Eric's conscience continued for him; 'and just as he had ceased doing this for one brother, the other brother, for whom he has often done the same, treated him with coarseness, violence, and insolence.'

'Oh, I am utterly wretched, Verny. I hate myself. And to think that while I'm like this, they are yet loving and praising me at home. And, oh, Verny, I was so sorry to hear from Duncan how you were talking the other day.'

Vernon hid his face on Eric's shoulder; and as his brother stooped over him and folded him to his heart, they cried in silence, for there seemed no more to say, until wearied with sorrow, the younger fell asleep; and then Eric carried him tenderly downstairs, and laid him, still half-sleeping, upon his bed.

He laid him down, and looked at him as he slumbered. The other boys had not been disturbed by their noiseless entrance, and he sat down on his brother's bed to think, shading off the light of the candle with his hand. It was rarely now that Eric's thoughts were so rich with the memories of childhood, and sombre with the consciousness of sin, as they were that night, while he gazed on his brother Vernon's face. He did not know what made him look so long and earnestly; an indistinct sorrow, an unconjectured foreboding, passed over his mind, like the shadow of a summer cloud. Vernon was now slumbering deeply; his soft childish curls fell off his forehead, and his head nestled in the pillow; but there was an expression of uneasiness on his sleeping features, and the long eyelashes were still wet with tears.

'Poor child,' thought Eric; 'dear little Vernon: and he is to be flogged, perhaps birched, tomorrow.'

He went off sadly to bed, and hardly once remembered that *he* too would come in for certain punishment the next day.

THE ALPHA-WAVE EXPERIMENT
Anthea Courtenay

That Friday night only three people from Form M noticed anything strange in the sky. Only Annabel Lewis, Timmy Norton and Gerry Moodie were awake, for different reasons.

Annabel was staring despondently out of her window. She'd got up after lying for hours worrying about the forthcoming exams. 'Worrying won't help,' her father was always saying, but that only made Annabel worry about how to stop worrying.

Timmy was looking through a telescope which he had rehabilitated from pieces bought in a junk-shop. He was a dark, rosy-cheeked boy with spectacles, sometimes known as 'Professor', more often as 'Tiny Tim'. Occasionally he wished he could acquire another few inches, but mostly he was too interested in what was going on around him to be bothered by his lack of height.

Gerry was puffing cigarette smoke out of his window and wondering how best to annoy their form teacher, Miss Howarth, next Monday. She'd been picking on him again, called him a lazy, idle trouble-maker. Right, if that's what she thought, that's what he'd be.

What all three saw was very brief but quite clear. At 2 a.m. precisely the sky towards the west, where Fellfields Comprehensive School lay, turned a brilliant orange. The glow made the three watchers blink, and for moments afterwards the sky looked green. Then, as their vision cleared, they saw a round red light descending slowly at an angle of forty-five degrees. Above the school roof it made an enquiring sort of circle, before resuming its descent and disappearing somewhere behind the school buildings. It was all over in less than two minutes.

At breakfast Annabel said, 'I saw something funny in the sky last night'.

'Oh, Annabel!' wailed her mother, 'couldn't you get to sleep again? You are a worry, dear, really!' That was another thing that worried Annabel; her own worrying got her mother worried too.

When she met her friend Aileen as usual on the way to school she asked her if she'd seen anything, but Aileen began talking about the disco she was going to that night. 'You coming, Annabel?'

'Depends how much homework we get. You know my mum. . . .'

Perhaps she'd dreamed it. She did have very vivid dreams.

★ ★ ★ ★

The following Monday Miss Howarth didn't turn up for registration, and Form M was getting restive in its own unique fashion when Mrs Bins, the Deputy Head, came in accompanied by a stranger. 'Is this the senior class in the Lower School or the monkey house at the zoo?' she demanded.

Gerry Moodie began scratching himself and making gibbering noises.

'That'll *do*! Gerry, that's completely childish. *Quiet*! I want your attention, please. I'm sorry to tell you that Miss Howarth is ill with glandular fever. Mr Falconer will be taking over in her absence.'

A buzz broke out.

'Miss! Miss! What's glandular fever?'

'Isn't it something pigs get?' That was Gerry.

'We can't do our exams now, can we?'

'If it's infectious perhaps we should all go home,' suggested Timmy.

Mrs Bins raised her hand for silence. 'Glandular fever is non-infectious, and has nothing to do with pigs, Gerry – unless there is some connection with the strain of having to teach you. Now, will you please show Mr Falconer that you can behave like normal, responsible human beings, and give him all the help you can?' At the door she added, with some satisfaction, 'Your exams will take place as usual.'

Thirty pairs of eyes stared appraisingly at the supply teacher. He was tall, slim, young, with dark hair and a short beard. He looked round, half-smiling, meeting the eyes of each individual in turn. Annabel had never seen such dark eyes; almost black, they were – and disconcerting. It seemed as if the whole of her had been taken in and judged in one glance.

After taking the register, Mr Falconer perched himself on Miss Howarth's desk, one long leg swinging, and said, 'Fine. As I may be around for some time, let's get to know each other. I'd like you to do a little test for me.' There were groans at this, but he went on: 'OK, let's call it an experiment, since you don't like the word "test". Tell me, do any of you ever get told off for day-dreaming?' Annabel was among those who nodded. 'Well, I *want* you to day-dream. I want you to sit quite comfortable and relaxed, and close your eyes. . . .'

One or two people giggled, but Mr Falconer had Form M's interest. 'Yes, all of you – and just imagine you're somewhere very pleasant. Anywhere you like – by the sea, maybe, in a garden, a skating rink, whatever.'

Annabel closed her eyes. Imagining herself away from this classroom with its peeling yellow paint was something she often did. This time, though, it was different. She knew perfectly well that she was sitting in her school desk, with Jennifer Pims – who had a permanent cold – snuffling beside her. But at the same time, what she experienced was totally real. She was floating, hovering, over a green field rich with wild flowers. In the distance she could see mountains and the sea, and below her a little round white building surrounded by pillars, like a temple. She sailed towards it, came gently to earth, and started up the steps—'

'Open your eyes.' Mr Falconer's voice cut through the silence.

Annabel opened heavy eyes and looked at Jennifer, who was blinking in a dazed fashion. She felt dazed herself, but calm and peaceful too, as though she could float through the rest of the day without worrying once.

Mr Falconer continued: 'Now, I want you to write down a description of what you imagined. Have you all got paper?'

For a few minutes the class wrote feverishly. Mr Falconer glanced rapidly through their papers, stacked them together and said, 'Thank you all very much. Interesting.'

Everyone felt vaguely let down. Wasn't he going to say any more?

Timmy Norton said, 'Sir, do you do speed-reading?'

He smiled. 'I'll read them properly later.'

The dinner money was collected and the bell rang for the first class. Before he left, Mr Falconer said quietly to Annabel, 'Oh, Annabel, would you come and see me here during break?'

Surprised that he already knew her name, and wondering what she'd done wrong, Annabel felt the familiar little worm of worry creep back into her stomach. But she still felt so nice and floaty that she couldn't stay anxious for long. Nor did she notice that Gerry Moodie had overheard Mr Falconer's quiet summons.

When he came in at break-time, she saw he was holding the paper she'd written. He gave her a reassuring smile. 'Sit down, Annabel. I was very interested in what you wrote this morning – you've got a vivid imagination, as I daresay you know.'

Annabel felt her freckled cheeks go pink.

'And that's why I'm going to ask your help in a further experiment. You don't have to, but I'll explain what it's about, and you can decide, OK? Curious, she nodded again. 'You may know,' he went on slowly, 'that many scientists believe that people only use a tiny proportion of their actual brain-power. Now, I'm taking part in a survey on learning methods, sponsored by a group that's found a natural way of tapping the brain's electrical energy so that you can use your mind much more efficiently.'

The words 'survey', 'learning methods' and 'sponsored' reminded Annabel of something. She frowned.

Mr Falconer laughed. 'It's OK, I'm not selling junior encyclopedias, and it won't cost you anything – or your parents.' Annabel smiled too – that was exactly what she'd been thinking of. 'In fact, if you do take part in this you mustn't say anything to anyone; it could destroy the value of the experiment. Now, what it consists of is this. . . .'

Ten minutes later Annabel left the classroom deep in thought, and bumped into Gerry Moodie. He often seemed to be hanging around where she was, and she wished he wouldn't.

'What did *he* want then?' demanded Gerry, scuffing the toe of his boot on the stone floor.

'Nothing much. Just wanted to talk about my composition.'

'Oh yeah? More likely he fancies you.'

'Oh, don't be stupid!' Annabel turned away, wishing she didn't blush so easily.

Gerry called after her: 'But he hadn't read your composition when he told you to come and see him!'

Annabel walked off, not really listening.

★   ★   ★   ★

Annabel sat in her room that evening, staring curiously at the object Mr Falconer had given her. It was a rectangular pendant on a chain, made of a darkish metal, with an intricate design that reminded her of the insides of a transistor. An alpha-inducer, he'd called it; it would help her to use her brain properly, do her homework in half the time, remember the answers to things straight away instead of getting all nervous – it all sounded fantastic. She couldn't really understand how it worked, but they'd had what he called a practice run, and there was nothing to it. Back there in the classroom with Mr Falconer, the experiment had seemed quite normal, ordinary, even. Now though, now she was alone, it seemed a strange thing to be doing.

Here goes. She closed her eyes and held the pendant to her forehead. Immediately, she experienced the same pleasant, tingling sensation in her head and down her spine as she had during the practice run, and the same delicious floatiness. . . . Five minutes, he'd told her, no more, and though she could have gone on much longer she opened her eyes after a while and looked at her watch. Four and a half minutes – not bad.

There was a French vocabulary list to learn. She took out her book, read the page quickly, closed her eyes – and found that she could remember every word, as though she were still looking at the page.

'*Fantastic!*' whispered Annabel, another sort of tingle going down her spine. She turned to her history book. There was a chapter they were being tested on tomorrow. . . .

When she finally got to sleep that night she dreamed she was again floating towards the little white temple. If only she could get inside,

Then she was inside the Temple and inside the golden glow.

she knew there was something very precious in there. But as she began to climb the steps, her mother's voice hauled her into morning. 'Annabel! For goodness' sake, you'll be late for school!'

★   ★   ★   ★

By Friday Annabel had come out top in just about every subject for the entire week. It was all so *easy*. Anything she read after using the alpha-inducer, she could remember. In class the answers popped into her mind and out of her mouth like toast out of a toaster. It wasn't just her memory that was getting better: she found she could reason things out more easily too. Only one thing she couldn't work out – why hadn't he given these things to everyone? Why *her*?

The Falcon – as Mr Falconer inevitably came to be called – gave no indication that he'd picked Annabel out for something special. In fact he was one of the fairest teachers Form M had ever come across; even Gerry Moodie, who pursued a policy of unremitting non-cooperation with all teachers, came in for the Falcon's praise.

'This is a good composition, Gerry,' he said, during one English lesson. The subject he'd given them was 'The School of the Future.' Gerry glowered; he felt he was being got at. 'Read much science fiction, do you?'

Gerry nodded. 'A bit.'

'Maybe you'll end up as a sci-fi writer yourself one day.' The Falcon read from Gerry's almost illegible scrawl: ' "In the school of the future there won't be any exams . . ." I hope you're right, Gerry, exams are no way to judge people.' Most of Form M looked slightly shocked. Mr Falconer's dark eyes were fixed somewhere out of the window. 'Exams, competitiveness, one-upmanship – it's all *wrong*! People talk about progress, when they mean pollution, more efficient means of killing more people. . . . So,' he turned back to the class. 'How could we do things differently? Gerry, I'd like to hear some more of your ideas. Supposing the future were *now*?'

There was an expectant pause during which the Falcon's eyes met Gerry's and held them. But Gerry, crimson-faced and mute, slumped further into his seat, and Tiny Tim Norton began jumping up and down.'

'Sir, Sir! The future *is* now, isn't it? For people from the past?'

During the lively discussion that followed, Annabel fingered the pendant hidden under her blouse. If Falconer didn't go along with exams, why had he given her this? Perhaps it wasn't about exams, after all. She'd like to ask him. He'd said he'd see her again soon, but he seemed to have forgotten about her.

She was walking out of the school gate that afternoon when Gerry loomed up beside her. 'I want to talk to you.'

Annabel shrugged. 'Can't stop you, I suppose.'

After a pause, Gerry said: 'How are you doing it?'

'Doing what?'

'Cheating, of course!'

'I'm *not* cheating!' she said furiously.

'Oh, come off it! You've known all the answers to everything for the last week. No-one could be that brainy, and you're not even brainy.'

Annabel stuck her chin out and said, 'It's a well known fact that most people only use a small bit of their brains. I just happen to be using all of mine, that's all.'

'He tell you that did he – the Falcon? Oh, I know he's behind this. It's just since he came, this has happened to you. There's something really weird about that man.'

Annabel stood still. 'What d'you mean?'

'Haven't you noticed? He can read people's minds. He's *getting* at you, Annabel!' Gerry narrowed his eyes. 'Listen, a few nights before he arrived, I saw a UFO landing. No-one else saw it—'

'I did,' said Annabel, and wished she hadn't.

'Well, then, can't you see? *That UFO was the Falcon arriving!*'

'You're mad, Gerry Moodie, it's all that science fiction you read!'

Gerry grabbed her arm. 'He gave you something, didn't he?'

Annabel pulled away. 'No he didn't, nothing – stop *spying* on me! Leave me alone!'

Gerry let her go. She was definitely in the Falcon's clutches, he decided. That man scared him – those dark eyes, the way they could see the whole of you, even the hidden, secret bits. Someone had to put a stop to his activities, and that someone was Gerry Moodie.

$$\star \qquad \star \qquad \star \qquad \star$$

It was during the following week that things began to get really uncomfortable for Annabel. It wasn't just Gerry, whose sombre stare seemed to follow her every move. At first, she tried to believe she was imagining the whispered remarks, the turned backs in the playground, the way Aileen always seemed to be sitting with someone else at dinner. But it got worse. She could almost hear her friend thinking, 'Keep away!'

She decided to test things out. In the cloakroom at the end of school on the Wednesday, she went up to Aileen and said, 'Let's go for an ice-cream before we go home.'

Aileen gave her a dark look. 'I'm going with Jennifer.'

'Well, I can come too, can't I?'

Jennifer Pims appeared from behind the shoe-lockers and said, '*You're* not wanted, Miss Brains of Britain!' She linked arms with Aileen, and they walked out together. Annabel stared after them, feeling hot all over. If only she could *explain*.

Sitting up in bed that night she looked a long time at the pendant round her neck. She hadn't used it before doing her homework that evening. What was the point of using all your brain-power if everyone hated you? And why should she be the only one? It wasn't fair.

Automatically, she pressed the alpha-inducer to her aching forehead. Immediately, the tingle, the sense of peacefulness. She began to think more clearly. Maybe she wasn't the only one. Maybe someone else was secretly experimenting, too. But who . . .? Not Aileen or Jennifer. Not Gerry, with his crazy ideas. Reading people's minds! But wait, was that so crazy? Using more of your mind needn't just mean learning verbs.

She closed her eyes, visualizing the classroom. A picture of Timmy Norton flashed into her mind, jumping up and down, eager to show off his knowledge. But he'd always been like that, bumptious little pig, he hadn't suddenly got cleverer.

'Oh, *show* yourself, whoever you are,' she urged silently.

'Annabel, you're not still reading, are you?' Her mother's voice outside the door made her jump.

'No, Mum,' she said, quickly turning out the light. She snuggled down in bed, still holding the pendant to her brow. Who, who? She didn't want to be alone in this any more . . . have to see Mr Falconer – yes, see the Falcon – ask him. . . .

All at once she was both asleep and not asleep, dreaming and not dreaming. She was walking up the steps of the Temple, and they were solid beneath her feet, though her feet made no sound. From the heart of the building, between the two white pillars ahead of her, came such a golden glow of light that she couldn't make out what was beyond.

Then she was inside the Temple and inside the golden glow. She was in a circular chamber with a domed roof; at its heart a shimmering, sparkling fountain splashed noiselessly into the waters of a round marble pool. From this came the glow that filled the room, turning the white pillars to gold, a dancing light, intense yet fluctuating, making it hard to see anything quite clearly. Only later did she think, 'But light doesn't come from water!'

Standing beside the pool was the Falcon. When she tried to remember it all next morning she knew he had not been dressed in ordinary clothes, but could recall no details – only his face and his eyes and his smile. He didn't speak, but she knew he was telling her he was glad to see her. He gestured towards the entrance opposite the one she had entered by, and she was not at all surprised to see a boy coming in. He came towards her, and they clasped right hands, and Annabel knew she was looking at Timmy Norton, only not Timmy as she knew him: he was Timmy and more besides. And she knew he was seeing Annabel, and more besides.

On their two joined hands the Falcon laid his own. And everything was right; everything was absolutely as it should be.

*   *   *   *

All through lessons next morning Annabel avoided looking at Timmy. At break he came up to her. 'Hey, Annabel, we've got to have a talk – somewhere private!'

'What about the Arts Block? No-one'll see us there.'

As they crossed the playground and entered the empty building, neither of them spoke. Timmy closed the door; still silent, he fished out from under his seater an oblong metal object on a chain. Annabel put her own hand to her collar. The two alpha-inducers were identical.

Annabel stared at him, Tiny Tim Norton, half a head shorter than herself, with a smudge of biro on his cheek. An ordinary boy she'd never much liked. She broke the awkward silence. 'I didn't know – I'd never have guessed—'

Timmy grinned. 'Wasn't hard to guess about you. Top of the class all of a sudden – not very subtle, are you? People were bound to notice.'

'Hasn't it worked with you, then?'

'Oh, it's worked, all right. But I've been – cheating the wrong way round, you could call it.'

Annabel was annoyed with herself for not thinking of that, and annoyed with Timmy for being so smug about it. After a pause, Timmy said,

'Well, you did want to talk to me, didn't you? Last night, you were trying to contact me.'

Annabel felt weak at the knees. 'Telepathy . . .?' she said.

'Telepathy, thought transference . . . I've been picking up quite a lot of people's thoughts lately. I've been practising. It's funny, at first you think it's your own thoughts, or you're just guessing, and then you realize you can sort of tune in to other people.'

Annabel remembered what Gerry had said, remembered feeling she could hear Aileen willing her to stay away at dinner. She nodded.

'And last night,' went on Timmy, 'it was like you were calling, quite loudly.'

'And I didn't know it was you I was calling!'

'Weird, isn't it? We won't need telephones any more! And that's not all these things can make us do!' he added. 'There's precognition, too – that's seeing the future, dimbo. And other things. Listen, I've been reading up about alpha waves – that's the brainwaves people produce when they meditate and do bio-feedback and stuff like that – there's a lot of people doing experiments with them. But not with *these*. I'd love to know where he got *these*. I reckon we've had the equivalent of ten or twenty years' meditating in the last ten days. Mind-blowing, isn't it!'

She wasn't in a golden temple, she was in a large, dusty art room lined with Form R's interpretations of dinosaurs.

'I don't want my mind blown! I don't want to read people's thoughts, and all that stuff. It's scary. Maybe Gerry was right.' She told Timmy about Gerry's theories.

Timmy frowned. 'That's very interesting. Because, I saw that UFO too. And one mind I can't get anywhere near is the Falcon's. It's not like other people's, it sort of gives off different vibes.'

THE ALPHA-WAVE EXPERIMENT

Annabel shivered. 'Let's stop it. Let's give them back.'

'Trouble with you girls is you lack the spirit of scientific enquiry. I want to get all I can out of this. Besides, the more we know, the better we can protect ourselves.'

'Protect? Against what? Who?'

Timmy looked solemn. 'There was a bit in the paper on Sunday about psychic warfare. Using electrical energy to get control of people's minds. The warfare of the future, they called it.'

'What was it he said – about the future being now?'

They stared at each other. 'The question is,' said Annabel, 'whose side is he on? And why does he want *us*?'

'I think Gerry's got it the wrong way round,' said Timmy. 'I'm pretty sure the Falcon's OK.'

Something in his tone made Annabel ask the question she hadn't really wanted to ask. The Temple was her own, private thought-place. 'Timmy, last night, I had a sort of dream. . . . You didn't – ?'

Timmy's eyes met hers and he flushed. 'Yup,' he said briefly, and went on, 'Anyway, the only way to find out what's really going on is to use the alpha-inducers *more*.'

'D'you think we should?'

He made an exasperated gesture. 'Where's the harm? Look, I'll come round to your place on Saturday. Tell your Mum we're doing a project together, OK?'

As they left, Gerry Moodie slipped away from the open window at the side of the building.

★   ★   ★   ★

'*Timmy*! What on earth happened?' It was Saturday morning, and luckily Annabel's mother had gone out shopping, for Tiny Tim Norton was standing on the doorstep in a terrible state: mud on his hands and knees, his sweater torn, his glasses askew, and almost incoherent. She took him quickly to her room, where he sat down spluttering, 'That Gerry! That bully! He must have heard us – he was waiting for me in the park! Bloody hell! If only I was bigger!'

To the embarrassment of both, he burst into tears. Annabel hunted for a hanky in her drawer and handed it to him silently. Timmy blew his nose with a loud masculine trumpeting.

'Annabel . . . he's taken my alpha-inducer!'

She couldn't be annoyed with him, he was suddenly such a little boy. But visions flashed through her mind of what Gerry might do with an alpha-inducer – Gerry, who was so anti everyone and everything.

'We'll have to tell the Falcon,' she said.

'How *can* we? We don't even know where he lives!'

Annabel found herself very cool, very calm. 'There's one place we can find him. The temple.'

Timmy looked at her helplessly.

'If I use my alpha-inducer and we hold hands and think very hard . . . I'm sure we can do it.' She held her hand out to Timmy.

★   ★   ★   ★

In the park there was a summerhouse, used in summer by courting couples. Here Gerry was sitting, examining his loot. So this is what the Falcon had given them. . . . He turned it around held it up to the light, listened to it. He couldn't have said what made him put it to his forehead and close his eyes.

He was slipping, flying, floating unwillingly through an air dense with cloud and fog. It was real and unreal, he knew he could stop, open his eyes, be back in the park, but something held him to the vision. And then he was in a round room, shimmering with light, and Timmy and Annabel were there, but different, strange, and there was something in that room that drew him, beckoned him, tempting him to let his toughness melt, give in . . . give in. . . . And there was the Falcon, staring at him with those all-seeing eyes. He didn't look hostile or angry, and that made him all the more frightening. He put out his hand and Gerry knew what he wanted. 'I won't – give – in!' he tried to say, but no sounds came, and his own hand went out of its own accord.

As the alpha-inducer left his grasp a kind of thud shook his whole being, and he was back in the summerhouse, trembling and furious.

'Imagination!' he muttered. But his hand was empty. 'Must've dropped it!' He searched on the floor, more and more frantically, but the alpha-inducer had most certainly gone.

Must *do* something! Tell Dad! If he told exactly what had happened, no-one would believe him. But there was enough that he could tell, and if he had to embroider a little, well he had to, before everyone found themselves being taken over, like he'd been just now.

★   ★   ★   ★

On Monday morning Mrs Bins took Form M's registration. Mr Falconer had been called away; she said; fortunately Miss Howarth would be back soon. Timmy and Annabel looked at each other, and then they both looked at Gerry Moodie. Without a word spoken, they knew what had happened. And without a word spoken, at break they both headed for the Arts Block.

The Falcon was there, half perched on a desk, one long leg swinging. His hands were plunged into the pockets of his coat, his shoulders hunched. He looked sad, though Annabel, and not grown-up, somehow. But he smiled at them and said quite cheerily:

'Well, you guessed it. No, you *know*, don't you? I've got to leave sooner than I planned. There have been complaints – 'he gave a good imitation of the Headmaster's voice' – Favouritism – trying to hypnotise pupils – wanting to overthrow the exam system – subversive ideas – you name it, I'm guilty.'

'That Gerry!' exploded Tim. 'If I was bigger, I'd—'

'Don't blame Gerry. He was scared, because he didn't understand. He really thought he was doing the right thing. And it wasn't just him. There've been mutterings about "encouraging day-dreaming" right from the start. Parents half-listen to what their kids tell them, and some garbled version gets back to the Head. . . . But yes, Gerry's father went to see the Head yesterday with a pretty strong story.' He rose and walked down the room, examining Form R's dinosaurs. 'What a world!'

He turned, and said, 'You were right, Gerry, it's not *my* world.'

Annabel and Timmy swung round. Gerry was standing in the doorway, a curious expression in his face. Annabel remembered a stray cat that used to come to the door to be fed, and then ran away immediately afterwards, as if expecting to be kicked.

The Falcon went on, 'But I didn't come here to harm you. On the contrary. We've been watching your world for some time, watching the mess humanity's been making of things – how close you are to destroying yourselves – and it's so *unnecessary*! We had to step in.

Everything that happens on Earth affects the rest of the Universe, too. We thought if we could only reach the young, we could help.'

'Help, how?' demanded Gerry.

'Simply by showing you how to use the powers you've already got. Think of using mind-energy to grow bigger and better crops, without having to use chemicals. Think of doctors healing their patients without resorting to drugs and surgery. . . . Oh, there's so many ways. It's all there, in your heads and hearts, every one of you. It's happening already, but it's too *slow*! The alpha-inducers act as a boost. I'm afraid I'll have to take them back, by the way.'

Slowly, Annabel took the pendant from her neck. She was near to tears.

'Why should we believe you?' Gerry persisted. 'How do we know you're not trying to take us over – get control of our minds?'

'You know the answer to that, Gerry. If I'd wanted to control your mind I'd have stopped you saying anything, stopped your father going to the Head. But I had to leave you free. That's part of the deal. Like I've had to leave Timmy and Annabel free to find things out for themselves. I'd have liked to include you in on it – you've probably got the most creative mind in your form. It's only fear that stops you seeing clearly. Well, next time, maybe. . . .'

That night, only three people from Form M saw anything strange in the sky. Timmy, Annabel and Gerry sat at their separate windows, watching the skyline above Fellfields Comprehensive School. At 2 a.m. precisely an orange glow lit the whole sky, and in the green aftermath a red ball lifted slowly from the horizon, circled once round the school in a kind of farewell, and then shot upwards and out of sight.

'He'll be back,' thought Timmy. Across the streets, Annabel heard his thought. 'Yes, he'll be back,' she thought. 'I wonder when . . .'

Alone in his room, Gerry, too, was thinking, 'He'll be back. And next time, maybe. . . .'

CHISWICK MALL
William Makepeace Thackeray

While the present century was in its teens, and on one sunshiny morning in June, there drove up to the great iron gate of Miss Pinkerton's academy for young ladies, on Chiswick Mall, a large family coach, with two fat horses in blazing harness, driven by a fat coachman in a three-cornered hat and wig, at the rate of four miles an hour. A black servant, who reposed on the box beside the fat coachman, uncurled his bandy legs as soon as the equipage drew up opposite Miss Pinkerton's shining brass plate, and as he pulled the bell, at least a score of young heads were seen peering out of the narrow windows of the stately old brick house. Nay, the acute observer might even have recognized the little red nose of good-natured Miss Jemima Pinkerton herself, rising over some geranium pots in the window of that lady's own drawing-room.

'It is Mrs Sedley's coach, sister,' said Miss Jemima. 'Sambo, the black servant, has just rung the bell; and the coachman has a new red waist-coat.'

'Have you completed all the necessary preparations incident to Miss Sedley's departure, Miss Jemima?' asked Miss Pinkerton herself, that majestic lady – the Semiramis of Hammersmith, the friend of Dr Johnson, the correspondent of Mrs Chapone herself.

'The girls were up at four this morning, packing her trunks, sister,' replied Miss Jemima; 'we have made her a bow-pot.'

'Say a bouquet, sister Jemima – 'tis more genteel.'

'Well, a booky as big almost as a haystack. I have put up two bottles of the gillyflower-water for Mrs Sedley, and the receipt for making it, in Amelia's box.'

'And I trust, Miss Jemima, you have made a copy of Miss Sedley's account. This is it, is it? Very good – ninety-three pounds, four shillings. Be kind enough to address it to John Sedley, Esquire, and to seal this billet which I have written to his lady.'

In Miss Jemima's eyes an autograph letter of her sister, Miss Pinkerton, was an object of as deep veneration as would have been a letter from a sovereign. Only when her pupils quitted the establishment, or when they were about to be married, and once, when poor Miss Birch died of the scarlet fever, was Miss Pinkerton known to write personally to the parents of her pupils; and it was Jemima's opinion that if anything *could* console Mrs Birch for her daughter's loss, it would be that pious and eloquent composition in which Miss Pinkerton announced the event.

In the present instance Miss Pinkerton's 'billet' was to the following effect:

'THE MALL, CHISWICK, *June* 15, 18 – .

'MADAM, – After her six years' residence at the Mall, I have the honour and happiness of presenting Miss Amelia Sedley to her parents, as a young lady not unworthy to occupy a fitting position in their polished and refined circle. Those virtues which characterize the young English gentlewoman, those accomplishments which become her birth and station, will not be found wanting in the amiable Miss Sedley, whose *industry* and *obedience* have endeared her to her instructors, and whose delightful sweetness of temper has charmed her *aged* and her *youthful* companions.

'In music, in dancing, in orthography, in every variety of embroidery and needlework, she will be found to have realized her friends' *fondest wishes*. In geography there is still much to be desired; and a careful and undeviating use of the backboard, for four hours daily during the next three years, is recommended as necessary to the acquirement of that dignified *deportment and carriage*, so requisite for every young lady of *fashion*.

'In the principles of religion and morality, Miss Sedley will be found worthy of an establishment which has been honoured by the presence of *The Great Lexicographer*, and the patronage of the admirable Mrs Chapone. In leaving the Mall, Miss Amelia carries with her the hearts of her companions, and the affectionate regards of her mistress, who has the honour to subscribe herself,

'Madam, your most obliged humble servant,

'BARBARA PINKERTON.

'*P.S.* – Miss Sharp accompanies Miss Sedley. It is particularly requested that Miss Sharp's stay in Russell Square may not exceed ten days. The family of distinction with whom she is engaged desire to avail themselves of her services as soon as possible.'

This letter completed, Miss Pinkerton proceeded to write her own name and Miss Sedley's in the fly-leaf of a Johnson's Dictionary – the interesting work which she invariably presented to her scholars on their departure from the Mall. On the cover was inserted a copy of 'Lines addressed to a young lady on quitting Miss Pinkerton's school, at the Mall; by the late revered Doctor Samuel Johnson.' In fact, the Lexicographers' name was always on the lips of this majestic woman, and a visit he had paid to her was the cause of her reputation and her fortune.

Being commanded by her elder sister to get 'the Dictionary' from the cupboard, Miss Jemima had extracted two copies of the book from the receptacle in question. When Miss Pinkerton had finished the inscription in the first, Jemima, with rather a dubious and timid air, handed her the second.

'For whom is this, Miss Jemima?' said Miss Pinkerton coldly.

'For Becky Sharp,' answered Jemima, trembling very much, and blushing over her withered face and neck, as she turned her back on her sister. 'For Becky Sharp: she's going too.'

'MISS JEMIMA!' exclaimed Miss Pinkerton, in the largest capitals; 'are you in your senses? Replace the Dixonary in the closet, and never venture to take such a liberty in future.'

'Well, sister, it's only two and ninepence, and poor Becky will be miserable if she don't get one.'

'Send Miss Sedley instantly to me,' said Miss Pinkerton. And so, venturing not to say another word, poor Jemima trotted off, exceedingly flurried and nervous.

Miss Sedley's papa was a merchant in London, and a man of some wealth; whereas Miss Sharp was an articled pupil, for whom Miss Pinkerton had done, as she thought, quite enough, without conferring upon her at parting the high honour of the Dixonary.

Although schoolmistresses' letters are to be trusted no more nor less than churchyard epitaphs; yet, as it sometimes happens that a person departs this life who is really deserving of all the praises the stonecutter carves over his bones; who *is* a good Christian, a good parent, child, wife, or husband; who actually *does* leave a disconsolate family to mourn his loss; so in academies of the male and female sex it occurs every now and then that the pupil is fully worthy of the praises bestowed by the disinterested instructor. Now, Miss Amelia Sedley was a young lady of this singular species, and deserved not only all that Miss Pinkerton said in her praise, but had many charming qualities which that pompous old Minerva of a woman could not see, from the differences of rank and age between her pupil and herself.

For she could not only sing like a lark, or a Mrs Billington, and dance like Hillisberg or Parisot; and embroider beautifully; and spell as well as a Dixonary itself; but she had such a kindly, smiling, tender, gentle, generous heart of her own, as won the love of everybody who came near her, from Minerva herself down to the poor girl in the scullery and the one-eyed tart-woman's daughter, who was permitted to vend her wares once a week to the young ladies in the Mall. She had twelve intimate and bosom friends out of the twenty-four young ladies. Even envious Miss Briggs never spoke ill of her; high and mighty Miss Saltire (Lord Dexter's grand-daughter) allowed that her figure was genteel; and as for Miss Swartz, the rich woolly-haired mulatto from St Kitts, on the day Amelia went away, she was in such a passion of tears, that they were obliged to send for Dr Floss, and half tipsify her with sal volatile. Miss Pinkerton's attachment was, as may be supposed, from the high position and eminent virtues of that lady, calm and dignified; but Miss Jemima had already whimpered several times at the idea of Amelia's departure; and, but for fear of her sister, would have gone off in downright hysterics, like the heiress (who paid double) of

St. Kitts. Such luxury of grief, however, is only allowed to parlour-boarders. Honest Jemima had all the bills, and the washing, and the mending, and the puddings, and the plate and crockery, and the servants to superintend. But why speak about her? It is probable that we shall not hear of her again from this moment to the end of time, and that when the great filigree iron gates are once closed on her, she and her awful sister will never issue therefrom into this little history.

But as we are to see a great deal of Amelia, there is no harm in saying, at the outset of our acquaintance, that she was a dear little creature; and a great mercy it is, both in life and in novels, which (and the latter especially) abound in villains of the most sombre sort, that we are to have for a constant companion so guileless and good-natured a person. As she is not a heroine, there is no need to describe her person; indeed I am afraid that her nose was rather short than otherwise, and her cheeks a great deal too round and red for a heroine; but her face blushed with rosy health, and her lips with the freshest of smiles, and she had a pair of eyes which sparkled with the brightest and honestest good-humour, except indeed when they filled with tears, and that was a great deal too often; for the silly thing would cry over a dead canary-bird; or over a mouse, that the cat haply had seized upon; or over the end of a novel, were it ever so stupid; and as for saying an unkind word to her, were any persons hard-hearted enough to do so – why, so much the worse for them. Even Miss Pinkerton, that austere and godlike woman, ceased scolding her after the first time, and though she no more comprehended sensibility than she did Algebra, gave all masters and teachers particular orders to treat Miss Sedley with the utmost gentleness, as harsh treatment was injurious to her.

So that when the day of departure came, between her two customs of laughing and crying, Miss Sedley was greatly puzzled how to act. She was glad to go home, and yet most woefully sad at leaving school. For three days before, little Laura Martin, the orphan, followed her about, like a little dog. She had to make and receive at least fourteen presents – to make fourteen solemn promises of writing every week: 'Send my letters under cover to my grandpapa, the Earl of Dexter,' said Miss Saltire (who, by the way, was rather shabby): 'Never mind the postage, but write every day, you dear darling,' said the impetuous and woolly-headed, but generous and affectionate, Miss Swartz; and the orphan little Laura Martin (who was just in round-hand), took her friend's hand and said, looking up in her face wistfully, 'Amelia, when I write to you I shall call you Mamma.' All which details, I have no doubt, JONES, who reads this book at his Club, will pronounce to be excessively foolish, trivial, twaddling, and ultra-sentimental. Yes; I can see Jones at this minute (rather flushed with his joint of mutton and half-pint of wine) taking out his pencil and scoring under the words 'foolish, twaddling,' etc., and adding to them his own remark of *'quite true.'* Well, he is a lofty man of genius, and admires the great and heroic in life and novels; and so had better take warning and go elsewhere.

Well, then. The flowers, and the presents, and the trunks, and bonnet-boxes of Miss Sedley having been arranged by Mr Sambo in the carriage, together with a very small and weather-beaten old cow's-skin trunk with Miss Sharp's card neatly nailed upon it, which was delivered by Sambo with a grin, and packed by the coachman with a corresponding sneer – the hour for parting came; and the grief of that moment was considerably lessened by the admirable discourse which Miss Pinkerton addressed to her pupil. Not that the parting speech caused Amelia to philosophize, or that it armed her in any way with a calmness, the result of argument; but it was intolerably dull, pompous, and tedious; and having the fear of her schoolmistress greatly before her eyes, Miss Sedley did not venture, in her presence, to give way to any ebullitions of private grief. A seed-cake and a bottle of wine were produced in the drawing-room, as on the solemn occasions of the visits of parents, and these refreshments being partaken of, Miss Sedley was at liberty to depart.

'You'll go in and say good-bye to Miss Pinkerton, Becky!' said Miss Jemima to a young lady of whom nobody took any notice, and who was coming downstairs with her own hand box.

'I suppose I must,' said Miss Sharp calmly, and much to the wonder of Miss Jemima; and the latter having knocked at the door, and receiving permission to come in, Miss Sharp advanced in a very un-concerned manner, and said in French, and with a perfect accent, 'Mademoiselle, je viens vous faire mes adieux.'

Miss Pinkerton did not understand French; she only directed those who did; but biting her lips and throwing up her venerable and Roman-nosed head (on the top of which figured a large and solemn

There was such a scuffling, and hugging, and kissing, and crying.

turban), she said, 'Miss Sharp, I wish you a good-morning.' As the Hammersmith Semiramis spoke she waved one hand, both by way of adieu, and to give Miss Sharp an opportunity of shaking one of the fingers of the hand which was left out for that purpose.

Miss Sharp only folded her own hands with a very frigid smile and bow, and quite declined to accept the proffered honour; on which Semiramis tossed up her turban more indignantly than ever. In fact, it was a little battle between the young lady and the old one, and the latter was worsted. 'Heaven bless you, my child,' said she, embracing Amelia, and scowling the while over the girl's shoulder at Miss Sharp. 'Come away, Becky,' said Miss Jemima, pulling the young woman away in great alarm, and the drawing-room door closed upon them.

Then came the struggle and parting below. Words refused to tell it. All the servants were there in the hall – all the dear friends – all the young ladies – the dancing-master who had just arrived; and there was such a scuffling, and hugging, and kissing, and crying, with the hysterical *yoops* of Miss Swartz, the parlour-boarder, from her room, as no pen can depict, and as the tender heart would fain pass over. The embracing was over; they parted – that is, Miss Sedley parted from her friends. Miss Sharp had demurely entered the carriage some minutes before. Nobody cried for leaving *her*.

Sambo of the bandy legs slammed the carriage-door on his young weeping mistress. He sprang up behind the carriage. 'Stop!' cried Miss Jemima, rushing to the gate with a parcel.

'It's some sandwiches, my dear,' said she to Amelia. 'You may be hungry, you know; and Becky, Becky Sharp, here's a book for you that my sister – that is, I – Johnson's Dixonary, you know; you mustn't leave us without that. Good-bye. Drive on, coachman. God bless you!'

And the kind creature retreated into the garden, overcome with emotion.

But, lo! and just as the coach drove off, Miss Sharp put her pale face out of the window and actually flung the book back into the garden.

This almost caused Jemima to faint with terror. 'Well, I never!' – said she – 'what an audacious– ' Emotion prevented her from completing either sentence. The carriage rolled away; the great gates were closed; the bell rang for the dancing lesson. The world is before the two young ladies; and so, farewell to Chiswick Mall.

THE BUS
Margaret Biggs

The first morning Alan started at our school, Brambley Comprehensive, I was having trouble with some of the morons in 1B.

The problem is, I'm the smallest boy in the form, and they think it's funny and try to get under my skin. I've always had to put up with this, and I can usually take it because I've had plenty of practice. I don't mind people calling me Titch, at least I'm resigned to it, but that particular morning before registration a whole gang of them, led by Mark Simms, who thinks he's witty, got onto me. Mark was mad because I'd scored past him during a five-a-side football game the day before – he's hopeless in goal. So his mates were standing round grinning while he called me a garden gnome, and other daft things, and pointed to a crack in the floor near my desk and told me to watch out, or I'd fall through and be screaming for help. I suddenly lost my cool, and when Mr Sunderland our form tutor came in with Alan I'd got Mark round the throat, and was doing my best to choke him, while the others were vainly trying to pull me off. I may be small, but I've learnt how to fight.

'Cut it out, Paul,' old Slumberland said, striding across and yanking me away. 'Cut it *out*, I tell you!'

'He's nearly throttled me, sir,' Mark gasped.

But old Slumberland knew the score. 'As you're twice Paul's size,

Mark, I assume you asked for it, so don't waste my time. Sit down, the lot of you,' he said coldly. He gave me a glare, but he left it at that. 'Listen, this is a new boy, Alan Frazer, and he'll be sitting next to you, Paul, and I want you to show him the ropes. OK?'

'Yes, sir, I will,' I said, trying to get my breath and smooth my hair. 'Hi,' I said to Alan, as he sat down beside me.

'Hi,' he said rather warily, and I didn't blame him. I sized him up and liked the look of him. He was taller than me – he would be! – and very neat and tidy, but he didn't look a sissy.

When Mr Sunderland had taken the register he told us to watch our step, and left us. Mark called over to Alan: 'Better watch out he doesn't go for you – he's got a crazy temper!'

'Thanks for the advice,' Alan said coolly, and I could see he wasn't impressed. He looked at me and asked: 'Was he getting at you?'

I nodded. 'It's because I'm small,' I told him. 'I don't make a habit of throttling people, but he went on and on.'

'I don't blame you. He looks an idiot,' Alan said. He smiled at me, and I began to cheer up. After that we got talking, and before the first period we found we were almost exactly the same age, twelve and a half, and that we were both mad on football. He was quiet, but easy to talk to, and he took in everything I told him. I think he was glad to have me to show him around. It's not easy starting at a new school in the middle of term after everyone else, and Brambley's pretty enormous.

I liked him from the word go, and he seemed to like me which was a boost for my morale. But straight away I felt there was something mysterious about him, that I just couldn't understand.

For example, at break we were talking and it turned out he'd come to live in the next road to me. 'Oh great, you'll be coming on the bus with me, I catch the eight twenty every morning,' I said. It's about a mile to school from where we live, and quite a few of us first years go together.

But Alan shook his head at once and said, 'No, Paul, I shan't go on the bus.'

'Oh, won't you?' I warn you, old Slumberland isn't keen on first years cycling through the town centre,' I said.

'I shan't be cycling, I haven't got a bike. I'll be walking,' Alan answered.

'Walking? Coo, it's a bit of a trek,' I said, surprised. Walking was boring, in my opinion.

Alan didn't say anything in reply, but after a pause asked me what school dinners were like, and where we had to queue. It seemed strange to me but I had the sense not to bother him about it, because I could see plainly he didn't want to answer questions.

Apart from that, we got on fine all day. On the bus going home Rachel, my twin sister, who's in 1B with me – there's no getting away from her, she tags round after me whatever I tell her, she can't take a hint – started saying how good-looking Alan was. I ask you! Girls are like that, bird-witted. Who cared if Alan was good-looking? Much more to the point, I'd found out he was brilliant at football, and I told her. But she wasn't interested. Sport's a closed book to her.

'Football's all you think about,' she said in a scathing voice copied from Mum. 'No, this new boy's really nice looking. He's got lovely blue eyes. Like John Travolta.'

I made a yukky sick noise and rolled *my* eyes, but she went on like a steamroller, 'But that's a funny scar down one side of his face. I wonder how he got it?'

'Didn't notice a scar,' I said.

Rachel gave me a superior look. 'You don't notice *anything*, Paul.' At least she doesn't call me 'Titch' – she knows better.

'Yes I do,' I retorted. 'I noticed he's got a great kick with his left foot – he's a useful striker, Alan.'

'I give you up,' Rachel said. And I told her that really broke my heart, and tickled her until she got the giggles and fell off the seat, and people turned round and glared, and the conductor, who's a spoilsport, told us he'd put us off if he had any trouble. I ask you!

Brambley's not a bad school, though there are too many boring rules, and you get a detention if you don't watch out. Now it's our second term I've got used to it, but after primary school it seemed huge and unfriendly at first. Rachel used to be scared of getting lost, and though I never said so, I felt exactly the same. And starting at the bottom all over again seemed weird after being in the top class at our old school. And some of the seniors pushed you over if you didn't get out of their way quick. But I soon got to know my way around all the long corridors, and up and down the flights of iron stairs, and to find the different faculties – you had to walk miles for some. The staff weren't bad when you got to know them, though some of them were really tough, and were onto you like a ton of bricks if you forgot something. Old Slumberland pretended to be tough, but I could tell it was an act. He was bearable really, and he supported City like I did, so he couldn't be all bad.

Apart from being 1 B's form tutor, he taught humanities – geography, history, all that stuff – but as far as I could see his main interest was looking after the school bus we used for trips and sometimes for away matches and going swimming. It was as old as the hills, painted green and white in the Brambley colours, and everyone called it Grandad. Well, it looked like the grandad of all buses. It jolted and wheezed along, the engine made as much noise as a plane coming in to land, and it was a standing joke how often it broke down. It was notorious in our town. But old Slumberland always stuck up for it and got quite heated if anybody criticized it. 'That's a vintage bus, that is,' he was always saying. 'What can you expect, with the loads it has to carry?' And I often saw him crawling round it in the dinner hours, working on it until the bell went, fiddling with its innards with the bonnet open. He could hardly tear himself away. A group of seniors used to help him sometimes, but he'd still be there when they'd gone. Grandad used to stand out in the car park, which was just under our form room window, in all weathers, and when it snowed or poured with rain old Slumberland would keep drifting over to the window and giving it worried looks. He was nutty about it.

Anyhow, as I say, Alan settled down in 1 B without any trouble, and everybody accepted him. He could take a joke, he listened to what you said, he wasn't a bighead though he had plenty of brains and was soon top of the form. The staff liked him too, not that that's much to go by. Within a week he got into the football team with me, and he and I went around together most of the time, and stuck up for each other. He supported Southampton, which was a big snag, but you can't have everything, and I tolerantly made allowances for him.

The only thing we didn't do together was travel to and from school. When we were all in the bus we used to whizz past him trudging along, but he never once came on it himself, even when it was rotten weather. I'd bang on the glass to him, and he'd look round and wave, and keep on walking. Mark Simms, who lived down our road, teased him about it, but Alan smiled and didn't react. He didn't let Mark get under his skin.

At the end of the first week, when we were packing up to go home, I said, 'Like me to call for you tomorrow morning? Maybe we could go down to the town.' I usually had a look round on a Saturday morning, checked up on the top ten, did a bit of shopping for Mum and spent my pocket money on sweets and biros and maybe a record.

Alan hesitated. 'I'd like to, but I'm not sure. Tell you what, I'll call for you about ten if I can make it, OK?'

'Fair enough,' I said.

I didn't realize it then, but Alan never wanted anybody to call round at his house. And he never mentioned his family. He called at mine sometimes, but nobody ever got an invite to his. He always had some good reason why it wasn't on, but it gradually dawned on me. As I say, he had this hidden, mysterious streak.

My Mum took a fancy to him, and always told me to get out the biscuit tin when he turned up. And Rachel of course used to hang about and get in the way as usual, if she could.

'He's a nice polite boy,' Mum said, after Alan had been round a couple of times. 'Much better mannered than you two. I hope you take a leaf out of his book! He seems older, somehow, though I know he isn't. If I bump into his mother I'll ask her in for coffee.'

It was true, Alan *did* seem older. There was a look on his face sometimes, as if he was a million miles away. He'd answer you but he wasn't really with you. It was as if he was watching something that had happened years ago. It was weird and disconcerting. Then he'd snap out of it, and come back to normal again.

One day in the second week I knew him he went home before me. I had a half hour detention for time-wasting, old Slumberland had the nerve to say. Just because I'd been discussing tactics with some of the others for our match against Adderley, when we were supposed to be copying a boring map of South America. Honestly, we had to *slave* at times! Anyhow, when I finished detention I had to go and pick up my bag from 1B, and I noticed Alan had left his football shorts dropped under his desk, so I thought I'd take them on my way home. To tell the truth, I wasn't sorry – I was eager to see Alan's home.

It looked perfectly normal like all the other houses in the street. I marched up the front path and rang the bell. There was a long pause, and I was beginning to think they were all out, and I'd have to shove the football shorts through the letterbox, when the door opened and it was Alan.

He didn't look a bit pleased – he just said: 'Hi, what do *you* want?'

'I've brought your shorts,' I said, handing them over.

'Oh – thanks,' Alan said. Then a woman's voice called him from inside, and he said quickly: 'I've got to go. Thanks, Titch,' and shut the door in my face.

I felt a bit mad with him – after all, I *had* been doing him a favour. Next time he can find his own things, I thought crossly. He might have asked me in for a coke, at least. But in a way I had to admit it was partly my own fault. I knew well enough Alan hadn't wanted me to call.

Next day neither of us said anything. Well, what was there to say? I tried to be a bit cool and curt, but I didn't keep it up, it seemed stupid. I liked him, and I had a feeling he was sorry. He gave me half a bar of chocolate, and I knew it was a peace offering.

At tutorial time old Slumberland started talking about our form trip. It was in a couple of weeks – all the first years were going to various places. 1B was to go to Palgrave Manor, he told us. One or two people groaned under their breath, but old Slumberland gave us a glowing multicoloured account of what a great time we'd have, what a lot there was to see and how we'd all enjoy it. 'It's a perfect example of an Elizabethan manor,' he said in his enthusiastic way. He does go on sometimes. 'It's supposed to be haunted, though I'm sure the ghosts will be too terrified of you crowd to put in an appearance! We'll go round the house and do the thing properly, and then we'll find plenty to do in the grounds. We'll eat outside if it's possible. There's a maze, I understand, and a lake, and an adventure playground you can expend your surplus energy on.'

We looked at each other and cheered up a bit. That sounded more promising. 'And we'll be going in the school bus,' he went on proudly, as if giving us an incredible treat. 'It's about thirty-five miles, and it should be a really pleasant journey. We'll go along the motorway and turn off at Buxton.'

We sat on a wooden seat and chewed some gum.

'Oh sir, have we got to go in Grandad? It's bound to break down,' Rachel wailed, just to needle him. And we all started agreeing, saying we'd never get there, just to kid him.

Old Slumberland tried to laugh it off, but he got quite hot and bothered. 'You're all talking rubbish, and don't use that stupid nickname. It's in tiptop condition. You know I service it myself regularly.'

'It broke down last week, sir, with 1D,' put in Mark Simms. 'I heard all about it. Mr James was driving it, and it stalled at the lights, and – '

'Never mind that, Mr James isn't *au fait* with the controls like I am,' old Slumberland cut in sharply. 'You're all ignoramuses on the subject, and that's enough. What I want to emphasize is, I hope you'll all come on the trip, as it's excellent value, highly educational and in addition will be a great day out. But I must have the money, one pound fifty, by next Monday, that's definitely the last day. Remember, Monday's your last chance. Take these slips home to your parents this afternoon, and get their signatures and the money back to me as soon as you can.'

At break we discussed it. Most people were keen, as at least it made a change from school routine, but Alan kept silent. In the end I asked him if he'd be going. 'I don't think so,' he said, his forehead all puckered.

'Why on earth not? You'll only be stuck at school on your own if you don't,' I said impatiently. 'That'll be dead boring.'

'I'll think about it,' Alan said. 'Have we got to go on the bus?'

'You bet, it's the highspot of the trip, according to old Slumberland,' I said. 'What's the matter, you get sick in buses?' But Alan only shook his head and changed the subject. Honestly, he could be maddening sometimes. And I did want him to come.

On the Friday after school we had a match and beat Adderley three one. Alan and I were delighted with ourselves, because we'd practised a move over and over again in the dinner hour, and at last it had worked and we'd scored a goal between us. 'Great teamwork, lads, you're starting to put it together,' Mr Lamb the sports master told us, which was unheard of for him, and he handed round glucose sweets. While we were in the showers I called to Alan, 'Made up your mind about the trip, then?'

He came out, rubbing himself with the towel. 'I'd like to, Titch, honest.' I noticed the scar on his face pink from the shower, and wished I dared ask him how he got it.

'Well, what's stopping you? Is it the money? Maybe I could lend you some.' Though I hadn't much to spare, and as soon as I said it I felt worried.

'No, it's not that.' Alan started pulling on his clothes. 'D'you think we'd get back to school the usual time?'

'Yeah, four o'clock, same as usual. Why?'

'Right, I'll come,' Alan said. 'Why not, why shouldn't I?' He sounded as if he was talking to himself.

'That's great, we'll have a brilliant time, you see,' I said.

'Hope so,' Alan said, as he half doubted it. But he smiled at me suddenly, and I knew he was pleased too.

So Alan handed in his money to old Slumberland on the Monday with the form, and old Slumberland said warmly: 'That's fine, Alan, I'm glad you're coming.' I think he felt rather as I did – he liked Alan but couldn't entirely make him out. 'Your father or mother have signed this, have they? Yes, I see. Right, thanks.' Alan came back to his place looking a bit red, and I wondered vaguely why, but immediately forgot about it. He was coming, that was the main thing.

On the day of the trip we all got to school early though we weren't leaving till nine thirty, after first year assembly. Rachel and I had made stacks of corned beef and tomato sauce sandwiches the night before, and there wasn't enough bread at breakfast for toast, which annoyed Mum. Still, she'd insisted we do them ourselves, so it wasn't our fault. We left her and Dad arguing about whose fault it was, and hurried off. All our gang on the bus were a bit excited, and Mark Simms ate half his sandwiches then and there, to check if they were any good. We even began a singsong, but the conductor came stomping along and told us to belt up. He really was a kill-joy. We passed Alan halfway, and when I banged on the glass and waved at him he gave me the thumbs-up sign and looked much more excited than usual.

As we walked up the drive I spotted old Slumberland in the car park, a rag in his hand, fussing over Grandad. In the formroom a few minutes later he came bounding in, all smiles, a spot of grease on his chin. After registration he began giving us the usual lecture about behaving responsibly, and not letting the school down, but luckily the bell for assembly cut him short.

Assembly was mercifully short – the first year head must have sensed the atmosphere – and just before nine thirty we were charging into Grandad, shouting and bagging seats. Old Slumberland had to bellow to make himself heard. He was driving of course, and Mrs Peters, who took us for English, was coming as well. She wasn't bad – she read a lot and often didn't notice what was going on, which was in her favour.

Alan had only brought two apples and a chocolate biscuit. 'Slimming, are you?' Mark Simms said. But Alan took no notice. I told him we'd got some spare sandwiches if he wanted any. 'Thanks, Titch,' he said, looking excited and somehow worried at the same time.

It took about an hour and a quarter to get to Palgrave Manor. We got held up in the town, but once we were on the motorway we made steady progress. Mind you, Grandad never got out of the slow lane, and we didn't pass anything, not even a heavy lorry, but at least we kept grinding along. Old Slumberland was having a great time driving, I could tell, he was in his element changing the enormous gears, and when we had a five minute stop at the motorway café to use the lavatories, I heard him going on to Mrs Peters about how well the engine was performing. She tried to look interested, but I could see she'd rather have been reading her book.

It rained a bit just before we got there, but as we drove between some huge iron gates and then up the manor drive between dripping rhododendron bushes, the sun came faintly out, and there was Palgrave Manor ahead of us, a huge sprawling place in red brick with lots of crooked tall chimneys. We all gave a cheer, because we were tired of sitting still.

'Right, out you all get,' old Slumberland said, when Grandad had juddered to a halt. 'We'll go round the house first, and I expect sensible behaviour, remember, or there'll be trouble.'

So we went round the house with one of the guides, an old chap who walked very slowly and kept stopping and pointing things out. I couldn't hear what he said half the time. He seemed to think we wanted to see every picture and every ornament, and there were thousands of both, and he kept telling us in detail about the Palgrave family, and how many hundred years they'd lived here, and how one had been a courtier to Queen Elizabeth I, and another had had his head chopped off in the Civil War in sixteen something. *He* was supposed to haunt the ministrels' gallery. It was interesting up to a point, but by the time we'd done most of the ground floor and then trailed up huge wooden stairs to go over the state bedrooms and the library and the portrait galley we'd all had enough. I even saw old Slumberland stifle a yawn at one point, and nudged Alan, but he seemed riveted. Still, at the end we all thanked the old chap profusely, and then at last clattered out through the old kitchen into the fresh air.

'Right, you've got about an hour to explore the grounds, but be back here by one fifteen and we'll have dinner – there's a clock on the stables – and behave sensibly or I'll wring your necks!' Old Slumberland ended in a shout and an old lady going past jumped and dropped her handbag. He picked it up for her looking sheepish, and we all had a job keeping a straight face.

Alan and I slipped away to find the maze. It looked pretty impressive, a vast circle of high hedges. We were both keen to see what it was like. The old chap who took the money at the entrance mumbled something about how to find the middle, but I told him we wouldn't have any trouble. 'Come on, before they catch us up,' I said, seeing Rachel and two of her friends trying to catch us up. We certainly didn't want to get lumbered with *them*. So we hurried in.

It was much harder than I thought. At first I suggested we kept going left, but that brought us back where we started. Then Alan suggested we went first left, then right alternatively, and *that* brought us back where we started as well, but took much longer. After that we just wandered round and just when we'd given up hope we stumbled on the middle of the maze, and collapsed on the wooden seat. We sat and chewed some gum, and I looked round and said 'Mum would like this, she likes old places. Does your Mum?'

'She doesn't go anywhere, ever,' Alan said slowly. I stared, and he said: 'Swear not to tell anybody, Titch?' And then at last he told me.

He said that five years ago his older sister had been taking him to school, and they'd been crossing the main road when a bus ran into them. They were on a zebra crossing, Alan said not looking at me, but the brakes of the bus failed, and they didn't have a chance. Alan's sister was killed, and Alan was slightly injured. 'My face and one shoulder, nothing much,' he said quickly. But I could see by his expression how awful it must have been. And afterwards his mother had a breakdown, and though since then she'd got better very slowly, she was absolutely terrified of buses, and never let any of the family travel on one. 'She can't forget, you see,' Alan said. 'Dad and I understand, we try and help, but sometimes it gets me down. It's gone on so long. She won't have anybody come to the house either, and she used to have lots of friends popping in before. And she never wants us to do anything or go anywhere. It's like living in prison.'

'It sounds rotten,' I said awkwardly. 'How come she let you come today?' I could understand why he was so secretive now.

'She didn't, I never asked her,' Alan said. 'I knew it was no good, and I did want to come. But if we're late and she finds out, I'd feel awful. I feel sort of responsible for her, you see, she worries about me all the time. I paid the money and signed the form myself, and I daren't make any sandwiches or Mum would have found out. But it's not her fault, it's such a mess,' he added bleakly.

I didn't know what to say. I felt terribly sorry for him. 'I expect she'll get over it,' I said at last uncomfortably, and Alan said, 'Yes, that's what Dad says, but *when*?' and we left it at that.

Suddenly Rachel and her friends appeared, and in a way it was a relief. Rachel beamed delightedly and said, 'Are you lost? We know the way out, you can come with us if you like.'

'Big deal,' I said. 'Still, we'll keep you company.'

I was sure she was just boasting, but to my annoyance she *did* find the right path. It was maddening, just like her. She looked complacently at us when we got out and said, 'There you are, you'd still be in there but for me.'

It wasn't worth arguing with her, but I said gloomily to Alan: 'You're lucky you haven't got a sister – you can't win.' Then I remembered and felt awful, but Alan only said, 'It's all right, Titch.' No doubt he was used to remarks like that. He seemed to feel better now he'd told me, so I was glad he had. It proved he trusted me, for one thing.

We had lunch and played about, then spent an hour in the adventure playground, which was brilliant, till old Slumberland hauled us out saying he'd promised the head we would be back by four. We'd charged madly round on the rope ladders and tree-houses, so it wasn't too unwelcome to slump back inside Grandad. But as we chugged through Buxton the engine started to make nasty grinding sounds, as if it was chewing up bricks, and we had to pull into a lay-by. Old

Slumberland jumped out and Alan started looking at his watch and getting all strained and white. Everybody else was laughing and talking, but I could guess how he felt.

Mrs Peters told us to stay where we were, and got out to see if she could help. We were sitting near the front, and could hear old Slumberland telling her something about the fanbelt, and how he was trying to fix it temporarily, while she made soothing noises. It started to rain again, black clouds swamped the sky, and suddenly everything felt depressing.

'We'll be late,' Alan said. 'I shouldn't have come, I knew I wouldn't get away with it. Something like this was bound to happen.' He started to bite his nails.

'He'll fix it, don't worry,' I said, trying to sound confident.

We got going again after awhile, but old Slumberland had to drive in second gear all the way home, so we just crawled along. It was nearly five when we got back to Brambley, and Alan was a bundle of nerves by then. And as at last we pulled thankfully into the school car park I saw a woman in a mac waiting staring at the bus, looking dreadfully white and agitated, and I glanced sideways at Alan and knew it was his mother.

The moment we stopped Mrs Frazer came rushing over. She was nearly crying, it was awful for Alan. He got out quickly and I followed, pushing ahead of everybody else, wondering uneasily if I could help, because it was partly my fault, I'd persuaded him to come.

'Oh Alan, how could you? I came up to school when you were late and they told me – how *could* you go on a bus, when you know how I feel about them? And you never ever told me—'

Old Slumberland came up trying to be jolly and apologize for the delay, but Mrs Frazer took no notice of him. Her hands were shaking, she was in a dreadful state. She pulled Alan along by his arm, talking all the time, and left old Slumberland standing there dumbfounded.

Rachel came running to catch me up, and I said, 'You go on the bus, I'm walking back – for heaven's sake don't argue!' Rachel saw something was wrong so for once she just nodded. 'I'll explain later,' I told her, and followed Alan and his mother.

She was marching Alan along at such a rate I had a job to keep up, and they never noticed me. Alan was still vainly trying to calm her down, to explain. I caught snatches of what he was saying. 'But Mum, it was safe, honestly, it was just a school trip – ' Then Mrs Frazer interrupted. 'But you promised me faithfully you'd never go on a bus after what happened. I thought I could trust you, and now you've let me down!' And I caught sight of Alan's miserable face.

We got onto the main road. It was the rush hour, and cars and lorries were slithering by in an unending stream. It was getting dark, drivers were switching their headlights on, and I decided to try and help, though I didn't have much hope. 'Mrs Frazer, wait a minute, please can I explain—' I began, overhauling them.

Alan's mum stared at me unwelcomingly. 'It's Titch, Mum, I've told you about him,' Alan said.

'We were only late back because our bus broke down. It's always doing that, nothing dangerous happened, cross my heart, we had a great day,' I said.

'I don't want to talk about it,' Mrs Frazer said. 'Leave us alone, go away. Come on with me, Alan.' And she was so worked up and panicky she seized his arm and stepped off the curb in a great rush – mainly to get away from me.

Then lots of things happened simultaneously, and somehow everything slowed up, like an action replay, and that made it worse. A car was right near and had to brake like mad to miss them. I saw the driver's face, shouting and swearing as he wrenched at the wheel. Mrs Frazer screamed, the car skidded, brakes screeching. People spun round in horror, and in all the hubbub Alan grabbed his mother with all his strength and yanked her back onto the pavement with inches to spare. The car halted sideways on the wet gleaming road, and other cars' horns blared deafeningly.

'Want to kill yourself, lady? You're not fit to be out!' the driver yelled angrily – then started up his engine and drove on. People stared, then moved on again, shaking their heads. We three stood there.

Mrs Frazer stood whitefaced, motionless. Alan peered anxiously at her. 'Mum, are you all right?' She didn't answer. '*Mum*, are you OK? Do say something,' he said urgently, gripping her arm.

His mother seemed to jerk back to awareness again. She looked dazedly at Alan, then at me. She muttered something, 'What a fool' was all I caught.

'It's all right, Mum, we're safe, don't worry,' Alan said.

His mother looked hard at him, as if she had never seen him before. 'All I could think of was you going on that bus,' she said slowly. 'I was so stupidly obsessed I nearly killed us both!' She shivered.

I shivered too. It was cold, standing there in the twilight drizzle, and suddenly I longed to be home, wolfing down egg and chips and watching something funny on TV, away from Alan and his mother.

We walked on, and now Mrs Frazer made no objection to me being with them. She said nothing, just held Alan's arm. But when I said goodbye at the corner, to my surprise she said 'Goodbye, Titch,' and managed a wavering smile. I saw then she must have been very pretty once. 'Bye, Titch, see you at school tomorrow,' Alan said, and I ran on home.

Next morning Rachel had a cold, and Mum made her stay at home. I hadn't, worse luck, and we were late up so I had to belt along to the bus stop. I'd missed the earlier bus, I saw it disappearing up the road, and there was only one lone figure at the stop, gazing up and down. When he saw me he started to wave, and I blinked disbelievingly. It was Alan.

'What are *you* doing?' I said stupidly, reaching him.

'What's it look like? Waiting for you, and the bus, of course,' he said.

I gazed at him, struck by his cheerful face and shining eyes. I'd never seen him look like that before. 'What's happened?' I said.

'Nothing much. Mum and Dad talked for hours last night, I heard them when I was in bed. Then at breakfast Mum gave me my fare, and told me to get a move on or I'd miss the bus and not see you, and Dad nodded. So here I am.' Alan's grin widened. 'You don't know how nice it will be not to walk for once, Titch.'

'That's great, really great,' I said warmly. 'Three cheers for your Mum!' We winked at each other. I didn't really understand, but grown-ups were a law unto themselves, and anyhow what did it matter? I found a liquorice at the bottom of my pocket, bit it in half and gave one half to Alan.

'Here it comes now,' I said. 'We'll get the front seat with a bit of luck.'

'You bet we will,' Alan said exuberantly.

I had a comfortable feeling that things were looking up.

SLAVES OF THE LAMP
Rudyard Kipling

The music-room on the top floor of Number Five was filled with the 'Aladdin' company at rehearsal. Dickson Quartus, commonly known as Dick Four, was Aladdin, stage-manager, ballet-master, half the orchestra, and largely librettist, for the 'book' had been rewritten and filled with local allusions. The pantomime was to be given next week, in the downstairs study occupied by Aladdin, Abanazar, and the Emperor of China. The Slave of the Lamp, with the Princess Badroul-badour and the Widow Twankey, owned Number Five study across the same landing, so that the company could be easily assembled. The floor shook to the stamp-and-go of the ballet, while Aladdin, in pink cotton tights, a blue and tinsel jacket, and a plumed hat, banged alternately on the piano and his banjo. He was the moving spirit of the game, as befitted a senior who had passed his Army Preliminary and hoped to enter Sandhurst next spring.

Aladdin came to his own at last, Abanazar lay poisoned on the floor, the Widow Twankey danced her dance, and the company decided it would 'come all right on the night.'

'What about the last song, though?' said the Emperor, a tallish, fair-headed boy with a ghost of a moustache, at which he pulled manfully. 'We need a rousing old tune.'

Stalky whistled lazily where he lay on top of the piano.

' "John Peel"? "Drink, Puppy, Drink"?' suggested Abanazar, smoothing his baggy lilac pyjamas. 'Pussy' Abanazar never looked more than one-half awake, but he owned a soft, slow smile which well suited the part of the Wicked Uncle.

'Stale,' said Aladdin. 'Might as well have "Grandfather's Clock." What's that thing you were humming at prep. last night, Stalky?'

Stalky, The Slave of the Lamp, in black tights and doublet, a black silk half-mast on his forehead, whistled lazily where he lay on the top of the piano. It was a catchy music-hall tune.

Dick Four cocked his head critically, and squinted down a large red nose.

'Once more, and I can pick it up,' he said, strumming. 'Sing the words.'

'Arrah, Patsy, mind the baby! Arrah, Patsy, mind the child!
Wrap him up in an overcoat, he's surely goin' wild!
Arrah, Patsy, mind the baby; just ye mind the child awhile!
He'll kick an' bite an' cry all night! Arrah, Patsy, mind the child!'

'Rippin'! Oh, rippin'!' said Dick Four. 'Only we shan't have any piano on the night. We must work it with the banjos – play an' dance at the same time. You try, Tertius.'

The Emperor pushed aside his pea-green sleeves of state, and followed Dick Four on a heavy nickel-plated banjo.

'Yes, but I'm dead all this time. Bung in the middle of the stage, too,' said Abanazar.

'Oh, that's Beetle's biznai,' said Dick Four. 'Vamp it up, Beetle. Don't keep us waiting all night. You've got to get Pussy out of the light somehow, and bring us all in dancin' at the end.'

'All right. You two play it again,' said Beetle, who, in a grey skirt and a wig of chestnut sausage-curls, set slantwise above a pair of spectacles mended with an old boot-lace, represented the Widow Twankey. He waved one leg in time to the hammered refrain, and the banjos grew louder.

'Um! Ah! Er – "Aladdin now has won his wife," ' he sang, and Dick Four repeated it.

' "Your Emperor is appeased," ' Tertius flung out his chest as he delivered his line.

278

'Now jump up, Pussy! Say, "I think I'd better come to life!" Then we all take hands and come forward: "We hope you've all been pleased." *Twiggez-vous?*'

'*Nous twiggons.* Good enough. What's the chorus for the final ballet? It's four kicks and a turn,' said Dick Four.

'Oh! Er!

John Short will ring the curtain down,
And ring the prompter's bell;
We hope you know before you go,
That we all wish you well.'

'Rippin'! Rippin'! Now for the Widow's scene with the Princess. Hurry up, Turkey.'

M'Turk, in a violet silk skirt and a coquettish blue turban, slouched forward as one thoroughly ashamed of himself. The Slave of the Lamp climbed down from the piano, and dispassionately kicked him. 'Play up, Turkey,' he said; 'this is serious.' But there fell on the door the knock of authority. It happened to be King, in gown and mortar-board, enjoying a Saturday evening prowl before dinner.

'Locked doors! Locked doors!' he snapped with a scowl. 'What's the meaning of this; and what, may I ask, is the intention of this – this epicene attire?'

'Pantomine, sir. The Head gave us leave,' said Abanazar, as the only member of the Sixth concerned. Dick Four stood firm in the confidence born of well-fitting tights, but the Beetle strove to efface himself behind the piano. A grey princess-skirt borrowed from a day-boy's mother and a spotted cotton-bodice unsystematically padded with imposition-paper make one ridiculous. And in other regards Beetle had a bad conscience.

'As usual!' sneered King. 'Futile foolery just when your careers, such as they may be, are hanging in the balance. I see! Ah, I see! The old gang of criminals – allied forces of disorder – Corkran' – the Slave of the Lamp smiled politely – 'M'Turk' – the Irishman smiled – 'and, of course, the unspeakable Beetle, our friend Gigadibs.' Abanazar, the Emperor, and Aladdin had more or less of characters, and King passed them over. 'Come forth, my inky buffoon, from behind yonder instrument of music! You supply, I presume, the doggerel for this entertainment. Esteem yourself to be, as it were, a poet?'

'He's found one of 'em,' thought Beetle, noting the flush on King's cheek-bone.

'I have just had the pleasure of reading an effusion of yours to my address, I believe – an effusion intended to rhyme. So – so you despise me, Master Gigadibs, do you? I am quite aware – you need not explain – that it was ostensibly *not* intended for my edification. I read it with laughter – yes, with laughter. These paper pellets of inky boys – still a boy we are, Master Gigadibs – do not disturb my equanimity.'

' 'Wonder which it was,' thought Beetle. He had launched many lampoons on an appreciative public ever since he discovered that it was possible to convey reproof in rhyme.

In sign of his unruffled calm, King proceeded to tear Beetle, whom he called Gigadibs, slowly asunder. From his untied shoe-strings to his mended spectacles (the life of a poet at a big school is hard) he held him up to the derision of his associates – with the usual result. His wild flowers of speech – King had an unpleasant tongue – restored him to good humour at the last. He drew a lurid picture of Beetle's latter end as a scurrilous pamphleteer dying in an attic, scattered a few compliments over M'Turk and Corkran, and, reminding Beetle that he must come up for judgement when called upon, went to Common-room, where he triumphed anew over his victims.

'And the worst of it,' he explained in a loud voice over his soup, 'is that I waste such gems of sarcasm on their thick heads. It's miles above them, I'm certain.'

'We-ell,' said the school chaplain slowly, 'I don't know what Corkran's appreciation of your style may be, but young M'Turk reads Ruskin for his amusement.'

'Nonsense! He does it to show off. I mistrust the dark Celt.'

'He does nothing of the kind. I went into their study the other night, unofficially, and M'Turk was gluing up the back of four odd numbers of *Fors Clavigera*.'

'I don't know anything about their private lives,' said a mathematical master hotly, 'but I've learned by bitter experience that Number Five study are best left alone. They are utterly soulless young devils.' He blushed as the others laughed.

But in the music-room there was wrath and bad language. Only Stalky, Slave of the Lamp, lay on the piano unmoved.

'That little swine Manders minor must have shown him your stuff. He's always suckin' up to King. Go and kill him,' he drawled. 'Which one was it, Beetle?'

'Dunno,' said Beetle, struggling out of the skirt. 'There was one about his hunting for popularity with the small boys, and the other one was one about him in hell, tellin' the Devil he was a Balliol man. I swear both of 'em rhymed all right. By gum! P'raps Manders minor showed him both! *I'll* correct his caesuras for him.'

He disappeared down two flights of stairs, flushed a small pink and white boy in a form-room next door to King's study, which, again, was immediately below his own, and chased him up the corridor into a form-room sacred to the revels of the Lower Third. Thence he came back, greatly disordered, to find M'Turk, Stalky, and the others of the company in his study enjoying an unlimited 'brew' – coffee, cocoa, buns, new bread hot and steaming, sardine, sausage, ham-and-tongue paste, pilchards, three jams, and pounds of Devonshire cream.

'My Hat!' said he, throwing himself upon the banquet. 'Who stumped up for this, Stalky?' It was within a month of term end, and blank starvation had reigned in the studies for weeks.

'You,' said Stalky serenely.

'Confound you! You haven't been popping my Sunday bags, then?'

'Keep your hair on. It's only your watch.'

'Watch! I lost it – weeks ago. Out on the Burrows, when we tried to shoot the old ram – the day our pistol burst.'

'It dropped out of your pocket (you're so beastly careless, Beetle), and M'Turk and I kept it for you. I've been wearing it for a week, and you never noticed. 'Took it into Bideford after dinner to-day. 'Got thirteen and sevenpence. Here's the ticket.'

'Well, that's pretty average cool,' said Abanazar behind a slab of cream and jam, as Beetle, reassured upon the safety of his Sunday trousers, showed not even surprise, much less resentment. Indeed, it was M'Turk who grew angry, saying:

'You gave him the ticket, Stalky? You pawned it? You unmitigated beast! Why, last month you and Beetle sold mine! 'Never got a sniff of any ticket.'

'Ah, that was because you locked your trunk and we wasted half the afternoon hammering it open. We might have pawned it if you'd behaved like a Christian, Turkey.'

'My Aunt!' said Abanazar, 'you chaps are communists. Vote of thanks to Beetle, though.'

'That's beastly unfair,' said Stalky, 'when I took all the trouble to pawn it. Beetle never knew he had a watch. Oh, I say, Rabbits-Eggs gave me a lift into Bideford this afternoon.'

Rabbits-Eggs was the local carrier – an outcrop of the early Devonian formation. It was Stalky who had invented his unlovely name. 'He was pretty average drunk, or he wouldn't have done it. Rabbits-Eggs is a little shy of me, somehow. But I swore it was *pax* between us, and gave him a bob. He stopped at two pubs on the way in, so he'll be howling drunk to-night. Oh, don't begin reading, Beetle; there's a council of war on. What the deuce is the matter with your collar?'

' 'Chivied Manders minor into the Lower Third box-room. 'Had all his beastly little friends on top of me,' said Beetle, from behind a jar of pilchards and a book.

'You ass! Any fool could have told you where Manders would bunk to,' said M'Turk.

'I didn't think,' said Beetle meekly, scooping out pilchards with a spoon.

' 'Course you didn't. You never do.' M'Turk adjusted Beetle's collar with a savage tug. 'Don't drop oil all over my "Fors", or I'll scrag you!'

'Shut up, you – you Irish Biddy! 'Tisn't your beastly "Fors". It's one of mine.'

The book was a fat, brown-backed volume of the later Sixties, which King had once thrown at Beetle's head that Beetle might see whence the name Gigadibs came. Beetle had quietly annexed the book, and had seen – several things. The quarter-comprehended verses lived and ate with him, as the be-dropped pages showed. He removed himself from all that world, drifting at large with wondrous Men and Women, till M'Turk hammered the pilchard spoon on his head and he snarled.

'Beetle! You're oppressed and insulted and bullied by King. Don't you feel it?'

'Let me alone! I can write some more poetry about him if I am, I suppose.'

'Mad! Quite mad!' said Stalky to the visitors, as one exhibiting strange beasts. 'Beetle reads an ass called Brownin', and M'Turk reads an ass called Ruskin; and—'

'Ruskin isn't an ass,' said M'Turk. 'He's almost as good as the Opium-Eater. He says "we're children of noble races trained by surrounding art." That means me, and the way I decorated the study when you two badgers would have stuck up brackets and Christmas cards. Child of a noble race, trained by surrounding art, stop reading, or I'll shove a pilchard down your neck!'

'It's two to one,' said Stalky warningly, and Beetle closed the book, in obedience to the law under which he and his companions had lived for six checkered years.

The visitors looked on delighted. Number Five study had a reputation for more variegated insanity than the rest of the school put together; and so far as its code allowed friendship with outsiders it was polite and open-hearted to its neighbours on the same landing.

'What rot do you want now?' said Beetle.

'King! War!' said M'Turk, jerking his head towards the wall, where hung a small wooden West-African war-drum, a gift to M'Turk from a naval uncle.

'Then we shall be turned out of the study again,' said Beetle, who loved his flesh-pots. 'Mason turned us out for – just warbling on it.' Mason was that mathematical master who had testified in Common-room.

'Warbling? – Oh, Lord!' said Abanazar. 'We couldn't hear ourselves speak in our study when you played the infernal thing. What's the good of getting turned out of your study, anyhow?'

'We lived in the form-rooms for a week, too,' said Beetle tragically. 'And it was beastly cold.'

'Ye-es; but Mason's rooms were filled with rats every day we were out. It took him a week to draw the inference,' said M'Turk. 'He loathes rats. 'Minute he let us go back the rats stopped. Mason's a little shy of us now, but there was no evidence.'

'Jolly well there wasn't,' said Stalky, 'when I got out on the roof and dropped the beastly things down his chimney. But, look here – question is, are our characters good enough just now to stand a study row?'

'Never mind mine,' said Beetle. 'King swears I haven't any.'

'I'm not thinking of you,' Stalky returned scornfully. 'You aren't going up for the Army, you old bat. I don't want to be expelled – and the Head's getting rather shy of us, too.'

'Rot!' said M'Turk. 'The Head never expels except for beastliness or stealing. But I forgot; you and Stalky *are* thieves – regular burglars.'

The visitors gasped, but Stalky interpreted the parable with large grins.

'Well, you know, that little beast Manders minor saw Beetle and me hammerin' M'Turk's trunk open in the dormitory when we took his watch last month. Of course Manders sneaked to Mason, and Mason solemnly took it up as a case of theft, to get even with us about the rats.'

'That just put Mason into our giddy hands,' said M'Turk blandly. 'We were nice to him, 'cause he was a new master and wanted to win the confidence of the boys. 'Pity he draws inferences, though. Stalky went to his study and pretended to blub, and told Mason he'd lead a new life if Mason would let him off this time, but Mason wouldn't. 'Said it was his duty to report him to the Head.'

'Vindictive swine!' said Beetle. 'It was all those rats! Then *I* blubbed, too, and Stalky confessed that he'd been a thief in regular practice for six years, ever since he came to the school; and that I'd taught him – *à la* Fagin. Mason turned white with joy. He thought he had us on toast.'

'Gorgeous! Oh, fids!' said Dick Four. 'We never heard of this.'

' 'Course not. Mason kept it jolly quiet. He wrote down all our statements on impot-paper. There wasn't anything he wouldn't believe,' said Stalky.

'And handed it all up to the Head, *with* an extempore prayer. It took about forty pages,' said Beetle. 'I helped him a lot.'

'And then, you crazy idiots?' said Abanazar.

'Oh, we were sent for; and Stalky asked to have the "depositions" read out, and the Head knocked him spinning into a waste-paper basket. Then he gave us eight cuts apiece – welters – for – for – takin' unheard-of liberties with a new master. I saw his shoulders shaking when we went out. Do you know,' said Beetle pensively, 'that Mason can't look at us now in second lesson without blushing? We three stare at him sometimes till he regularly trickles. He's an awfully sensitive beast.'

'He read *Eric; or, Little by Little*,' said M'Turk; 'so we gave him *St*

Winifred's; or, The World of School. They spent all their spare stealing at St Winifred's, when they weren't praying or getting drunk at pubs. Well, that was only a week ago, and the Head's a little bit shy of us. He called it constructive deviltry. Stalky invented it all.'

' 'Not the least good having a row with a master unless you can make an ass of him,' said Stalky, extended at ease on the hearth-rug. 'If Mason didn't know Number Five – well, he's learn't, that's all. Now, my dearly beloved 'earers' – Stalky curled his legs under him and addressed the company – 'we've got that strong, perseverin' man King on our hands. He went miles out of his way to provoke a conflict.' (Here Stalky snapped down the black silk domino and assumed the air of a judge.) 'He has oppressed Beetle, M'Turk, and me, *privatim et seriatim*, one by one, as he could catch us. But now he has insulted Number Five up in the music-room, and in the presence of these – these ossifers of the Ninety-third, wot look like hairdressers. Binjimin, we must make him cry "*Capivi!*" '

Stalky's reading did not include Browning or Ruskin.

'And, besides,' said M'Turk, 'he's a Philistine, a basket-hanger. He wears a tartan tie. Ruskin says that any man who wears a tartan tie will, without doubt, be damned everlastingly.'

'Bravo, M'Turk,' cried Tertius; 'I thought he was only a beast.'

'He's that, too, of course, but he's worse. He has a china basket with blue ribbons and a pink kitten on it, hung up in his window to grow musk in. You know when I got all that old oak carvin' out of Bideford Church, when they were restoring it (Ruskin says that any man who'll restore a church is an unmitigated sweep), and stuck it up here with glue? Well, King came in and wanted to know whether we'd done it with a fret-saw! Yah! He is the King of basket-hangers!'

Down went M'Turk's inky thumb over an imaginary arena full of bleeding Kings. '*Placetne*, child of a generous race!' he cried to Beetle.

'Well,' began Beetle doubtfully, 'he comes from Balliol, but I'm going to give the beast a chance. You see I can always make him hop with some more poetry. He can't report me to the Head, because it makes him ridiculous. (Stalky's quite right.) But he shall have his chance.'

Beetle opened the book on the table, ran his finger down a page, and began at random:

> 'Or who in Moscow toward the Czar
> With the demurest of footfalls,
> Over the Kremlin's pavement white
> With serpentine and syenite,
> Steps with five other generals——'

'That's no good. Try another,' said Stalky.

'Hold on a shake; I know what's coming.' M'Turk was reading over Beetle's shoulder –

> 'That simultaneously take snuff,
> For each to have pretext enough
> And kerchiefwise unfold his sash,
> Which – softness' self – is yet the stuff

(Gummy! What a sentence!)

> To hold fast where a steel chain snaps
> And leave the grand white neck no gash.

(Full stop.)'

' 'Don't understand a word of it,' said Stalky.

'More fool you! Construe,' said M'Turk. 'Those six bargees scragged the Czar and left no evidence. *Actum est* with King.'

'He gave me that book, too,' said Beetle, licking his lips:

> 'There's a great text in Galatians,
> Once you trip on it entails
> Twenty-nine distinct damnations,
> One sure if another fails.'

Then irrelevantly:

> 'Setebos! Setebos! and Setebos!
> Thinketh he liveth in the cold of the moon.'

'He's just come in from dinner,' said Dick Four, looking through the window. 'Manders minor is with him.'

' 'Safest place for Manders minor just now,' said Beetle.

'Then you chaps had better clear out,' said Stalky politely to the visitors. ' 'Tisn't fair to mix you up in a study row. Besides, we can't afford to have evidence.'

'Are you going to begin at once?' said Aladdin.

'Immediately, if not sooner,' said Stalky, and turned out the gas. 'Strong, perseverin' man – King. Make him cry "*Capivi*." G'way, Binjimin.'

The company retreated to their own neat and spacious study with expectant souls.

' When Stalky blows out his nostrils like a horse,' said Aladdin to the Emperor of China, 'he's on the war-path. Wonder what King will get.'

'Beans,' said the Emperor. 'Number Five generally pays in full.'

' 'Wonder if I ought to take any notice of it officially,' said Abanazar, who had just remembered that he was a prefect.

'It's none of your business, Pussy. Besides, if you did, we'd have them hostile to *us*; and we shouldn't be able to do any work,' said Aladdin. 'They've begun already.'

Now that West-African war-drum had been made to signal across estuaries and deltas. Number Five was forbidden to wake the engine within earshot of the school. But a deep devastating drone filled the passages as M'Turk and Beetle scientifically rubbed its top. Anon it changed to the blare of trumpets – of savage pursuing trumpets. Then, as M'Turk slapped one side, smooth with the blood of ancient sacrifice, the roar broke into short coughing howls such as the wounded gorilla throws in his native forest. These were followed by the wrath of King – three steps at a time, up the staircase, with a dry whirr of the gown. Aladdin and company, listening, squeaked with excitement as the door crashed open. King stumbled into the darkness, and cursed those performers by the gods of Balliol and quiet repose.

'Turned out for a week,' said Aladdin, holding the study door on the crack. 'Key to be brought down to his study in five minutes. "Brutes! Barbarians! Savages! Children!" He's rather agitated. "Arrah, Patsy, mind the baby," ' he sang in a whisper as he clung to the door-knob, dancing a noiseless war-dance.

King went downstairs again, and Beetle and M'Turk lit the gas to confer with Stalky. But Stalky had vanished.

' 'Looks like no end of a mess,' said Beetle, collecting his books and mathematical instrument case. 'A week in the form-rooms isn't any advantage to us.'

'Yes, but don't you see that Stalky isn't here, you owl?' said M'Turk.

287

'Take down the key, and look sorrowful. King'll only jaw you for half an hour. I'm going to read in the lower form-room.'

'But it's always me,' mourned Beetle.

'Wait till we see,' said M'Turk hopefully. 'I don't know any more than you do what Stalky means, but it's something. Go down and draw King's fire. You're used to it.'

No sooner had the key turned in the door than the lid of the coal-box, which was also the window-seat, lifted cautiously. It had been a tight fit, even for the lithe Stalky, his head between his knees, and his stomach under his right ear. From a drawer in the table he took a well-worn catapult, a handful of buckshot, and a duplicate key of the study; noiselessly he raised the window and kneeled by it, his face turned to the road, the wind-sloped trees, the dark levels of the Burrows, and the white line of breakers falling nine-deep along the Pebble-ridge. Far down the steep-banked Devonshire lane he heard the husky hoot of the carrier's horn. There was a ghost of melody in it, as it might have been the wind in a gin-bottle essaying to sing 'It's a way we have in the Army.'

Stalky smiled a tight-lipped smile, and at extreme range opened fire: the old horse half wheeled in the shafts.

'Where be gwaine tu?' hiccoughed Rabbits-Eggs. Another buckshot tore through the rotten canvas tilt with a vicious zipp.

'*Habet!*' murmured Stalky, as Rabbits-Eggs swore into the patient night, protesting that he saw the 'dommed colleger' who was assaulting him.

★　　　★　　　★　　　★

'And so,' King was saying in a high head voice to Beetle, whom he had kept to play with before Manders minor, well knowing that it hurts a Fifth-form boy to be held up to a fag's derision, – 'and so, Master Beetle, in spite of all our verses, which we are so proud of, when we presume to come into direct conflict with even so humble a representative of authority as myself, for instance, we are turned out of our studies, are we not?'

'Yes, sir,' said Beetle, with a sheepish grin on his lips and murder in his heart. Hope had nearly left him, but he clung to a well-established faith that never was Stalky so dangerous as when he was invisible.

'You are not required to criticize, thank you. Turned out of our studies, are we, just as if we were no better than little Manders minor. Only inky schoolboys we are, and must be treated as such.'

Beetle pricked up his ears, for Rabbits-Eggs was swearing savagely on the road, and some of the language entered at the upper sash. King believed in ventilation. He strode to the window, gowned and majestic, very visible in the gas-light.

'I zee 'en! I zee 'un!' roared Rabbits-Eggs, now that he had found a visible foe – another shot from the darkness above. 'Yiss, yeou, yeou long-nosed, fower-eyed, gingy-whiskered beggar! Yeu'm tu old for such goin's on. Aie! Poultice yeour long nose, I tall 'ee! Poultice yeour long nose!'

Beetle's heart leapt up within him. Somewhere, somehow, he knew, Stalky moved behind these manifestations. There was hope and the prospect of revenge. He would embody the suggestion about the nose in deathless verse. King threw up the window, and sternly rebuked Rabbits-Eggs. But the carrier was beyond fear or fawning. He had descended from the cart, and was stooping by the roadside.

It all fell swiftly as a dream. Manders minor raised his hand to his head with a cry, as a jagged flint cannoned onto some rich tree-calf bindings in the bookshelf. Another quoited along the writing-table. Beetle made zealous feint to stop it, and in that endeavour overturned a student's lamp, which dripped, *via* King's papers and some choice books, greasily onto a Persian rug. There was much broken glass on the window-seat; the china basket – M'Turk's aversion – cracked to flinders, had dropped her musk plant and its earth over the red rep cushions; Manders minor was bleeding profusely from a cut on the cheek-bone; and King, using strange words, every one of which Beetle treasured, ran forth to find the school-sergeant, that Rabbits-Eggs might be instantly cast into jail.

'Poor chap!' said Beetle, with a false, feigned sympathy. 'Let it bleed a little. That'll prevent apoplexy,' and he held the blind head skilfully over the table, and the papers on the table, as he guided the howling Manders to the door.

Then did Beetle, alone with the wreckage, return good for evil. How, in that office, a complete set of 'Gibbon' was scarred all along the back as by a flint; how so much black and copying ink chanced to mingle with Manders's gore on the table-cloth; why the big gum-bottle, unstoppered, had rolled semicircularly across the floor; and in what manner the white china door-knob grew to be painted with yet more of Manders's young blood, were matters which Beetle did not explain when the rabid King returned to find him standing politely over the reeking hearth-rug.

'You never told me to go, sir,' he said, with the air of Casabianca, and King consigned him to the outer darkness.

But it was to a boot-cupboard under the staircase on the ground floor that he hastened, to loose the mirth that was destroying him. He had not drawn breath for a first whoop of triumph when two hands choked him dumb.

'Go to the dormitory and get me my things. Bring 'em to Number Five lavatory. I'm still in tights,' hissed Stalky, sitting on his head. 'Don't run. Walk.'

But Beetle staggered into the form-room next door, and delegated his duty to the yet unenlightened M'Turk, with an hysterial *précis* of the campaign thus far. So it was M'Turk, of the wooden visage, who brought the clothes from the dormitory while Beetle panted on a form. Then the three buried themselves in Number Five lavatory, turned on all the taps, filled the place with steam, and dropped weeping into the baths, where they pieced out the war.

'*Moi! Je! Ich! Ego!*' gasped Stalky. 'I waited till I couldn't hear myself think, while you played the drum! Hid in the coal-locker – and tweaked Rabbits-Eggs – and Rabbits-Eggs, rocked King. Wasn't it beautiful? Did you hear the glass?'

'Why, he – he – he,' shrieked M'Turk, one trembling finger pointed at Beetle.

'Why, I – I – I was through it all,' Beetle howled; 'in his study, being jawed.'

'Oh, my soul!' said Stalky with a yell, disappearing under water.

'The – the glass was nothing. Manders minor's head's cut open. La-la-lamp upset all over the rug. Blood on the books and papers. The gum! The gum! The gum! The ink! The ink! The ink! Oh, Lord!'

Then Stalky leaped out, all pink as he was, and shook Beetle into some sort of coherence; but his tale prostrated them afresh.

'I bunked for the boot-cupboard the second I heard King go downstairs. Beetle tumbled in on top of me. The spare key's hid behind the loose board. There isn't a shadow of evidence,' said Stalky. They were all chanting together.

'And he turned us out himself – himself – him*self!*' This from M'Turk. 'He can't begin to suspect us. Oh, Stalky, it's the loveliest thing we've ever done.'

'Gum! Gum! Dollops of gum!' shouted Beetle, his spectacles gleaming through a sea of lather. 'Ink and blood all mixed. I held the little beast's head all over the Latin proses for Monday. Golly, how the oil stunk! And Rabbits-Eggs told King to poultice his nose! Did you hit Rabbits-Eggs, Stalky?'

'Did I jolly well not? Tweaked him all over. Did you hear him curse? Oh, I shall be sick in a minute if I don't stop.'

But dressing was a slow process, because M'Turk was obliged to dance when he heard that the musk basket was broken, and, moreover, Beetle retailed all King's language with emendations and purple insets.

'Shockin'!' said Stalky, collapsing in a helpless welter of half-hitched trousers. 'So dam' bad, too, for innocent boys like us! Wonder what they'd say at "St Winifred's, *or* The World of School". By gum! That reminds me we own the Lower Third one for assaultin' Beetle when he chivied Manders minor. Come on! It's an alibi, Samivel; and besides, if we let 'em off they'll be worse next time.'

The Lower Third had set a guard upon their form-room for the space of a full hour, which to a boy is a lifetime. Now they were busy with their Saturday evening businesses – cooking sparrows over the gas with rusty nibs; brewing unholy drinks in gallipots; skinning moles with pocket-knives: attending to paper trays full of silkworms, or discussing the iniquities of their elders with a freedom, fluency, and point that would have amazed their parents. The blow fell without warning. Stalky upset a crowded form of small boys among their own cooking utensils; M'Turk raided the untidy lockers as a terrier digs at a rabbit-hole; while Beetle poured ink upon such heads as he could not appeal to with a Smith's Classical Dictionary. Three brisk minutes accounted for many silk-worms, pet larvae, French exercises, school caps, half-prepared bones and skulls, and a dozen pots of home-made sloe jam. It was a great wreckage, and the form-room looked as though three conflicting tempests had smitten it.

'Phew!' said Stalky, drawing breath outside the door (amid groans of 'Oh, you beastly ca-ads! You think yourselves awful funny,' and so forth). '*That's* all right. Never let the sun go down upon your wrath. Rummy little devils, fags. 'Got no notice o' combinin'.'

'Six of 'em sat on my head when I went in after Manders minor,' said Beetle. 'I warned 'em what they'd get, though.'

'Everybody paid in full – beautiful feelin',' said M'Turk absently, as they strolled along the corridor. ' 'Don't think we'd better say much about King, though, do you, Stalky?'

'Not much. Our line is injured innocence, of course – same as when old Foxibus reported us on suspicion of smoking in the Bunkers. If I hadn't thought of buyin' the pepper and spillin' it all over our clothes, he'd have smelt us. King was gha-astly facetious about that. 'Called us bird-stuffers in form for a week.'

'Ah, King hates the Natural History Society because little Hartopp is president. 'Mustn't do anything in the Coll. without glorifyin' King,' said M'Turk. 'But he must be a putrid ass, you know, to suppose at our time o' life we'd go out and stuff birds like fags.'

'Poor old King!' said Beetle. 'He's awf'ly unpopular in Common-room, and they'll chaff his head off about Rabbits-Eggs. Golly! How lovely! How beautiful! How holy! But you should have seen his face when the first rock came in! *And* the earth from the basket!'

So they were all stricken helpless for five minutes.

They repaired at last to Abanazar's study, and were received reverently.

'What's the matter?' said Stalky, quick to realize new atmospheres.

'You know jolly well,' said Abanazar. 'You'll be expelled if you get caught. King is a gibbering maniac.'

'Who? Which? What? Expelled for how? We only played the war-drum. We've got turned out for that already.'

'Do you chaps mean to say you didn't make Rabbits-Eggs drunk and bribe him to rock King's rooms?'

'Bribe him? No, that I'll swear we didn't,' said Stalky, with a relieved heart, for he loved not to tell lies. 'What a low mind you've got, Pussy! We've been down having a bath. Did Rabbits-Eggs rock King? Strong, perseverin' man King? Shockin'!'

'Awf'ly. King's frothing at the mouth. There's bell for prayers. Come on.'

'Wait a sec,' said Stalky, continuing the conversation in a loud and cheerful voice, as they descended the stairs. 'What did Rabbits-Eggs rock King for?'

'I know,' said Beetle, as they passed King's open door. 'I was in his study.'

'Hush, you ass!' hissed the Emperor of China. 'Oh, he's gone down to prayers,' said Beetle, watching the shadow of the house-master on the wall. 'Rabbits-Eggs was only a bit drunk, swearin' at his horse, and King jawed him through the window, and then, of course, he rocked King.'

'Do you mean to say,' said Stalky, 'that King began it?'

King was behind them, and every well-weighed word went up the staircase like an arrow. 'I can only swear,' said Beetle, 'that King cursed like a bargee. Simply disgustin'. I'm goin' to write to my father about it.'

'Better report it to Mason,' suggested Stalky. 'He knows our tender consciences. Hold on a shake. I've got to tie my bootlace.'

The other study hurried forward. They did not wish to be dragged into stage asides of this nature. So it was left to M'Turk to sum up the situation beneath the guns of the enemy.

'You see,' said the Irishman, hanging on the banister, 'he begins by bullying little chaps; then he bullies the big chaps; then he bullies some one who isn't connected with the College, and then he catches it. Serves him jolly well right. . . . I beg your pardon, sir. I didn't see you were coming down the staircase.'

The black gown tore past like a thunder-storm, and in its wake, three abreast, arms linked, the Aladdin Company rolled up the big corridor to prayers, singing with most innocent intention:

'Arrah, Patsy, mind the baby! Arrah, Patsy, mind the child!
Wrap him up in an overcoat, he's surely goin' wild!
Arrah, Patsy, mind the baby; just ye mind the child awhile!
He'll kick an' bite an' cry all night! Arrah, Patsy, mind the child!'

THE RAFFLE
V.S. Naipaul

They don't pay primary schoolteachers a lot in Trinidad, but they allow them to beat their pupils as much as they want.

Mr Hinds, my teacher, was a big beater. On the shelf below *The Last of England* he kept four or five tamarind rods. They are good for beating. They are limber, they sting and they last. There was a tamarind tree in the schoolyard. In his locker Mr Hinds also kept a leather strap soaking in the bucket of water every class had in case of fire.

It wouldn't have been so bad if Mr Hinds hadn't been so young and athletic. At the one school sports I went to, I saw him slip off his shining shoes, roll up his trousers neatly to mid-shin and win the Teachers' Hundred Yards, a cigarette between his lips, his tie flapping smartly over his shoulder. It was a wine-coloured tie: Mr Hinds was careful about his dress. That was something else that somehow added to the terror. He wore a brown suit, a cream shirt and the wine-coloured tie.

It was also rumoured that he drank heavily at weekends.

But Mr Hinds had a weak spot. He was poor. We knew he gave those 'private lessons' because he needed the extra money. He gave us private lessons in the ten-minute morning recess. Every boy paid fifty cents for that. If a boy didn't pay, he was kept in all the same and flogged until he paid.

We also knew that Mr Hinds had an allotment in Morvant where he kept some poultry and a few animals.

The other boys sympathized with us – needlessly. Mr Hinds beat us, but I believe we were all a little proud of him.

I say he beat us, but I don't really mean that. For some reason which I could never understand then and can't now, Mr Hinds never beat me. He never made me clean the blackboard. He never made me shine his shoes with the duster. He even called me by my first name, Vidiadhar.

This didn't do me any good with the other boys. At cricket I wasn't allowed to bowl or keep wicket and I always went in at number eleven. My consolation was that I was spending only two terms at the school before going on to Queen's Royal College. I didn't want to go to QRC so much as I wanted to get away from Endeavour (that was the name of the school). Mr Hinds's favour made me feel insecure.

At private lessons one morning Mr Hinds announced that he was going to raffle a goat – a shilling a chance.

He spoke with a straight face and nobody laughed. He made me write out the names of all the boys in the class on two foolscap sheets. Boys who wanted to risk a shilling had to put a tick after their names. Before private lessons ended there was a tick after every name.

I became very unpopular. Some boys didn't believe there was a goat. They all said that if there was a goat, they knew who was going to get it. I hoped they were right. I had long wanted an animal of my own, and the idea of getting milk from my own goat attracted me. I had heard that Mannie Ramjohn, Trinidad's champion miler, trained on goat's milk and nuts.

Next morning I wrote out the names of the boys on slips of paper. Mr Hinds borrowed my cap, put the slips in, took one out, said, 'Vidiadhar, is your goat,' and immediately threw all the slips into the wastepaper basket.

At lunch I told my mother, 'I win a goat today.'

'What sort of goat?'

'I don't know. I ain't see it.'

She laughed, but said: 'It would be nice, though.'

I was getting not to believe in the goat, too. I was afraid to ask Mr Hinds, but a day or two later he said, 'Vidiadhar, you coming or you ain't coming to get your goat?'

He led me to the back of the yard. There was a goat.

He lived in a tumbledown wooden house in Woodbrook and when I got there I saw him in khaki shorts, vest and blue canvas shoes. He was cleaning his bicycle with a yellow flannel. I was overwhelmed. I had never associated him with such dress and such a menial labour. But his manner was more ironic and dismissing than in the classroom.

He led me to the back of the yard. There *was* a goat. A white one with big horns, tied to a plum tree. The ground around the tree was filthy. The goat looked sullen and sleepy-eyed, as if a little stunned by the smell it had made. Mr Hinds invited me to stroke the goat. I stroked it. He closed his eyes and went on chewing. When I stopped stroking him, he opened his eyes.

Every afternoon at about five an old man drove a donkey-cart through Miguel Street where we lived. The cart was piled with fresh grass tied into neat little bundles, so neat you felt grass wasn't a thing that grew but was made in a factory somewhere. That donkey-cart became important to my mother and me. We were buying five, sometimes six bundles a day, and every bundle cost six cents. The goat didn't change. He still looked sullen and bored. From time to time Mr Hinds asked me with a smile how the goat was getting on, and I said it was getting on fine. But when I asked my mother when we were going to get milk from the goat she told me to stop aggravating her. Then one day she put up a sign:

RAM FOR SERVICE
Apply Within For Terms

and got very angry when I asked her to explain it.

The sign made no difference. We bought the neat bundles of grass, the goat ate, and I saw no milk.

And when I got home one lunch-time I saw no goat.

'Somebody borrow it,' mother said. She looked happy.

'When it coming back?'

She shrugged her shoulders.

It came back that afternoon. When I turned the corner into Miguel Street I saw it on the pavement outside our house. A man I didn't know was holding it by a rope and making a big row, gesticulating like anything with his free hand. I knew that sort of man. He wasn't going to let hold of the rope until he had said his piece. A lot of people were looking on through curtains.

'But why all–you want to rob poor people so?' he said, shouting. He turned to his audience behind the curtains. 'Look, all–you, just look at this goat!'

The goat, limitlessly impassive, chewed slowly, its eyes half-closed.

'But how all you people so advantageous? My brother stupid and he ain't known this goat but I know this goat. Everybody in Trinidad who know about goat know this goat, from Icacos to Mayaro to Toco to Chaguaramas,' he said, naming the four corners of Trinidad. 'Is the most uselessest goat in the whole world. And you charge my brother for this goat? Look, you better give me back my brother money, you hear.'

My mother looked hurt and upset. She went inside and came out with some dollar notes. The man took them and handed over the goat.

That evening my mother said, 'Go and tell your Mr Hinds that I don't want this goat here.'

Mr Hinds didn't look surprised. 'Don't want it, eh?' He thought, and passed a well-trimmed thumb-nail over his moustache. 'Look, tell you. Going to buy him back. Five dollars.'

I said, 'He eat more than that in grass alone.'

That didn't surprise him either. 'Say six, then.'

I sold. That, I thought, was the end of that.

One Monday afternoon about a month before the end of my last term I announced to my mother, 'That goat raffling again.'

She became alarmed.

At tea on Friday I said casually, 'I win the goat.'

She was expecting it. Before the sun set a man had brought the goat away from Mr Hinds, given my mother some money and taken the goat away.

I hoped Mr Hinds would never ask about the goat. He did, though. Not the next week, but the week after that, just before school broke up.

I didn't know what to say.

But a boy called Knolly, a fast bowler and a favourite victim of Mr Hinds, answered for me. 'What goat?' he whispered loudly. 'That goat kill and eat long time.'

Mr Hinds was suddenly furious. 'Is true, Vidiadhar?'

I didn't nod or say anything. The bell rang and saved me.

At lunch I told my mother, 'I don't want to go back to that school.'

She said, 'You must be brave.'

I didn't like the argument, but went.

We had Geography the first period.

'Naipaul' Mr Hinds said right away, forgetting my first name, 'define a peninsula.'

'Peninsula,' I said, 'a piece of land entirely surrounded by water.'

'Good. Come up here.' He went to the locker and took out the soaked leather strap. Then he fell on me. 'You sell my goat?' Cut. 'You kill my goat?' Cut. 'How you so damn ungrateful?' Cut, cut, cut. 'Is the last time you win anything I raffle.'

It was the last day I went to that school.

MY 'FIRST HALF' AT SALEM HOUSE
Charles Dickens

School began in earnest next day. A profound impression was made upon me, I remember, by the roar of voices in the schoolroom suddenly becoming hushed as death when Mr Creakle entered after breakfast, and stood in the doorway looking round upon us like a giant in a story-book surveying his captives.

Tungay stood at Mr Creakle's elbow. He had no occasion, I thought, to cry out 'Silence!' so ferociously, for the boys were all struck speechless and motionless.

Mr Creakle was seen to speak, and Tungay was heard, to this effect:

'Now, boys, this is a new half. Take care what you're about in this new half. Come fresh up to the lessons, I advise you, for I come fresh up to the punishment. I won't flinch. It will be of no use your rubbing yourselves; you won't rub the marks out that I shall give you. Now get to work, every boy!'

When this dreadful exordium was over, and Tungay had stumped out again, Mr Creakle came to where I sat, and told me that if I were famous for biting, he was famous for biting too. He then showed me the cane, and asked me what I thought of *that* for a tooth? Was it a sharp tooth, hey? Was it a double tooth, hey? Had it a deep prong, hey? Did it bite, hey? Did it bite? At every question he gave me a fleshy cut with it that made me writhe; so I was very soon made free of Salem House (as Steerforth said), and was very soon in tears also

Not that I meant to say these were special marks of distinction, which only I received. On the contrary, a large majority of the boys (especially the smaller ones) were visited with similar instances of notice, as Mr Creakle made the round of the schoolroom. Half the establishment was writhing and crying before the day's work began; and how much of it had writhed and cried before the day's work was over, I am really afraid to recollect, lest I should seem to exaggerate.

I should think there never can have been a man who enjoyed his profession more than Mr Creakle did. He had a delight in cutting at the boys, which was like the satisfaction of a craving appetite. I am confident that he couldn't resist a chubby boy especially; that there was a fascination in such a subject, which made him restless in his mind until he had scored and marked him for the day. I was chubby myself, and ought to know. I am sure, when I think of the fellow now, my blood rises against him with the disinterested indignation I should feel if I could have known all about him without having ever been in his power; but it rises hotly, because I know him to have been an incapable brute, who had no more right to be possessed of the great trust he held than to be Lord High Admiral or Commander-in-chief – in either of which capacities it is probable that he would have done infinitely less mischief.

Miserable little propitiators of a remorseless Idol, how abject we were to him! What a launch in life I think it now, on looking back, to be so mean and servile to a man of such parts and pretensions!

Here I sit at the desk again watching his eye – humbly watching his eye, as he rules a ciphering book for another victim whose hands have just been flattened by that identical ruler, and who is trying to wipe the sting out with a pocket-handkerchief. I have plenty to do. I don't watch his eye in idleness, but because I am morbidly attracted to it in a dread desire to know what he will do next, and whether it will be my turn to suffer or somebody else's. A lane of small boys beyond me, with the same interest in his eye, watch it too. I think he knows it, though he pretends he doesn't. He makes dreadful mouths as he rules the ciphering book; and now he throws his eye sideways down our lane, and we all droop over our books and tremble. A moment afterwards we are again eyeing him. An unhappy culprit, found guilty of imperfect exercise, approaches at his command. The culprit falters excuses and professes a determination to do better tomorrow. Mr Creakle cuts a joke before he beats him, and we laugh at it – miserable little dogs, we laugh, with our visages as white as ashes, and our hearts sinking into our boots.

Here I sit at the desk again on a drowsy summer afternoon. A buzz and hum go up around me, as if the boys were so many blue-bottles. A cloggy sensation of the luke-warm fat of meat is upon me (we dined an hour or two ago), and my head is as heavy as so much lead. I would give the world to go to sleep. I sit with my eye on Mr Creakle, blinking at him like a young owl; when sleep overpowers me for a minute, he still looms through my slumber, ruling these ciphering books, until he softly comes behind me and wakes me to plainer perception of him with a red ridge across my back.

Here I am in the playground, with my eye still fascinated by him, though I can't see him. The window, at a little distance from which I know he is having his dinner, stands for him, and I eye that instead. If he shows his face near it, mine assumes an imploring and submissive expression. If he looks out through the glass, the boldest boy (Steerforth excepted) stops in the middle of a shout or yell, and becomes contemplative. One day, Traddles (the most unfortunate boy in the world) breaks that window accidentally with a ball. I shudder at this moment with the tremendous sensation of seeing it done, and feeling that the ball has bounded onto Mr Creakle's sacred head.

Poor Traddles! In a tight sky-blue suit that made his arms and legs like German sausages, or roly-poly puddings, he was the merriest and most miserable of all the boys. He was always being caned – I think he was caned every day that half-year, except one holiday Monday when he was only ruler'd on both hands – and was always going to write to his uncle about it, and never did. After laying his head on the desk for a little while, he would cheer up somehow, begin to laugh again, and draw skeletons all over his slate, before his eyes were dry. I used at first to wonder what comfort Traddles found in drawing skeletons; and for some time looked upon him as a sort of hermit, who reminded himself by those symbols of mortality that caning couldn't last for ever. But I believe he only did it because they were easy, and didn't want any features.

He was very honourable, Traddles was, and held it as a solemn duty in the boys to stand by one another. He suffered for this on several occasions; and particularly once, when Steerforth laughed in church, and the beadle thought it was Traddles, and took him out. I see him now, going away in custody, despised by the congregation. He never said who was the real offender, though he smarted for it next day, and was imprisoned so many hours that he came forth with a whole churchyardful of skeletons swarming all over his Latin dictionary. But he had his reward. Steerforth said there was nothing of the sneak in Traddles, and we all felt that to be the highest praise. For my part, I could have gone through a good deal (though I was much less brave than Traddles, and nothing like so old) to have won such a recompense.

To see Steerforth walk to church before us, arm in arm with Miss Creakle, was one of the great sights of my life. I didn't think Miss Creakle equal to little Em'ly in point of beauty, and I didn't love her (I didn't dare); but I thought her a young lady of extraordinary attractions, and in point of gentility not to be surpassed. When Steerforth, in white trousers, carried her parasol for her, I felt proud to know him, and believed that she could not choose but adore him with all her heart. Mr Sharp and Mr Mell were both notable personages in my eyes; but Steerforth was to them what the sun was to two stars.

Steerforth continued his protection of me, and proved a very useful friend, since nobody dared to annoy one whom he honoured with his countenance. He couldn't – or, at all events, he didn't – defend me from Mr Creakle, who was very severe with me; but whenever I had been treated worse than usual, he always told me that I wanted a little of his pluck, and that he wouldn't have stood it himself – which I felt he intended for encouragement, and considered to be very kind of him. There was one advantage, and only one that I know of, in Mr Creakle's severity. He found my placard in his way when he came up or down behind the form on which I sat, and wanted to make a cut at me in passing. For this reason it was soon taken off, and I saw it no more.

An accidental circumstance cemented the intimacy between Steerforth and me, in a manner that inspired me with great pride and satisfaction, though it sometimes led to inconvenience. It happened on one occasion, when he was doing me the honour of talking to me in the playground, that I hazarded the observation that something or somebody – I forget what now – was like something or somebody in

'Peregrine Pickle'. He said nothing at the time; but when I was going to bed at night, asked me if I had got that book.

I told him no, and explained how it was that I had read it, and all those other books of which I have made mention.

'And do you recollect them?' Steerforth said.

Oh, yes, I replied; I had a good memory, and I believed I recollected them very well.

'Then I tell you what, young Copperfield,' said Steerforth, 'you shall tell 'em to me. I can't get to sleep very early at night, and I generally wake rather early in the morning. We'll go over 'em one after another. We'll make some regular Arabian Nights of it.'

I felt extremely flattered by this arrangement, and we commenced carrying it into execution that very evening. What ravages I committed on my favourite authors in the course of my interpretation of them, I am not in a condition to say, and should be very unwilling to know; but I had a profound faith in them, and I had, to the best of my belief, a simple earnest manner of narrating what I did narrate.

The drawback was, that I was often sleepy at night, or out of spirits and indisposed to resume the story, and then it was rather hard work, and it must be done; for to disappoint or displease Steerforth was of course out of the question. In the morning too, when I felt weary, and should have enjoyed another hour's repose very much, it was a tiresome thing to be roused, like the Sultana Scheherazade, and forced into a long story before the getting-up bell rang. But Steerforth was resolute; and as he explained to me, in return, my sums and exercises and anything in my tasks that was too hard for me, I was no loser by the transaction. Let me do myself justice, however. I was moved by no interested or selfish motive, nor was I moved by fear of him. I admired and loved him, and his approval was return enough. It was so precious to me, that I look back on these trifles now with an aching heart.

Steerforth was considerate too, and showed his consideration in one particular instance, in an unflinching manner that was a little tantalizing, I suspect, to poor Traddles and the rest. Peggotty's promised letter – what a comfortable letter it was! – arrived before 'the half' was many weeks old, and with it a cake in a perfect nest of oranges, and two bottles of cowslip wine. This treasure, as in duty bound, I laid at the feet of Steerforth, and begged him to dispense.

'Now, I'll tell you what, young Copperfield,' said he, 'the wine shall be kept to wet your whistle when you are story-telling.'

I blushed at the idea, and begged him, in my modesty, not to think of it. But he said he had observed I was sometimes hoarse – a little roopy was his exact expression – and it should be, every drop, devoted to the purpose he had mentioned. Accordingly, it was locked up in his box, and drawn off by himself in a phial, and administered to me through a piece of quill in the cork, when I was supposed to be in want of a restorative. Sometimes, to make it a more sovereign specific, he was so kind as to squeeze orange juice into it, or to stir it up with ginger, or dissolve a peppermint drop in it; and although I cannot assert that the flavour was improved by these experiments, or that it was exactly the compound one would have chosen for a stomachic the last thing at night and the first thing in the morning, I drank it gratefully, and was very sensible of his attention.

We seem, to me, to have been months over Peregrine, and months more over the other stories. The institution never flagged for want of a story, I am certain, and the wine lasted out almost as well as the matter. Poor Traddles – I never think of that boy but with a strange disposition to laugh, and with tears in my eyes – was a sort of chorus, in general, and affected to be convulsed with mirth and at the comic parts, and to be overcome with fear when there was any passage of an alarming character in the narrative. This rather put me out, very often. It was a great jest of his, I recollect, to pretend that he couldn't keep his teeth from chattering whenever mention was made of an Alguazil in connection with the adventures of Gil Blas; and I remember, when Gil Blas met the captain of the robbers in Madrid, this unlucky joker counterfeited such an ague of terror that he was overheard by Mr Creakle, who was prowling about the passage, and handsomely flogged for disorderly conduct in the bedroom.

Whatever I had within me that was romantic and dreamy was encouraged by so much story-telling in the dark; and in that respect the pursuit may not have been very profitable to me. But the being cherished as a kind of plaything in my room, and the consciousness that this accomplishment of mine was bruited about among the boys, and attracted a good deal of notice to me though I was the youngest there, stimulated me to exertion. In a school carried on by sheer cruelty, whether it is presided over by a dunce or not, there is not likely to be much learnt. I believe our boys were generally as ignorant a set as any schoolboys in existence; they were too much troubled and knocked about to learn; they could no more do that to advantage, than any one can do anything to advantage in a life of constant misfortune, torment, and worry. But my little vanity, and Steerforth's help, urged me on somehow; and without saving me from much, if anything, in the way of punishment, made me, for the time I was there, an exception to the general body, insomuch that I did steadily pick up some crumbs of knowledge.

In this I was much assisted by Mr Mell, who had a liking for me that I am grateful to remember. It always gave me pain to observe that Steerforth treated him with systematic disparagement, and seldom lost an occasion of wounding his feelings, or inducing others to do so. This troubled me the more for a long time, because I had soon told Steerforth, from whom I could no more keep such a secret than I could keep a cake or any other tangible possession, about the two old women Mr Mell had taken me to see; and I was always afraid that Steerforth would let it out, and twit him with it.

We little thought, any one of us, I dare say, when I ate my breakfast that first morning, and went to sleep under the shadow of the peacock's feathers to the sound of the flute, what consequences would come of the introduction into those alms-houses of my insignificant person. But the visit had its unforeseen consequences; and of a serious sort, too, in their way.

One day when Mr Creakle kept the house from indisposition, which naturally diffused a lively joy through the school, there was a good deal of noise in the course of the morning's work. The great relief and satisfaction experienced by the boys made them difficult to manage; and though the dreaded Tungay brought his wooden leg in twice or thrice, and took notes of the principal offenders' names, no great impression was made by it, as they were pretty sure of getting into trouble tomorrow, do what they would, and thought it wise, no doubt, to enjoy themselves today.

It was properly a half-holiday, being Saturday; but as the noise in the playground would have disturbed Mr Creakle, and the weather was not favourable for going out walking, we were ordered into school in the afternoon, and set some lighter tasks than usual, which were made for the occasion. It was the day of the week on which Mr Sharp went out to get his wig curled; so Mr Mell, who always did the drudgery, whatever it was, kept school by himself.

If I could associate the idea of a bull or a bear with anyone so mild as Mr Mell, I should think of him, in connection with that afternoon when the uproar was at its height, as of one of those animals baited by a thousand dogs. I recall him bending his aching head, supported on his bony hand, over the book on his desk, and wretchedly endeavouring to get on with his tiresome work, amidst an uproar that might have made the Speaker of the House of Commons giddy. Boys started in and out of their places, playing at puss-in-the-corner with other boys; there were laughing boys, singing boys, talking boys, dancing boys, howling boys; boys shuffled with their feet, boys whirled about him, grinning, making faces, mimicking him behind his back and before his eyes – mimicking his poverty, his boots, his coat, his mother, everything belonging to him that they should have had consideration for.

'Silence!' cried Mr Mell, suddenly rising up and striking his desk with the book. 'What does this mean? It's impossible to bear it. It's maddening. How can you do it to me, boys?'

It was my book that he struck his desk with; and as I stood beside him, following his eye as it glanced round the room, I saw the boys all stop, some suddenly surprised, some half afraid, and some sorry perhaps.

Steerforth's place was at the bottom of the school, at the opposite end of the long room. He was lounging with his back against the wall, and his hands in his pockets, and looked at Mr Mell with his mouth shut up as if he were whistling, when Mr Mell looked at him.

'Silence, Mr Steerforth!' said Mr Mell.

'Silence yourself,' said Steerforth, turning red. 'Whom are you talking to?'

'Sit down,' said Mr Mell.

'Sit down yourself,' said Steerforth, 'and mind your business.'

There was a titter, and some applause. But Mr Mell was so white that silence immediately succeeded; and one boy, who had darted out behind him to imitate his mother again, changed his mind, and pretended to want a pen mended.

'If you think, Steerforth,' said Mr Mell, 'that I am not acquainted

Steerforth lounged with his back against the wall.

with the power you can establish over any mind here' – he laid his hand, without considering what he did (as I supposed), upon my head – 'or that I have not observed you, within a few minutes, urging your juniors on to every sort of outrage against me, you are mistaken.'

'I don't give myself the trouble of thinking at all about you,' said Steerforth coolly; 'so I'm not mistaken, as it happens.'

'And when you make use of your position of favouritism here, sir,' pursued Mr Mell, with his lip trembling very much 'to insult a gentle-man—'

'A what? – where is he?' said Steerforth.

Here somebody cried out, 'Shame, J. Steerforth! Too bad!' It was Traddles, whom Mr Mell instantly discomfited by bidding him hold his tongue.

'To insult one who is not fortunate in life, sir, and who never gave you the least offence, and the many reasons for not insulting whom you are old enough and wise enough to understand,' said Mr Mell, with his lip trembling more and more, 'you commit a mean and base action. You can sit down or stand up as you please, sir. – Copperfield, go on.'

'Young Copperfield,' said Steerforth, coming forward up the room, 'stop a bit. I tell you what, Mr Mell, once for all: when you take the liberty of calling me mean or base, or anything of that sort, you are an impudent beggar. You are always a beggar, you know; but when you do that, you are an impudent beggar.'

I am not clear whether he was going to strike Mr Mell, or Mr Mell was going to strike him, or there was any such intention on either side. I saw a rigidity come upon the whole school as if they had been turned into stone, and found Mr Creakle in the midst of us, with Tungay at his side, and Mrs and Miss Creakle looking in at the door as if they were frightened. Mr Mell, with his elbows on his desk and his face in his hands, sat for some moments quite still.

'Mr Mell,' said Mr Creakle, shaking him by the arm – and his whisper was so audible now that Tungay felt it unnecessary to repeat his words – 'you have not forgotten yourself, I hope?'

'No, sir, no,' returned the Master, showing his face, and shaking his head, and rubbing his hands in great agitation. 'No, sir, no. I have remembered myself; I – no, Mr Creakle, I have not forgotten myself; I – I have remembered myself, sir. I – I – could wish you had remembered me a little sooner, Mr Creakle. It – it – would have been more kind, sir, more just, sir. It would have saved me something, sir.'

Mr Creakle, looking hard at Mr Mell, put his hand on Tungay's shoulder, and got his feet upon the form close by, and sat upon the desk. After still looking hard at Mr Mell from this throne, as he shook his head and rubbed his hands, and remained in the same state of agitation, Mr Creakle turned to Steerforth, and said, –

'Now, sir, as he don't condescend to tell me, what *is* this?'

Steerforth evaded the question for a little while, looking in scorn and anger on his opponent, and remaining silent. I could not help thinking even in that interval, I remember, what a noble fellow he was in appearance, and how homely and plain Mr Mell looked opposed to him.

'What did he mean by talking about favourites, then?' said Steerforth at length.

'Favourites?' repeated Mr Creakle, with the veins in his forehead swelling quickly. 'Who talked about favourites?'

'He did,' said Steerforth.

'And pray, what did you mean by that, sir?' demanded Mr Creakle, turning angrily on his assistant.

'I meant, Mr Creakle,' he returned in a low voice, 'as I said – that no pupil had a right to avail himself of his position of favouritism to degrade me.'

'To degrade *you?*' said Mr Creakle. 'My stars! But give me leave to ask you, Mr What's-your-name' (and here Mr Creakle folded his arms, cane and all, upon his chest, and made such a knot of his brows that his little eyes were hardly visible below them), 'whether, when you talk about favourites, you showed proper respect to me? To me, sir,' said Mr Creakle, darting his head at him suddenly, and drawing it back again, 'the principal of this establishment, and your employer.'

'It was not judicious, sir, I am willing to admit,' said Mr Mell. 'I should not have done so if I had been cool.'

Here Steerforth struck in.

'Then he said I was mean, and then he said I was base; and then I called him a beggar. If I had been cool, perhaps I shouldn't have called him a beggar; but I did, and I am ready to take the consequences of it.'

Without considering, perhaps, whether there were any consequences to be taken, I felt quite in a glow at this gallant speech. It made an impression on the boys too, for there was a low stir among them, though no one spoke a word.

'I am surprised, Steerforth – although your candour does you honour,' said Mr Creakle, 'does you honour, certainly – I am surprised, Steerforth, I must say, that you should attach such an epithet to any person employed and paid in Salem House, sir.'

Steerforth gave a short laugh.

'That's not an answer, sir,' said Mr Creakle, 'to my remark. I expect more than that from you, Steerforth.'

If Mr Mell looked homely in my eyes before the handsome boy, it would be quite impossible to say how homely Mr Creakle looked.

'Let him deny it,' said Steerforth.

'Deny that he is a beggar, Steerforth?' cried Mr Creakle, 'Why, where does he go a-begging?'

'If he is not a beggar himself, his near relation's one,' said Steerforth. 'It's all the same.'

He glanced at me, and Mr Mell's hand gently patted me upon the shoulder. I looked up with a flush upon my face and remorse in my heart; but Mr Mell's eyes were fixed on Steerforth. He continued to pat me kindly on the shoulder, but he looked at him.

'Since you expect me, Mr Creakle, to justify myself,' said Steerforth, 'and to say what I mean: what I have to say is, that his mother lives on charity in an alms-house.'

Mr Mell still looked at him, and still patted me kindly on the shoulder, and said to himself in a whisper, if I heard right, 'Yes, I thought so.'

Mr Creakle turned to his assistant with a severe frown and laboured politeness:

'Now you hear what this gentleman says, Mr Mell. Have the goodness, if you please, to set him right before the assembled school.'

'He is right, sir, without correction,' returned Mr Mell, in the midst of a dead silence; 'what he has said is true.'

'Be so good, then, as declare publicly, will you,' said Mr Creakle, putting his head on one side, and rolling his eyes round the school, 'whether it ever came to my knowledge until this moment?'

'I believe not directly,' he returned.

'Why, you know not,' said Mr Creakle. 'Don't you, man?'

'I apprehend you never supposed my worldly circumstances to be very good,' replied the assistant. 'You know what my position is, and always has been, here.'

'I apprehend, if you come to that,' said Mr Creakle, with his veins swelling again bigger than ever, 'that you've been in a wrong position altogether, and mistook this for a charity school. Mr Mell, we'll part, if you please. The sooner the better.'

'There is no time,' answered Mr Mell, rising, 'like the present.'

'Sir, to you!' said Mr Creakle.

'I take my leave of you, Mr Creakle, and all of you,' said Mr Mell, glancing round the room, and again patting me gently on the shoulder. 'James Steerforth, the best wish I can leave you is that you may come to be ashamed of what you have done today. At present I would prefer to see you anything rather than a friend to me or to anyone in whom I feel an interest.'

Once more he laid his hand upon my shoulder; and then taking his flute and a few books from his desk, and leaving the key in it for his successor, he went out of the school with his property under his arm. Mr Creakle then made a speech, through Tungay, in which he thanked Steerforth for asserting (though perhaps too warmly) the independence and respectability of Salem House, and which he wound up by shaking hands with Steerforth; while we gave three cheers – I did not quite know what for, but I supposed for Steerforth, and so joined in them ardently, though I felt miserable. Mr Creakle then caned Tommy Traddles for being discovered in tears instead of cheers, on account of Mr Mell's departure; and went back to his sofa, or his bed, or wherever he had come from.

We were left to ourselves now, and looked very blank, I recollect, on one another. For myself, I felt so much self-reproach and contrition for my part in what had happened, that nothing would have enabled me to keep back my tears but the fear that Steerforth, who often looked at me, I saw, might think it unfriendly – or, I should rather say, considering our relative ages and the feeling with which I regarded him, undutiful – if I showed the emotion which distressed me. He was very angry with Traddles, and said he was glad he had caught it.

Poor Traddles, who had passed the stage of lying with his head upon the desk, and was relieving himself as usual with a burst of skeletons, said he didn't care; Mr Mell was ill-used.

'Who has ill-used him, you girl?' said Steerforth.

'Why, you have,' returned Traddles.

'What have I done?' said Steerforth.

'What have you done?' retorted Traddles. 'Hurt his feelings, and lost him his situation.'

'His feelings!' repeated Steerforth disdainfully. 'His feelings will soon get the better of it, I'll be bound. His feelings are not like yours, Miss Traddles. As to his situation – which was a precious one, wasn't it? – do you suppose I am not going to write home and take care that he gets some money, Polly?'

We thought this intention very noble in Steerforth, whose mother was a widow, and rich, and would do almost anything, it was said, that he asked her. We were all extremely glad to see Traddles so put down, and exalted Steerforth to the skies – especially when he told us, as he condescended to do, that what he had done had been done expressly for us and for our cause, and that he had conferred a great boon upon us by unselfishly doing it.

But I must say that when I was going on with a story in the dark that night, Mr Mell's old flute seemed more than once to sound mournfully in my ears; and that when at last Steerforth was tired, and I lay down in my bed, I fancied it playing so sorrowfully somewhere that I was quite wretched.

I soon forgot him in the contemplation of Steerforth, who, in an easy amateur way, and without any book (he seemed to me to know everything by heart), took some of his classes until a new master was found. The new master came from a grammar-school, and before he entered on his duties dined in the parlour one day, to be introduced to Steerforth. Steerforth approved of him highly, and told us he was a brick. Without exactly understanding what learned distinction was meant by this, I respected him greatly for it, and had no doubt whatever of his superior knowledge; though he never took the pains with me – not that *I* was anybody – that Mr Mell had taken.

A TEMPEST IN THE SCHOOL TEAPOT
L.M. Montgomery

'What a splendid day!' said Anne, drawing a long breath. 'Isn't it good just to be alive on a day like this? I pity the people who aren't born yet for missing it. They may have good days, of course, but they can never have this one. And it's splendider still to have such a lovely way to go to school by, isn't it?'

'It's a lot nicer than going round by the road; that is so dusty and hot,' said Diana practically, peeping into her dinner basket and mentally calculating if the three juicy, toothsome, raspberry tarts reposing there were divided among ten girls how many bites each girl would have.

The little girls of Avonlea school always pooled their lunches, and to eat three raspberry tarts all alone or even to share them only with one's best chum would have for ever and ever branded as 'awful mean' the girl who did it. And yet, when the tarts were divided among ten girls you just got enough to tantalize you.

The way Anne and Diana went to school *was* a pretty one. Anne thought those walks to and from school with Diana couldn't be improved upon even by imagination. Going around by the main road would have been so unromantic; but to go by Lovers' Lane and Willowmere and Violet Vale and the Birch Path was romantic, if ever anything was.

Lovers' Lane opened out below the orchard at Green Gables and stretched far into the woods to the end of the Cuthbert Farm. Anne had named it Lovers' Lane before she had been a month at Green Gables.

'Not that lovers ever really walk there,' she explained to Marilla, 'but Diana and I are reading a perfectly magnificent book and there's a Lovers' Lane in it. So we want to have one, too. And it's a very pretty name, don't you think? So romantic! We can imagine the lovers into it, you know. I like that lane because you can think out loud there without people calling you crazy.'

Anne, starting out alone in the morning, went down Lovers' Lane as far as the brook. Here Diana met her, and the two little girls went on up the lane under the leafy arch of maples – 'maples are such sociable trees,' said Anne; 'they're always rustling and whispering to you,' – until they came to a rustic bridge. Then they left the lane and walked through Mr Barry's back field and past Willowmere. Beyond Willowmere came Violet Vale – a little green dimple in the shadow of Mr Andrew Bell's big woods. 'Of course there are no violets there now,' Anne told Marilla, 'but Diana says there are millions of them in spring. Oh, Marilla, can't you just imagine you see them? It actually takes away my breath. I named it Violet Vale. Diana says she never saw the beat of me for hitting on fancy names for places. It's nice to be clever at something, isn't it? But Diana named the Birch Path. She wanted to, so I let her; but I'm sure I could have found something more poetical than plain Birch Path. Anybody can think of a name like that. But the Birch Path is one of the prettiest places in the world, Marilla.'

It was. Other people besides Anne thought so when they stumbled on it. It was a little narrow, twisting path, winding down over a long hill straight through Mr Bell's woods, where the light came down sifted through so many emerald screens that it was as flawless as the heart of a diamond. It was fringed in all its length with slim young birches, white-stemmed and lissom-boughed; fern sand starflowers and wild lilies of the valley and scarlet tufts of pigeon berries grew thickly along it; and always there was a delightful spiciness in the air and music of bird calls. Down in the valley the path came out to the main road and then it was just up the spruce hill to the school.

The Avonlea school was a whitewashed building low in the eaves and wide in the windows, furnished inside with comfortable substantial old-fashioned desks that opened and shut, and were carved all over their lids with the initials and hieroglyphics of three generations of school-children. The schoolhouse was set back from the road and behind it was a dusky fir wood and a brook where all the children put their bottles of milk in the morning to keep cool and sweet until dinner hour.

Marilla had seen Anne start off to school on the first day of September with many secret misgivings. Anne was such an odd girl. How would she get on with the other children? And how on earth would she ever manage to hold her tongue during school hours?

Things went better than Marilla feared, however. Anne came home that evening in high spirits.

'I think I'm going to like school here,' she announced. 'I don't think much of the master, though. He's all the time curling his moustache and making eyes at Prissy Andrews. Prissy is grown-up, you know. She's sixteen and she's studying for the entrance examination into Queen's Academy at Charlottetown next year. Tillie Boulter says the master is *dead gone* on her. She's got a beautiful complexion and curly brown hair and she does it up so elegantly. She sits in the long seat at the back and he sits there, too, most of the time – to explain her lessons, he says. But Ruby Gillis says she saw him writing something on her slate and when Prissy read it she blushed as red as a beet and giggled; and Ruby Gillis says she doesn't believe it had anything to do with the lesson.'

'Anne Shirley, don't let me hear you talking about your teacher in that way again,' said Marilla sharply. 'You don't go to school to criticize the master. I guess he can teach *you* something and it's your business to learn. And I want you to understand right off that you are not to come home telling tales about him. That is something I won't encourage. I hope you were a good girl.'

'Indeed I was,' said Anne comfortably. 'It wasn't so hard as you might imagine, either. I sit with Diana. Our seat is right by the window and we can look down to the Lake of Shining Waters. There are a lot of nice girls in school and we had scrumptious fun playing at dinner-time. It's so nice to have a lot of little girls to play with. But of course I like Diana best and always will. I *adore* Diana. I'm dreadfully far behind the others. They're all in the fifth book and I'm only in the fourth. I feel that it's a kind of a disgrace. But there's not one of them has such an imagination as I have, and I soon found that out. We had reading and geography and Canadian History and dictation today. Mr Phillips said my spelling was disgraceful and he held up my slate so that everybody could see it, all marked over. I felt so mortified, Marilla; he might have been politer to a stranger, I think. Ruby Gillis gave me an apple and Sophia Sloane lent me a lovely pink card with 'May I see you home?' on it. I'm to give it back to her tomorrow. And Tillie Boulter let me wear her bead ring all the afternoon. Can I have some of those pearl beads off the old pincushion in the garret to make myself a ring? And oh, Marilla, Jane Andrews told me that Minnie MacPherson told her that she heard Prissy Andrews tell Sara Gillis that I had a very pretty nose. Marilla, that is the first compliment I have ever had in my life and you can't imagine what a strange feeling it gave me. Marilla, have I really a pretty nose? I know you'll tell me the truth.'

'Your nose is well enough,' said Marilla shortly. Secretly she thought Anne's nose was a remarkably pretty one; but she had no intention of telling her so.

That was three weeks ago and all had gone smoothly so far. And now, this crisp September morning, Anne and Diana were tripping blithely down the Birch Path, two of the happiest little girls in Avonlea.

'I guess Gilbert Blythe will be in school today,' said Diana. 'He's been visiting his cousins over in New Brunswick all summer and he only came home Saturday night. He's *awf'ly* handsome, Anne. And he teases the girls something terrible. He just torments our lives out.'

Diana's voice indicated that she rather liked having her life tormented out than not.

'Gilbert Blythe?' said Anne. 'Isn't it his name that's written up on the porch wall with Julia Bell's and a big "Take Notice" over them?'

'Yes,' said Diana, tossing her head, 'but I'm sure he doesn't like Julia Bell so very much. I've heard him say he studied the multiplication table by her freckles.'

'Oh, don't speak about freckles to me,' implored Anne. 'It isn't delicate when I've got so many. But I do think that writing take-notices up on the wall about the boys and girls is the silliest ever. I should just like to see anybody dare to write my name up with a boy's. Not, of course,' she hastened to add, 'that anybody would.'

Anne sighed. She didn't want her name written up. But it was a little humiliating to know that there was no danger of it.

'Nonsense,' said Diana, whose black eyes and glossy tresses had played such havoc with the hearts of Avonlea schoolboys that her name figured on the porch walls in half a dozen take-notices. 'It's only meant as a joke. And don't you be too sure your name won't ever be written up. Charlie Sloane is *dead gone* on you. He told his mother – his *mother*, mind you – that you were the smartest girl in school. That's better than being good-looking.'

'No, it isn't,' said Anne, feminine to the core. 'I'd rather be pretty than clever. And I hate Charlie Sloane. I can't bear a boy with goggle eyes. If anyone wrote my name up with his I'd *never* get over it, Diana Barry. But it *is* nice to keep head of your class.'

'You'll have Gilbert in your class after this,' said Diana, 'and he's used to being head of his class, I can tell you. He's only in the fourth book although he's nearly fourteen. Four years ago his father was sick and had to go out to Alberta for his health and Gilbert went with him. They were there three years and Gil didn't go to school hardly any until they came back. You won't find it so easy to keep head after this, Anne.'

'I'm glad,' said Anne quickly. 'I couldn't really feel proud of keeping head of little boys and girls of just nine or ten. I got up yesterday spelling "ebullition". Josie Pye was head and, mind you, she peeped in her book. Mr Phillips didn't see her – he was looking at Prissy Andrews – but I did. I just swept her a look of freezing scorn and she got as red as a beet and spelled it wrong after all.'

'Those Pye girls are cheats all round,' said Diana indignantly, as they climbed the fence of the main road. 'Gertie Pye actually went and put her milk bottle in my place in the brook yesterday. Did you ever? I don't speak to her now.'

When Mr Phillips was in the back of the room hearing Prissy Andrews' Latin, Diana whispered to Anne:

'That's Gilbert Blythe sitting right across the aisle from you, Anne. Just look at him and see if you don't think he's handsome.'

Anne looked accordingly. She had a good chance to do so, for the said Gilbert Blythe was absorbed in stealthily pinning the long yellow braid of Ruby Gillis, who sat in front of him, to the back of her seat. He was a tall boy, with curly brown hair, roguish hazel eyes and a mouth twisted into a teasing smile. Presently Ruby Gillis started up to take a sum to the master; she fell back into her seat with a little shriek, believing that her hair was pulled out by the roots. Everybody looked at her and Mr Phillips glared so sternly that Ruby began to cry. Gilbert had whisked the pin out of sight and was studying his history with the soberest face in the world; but when the commotion subsided he looked at Anne and winked with inexpressible drollery.

'I think your Gilbert Blythe *is* handsome,' confided Anne to Diana, 'but I think he's very bold. It isn't good manners to wink at a strange girl.'

But it was not until the afternoon that things really began to happen.

Mr Phillips was back in the corner explaining a problem in algebra to Prissy Andrews and the rest of the scholars were doing pretty much as they pleased, eating green apples, whispering, drawing pictures on their slates, and driving crickets, harnessed to strings, up and down the aisle. Gilbert Blythe was trying to make Anne Shirley look at him and failing utterly, because Anne was at that moment totally oblivious, not only of the very existence of Gilbert Blythe, but of every other scholar in Avonlea school and of Avonlea school itself. With her chin propped on her hands and her eyes fixed on the blue glimpse of the Lake of Shining Waters that the west window afforded, she was far away in a gorgeous dreamland, hearing and seeing nothing save her own wonderful visions.

Gilbert Blythe wasn't used to putting himself out to make a girl look at him and meeting with failure. She *should* look at him, that red-haired Shirley girl with the little pointed chin and big eyes that weren't like the eyes of any other girl in Avonlea school.

Gilbert reached across the aisle, picked up the end of Anne's long red braid, held it out at arm's length, and said in a piercing whisper:

'Carrots! Carrots!'

Then Anne looked at him with a vengeance!

She did more than look. She sprang to her feet, her bright fancies fallen into cureless ruin. She flashed one indignant glance at Gilbert from eyes whose angry sparkle was swiftly quenched in equally angry tears.

'You mean, hateful boy!' she exclaimed passionately. 'How dare you!'

And then – Thwack! Anne had brought her slate down on Gilbert's head and cracked it – slate, not head – clear across.

Thwack! Anne brought her slate down on Gilbert's head.

Avonlea school always enjoyed a scene. This was an especially enjoyable one. Everybody said, 'Oh,' in horrified delight. Diana gasped. Ruby Gillis, who was inclined to be hysterical, began to cry. Tommy Sloane let his team of crickets escape him altogether while he stared open-mouthed at the tableau.

Mr Phillips stalked down the aisle and laid his hand heavily on Anne's shoulder.

'Anne Shirley, what does this mean?' he said angrily.

Anne returned no answer. It was asking too much of flesh and blood to expect her to tell before the whole school that she had been called 'carrots'. Gilbert it was who spoke up stoutly.

'It was my fault, Mr Phillips. I teased her.'

Mr Phillips paid no heed to Gilbert.

'I am sorry to see a pupil of mine displaying such a temper and such a vindictive spirit,' he said in a solemn tone, as if the mere fact of being a pupil of his ought to root out all evil passions from the hearts of small imperfect mortals. 'Anne, go and stand on the platform in front of the blackboard for the rest of the afternoon.'

Anne would have infinitely preferred a whipping to this punishment, under which her sensitive spirit quivered as from a whiplash. With a white, set face she obeyed. Mr Phillips took a chalk crayon and wrote on the blackboard above her head:

'Anne Shirley has a very bad temper. Anne Shirley must learn to control her temper,' and then read it out loud, so that even the primer class, who couldn't read writing, should understand it.

Anne stood there the rest of the afternoon with that legend above her. She did not cry or hang her head. Anger was still too hot in her heart for that and it sustained her amid all her agony of humiliation. With resentful eyes and passion-red cheeks she confronted alike Diana's sympathetic gaze and Charlie Sloane's indignant nods and Josie Pye's malicious smiles. As for Gilbert Blythe, she would not even look at him. She would *never* look at him again! She would never speak to him!!

When school was dismissed Anne marched out with her red head held high. Gilbert Blythe tried to intercept her at the porch door.

'I'm awfully sorry I made fun of your hair, Anne,' he whispered contritely. 'Honest I am. Don't be mad for keeps, now.'

Anne swept by disdainfully, without look or sign of hearing. 'Oh, how could you, Anne?' breathed Diana as they went down the road, half reproachfully, half admiringly. Diana felt that *she* could never have resisted Gilbert's plea.

'I shall never forgive Gilbert Blythe,' said Anne firmly. 'And Mr Phillips spelled my name without an *e*, too. The iron has entered into my soul, Diana.'

Diana hadn't the least idea what Anne meant, but she understood it was something terrible.

'You mustn't mind Gilbert making fun of your hair,' she said soothingly. 'Why, he makes fun of all the girls. He laughs at mine because it's so black. He's called me a crow a dozen times; and I never heard him apologize for anything before either.'

'There's a great deal of difference between being called a crow and being called carrots,' said Anne with dignity. 'Gilbert Blythe has hurt my feelings *excruciatingly*, Diana.'

It is possible the matter might have blown over without more excruciation if nothing else had happened. But when things begin to happen they are apt to keep on.

Avonlea scholars often spent noon hour picking gum in Mr Bell's spruce grove over the hill and across his big pasture field. From there they could keep an eye on Eben Wright's house, where the master boarded. When they saw Mr Phillips emerging therefrom they ran for the schoolhouse; but the distance being about three times longer than Mr Wright's lane they were very apt to arrive there, breathless and gasping, some three minutes too late.

On the following day Mr Phillips was seized with one of his spasmodic fits of reform and announced, before going to dinner, that he should expect to find all the scholars in their seats when he returned. Anyone who came in late would be punished.

All the boys and some of the girls went to Mr Bell's spruce grove as usual, fully intending to stay only long enough to 'pick a chew.' But spruce groves are seductive and yellow nuts of gum beguiling; they picked and loitered and strayed; and as usual the first thing that recalled them to a sense of the flight of time was Jimmy Glover shouting from the top of a patriarchal old spruce, 'Master's coming.'

The girls, who were on the ground, started first and managed to reach the schoolhouse in time, but without a second to spare. The boys, who had to wriggle hastily down from the trees, were later; and Anne, who had not been picking gum at all but was wandering happily in the far end of the grove, waist deep among the bracken, singing softly to herself, with a wreath of rice lilies on her hair as if she were some wild divinity of the shadowy places, was latest of all. Anne could run like a deer, however; run she did with the impish result that she overtook the boys at the door and was swept into the schoolhouse among them just as Mr Phillips was in the act of hanging up his hat.

Mr Phillips' brief reforming energy was over; he didn't want the bother of punishing a dozen pupils; but it was necessary to do something to save his word, so he looked about for a scapegoat and found it in Anne, who had dropped into her seat, gasping for breath, with her forgotten lily wreath hanging askew over one ear and giving her a particularly rakish and dishevelled appearance.

'Anne Shirley, since you seem to be so fond of the boys' company we shall indulge your taste for it this afternoon,' he said sarcastically. 'Take those flowers out of your hair and sit with Gilbert Blythe.'

The other boys snickered. Diana, turning pale with pity, plucked the wreath from Anne's hair and squeezed her hand. Anne stared at the master as if turned to stone.

'Did you hear what I said, Anne?' queried Mr Phillips sternly.

'Yes, sir,' said Anne slowly, 'but I didn't suppose you really meant it.'

'I assure you I did' – still with the sarcastic inflection which all the children, and Anne especially, hated. It flicked on the raw. 'Obey me at once.'

For a moment Anne looked as if she meant to disobey. Then, realizing that there was no help for it, she rose haughtily, stepped across the aisle, sat down beside Gilbert Blythe, and buried her face in her arms on the desk. Ruby Gillis, who got a glimpse of it as it went down, told the others going home from school that she'd 'acksually never seen anything like it – it was so white, with awful little red spots in it.'

To Anne, this was at the end of all things. It was bad enough to be singled out for punishment from among a dozen equally guilty ones; it was worse still to be sent to sit with a boy; but that that boy should be Gilbert Blythe was heaping insult on injury to a degree utterly unbearable. Anne felt that she could *not* bear it and it would be of no use to try. Her whole being seethed with shame and anger and humiliation.

At first the other scholars looked and whispered and giggled and nudged. But as Anne never lifted her head and as Gilbert worked fractions as if his whole soul was absorbed in them and them only, they soon returned to their own tasks and Anne was forgotten. When Mr Phillips called the history class out Anne should have gone; but Anne did not move, and Mr Phillips, who has been writing some verses 'To Priscilla' before he called the class, was thinking about an obstinate rhyme still and never missed her. Once, when nobody was looking, Gilbert took from his desk a little pink candy heart with a gold motto on it, 'You are sweet,' and slipped it under the curve of Anne's arm. Where-upon Anne arose, took the pink heart gingerly between the tips of her fingers, dropped it on the floor, ground it to powder beneath her heel, and resumed her position without deigning to bestow a glance on Gilbert.

When school went out Anne marched to her desk, ostentatiously took out everything therein, books and writing tablet, pen and ink, testament and arithmetic, and piled them neatly on her cracked slate.

'What are you taking all those things home for, Anne?' Diana wanted to know, as soon as they were out on the road. She had not dared to ask the question before.

'I am not coming back to school any more,' said Anne.

Diana gasped and stared at Anne to see if she meant it.

'Will Marilla let you stay home?' she asked.

'She'll have to,' said Anne. 'I'll *never* go to school to that man again.'

'Oh, Anne!' Diana looked as if she were ready to cry. 'I do think you're mean. What shall I do? Mr Phillips will make me sit with that horrid Gertie Pye – I know he will, because she is sitting alone. Do come back, Anne.'

'I'd do almost anything in the world for you, Diana,' said Anne sadly. 'I'd let myself be torn limb from limb if it would do you any good. But I can't do this, so please don't ask it. You harrow up my very soul.'

'Just think of all the fun you will miss,' mourned Diana. 'We are going to build the loveliest new house down by the brook; and we'll be playing ball next week and you've never played ball, Anne. It's tremendously exciting. And we're going to learn a new song – Jane Andrews is practising it up now; and Alice Andrews is going to bring a new Pansy book next week and we're all going to read it out loud, chapter about, down by the brook. And you know you are so fond of reading out loud, Anne.'

Nothing moved Anne in the least. Her mind was made up. She would not go to school to Mr Phillips again; she told Marilla so when she got home.

'Nonsense,' said Marilla.

'It isn't nonsense at all,' said Anne, gazing at Marilla, with solemn, reproachful eyes. 'Don't you understand, Marilla? I've been insulted.'

'Insulted fiddlesticks! You'll go to school tomorrow as usual.'

'Oh, no.' Anne shook her head gently. 'I'm not going back, Marilla. I'll learn my lessons at home and I'll be as good as I can be and hold my tongue all the time if it's possible at all. But I will not go back to school I assure you.'

Marilla saw something remarkably like unyielding stubbornness looking out of Anne's small face. She understood that she would have trouble in overcoming it; but she resolved wisely to say nothing more just then.

'I'll run down and see Rachel about it this evening,' she thought. 'There's no use reasoning with Anne now. She's too worked up and I've an idea she can be awful stubborn if she takes the notion. Far as I can make out from her story, Mr Phillips has been carrying matters with a rather high hand. But it would never do to say so to her. I'll just talk it over with Rachel. She's sent ten children to school and she ought to know something about it. She'll have heard the whole story, too, by this time.'

Marilla found Mrs Lynde knitting quilts as industriously and cheerfully as usual.

'I suppose you know what I've come about,' she said, a little shamefacedly.

Mrs Rachel nodded.

'About Anne's fuss in school, I reckon,' she said. 'Tillie Boulter was in on her way home from school and told me about it.'

'I don't know what to do with her,' said Marilla. 'She declares she won't go back to school. I never saw a child so worked up. I've been expecting trouble ever since she started to school. I knew things were going too smooth to last. She's so high-strung. What would you advise, Rachel?'

'Well, since you've asked my advice, Marilla,' said Mrs Lynde amiably – Mrs Lynde dearly loved to be asked for advice – 'I'd just humour her a little at first, that's what I'd do. It's my belief that Mr Phillips was in the wrong. Of course, it doesn't do to say so to the children, you know. And of course he did right to punish her yesterday for giving way to temper. But today it was different. The others who were late should have been punished as well as Anne, that's what. And I don't believe in making the girls sit with the boys for punishment. It isn't modest. Tillie Boulter was real indignant. She took Anne's part right through and said all the scholars did, too. Anne seems real popular among them, somehow. I never thought she'd take with them so well.'

'Then you really think I'd better let her stay home,' said Marilla in amazement.

'Yes. That is, I wouldn't say school to her again until she said it herself. Depend upon it, Marilla, she'll cool off in a week or so and be ready enough to go back of her own accord, that's what, while, if you were to make her go back right off, dear knows what freak or tantrum she'd take next and make more trouble than ever. The less fuss made the better, in my opinion. She won't miss much by not going to school, as far as *that* goes. Mr Phillips isn't any good at all as a teacher. The order he keeps is scandalous, that's what, and he neglects the young fry and puts all his time on those big scholars he's getting ready for Queen's. He'd never have got the school for another year if his uncle hadn't been a trustee – *the* trustee, for he just leads the other two around by the nose, that's what. I declare, I don't know what education in this Island is coming to.'

Mrs Rachel shook her head, as much as to say if she were only at the head of the educational system of the Province things would be much better managed.

Marilla took Mrs Rachel's advice and not another word was said to Anne about going back to school. She learned her lessons at home, did her chores, and played with Diana in the chilly purple autumn twilights; but when she met Gilbert Blythe on the road or encountered him in Sunday school she passed him by with an icy contempt that was no whit thawed by his evident desire to appease her. Even Diana's efforts as a peacemaker were of no avail. Anne had evidently made up her mind to hate Gilbert Blythe to the end of life.

As much as she hated Gilbert, however, did she love Diana, with all the love of her passionate little heart, equally intense in its likes and dislikes. One evening Marilla, coming in from the orchard with a basket of apples, found Anne sitting alone by the east window in the twilight, crying bitterly.

'Whatever's the matter now, Anne?' she asked.

'It's about Diana,' sobbed Anne luxuriously. 'I love Diana so, Marilla. I cannot ever live without her. But I know very well when we grow up that Diana will get married and go away and leave me. And oh, what shall I do? I hate her husband – I just hate him furiously. I've been imagining it all out – the wedding and everything – Diana dressed in snowy garments, with a veil, and looking as beautiful and regal as a queen; and me the bridesmaid, with a lovely dress, too, and puffed sleeves, but with a breaking heart hid beneath my smiling face. And then bidding Diana good-bye-e-e-e——' Here Anne broke down entirely and wept with increasing bitterness.

Marilla turned quickly away to hide her twitching face; but it was no use; she collapsed on the nearest chair and burst into such a hearty and unusual peal of laughter that Matthew, crossing the yard outside, halted in amazement. When had he heard Marilla laugh like that before?

'Well, Anne Shirley,' said Marilla as soon as she could speak, 'if you must borrow trouble, for pity's sake borrow it handier home. I should think you had an imagination, sure enough.'

THE QUEEN'S BIRTHDAY
George Lamming

In one corner where the walls met there was a palm-tree laden with nuts, and in front on all sides an area of pebbles, marl and stone. That area wide and pebbled in every part was called the school yard. The school was in another corner, a wooden building of two storeys with windows all around that opened like a yawning mouth. Except when it rained, the windows supported from the sills by broomsticks were kept open. In another corner was the church, a stone building which extended across the yard to within a few yards of the school. The church seemed three times the size of the school, with dark stained hooded windows that never opened. Inside the air was dark and heavy and strange. The mystery of the church frightened the boys, and they never entered it except in their attempt to peeve the sexton by ringing the bell.

The church was not the church school as some churches were called, and the boys never really understood why these two buildings were erected within the same enclosure. The school inspector was an Englishman, and the school was supposed to be of anglican persuasion. The supervising minister of the church was also English, but he was Presbyterian. Twice a term the inspector visited the schools to record the attendance and give intelligence tests. On such occasions the teachers and boys all seemed frightened, and the head teacher who seldom laughed would smile for the length of the inspector's visit. Occasionally the supervising minister came in to give pep talks on the work of the church, and then no one seemed frightened. But the inspector and the minister never met in the school. The head teacher never arranged for them to meet except on special occasions like Empire Day. After the celebrations and parades, the head teacher took them to his house which occupied the fourth corner of the school yard. In one corner a palm-tree, and in the others three shrines of enlightenment that looked over the wall and across a benighted wooden tenantry.

★   ★   ★   ★

The children were arranged in thick squads over the school yard. One squad represented the primary school, and the remaining eight the classes that ranged from standard Lower First to Standard Seven. Standard Lower First comprised the boys between the age of five and six who were too old for the primary school and not clever enough for the upper school. On special occasions they were called Lower First, otherwise everyone referred to them as

a   b   ab   catch a crab

g   o   go   let it go

There were nine squads comprising about a thousand boys. The squads were packed close, and seen from the school porch the spectacle was that of an enormous ship whose cargo had been packed in boxes and set on the deck. The squads were all at ease. The boys stood leisurely, their hands met in a fist of knuckles somewhere between their buttocks. Some boys stole a chance to scratch with the index finger. The teachers stepped with great dignity between the rows, inspecting the discipline of the lines, and when they stopped and shouted with military urgency ' 'Tion!' the boys raised their left legs and brought them down heavily on the ground beside the right heels. Their heads were slightly tilted back, and the small hands pressed earnestly against their sides. Some failed to distinguish quickly between right and left and lifted the wrong leg. The naked ankles of the neighbouring colleagues collided and hurt. But no one winced. It was the twenty-fourth of May, the Queen's birthday.

The sun was big in the sky, and it shone, bright and steady, over the pebbles. The green coconuts shone, and the church windows and galvanized sheets of iron that roofed the school. Everything seemed a heaving tussle of light. The wind came in sharp spasms and the flags flew. The school wore a uniform of flags: doors, windows and partitions on all sides carried the colours of the school's king. There were small flags and big flags, round flags and square flags, flags with sticks and flags without sticks, and flags that wore the faces of kings and princes, ships, thrones and empires. Everywhere the red and the white and the blue. In every corner of the school the tricolour Union Jack flew its message. The colours though three in number had by constant repetition produced something vast and terrible, a kind of pressure or presence of which everyone was a part. The children in the lower school looked with wonder. They seemed to see a mystery that was its own revelation, and there was, therefore, no need to ask questions. The boys in the upper school looked with triumph. They saw a fact that was its own explanation. The red and the white and the blue. How strong and deep the colours were!

On all sides the walls were crowded with people. There were relatives of the children who were in the squads, or children who did not go to that school. The older people saw the flags and talked of the old days. Such a long time ago, but nothing had really changed. There were more flags now, the school was bigger and the children more clever. They could take and give orders, and parade for the inspector. And they understood the meaning of big words, but nothing had really changed. The flags were the same colour. It was a queen in their time. Now it was a king. But the throne was the same. Good old England and old Little England! They had never parted company since they met way back in the reign of James or was it Charles? They weren't sure, but it was a James or a Charles. God bless his name. Three hundred years, more than the memory could hold, Big England had met and held Little England and Little England like a sensible child accepted. Three hundred years, and never in all that time did any other nation dare interfere with these two. Barbados or Little England was the oldest and purest of England's children, and may it always be so. The other islands had changed hands. Now they were French, now they were Spanish. But Little England remained steadfast and constant to Big

England. Even to this day. Indeed, it was God's doing. The hand of the Lord played a great part in that union. And who knows? You could never tell. One day before time changed for eternity, Little England and Big England, God's anointed on earth, might hand-in-hand rule this earth. In the '14 war they went side by side together, and they would go again any time. Big England had only to say the word and Little England followed. Big England had the strongest navy, and Little England the best fishermen in this God's world. Together they were mistresses of the sea, and whenever, wherever, the two met on the same side, war or peace, there was bound to be victory.

★   ★   ★   ★

A car drove slowly through the school yard flying a flag on its bonnet and then there was only the sound of the wind in the trees. The inspector stepped from the car, and before he had found his feet one of the teachers had bellowed the order. With incredible precision every squad saluted, and there was silence but for the sound of the wind in the trees, and the silence moving gradually from squad to squad broke forth into an earnest, pleading resonance:

> God save our gracious King,
> Long live our noble King,
> God save the King.

At the order of the teachers the boys dropped the salute. They stood at attention, and when the second order was given relaxed. The head teacher led the inspector to a raised platform in the middle of the school yard. The inspector wore a white suit with a red, white and blue badge on the lapel of the jacket. He smiled all the time, while the head teacher grinned jovially as if he and the inspector were part of a secret the others were to guess. The inspector stood at the centre of the platform and all eyes were fastened on him. He looked around in all directions and then spoke. 'My dear boys and teachers, we are met once again to pay our respects to the memory of a great queen. She was your queen and my queen and yours no less than mine. We're all subjects and partakers in the great design, the British Empire, and your loyalty to the Empire can be seen in the splendid performance which your school decorations and the discipline of these squads represent. We are living,

With incredible precision every squad saluted.

my dear boys, in difficult times. We wait with the greatest anxiety the news of what is happening on the other side of the world. Those of you who read the papers may have read of the war in Abyssinia. You may have seen pictures of the King of Ethiopia, and the bigger boys may have wondered what it's all about. The British Empire, you must remember, has always worked for the peace of the world. This was the job assigned it by God, and if the Empire at any time has failed to bring about that peace it was due to events and causes beyond its control. But, remember, my dear boys, whatever happens in any part of this world, whatever happens to you here in this island of Barbados, the pride and treasure of the Empire, we are always on the side of peace. You are with us, and we with you. And together we shall always walk in the will of God. Let me say how impressed I am with the decorations. I hope I shall start no jealousy among the schools in the island under my control if I say that such a display as I see here could not have been bettered by the lads at home.'

The boys and teachers applauded and his voice was lost in the noise. The inspector waited till the shouting died down and concluded: 'Barbados is truly Little England!' He stepped from the platform and the applause was renewed with greater energy. The head teacher came forward and shook the inspector's hand gratefully, then he stepped on to the platform beaming with delight and yelled: 'Three cheers for the school. Hip pip pip . . . Hurararahhahrah Hippiippip . . . Hurrahhhaarararah . . . Hip pip pip . . . Hurrrrrrraaaahh. Hippiippip . . . Hurrahhhaarararah. . . .

The boys came to attention, and the teachers' voices were raised in a confusion of orders to the squads. They spoke at the same time, but the orders were different, and the movements of the squads taken on the whole were contradictory. When Class 6 was receiving the order to stand at ease, Class 5 was receiving the order to march. The inspector and the head teacher looked on from the platform and smiled at the innocent rivalry. After the orders were given and the lines were dressed to the teachers' satisfaction, the boys marched squad after squad after squad in circles round the platform. In the final circle they marched at the salute, and the inspector returned the salute and watched them march in single file into the school.

The parade had come to an end.

Four boys from the upper school returned for the platform. They lifted it into the school where it belonged, and the head teacher and the inspector were left in the school yard. They stood where the platform had been taken away, and talked quietly. The head teacher's hands were locked behind his back, and his teeth showed under the heavy lips. The inspector stood with a slight hump, his hands falling down in a straight, level stretch from the shoulders. His face was smooth and smiling. They looked very comfortable and at home in that easy and formal arrangement of appearances. They made a striking contrast in appearance, but they seemed in a way to belong to the same thing. The inspector was white and smooth and cool like a pebble. The head teacher's face richer and stronger burnt black in the sun. It was pleasing to watch them talk in that way the villagers called man to man, although it didn't seem altogether a case of man to man. They watched each other at times as a cat would watch a mouse, playfully but seriously. The inspector smiled and the head teacher smiled back, and the cat in each smiled too. It was not a reassuring smile. It was not inconceivable that the cat would spring and suck the blood of the other. And there was a terrifying suggestion of sucking about them. The inspector was smoother than anything you had ever seen, except perhaps a sore. Sometimes a villager caught a chigoe flea in his toe. He was careless in his attention, and the flea hatched in the flesh. Under the skin of the toe there would soon be a small bag fertile with fleas. The toe swelled up into a white and shining smoothness. It was an indescribable smoothness of skin under which the fleas lodged. When the toe was pricked with a pin, the skin cracked and the pus spilled out. The smoothness had slid away, but you couldn't forget it. You couldn't forget it when you saw the inspector smile. Smooth like the surface of pus. It gathered and secreted so much so quietly and so stealthily. The head teacher was smooth too, but his surface was coarse and bright and black like the leech the villagers had seen on Mr Foster's arm. When Mr Foster was suffering from blood poisoning, the doctor ordered that a leech be placed on the arm. The leech crouched over the arm, bright and black, and the neighbours watched it grow fat with the intake of blood. Walking beside the inspector towards the school the head teacher had that bright-black slouching carriage of the leech, and when he smiled the flesh of his face fattened with the new intake of feeling.

The second half of the celebrations began with the inspection of the classes. Three classes gave a special performance, and later it was announced which had won the inspector's shield.

The boys were all seated. The inspector sat in a chair on the platform. The head teacher alone stood. He indicated in turn the class which had to perform. The supervising teacher who was torn between fear and anxiety awaited the head teacher's signal, and when it was given he gave the class a quiet prompter and hoped for the best. Nearest the platform was the lower first which got up and recited the lesson they had been learning for the last three months. Their teacher gave them the signal and they intoned all together.

a	b	ab	catch a crab
g	o	go	let it go
a	b	ab	catch a crab
go	o	go	let it go.

They recited it faultlessly and the inspector applauded. The supervising teacher laughed and snapped his finger at the boys. They elbowed each other and grinned quietly. The scene shifted and a class from the upper school performed. Their teacher stood at the side and when he thought they had settled themselves he whispered, ready, steady, go; and the boys recited the lesson they had been learning for the last three months:

> Thirty days hath September,
> April, June and November;
> All the rest have thirty-one
> Except February which hath but twenty-eight
>   and twenty-nine in a Leap Year.

The inspector was pleased and applauded, and the scene shifted once more.

The next performance was a test of voice control, and standard 7 in the upper school was the class which performed. There were two teachers to standard 7, but on such occasions only one was allowed to make his appearance. The other stood as one of the boys. The teacher of standard 7 was also the teacher of music. He stood before the class with the ruler raised in his right hand, and the left hand poised. The arms extended making a half circle over his head, and when they met level and pointed direct at the class the voices rose. The first eight rows were trebles, the last three bass, and the one on the side alto. They sang the hymn which the school had sung every morning for the last three months.

> O God, our help in ages past,
> Our hope for years to come,
> Our shelter from the stormy blast,
> And our eternal home.

The performances had come to an end, and all were seated but the head teacher who made a speech. He was pleased with the attendance, which he said was the best the school had had in many years. He announced that standard 5 had won the inspector's shield. The monitor of standard 5 came forward amid applause and took the shield. He gave it to the teacher who hung it on a nail against the partition directly behind standard 5. Then the headmaster announced that three boys would be leaving this term to enter High School. They had won exhibition scholarships, and he was proud. He spoke with great feeling about their achievement.

'They will pursue what we call the higher studies,' he said. 'Mathematics and Science and such things. Here as you all know we do arithmetic up to and sometimes beyond compound interest. The boys in standard 7 can tell you everything about Stocks and Shares. Algebra and Geometry we leave to the higher school. But without that firm foundation which we give in arithmetic, these boys could not understand those subjects. We are proud of them. The future is theirs, and they will always remember with gratitude the school which taught them the first things they ever learnt.'

The school applauded, and the three boys walked forward and shook the inspector's hand.

'As you know,' the head teacher went on, 'every Empire Day we give pennies to the children. It's the gift of the Queen, and a great old Queen she was. And it is our custom here as in all the schools, to give a penny to the boys in the lower school and those in the upper school up to standard 4. The others get two pennies. Our three exhibitioners will get three pennies each. You must all when you go to spend your penny think before you throw it away. Queen Victoria was a wise queen, and she would have you spend it wisely. Some of those boys in standard 7 think they know what it is to be a king. Victoria was a real queen.'

There was a loud giggle from one corner of the school. The head teacher stiffened, and everyone felt the terror of the change that had come over him.

'And now for the pennies,' he said abruptly, and stepped from the platform.

The pennies were brought in, and the inspector who never waited to witness the distribution got up and made ready to leave. The head teacher blew his whistle and the whole school stood and saluted as the inspector walked out. The head teacher blew the whistle again, and everyone sat. He went back to the platform and surveyed the school. His face was coarse and savage and sad. It was difficult to understand when he spoke. His voice was low and choked with a kind of terror. 'I've never wanted it said that my boys are hooligans,' he said, 'grinning like jackasses when respectable people are around. I've always wanted it said that the boys at Groddeck's Boy School were gentlemen. But gentlemen don't grin and giggle like buffoons, and in the presence of respectable people, people of power and authority.' The school was silent, and everybody seemed to shiver under the threat of his tone. 'Who was it laughed when I said what I said about the queen?' he asked. No one moved.

'Who was it, I asked?' he shouted, taking the thick leather from his desk. It was the cured hide of the cow which had been soaked in resin, and which he used to punish. He took a step forward.

'Who was it, I ask again?' he shouted. 'Speak up or I'll beat every blasted one of you from top to bottom.' The terror mounted. The silence was heavy and terrible, like the certainty of death.

A boy got up from standard 7 and started to speak.

'Come out,' the head teacher snapped, cutting him short. The boy stood where he was, trying to make some explanation. No one knew whether he was the offender or whether he was informing on someone. The boy stepped forward, trying to speak. The head teacher stood trembling as if he feared the full responsibility of what he was going to do. He took the leather from his neck where he had strung it and waited for the boy to approach. The boy refused to walk further

337

forward and the head teacher glowered. 'Come up,' he said again, and stared at the boy as if he were a human symbol of the blackest sin. Suddenly the boy in terror leapt over the desks and benches, tripping over the other boys' heads, and fled towards the door. The teachers caught him as he tried to leap over the banister and brought him forward. He could not speak. Four boys were summoned, and they bound him hands and feet and stretched him flat over a bench. The head teacher removed his jacket and gripped the leather. The first blow rent the pants and left the black buttocks exposed. The boy made a brief howl like an animal that had had its throat cut. No one could say how long he was beaten or how many strokes he received. But when he stood supported by the four boys who had held him down he was weak. The knees tottered and the filth slithered down his legs. The boys lifted him out of the school and carried him under the pipe in the school yard.

BLOOD ON THE MOUNTAIN
Ann Spano

The history lesson dragged on and on. It was rather like the history of England itself, thought Tutkwe; his hand holding his head, trying to force himself to make sense of it all. He had so many new facts to learn. A succession of unfamiliar monarchs, parading through centuries of conflict, battles and change.

It was all so different from the history of his own land, which was passed down verbally from generation to generation. They had known a few great men, but no kings. Skirmishes and raids for cattle; good years and lean ones. The events were remembered in cycles and their beginnings receded in the distance of time.

'Tutkwe! Write the homework up on the blackboard,' rapped out the master, irritated by the black boy's constantly bowed head.

There was a burst of laughter from one of the boys behind Tutkwe.

'What's so funny, Nick?'

'I just wondered, sir. Do they use *white*boards in Africa, sir?'

There was just a hint of a smile on the history master's thin lips.

'You deserve an old fashioned black mark. *You* can write up the homework instead.'

Reluctantly Nick went to the blackboard and wrote until the bell rang. In twos and threes the boys straggled out of the classroom and

339

across a concrete yard to their class in the gymnasium. Only Tutkwe walked alone.

Some of the English boys were friendly enough but the black boy had not yet made any real friends. He missed the companions he had left behind in Nuerland, his home country in the central Sudan in Africa.

Only a year ago, when he was fourteen, he had been initiated into manhood with the other boys of his own 'age-set'. Silently they had endured together the great pain of six deep cuts slashed one above the other across their foreheads, from ear to ear. The scars they would carry for life: a declaration to all the world of their full membership of proud Nuer manhood. At the same time, the boys had sworn loyal brotherhood to one another.

Within six months of his initiation, Tutkwe had won a national Sudanese scholarship and had flown to England to take his place at an English public school. Far from welcoming him, the English boys had treated him as a source of amusement and looked upon his six prized marks of manhood with contempt. They regarded them as a sign of a backward culture. They mocked him for wanting to learn from their civilization when he bore such primitive tribal marks on his face. This shock came on top of the loneliness Tutkwe felt in a strange land and he remained silent to their taunts.

He was used to sleeping and eating with young people other than his immediate family, but the regimentation of the boarding school and the strict timetable were to get used to. The spartan furnishing of the dark classrooms and recreation rooms did not worry him, but he hated the cold draughtiness of the Victorian stone buildings, the melancholy of the yew trees in the overgrown grounds and the dreariness of leaky drains and damp walls. He was homesick for his own age-mates. At this time of the year when it was cold, wet winter in England, it would be the beginning of the dry season in Nuerland. The young boys and girls would be herding the cattle out of the villages and making camps near pools or streams, left after the rains had burst the banks of the Nile. A time of freedom, fun and companionship in the vast plains of the hot, flat, treeless savannah. He loved too, the work with the cattle and was starting his own herd.

The elders had told Tutkwe that the scholarship he had won had

340

brought honour to his people. He knew that they would be unhappy that he had not retaliated against the white boys' insults to himself and the forefathers of his tribe, for the Nuer thinks himself superior to all foreigners. But he had done nothing. He had even discovered a certain manly triumph in ignoring their jibes and controlling the bitterness simmering within him.

Of all the boys, one was the most persistent in his ridicule: Nick, the boy who had called out at the end of the history lesson. Encouraging his friend Tony to join him, he would taunt the Nuer at every opportunity. They tagged him even now, as the class made its way to the gymnasium.

'Tutkwe's in one of his black moods,' Tony hissed to Nick as they drew near him.

Nick stopped in front of Tutkwe. 'Know what the beef cattle are called in Wales?' he demanded. 'Welsh Blacks. You ought to feel at home when we get there this weekend.'

There was a shrill whistle and the file of boys hurried into the hall. In the chill changing room they changed into white singlets and shorts under the continual barking of a short, sinewy man in a blue track suit. When he had assembled them in the hall, he put them through some tough training exercises. Finally he allowed them to relax while he sat on the vaulting horse and addressed them.

'The trip we will be going on, up the Cambrian Mountains, isn't a picnic. No easy ride for any of you. In fact, in this weather, it could mean a physical challenge that most of you have never experienced. One cardinal rule is that, at all times, we must stick together and work as a team.'

From that moment on, any spare time before the expedition left for Wales was spent preparing the food supplies and camping and climbing equipment. Tutkwe enjoyed the excitement, but found it hard to visualize what he was in for.

Once on the mountain, he found it very different from what he had imagined. It was a sterile and frozen landscape of ice and snow. And it covered the whole world about him. His own Nuerland always became a floodplain in the rainy season, but the sun shone a hospitable heat and the water was warm and alive with fish.

'Is there really rock beneath all this ice?' Tutkwe wondered, stopping a moment to kick the snow. He could see mountain faces looming around them. They were hostile slabs of darkness and shadow; some faces were solid granite.

Tutkwe pulled his scarf up over his nose. The wind seemed to cut into his being with a relentless force. He saw that Nick and Tony had moved back to where he trailed the climbers, battling to keep up against the forbidding elements. Their nearness made Tutkwe feel even more isolated. Finally they stopped and confronted him.

'I've never seen a black person in the snow before,' laughed Nick. 'If you take all your clothes off as you do in Africa, you'll *never* get lost.'

Tutkwe made a low, grunting noise. From earliest childhood he had been taught that fighting was the only way for a Nuer man to square with an insult. As a boy, he had fought others with spiked bracelets. As men, they would fight with clubs and occasionally, spears. Courage is prized as the highest virtue but until now he had remained strangely subdued in the sophisticated world of his boarding school.

Now, on the bare, white mountain, honour and courage had become a reality once more. He must confront his aggressor. Uncontrollably, he felt a primeval anger growing inside him. He must fight a duel and avenge himself. A fight to the death if needs be.

He became aware of Tony saying urgently, 'We'll get lost if we don't hurry up and catch up with the others.' The others had gone ahead and were already out of sight.

'Come on. Follow their tracks,' said Nick, plunging upward, with the others close behind.

Not long afterwards it began to snow heavily and very soon there was no trail of footsteps to follow.

They shouted, but could hear no answering calls. They had become completely separated from the main group. Each fighting his despair in his own way, they continued to move upwards. Then Tony stumbled into a drift and they knew they would have to make a detour which might not be the one taken by the main party. They feared that they could well be moving farther and farther away from the others.

They had no choice but to continue edging along the mountain, keeping to the packed snow and icy ridges.

Tutkwe let out some of the fury simmering within him in an angry shout to Nick.

'You are a damned idiot,' he accused in the new and arrogant style of English he was learning. 'If it hadn't been for you and your stupid jokes we wouldn't be lost.'

'So what do you think you know?' jeered Nick. 'You've only just come down from the trees.'

'Oh, shut up, both of you,' snapped Tony. 'It's too cold to stand still. We must keep moving.'

But Tutkwe had stopped and was slowly sliding off his pack. His dark eyes glinted as he challenged Nick, his voice low and deliberate.

'This is the moment. This is the moment when I have to avenge my manhood and all the fathers of my tribe.'

Nick's burst of laughter froze. There was no doubting that the black youth meant what he was saying.

It had not been entirely malice which had provoked Nick to taunt Tutkwe at every opportunity. In the black schoolboy he had seen someone as haughty and aristocratic as he liked to think he was himself. That Tutkwe's cold and indifferent arrogance had even suggested that he thought himself Nick's superior was insufferable. And so Nick had retaliated with condescension and relentless teasing.

Sometimes, reading the fire in Tutkwe's eyes, Nick had felt a fearful panic that he was touching something completely out of his ken – something deep and unknown. In those moments he had been glad of the complicity of Tony, backing him in his attacks.

Nick paced back from Tutkwe. 'Look, we're in Britain. You can't bring any of your savage notions here. We'll talk about it.'

In answer Tutkwe unclipped a knife from his belt and flicked it open.

Nick hesitated, holding on to the straps of his pack. 'Look, I'm sorry. Honestly, half of what I said was joking. You can't be *serious*.'

Tony could sense the electric tension between the two boys. It had to be broken. He leaped between them.

'You don't know what you're doing,' he yelled. 'Are you *mad*? Can't you see we're *lost*. We're going to need all our strength to get off this mountain? All we need is for one of you to be hurt. We've got a whole night to face yet.'

Tutkwe brought his knife between Tony's eyes and nicked a small surface cut on his forhead. 'You stay out of this, Tony. You'll get more than that if you don't.'

343

Tony put a finger to the cut and licked the blood from the graze.

The fear that Nick had experienced before in the presence of the African boy, welled and choked him. He stared at Tutkwe.

The Nuer are among the tallest people in the world. At just sixteen, Tutkwe was well over six feet tall, long and lithe-limbed with narrow hips and shoulders. His head was finely shaped, his nose ridged low like a boxer's before it splayed with high arched nostrils. His eyes, naturally almond-shaped, were narrowed now with menace, smouldering with deep contempt.

Nick flexed his shoulders and slowly released his pack. It fell to the snow with a thud. He was not as tall as the Nuer, but his muscles were better developed, his build altogether heavier. His features were defined in cleanly angled bone structure below windblown brown hair. His lips were clamped against the cold and a fear for the reality of Tutkwe's threat.

The two tall boys facing each other were well matched. It was Tony who was in another class. He was plump, with springy red hair and a face speckled with pimples and freckles. He had taken off his glasses because of the sleet and wind, and now watched the others with myopic lack of definition and hopelessness.

'You must be *mad*!' repeated Nick.

The Nuer had thrown off his anorak and scarf and was pacing weird rhythmic steps in the snow. He appeared no longer to feel the cold and his black skin had begun to glisten with sweat. He was chanting in his own language and they could understand him calling his own name. The eerie light cast his shadow, blue, pale and grotesquely cavorting on the snow. His chanting was interjected with grunts. He seemed to be in some sort of trance. They knew there was no stopping him now.

'I am Tutkwe and I am insulted.
Even to the origins of Gwang-Jok,
Founder of my father's line.
I am Tutkwe and I call on Tut, my bull ox,
Gift of my father when I joined him
In manhood.
My black ox with the white face like Kwe,
The fish eagle,
With horns spread like wings balance in an air column.'

He made a harsh gull-like call, haunting and terrifying on the sombre mountain and spread out his arms, angled outwards from his head. Nick realized that this pagan ritual involved him. He had to fight.

Tutkwe stopped in front of him, slightly crouched on widely spaced legs, the knife poised erect in his hand. 'There are no trees in Nuerland.' His voice was cold and menacing. The threat from the Nuer was unmistakable; a call to the duel. But before Nick could move, Tony hurled himself at Tutkwe and knocked the knife from his hand. Tutkwe hardly noticed Tony's attack. He brushed him aside and sprang at Nick. The two locked and swayed and broke apart.

Tony retrieved the knife from where it had fallen. The fight was on in deadly earnest and there was nothing he could do. The boys struggled wildly with powerful blows and fierce grapple holds. It was a battle of life and death. They lunged and thrust and parried, and their heavy breathing told of the toll of combat. As they weakened, their limbs moved with clumsy inaccuracy, increased by the cold and the uncertainty of their footholds in the trampled snow.

Finally Nick collapsed, defeated not only by a hard upper cut from the Nuer which slammed a knock-out blow on his jaw, but also from sheer exhaustion and despair. He had felt in the Nuer an inner strength that he could not hope to match. He had known from the start that he could only hope to delay the inevitable end.

Tutkwe walked slowly over to his anorak, shook it free of snow and drew it on. Its padded warmth soothed the ache in his limbs from the pounding and the cold. He wound his scarf slowly about his neck. He wanted only to sink into sleep to escape a horrifying reality – that he may well have killed Nick.

With a heavy heart, Tony went to his friend. He was unconscious but breathing, limp and inert as he lay in the snow. The futility of it all angered him with a deep and bitter fury. He looked at Tutkwe. The Nuer was standing on one leg with the other bent and the sole of its foot pressed close against the back of his knee. They had teased him many times for relaxing like this, his body generally balanced by a long stick upon which he leant. He looked like some gaunt and mystic totem pole, silhouetted dramatically in the strange metallic light which reflected from the snow and encased them in a limbo between earth and sky.

It was a battle of life and death.

He had come into their lives with his remote and mysterious beliefs. They had mocked him, and he had avenged himself. They were lost on the mountain, and Nick was so exhausted that, in this harsh environment, he could very well die.

Tony laid Nick's head back in the snow. He gathered up all the packs and unrolled them one by one. They all had groundsheets and sleeping bags and extra sweaters. With the groundsheets he could make some sort of shelter and Nick must be got into his sleeping bag as soon as possible. They had only about an hour's daylight left, if this harsh, glinting light could be called daylight.

Silently, Tutkwe came to help him and they built up a high windbreak of snow which they lined with groundsheets. They struggled to get Nick's body into his sleeping bag and then dragged him to the windbreak. They pulled on their extra sweaters, wrapped Nick's about his head and climbed into their own sleeping bags. They had nothing left to eat or drink and had even finished the last of the sweets they had had.

'We *must* stay awake. It's the only way we'll live through the night,' said Tony. That was all he said. He had no words to utter the despair that he felt.

The two boys sat in silence with the unconscious body between them. On occasions Tony would try to rub some warmth into Nick, but his own hands were so cold that all he could manage were clumsy prodding. Slowly the darkness closed in around them until they could only feel each other's presence.

As the hours wore on it became harder and harder for them to keep awake. Around midnight Nick regained consciousness. He was tremendously weak and exposure on the mountain didn't help his condition. Tony wished they had some hot coffee, soup or, better still, some brandy to revive him. They could not hope for a search party until the morning and he knew that their only chance of survival was to keep awake until then.

'If anyone thinks anyone else has dropped off to sleep, kick him, punch him, do anything. But keep him awake,' said Tony. Then he turned to Tutkwe. 'What was that you were singing when you were dancing in the snow before you fought Nick?'

Tutkwe stiffened. He didn't feel like talking, and he answered slowly. 'I have an ox which I love. He was given to me by my father when I became a man. He is a very handsome bull with a fine hump and long wide horns. He is called Kwe because he is black with a white face like the fish eagle. I was singing about him. Tutkwe is my ox name. We call out our ox name when we dance or sing or fight. They are the names of our initiation.'

'Does every boy have an ox in Nuerland?' asked Tony.

'Yes. We are cattle people. Our oxen are the most prized possessions in our lives. We grow up with the cattle around us. As small children we play with the sheep and goats in the byres.'

Tutkwe talked faster now, with increasing warmth and animation. Nick and Tony listened enthralled, asking many questions so that they hardly noticed when the dawn began to lighten the heavy cloud in the sky. Tutkwe had many stories about home; stories about fishing and hunting. Fishing with spears in dammed streams, or with harpoons fired from lengthy, slender bows as they paddled waist deep in flooded pools or stood in dugout canoes. Hunting was a tale of tracking fleet-footed giraffe, antelope and occasionally elephant in the open grassland, armed with only a spear and accompanied by a small pack of dogs.

It was a magic world and as the two English boys listened, they began to understand the Nuer and his way of life, and to realize that it had a richness that their modern world lacked. As day broke they had no more hostility, only a knowledge that the bond that had grown between them would help overcome their shared adversity.

The wind had died, but it was still bitterly cold. Tony and Tutkwe packed their sleeping bags around Nick. They decided to climb down the mountain and to carry Nick between them. Slowly and laboriously they began their descent.

As the day advanced, they had to stop more and more frequently for rests. Their breath came in short, painful gulps and their limbs ached. All they wanted to do was sleep.

'Come on! We've made it this far,' urged Tony. 'We've just got to get to the bottom. I'm sure there's a road that goes round the base of this mountain.'

With Nick injured and Tutkwe completely unused to cold and height, Tony knew that he must be the fittest of the three. This gave him an unaccustomed confidence and he bullied and badgered them to keep going. Then suddenly, as though he had become frozen himself, the

Nuer stopped and refused to move. And yet, strangely, he *was* moving. The ground was giving beneath his feet.

Tutkwe looked at his feet in terror. 'It's the Leopard-Skin Chief,' he muttered from riveted lips as he was drawn down into the snow.

'Whaaat?'

'He who has mystical connections with the earth. It is He, and He has come to punish me because I have not made my sacrifice of a steer or a ram or a he-goat.'

Tutkwe imagined the magnificent old man with the full length leopard cloak, the legs and tail swinging about him as he walked. He had worked his magic and was coming for retribution out of the depths of the earth. It made no difference that Nick was alive. The sacrifice should have been made when he had thought he was dead the previous afternoon.

'A sheep! It must be a sheep buried in the snow,' called Nick from his sleeping bag.

Tony pushed Tutkwe aside and began to dig down in the snow. He soon uncovered the muzzle of a beast that was distinctly a sheep.

'Wait. Go slowly. Don't let it get away,' shouted Tutkwe, digging with Tony.

'What do you want to do? Let it suffocate until it dies?'

'No. We can get some strength from the animal.' As the woolly body, blotched with snow, was freed, he sat on its side to pin it down. The sheep struggled and swivelled its eyes in terror. Tutkwe slipped his hand under its belly and felt for its udder. It was, as he hoped, full.

'Tony, sit on the animal,' he ordered.

Gingerly, Tony sat astride the warm body. He had never been this close to a sheep before and was nervous of its lunging movements and repulsed by its musky smell.

Tutkwe started to dig deeper in the snow under the ewe.

'The udder is full. Her lamb must be somewhere here,' he said.

With a short sharp cry he lifted something out of the snow. It was a limp body with thin dangling legs and neck, a small black head with staring eyes. The lamb was dead but the warmth was still in its body. He laid it gently in front of the ewe.

'Now, listen,' said Tutkwe. 'When I was a small child I used to drink straight from the sheep and the goats. We all did. In fact, our mothers put us to suckle them as soon as we could drink animal milk. I will show you how and then you must do the same. It will give us strength.' Then he laughed.

'Nick,' he said. 'If I had killed you, I would not have been able to eat or drink until I had been cleansed by the Leopard-Skin Chief. You had better go first when I have shown you how.'

Expertly, Tutkwe moved the sheep's body so that its udder was exposed. He began to work it and soon a trickle of warm, sweetish liquid oozed into his mouth. In his hunger, he wanted to devour more and more, but he forced himself to drag Nick near the sheep. Starving though he was, he could not bring himself to drink and, in his weakness, he didn't care.

'I can't. I simply can't,' he muttered.

Without the strength to argue, Tony took Nick's place and drank his fill from one of the teats. The milk was warm and good. Tutkwe tried again to persuade Nick to drink, then satisfied himself.

When he was finished he told Tony not to move off the sheep and went to look at Nick. His face was pale and still and his breathing was shallow. He had closed his eyes and only fierce slapping would rouse him. If only he had taken the strength-giving milk from the sheep.

'Give me my knife. I think you picked it up. We've got to revive Nick.'

Tony thought for a horrible moment that Tutkwe would use the knife on Nick, but he had come back to the ewe. He took off his belt and fastened it tightly round the animal's neck. He made a funnel out of the plastic folder from his bus pass, secured with rubber bands which he found in his pocket. He took his knife from Tony and held it between his teeth while he ran his hands carefully into the thick wool to feel for the structure of sinews and muscle beneath. He found the vein he was looking for, the jugular vein, thickly distended by the restricting thong around the animal's neck.

Tony watched, fascinated, while the Nuer expertly thrust in the blade of the knife just far enough to release a spurt of bright red blood. The intensity of the colour gave him a sickening shock. It violated the white landscape with a substance of its own, the substance of life and death. He knew instinctively it was life-giving and could prevent the death of his friend. To be saved, Nick must drink the animal's blood.

The Nuer was holding the nose of the wild-eyed ewe and filling the plastic funnel with the blood. He then released the belt. The vein closed and the flow of blood stopped. He indicated to Tony to free the animal and come to help him.

The ewe lay for a moment, dazed in the snow. Then, slowly and laboriously, she hoisted herself from the drift and lumbered a few steps away. There she stopped so that she would not be far from the dead lamb.

'Will she be all right?' asked Tony, surprised at the normality of the sheep.

Tutkwe nodded. He supported Nick's head on his knees and gently prized open his mouth. Nick didn't resist. He was past caring. Tutkwe carefully poured in the blood, a little at a time. He finished the last drops himself, turning his tongue round the inside of the funnel.

'Tony, you will never believe what a delicacy this is when it coagulates and is roasted in embers and sliced. The blood will revive Nick and the act of bleeding will cleanse me.'

'I thought you said your sacrifice had to be a steer or a ram or a he-goat. That was a ewe.'

The Nuer laughed. 'I know. But allowances will have to be made for an alien country. The ewe was sent by the spirits for our survival. You can't get milk from a ram.'

Tony was staring down the mountain. Far below he could make out the shape of a snow plough, abandoned on the verge of the road. The road looked as if it had been cleared enough to allow traffic to pass along it.

Excitedly, he pointed it out to Tutkwe. At first, the glare from the snow was too much and the Nuer, who was skilled in picking out the flick of an ear that would betray a buck in a thicket, could not see it. Then he let out a yell.

'Do you think we can make it? It looks a long way off.'

'I certainly feel stronger now,' answered Tony. 'Thanks to you knowing what to do with that sheep. Even Nick won't be able to scoff at primitive backgrounds now he has drunk the blood of a sheep to survive!'

Saying no more, they both worked to manoeuvre Nick between them and begin their long downward journey to the road, sustained by milk and blood and hope.

Acknowledgments

The publishers would like to extend their grateful thanks to the following authors, publishers and others for kindly granting them permission to reproduce the copyrighted extracts and stories included in this anthology.

VILLAGE SCHOOL from *Cider with Rosie*. Reprinted by kind permission of The Hogarth Press and the author.

SCHOOL from *Lark Rise to Candleford* by Flora Thompson (1939). Reprinted by permission of Oxford University Press.

I MITE HAVE KNOWN from *Back in the Jug Agane* by Geoffrey Willans. Reprinted by kind permission of Irene Josephy.

THE SPORTS from *Decline and Fall* by Evelyn Waugh. Reprinted by kind permission of A. D. Peters & Co Ltd and Harold Matson Company.

THE CRYSTAL GAZERS from *The Madcap of the School* by Angela Brazil. Reprinted by kind permission of Blackie and Son Limited.

THE IDEALIST from *The Stories of Frank O'Connor* by Frank O'Connor. Reprinted by kind permission of A. D. Peters and Co Ltd and Joan Daves.

THE MUSEUM OUTING, an abridged version of Chapter 12 of *To Sir With Love* by E. R. Braithwaite. Reprinted by kind permission of The Bodley Head and Prentice-Hall Inc.

THE MAN'S WORLD from *The Rainbow* by D. H. Lawrence. © 1915 D. H. Lawrence. © 1943 Frieda Lawrence. Reprinted by kind permission of Laurence Pollinger Ltd, the Estate of the late Mrs Frieda Lawrence Ravagli and The Viking Press Inc.

NO ANGELS, from *No Angels* by Francesca Enns. Reprinted by kind permission of Routledge & Kegan Paul Ltd and John Johnson.

DON'T KNOCK THE CORNERS OFF, Chapter 8 of *Don't Knock the Corners Off* by Caroline Glyn. Reprinted by kind permission of Victor Gollancz Ltd.

A SCHOOL STORY from *The Day We Got Drunk on Cake* by William Trevor. Reprinted by kind permission of John Johnson.

TREACLE TART from *The Shout and Other Stories* by Robert Graves. Reprinted by kind permission of A. P. Watt Ltd and Curtis Brown.

FROM MY SCHOOLDAYS from *Autobiographical Writings* by Hermann Hesse. Reprinted by kind permission of Joan Daves and Farrar, Straus & Giroux Inc.

LAST YEAR AT SCHOOL from *Memoirs of a Dutiful Daughter* by Simone de Beauvoir. Reprinted by kind permission of André Deutsch.

SNOWDROPS from *Sliding* by Leslie Norris. Reprinted by kind permission of J. M. Dent & Sons Ltd and Brandt & Brandt.

FIRST DAY AT MILLINGTON by Jennifer Zabel. © 1980 Jennifer Zabel.

MR EVANS by Hayden McAllister. © 1980 Hayden McAllister.

THE ALPHA-WAVE EXPERIMENT by Anthea Courtenay. © 1980 Anthea Courtenay.

THE BUS by Margaret Biggs. © 1980 Margaret Biggs.

SLAVES OF THE LAMP from *Stalky & Co* by Rudyard Kipling. Reprinted by kind permission of The National Trust and the Macmillan Co. of London and Basingstoke.

THE RAFFLE from *A Flag on the Island* by V. S. Naipaul. Reprinted by kind permission of André Deutsch and Curtis Brown.

BLOOD ON THE MOUNTAIN by Ann Spano. © 1980 Ann Spano.

THE QUEEN'S BIRTHDAY from *In the Castle of My Skin* by George Lamming. Reprinted by kind permission of the author.

Every effort has been made to clear copyrights and the publishers trust that their apologies will be accepted for any errors or omissions.